The Price of Time

Tim Tigner

ACKNOWLEDGMENTS

Writing novels full of twists and turns is relatively easy. Doing so logically and coherently while maintaining a rapid pace is much tougher. Surprising readers without confusing them is the real art.

I draw on generous fans for guidance in achieving those goals, and for assistance in fighting my natural inclination toward typos. These are my friends, and I'm grateful to them all.

Errol Adler, William Babitt, Martin Baggs, Suzanne S. Barnhill, Dave Berkowitz, Doug Branscombe, Kay Brooks, Anna Bruns, Diane Bryant, Pat Carella, John Chaplin, Ian Cockerill, Doug Corneil, Lars de Kock, Robert Enzenauer, Hugo Ernst, Rae Fellenberg, Geof Ferrell, Andrew Gelsey, Emily Hagman, Cliff Jordan, Andrea Kerr, Robert Lawrence, Margaret Lovett, Debbie Malina, Judy Marksteiner, Peter Mathon, Ed McArdle, Joe McKinley, Jim Niles, Brian Pape, Rosemary Paton, Michael Picco, Connie Poleson, Lee Proost, Sharon Ring, Robert Rubinstayn, Ron Spunt, Gwen Tigner, Robert Tigner, Wendy Trommer, Alan Vickery and Sandy Wallace.

For more information on this novel or Tim Tigner's other thrillers, please visit timtigner.com

You and I will never know if The Fountain of Youth exists. There is one simple reason for this. Revealing such a grand discovery would be foolish—and no fool is going to find it.

This novel is dedicated to Robert Gottlieb, the extraordinary agent who gave generously of his precious time to help make it a success. Thank you, my friend.

1

One Problem

Palo Alto, California

December 24, 1999

PIERCE DUBOIS bunched his beefy fists, attempting to mask his irritation. He was unaccustomed to discourtesy. Certainly not from people whose paychecks depended on his support. Certainly not after being summoned a thousand miles on Christmas Eve.

What couldn't wait a few weeks until the quarterly meeting? Did the offending executives somehow sense what their angel investor had planned? Had they divined that he wanted to call it quits after seven disappointing years, to enter the new millennium free from past mistakes—and quarterly million-dollar payments? Could this power play be the CEO's last grasp at dignity, at going out on her terms?

Pierce hoped he had it wrong. That they'd found another investor. Someone who'd keep the research progressing toward a possible payout. But as he sat there waiting for the tardy executives to arrive, he wasn't holding his breath.

He shifted his gaze from the three empty chairs to the five faces that had gathered around the Silicon Valley conference room table. A table that, like everything else in the adjacent offices and laboratory, Pierce had paid for. Three bright-eyed scientists, an administrative assistant, and the CFO all sat quietly, studying papers and avoiding their investor's eye.

Despite their cloaked responses and coy behavior, Pierce sensed suppressed energy in the room. Something was up and dammit they knew what it was. But they weren't sharing.

Irritated by the petty game, he picked up his phone and

called his driver—who was also his pilot. Pierce hadn't become wealthy by wasting money. "We may be heading home momentarily. Be sure the plane's ready."

"Yes, sir."

Yes, sir. Now that was a proper response. *We don't know where they are, but surely they'll be here shortly sounded infinitely less satisfying.*

Punching off his phone, Pierce decided that he had never really cared for any of the Eos team. Their science, yes. He loved that. Their work ethic, fine. Seven of the eight were married to the job and only the job, so they put in the hours. But the lot of them were more sheep than wolf. Sure, Lisa Perera, the CEO, could show some tooth. And Felix Gentry, the CFO, occasionally displayed a full set of incisors. Neither, however, was a true carnivore. Neither was part of his pack.

Sounds of activity resonated from the outer office as Pierce picked at a pesky splinter in his left forefinger. A remnant of his last wood-chopping workout. The commotion had to be coming from the missing execs. Eos Pharmaceuticals only had eight employees.

All heads turned toward the door as Lisa Perera and David Hume entered the conference room. She wore the confident countenance of the consummate CEO but appeared more shaken than defiant. The Chief Scientific Officer was much less guarded. He wore a dazed stare and strode without his usual spring.

Neither apologized for being late.

Lisa sat at the end of the table opposite Pierce. David settled into one of the two empty chairs to her left. She took a deep breath and said, "We've just come from Kirsten Besanko's house."

All eyes turned toward the sole empty seat while Lisa continued. "She passed away this morning. Her husband found her in the pool when she didn't come in for breakfast after her morning swim."

Gasps erupted around the table.

Allison began sobbing without abandon.

Lisa answered the obvious question. "The paramedics

aren't sure what happened. Probably a stroke or heart attack."

"She was only thirty-three," Ries said.

"She was six months pregnant," Allison sobbed, adding, "She didn't want anyone to know."

Pierce saw shock register on a few faces—but not all. To him, the information was anything but surprising. It implied the answer. Pregnancy significantly increased the odds of having a stroke.

He didn't mention the connection. He hadn't flown all the way from northern Montana to talk about Kirsten. Best to move things along. "Why don't we knock out this meeting so you can move on to personal matters? Lisa, you said we had something supremely important to discuss."

The CEO struggled to pull herself together, taking a deep breath while momentarily closing her eyes. It was the first time Pierce had seen her anything but perky and polished.

With a photogenic face and an all-American fencer's quick wits, Lisa Perera was more handsome than pretty. She had shoulder-length brown hair complemented by bright brown eyes and a smile that effectively camouflaged a computer-like brain. Pierce expected her to end up hosting a talk show—once her biotech career bombed.

"Yes, of course," Lisa said, snapping herself back into form with a transformation that was both audible and visible. "Thank you for interrupting your holiday to join us on such short notice."

Pierce decided to set the tone then and there. "You didn't give me much choice on the phone. Or much information."

"As I said, some messages really must be delivered in person. On that note, I'm going to pass the baton to David. He's earned the honor."

David Hume, MD, PhD, and CSO, was the reason Pierce had funded Eos Pharmaceuticals. When he invested, Pierce bet on people. Despite delivering disappointing results for seven consecutive years, the Chief Scientific Officer still struck Pierce as the smartest man he'd ever met.

Unfortunately, intelligence wasn't everything.

David stepped up to the proverbial plate by lifting his head. As he prepared to speak, the fire reignited in his eyes. "It took forty-two more iterations than I would have liked, and nearly twice as many as I predicted when we first took your money, but forty-three proved to be the lucky number."

Pierce felt his heart palpitate. *Did David just say lucky?* "You succeeded?"

"We did," David confirmed, his exuberant expression blasting away all doubt. "Our latest compound keeps telomeres completely intact through thousands of cellular reproductive cycles. There's zero degradation."

Telomeres were like metal tips on the ends of DNA zippers. They kept the long strands from getting fouled up during the unzipping and re-zipping process at the core of cellular reproduction. When telomeres malfunctioned, people got cancer. When they wore down, people aged. By keeping telomeres in pristine condition, Eos—the name of both their product and their company—would act like the elixir of immortality.

At least in theory.

Pierce couldn't believe his ears, even though he had been fantasizing about this moment for seven years. "What are you telling me?"

David's enthusiastic gaze didn't waver. "Without extensive, long-term clinical trials, I can't be definitive. But at this point, and by all indications, we believe we can arrest human aging with two shots of Eos a year."

"What!"

"People won't age a day after their first injection."

Pierce found himself speechless but quickly recovered. This was definitely too good to be true. "How confident are you in your findings?"

"Confident enough to start using it." David gestured around the table. "All of us have."

Pierce felt like they'd just attached jumper cables to his dreams. If David and the others believed in the safety and efficacy of Eos enough to use it on themselves, then they weren't puffing him up as part of a pitch. When it came to science and safety, these were serious people. The leaders in their field. "I was only hoping for a slow-down. The ability to buy a few more years. Maybe a decade. You're telling me you invented immortality?"

David raised a palm, but the other research scientists' microexpressions might as well have been nods. Ries, Eric, and even Allison grew glows of pure pride. "No, far from it. People who take Eos can still die from any number of causes."

"Just not old age," Pierce confirmed.

"That's what all our evidence indicates."

Pierce found himself propelled to his feet by an irrepressible burst of energy. "Well, Merry Christmas! We're about to become the richest people on the planet."

His mind plowed forward as he paced. "If what you say is true, Eos is worth more than all the oil in Saudi Arabia. There's nothing people won't pay, and there's nobody who won't pay it. The big pharmaceutical companies will go nuts at auction. We'll get hundreds of billions for the rights." Pierce ran rough calculations as his lips and legs expelled excess energy. Expected purchase price. Anticipated royalty stream. His percentage ownership. He'd just become the wealthiest man alive—even if nobody knew it.

David raised his other palm, halting Pierce's pacing. "There is one problem. We can't sell it."

2
One Solution

LISA PERERA studied her company's chairman while trying to ignore the empty chair to her left. She'd long suspected that Pierce's parents had only named him after seeing his eyes, which were as penetrating as any she'd ever encountered. She felt that stare now and she shot it right back.

Pierce had visibly run half the range of human emotions in the span of a few seconds. From irritated to confused to disbelieving to hopeful to elated to despondent, and now he was quickly coming around the bend toward enraged.

She would lasso her cowboy and land him in a happy place, but only after he sweated a bit. He had intended to cut them off. To starve her company of oxygen. Best he suffer for a few seconds now, feeling her greater power at his moment of greatest triumph, lest he hesitate the next time she needed support.

"Why can't we sell Eos?" Pierce asked, his molars practically grinding.

"Consider the consequences," she said.

"The consequences were exactly what I was considering the twenty-eight times I handed you a million-dollar check."

"Set the money aside for a second and think big picture."

Pierce flung his hands like a frustrated ape. "You're telling the man who funded your dreams and livelihood for the past seven years to set the money aside. That's awfully convenient. And completely unrealistic."

Silicon Valley attracted the best and brightest. The toughest and most tactful. All were eager to participate in promising projects, to work around the clock in hopes of fame and fantastic financial rewards. This was one of those rare moments where the lives of those select scientists and engineers actually exceeded expectations. Where dreams and reality converged.

Lisa was determined to savor every moment. And to let her team participate.

She turned to David, passing him the proverbial baton.

"What does the world look like when nobody is getting old?" David asked, his expression unfazed by the chairman's outburst, his tone genteel.

Lisa marveled at the way her CSO could connect with just about anyone at any time. There was something about him that people found both disarming and inspiring, regardless of the circumstance. Her hypothesis was that he naturally evoked their better angels by using his big brain to see things from their points of view. That and that he had a Christlike appearance—complete with long hair, chiseled features, and soulful eyes.

Pierce's expression softened a second before he answered the question. "Without aging, the world looks a lot less wrinkly. And competition for slots in the *Sports Illustrated* swimsuit issue gets mighty fierce."

Chuckles erupted around the table. From everyone but David. "Actually, the world becomes considerably more crowded and dirty. It—"

Lisa zoned out while David took Pierce through his description of the dystopian world they'd create by decimating the death rate. They'd discussed it many times—with shouts and tears and shivering spines.

She found it odd that none of them had considered the costs of victory during their early years. Her explanation for that collective shortcoming was that the goal seemed so mythical and elusive that everyone had been 100 percent focused on achieving it. On the public glory and personal rewards of cracking history's greatest medical mystery.

Only when her team reached the point where they were plunging needles into their own flesh had their thoughts turned to the broader future ramifications. To the impact on the ecosystem, the economy, and the human psyche.

Pierce smacked his fist against the table, ending Lisa's reverie and refocusing her attention. "People will figure it out. They'll cope. They always do. It's what humans do. We adapt to challenges." His eyes were shooting lightning at the man destined to make all his dreams come true.

Lisa knew that evoking this reaction was part of David's plan. Not a failure of tact or tactic.

"I'm not going to walk away from billions just to ease your conscience," Pierce continued. "You can buy yourself all the therapy in the world, if that's what you need. Hell, you can found an entire university named in your honor and dedicated to the subject. Do what you want with your money. Just don't attempt to stand between me and mine."

Lisa intercepted the challenge, just as they'd planned. "No one's attempting to come between you and your big payday, Pierce. We'd just like to propose an alternative method for obtaining it. One that will make your new life much more enjoyable."

Pierce pivoted in her direction. At fifty-four, he was twenty years older than anyone else at the table, although few would guess that by looking at him. Or postulate that he'd made countless millions off a petroleum-processing patent.

Pierce looked like the healthy outdoorsy recluse that he was. The kind of guy you could send into the woods with a knife and expect to come back with a bear. Always dressed in jeans and a flannel shirt, he had intense green eyes, permanently tousled hair, and a stubble beard.

"You know a better way to cash in on Eos than selling it to Big Pharma?" Pierce asked.

Lisa smiled. "Much better. Please allow us to elaborate."

"All right." Pierce pushed back and put his feet up on the table. His boots were of the hiking kind, not cowboy and certainly not the polished leather loafers you'd expect to see descending the airstair of a private jet. She didn't object. She could ignore the insignificant slight if it would allow her investor to feel like a leader while he was actually following.

"Big Pharma is powerful because it has the mechanisms required to market to the masses. Sales representatives. Physician relationships. Advertising resources. But why should we market to the masses?"

The feet came down and Pierce leaned forward. "You want to limit sales to the elite?"

Lisa ignored his question. "Suppose we priced Eos at a million dollars. There are about forty million millionaires in the world, many of whom have many millions. Taking into account their families and friends, we could probably get a hundred million customers worth a million dollars each quite easily. That would gross the company one hundred thousand billion dollars. That's a one followed by fourteen zeroes, and it's more than the eight of us could spend in a million years."

Lisa was certain that Pierce had done the personal wealth math. With just one billion dollars in the bank, a person could spend a thousand an hour for a hundred years and still have a fortune left over.

"Go on," Pierce said. "Get me to your conclusion."

"When the numbers are this big, seeking to maximize financial return is foolish. What would be the point when we could never spend the money?"

Pierce gave an honest answer. "The point would be having a hell of a time trying."

Lisa closed the trap. "Not really. The minute word gets out that immortality is for sale, anyone who has it will become the target of extreme animus and prejudice from everyone who doesn't. We'd eventually be lynched in a populist revolution during which the formula would be stolen. Ultimately everybody would gain immortality—"

"Plunging the planet into David's dystopian scenario. I get it," Pierce said. "And I see the allure of finding another option. One of the reasons I live in Montana is that with so few people polluting you can still see the stars. But what's the alternative? Don't fool yourself into thinking you can keep the discovery secret. That won't work. People will talk."

"You're right. People will talk. Even if we priced it at $100 million and only approached customers we knew could afford it, the news would still leak. It's just too juicy to contain. Then there would be an investigation, and eventually our ivory tower would come tumbling down."

"So you want to walk away from the money? Be satisfied with immortality alone?"

Lisa rose, walked around the table and sat on the corner at Pierce's side. "Would that be so bad?"

She waited in that cozy pose through a full sixty seconds of silence while the rest of the room barely breathed. It was uncomfortable, but it did the trick. Pierce was nothing if not quick witted. "In essence, my $28 million investment will have bought me immortality."

"And the contentment that comes from being one of the only people to have it. Never in the history of the world has there been a special status so elite."

Another breathless pause ensued while Pierce ruminated and Lisa returned to her end of the table. He'd been about to walk away—to write off his $28 million. Now he was being offered an incalculably high return on his investment, albeit a non-financial one. "I could live with that," he said with a wink. "Is that your proposal?"

Lisa placed both hands on the back of her chair and leaned in. "No."

The chairman's face darkened even as his eyes grew brighter, but he bit his tongue. He knew the kicker was coming.

"There's a way for us to have our cake and eat it too. For us to become rich and immortal without getting lynched or overcrowding the planet."

Pierce smiled, as much from the realization that he'd been steered full circle as from the anticipation of another titillating revelation. "Now you're talking my language. What way is that?"

"Instead of selling Eos to a billion people, or even a million, we sell it to just one."

Pierce nodded slowly, then faster. "One extremely wealthy person. But at what price?"

"A price that puts all the Immortals on the same financial footing. We ask for an even division of the fortune—ten ways around."

"You mean nine," Pierce corrected, nodding toward the empty chair.

All eyes turned toward Lisa as her stomach fluttered. "Nine," she confirmed.

"And I suppose you already have the lucky man in mind?" Pierce pressed, now unable to repress his excitement.

"Woman, actually. My Stanford roommate married Jacques Eiffel, the late oil magnate."

AUTHOR'S NOTE

You may find it helpful to note that Immortals have
an "i" in their first names, while mortals do not.

3
The Fix Is In

Twenty years later
Seven Star Island, the Bahamas

ARIA EIFFEL experienced déjà vu as she entered her library to find eight attentive faces waiting. She shouldn't have been surprised. The faces appeared exactly as they had twenty years earlier when the same crew had ambushed her in that very room.

The pitch that started their everlasting association had begun an hour before midnight on millennium eve. Perfect timing. Poetic even. The end of an old era and the start of a new age. Lisa had even timed her presentation to climax as the fireworks began bursting overhead. Immortality could be hers—if she shared her wealth.

Although today's date was nothing special, Aria got the sudden sense that there might be fireworks ahead. The atmosphere felt different from the preceding Immortals meetings. She sensed an unusual energy in the room.

Back at that grand soirée on millennium eve, Lisa had been the only one of the eight on the guest list. She'd snuck the other seven onto Aria's private island.

Today they were all invited, of course, as they were once a year, when it was Aria's turn to host the Immortals' semiannual meeting. The other times, Lisa hosted them in California.

Back then, the deal had been immortality—in exchange for equal slices of her fortune. Or as Lisa had pitched it, "With Eos, you *can* take it with you. At least, one-ninth of it." Since that split still left Aria with more than a billion in the bank—plus the island, the plane, the yacht, et cetera— her decision had been a no-brainer.

What did her Stanford sorority sister have planned today? Aria could see a special glint in her eye. It was no less telling than a feather on a cat's mouth. But what bird was she hunting?

Back on millennium eve, Aria had been unable to pull herself from the compelling presentation and extraordinary pitch that followed, despite having a hundred affluent guests waiting for her attention.

These days she rarely had guests.

That was the one big thing Aria hadn't realized back then, standing on the same spot, surveying the same guests. The hidden cost of becoming one of only nine Immortals on the planet.

By making that enviable move, she had effectively forsaken her right to be a social butterfly. She had tethered herself to the only others whose lives had no horizon. Her secret accomplices. Her new forever family.

She studied the room, wondering what ambush they had planned. The Immortals were a mix of scientists and businesspeople, liberals and conservatives, but nonetheless they were tight. Kind of like cousins. They had to be. It was ultimately too uncomfortable to associate with anyone outside their circle. Any person still subject to the scythe of time.

Pierce immediately confirmed her intuition as he kicked off the Immortals' fortieth semiannual meeting. "There's a big decision before us today. Arguably the most difficult and consequential one we'll ever have to make."

Aria studied her friends' faces as she wondered what the big decision was. She saw that most were similarly surprised. Only Lisa and Camilla appeared to know what was coming. Why was it that no matter how small the group, you always had factions?

"As you have all undoubtedly considered in private, we are faced with the enviable but precarious predicament of having appearances that are now twenty years younger than our identities. Good genes and luxurious lifestyles go a long way toward explaining the discrepancy to inquiring minds, but we're approaching the practical limit."

Everyone nodded.

Aside from Pierce, who had twenty years on them, the Immortals were in their fifties but looked as they had in their thirties, if not better, thanks to Eos. Aria had in fact mentioned the aging problem to Lisa the last time they were alone together. The two still shared the connection of sorority sisters, despite the fact that their lives and outlooks had diverged considerably after college.

"Purchasing false identities might appear to be the perfect solution," Pierce continued, "but unfortunately it is not. Lisa and I conducted extensive research and consulted multiple experts. They informed us that using fake documents for an extended period would be extremely risky, given all the attention going to preventing and prosecuting illegal immigration. The experts also noted that people of great means face an additional level of government scrutiny, given their value to the IRS. So we can't just *purchase papers*, as they say."

"What alternative is there?" Felix interjected.

Felix Gentry was Aria's least favorite Immortal. He had been the CFO back when Eos was a company rather than a lifestyle. The numbers guy suffered from the ironic affliction of prematurely gray hair, which he combed straight back. His eyes were dark, his mouth serious, and his nose looked like it had been crimped with pliers. While she found the combination unappealing, others called it interesting. Apparently, the look attracted women who were drawn to power.

"That's what we need to discuss," Pierce said, his tone implying that what followed would not be a comfortable conversation. "The alternative to fake documents—is real documents."

"You mean replacing real people?" David asked. "Surely you're not considering something so barbaric?"

"He means scooping up the social security numbers of people who died young, and using them to get genuine documents," Felix said.

Pierce rose and began pacing. "No, unfortunately I don't. The government is all too aware of that favorite old tactic.

Given that knowledge, and the rise of interconnected databases, the experts have eliminated it as an advisable option. David was right. Our only permanent alternative is to replace real people."

"Except it wouldn't be permanent," David said. "It would need to be repeated every twenty years."

"Point taken," Pierce said, pausing behind David's chair and thereby making it awkward for him to respond.

"What exactly are you proposing?" Aria asked, her stomach suddenly unsettled.

Pierce turned his laser-like focus her way. "There are men who specialize in solving problems and shutting mouths. They're fixers. Usually former military or law enforcement officers, often with a law degree or private security background. Most live like ghosts off the grid. All know how to keep a secret.

"Lisa and I are asking for the go-ahead to identify and hire the best of their best."

"The fixer will find suitable physical matches for each of us and attempt to meet additional requirements if presented," Lisa added.

"Is that even possible?" Aria asked. "Finding our twins?"

"There are already commercial websites that do just that. *Twinstrangers, twinlets,* and *ilooklikeyou* for example. Obviously, minor cosmetic changes will be required, as will relocation to a place neither you nor your replacement previously lived."

Felix looked up from deep thought. "Physical appearances aside, how can we be expected to fool these replacements' families and friends?"

Lisa fielded the question with her typical diplomatic aplomb. "Good point. We'll need to target people without either. While that sounds like a big ask, there's actually a significant percentage of the population that either has no family or doesn't communicate with them. And friends tend to come and go with geography, so the move will take care of that.

"Obviously, there are a lot of considerations. Pierce and I have thought through many of them, but I'm sure there are some we've missed. That's another reason why we want to involve expert help."

"Will this expert know why we need replacements?" Felix pressed.

Lisa shook her head. "No. He won't know who we are or what we are. Just what we look and sound like. Obviously, that's data he'll need to do the matchmaking."

"We'll pay him extremely well," Pierce added. "Well enough to effectively own him. Both during the replacement process and going forward, since we'll need someone to troubleshoot any problems which may arise."

Aria was about to ask what problems they foresaw, when Lisa said, "I'd like to put the proposal forward for a vote."

Majority approval of the group was required when any Immortal wanted to take an action that might impact the rest of them. Aria, having joined late, voted only in case of a tie. To date, her vote had never been necessary.

"I can't believe we're actually considering this," David said. "Replacement is a euphemism for murder. We're not murderers."

"Of course we are," Pierce said. "We're simply not in the habit of tracing the provenance of our dinners—or our shoes, belts, bags, furniture… But just as we justify putting veal on our plates with the argument that humans are one rung up the food chain from cows, so we can condone replacing mortals. They are, unquestionably, one rung below us. I second the motion for a vote."

"Is there really no other way?" Aria asked.

"Surely we can find one!" David said. "Some way to make fake identities work. Through bribes or regular swaps, for example."

Lisa cut off Pierce's reply with a glance. "We considered those options. Both jeopardize the prime directive we agreed on during our very first meeting, twenty years ago, right here in this room."

"Secrecy," Aria muttered.

"Exactly. We must keep the world unaware of what we've achieved. All the alternatives to the replacement process jeopardize our very existence by requiring regular and repeated interactions with scores of outsiders. With the replacement option, by contrast, we only have a single exposure. It's an unfortunate circumstance, but an easy decision."

Lisa concluded by raising her hand. "All those in favor."

Aria watched with fascination as other hands went up one by one. First Camilla, Lisa's longtime executive assistant. The spoiled sycophant who undoubtedly held the record for best-compensated secretary in human history. Then Pierce, Lisa's co-sponsor. Felix didn't hesitate. No surprise there. The finance guy's calculations rarely escalated beyond number one.

The four researchers shared furtive glances among themselves. If one of them went along, the motion would pass.

Aria knew she was watching history unfold, right there, right then, with stilled breath. The big coin was flipping. Their humanity was spinning in the air. Would it be heads or tails?

She caught a slight nod between Eric and Ries a second before both raised their hands. As the proposal passed, Allison and David met eyes. Their votes were now superfluous. The only question was whether there would be a protest or unanimity.

After a protracted pause that grew more uncomfortable by the second, the last two relented. Most likely out of solidarity rather than consensus.

"The motion passes," Pierce said, maintaining a neutral tone. "We'll begin searching for our fixer tomorrow morning."

"No need," Felix said. "I've heard of the perfect guy."

4
About Face

That same day
London, England

WHEN SOMEONE WHACKS YOU in the back of the head, you don't know what's going on. Your brain simply registers a bright flash a split second before everything goes dark. With luck, you live to see the light again.

I lived, but I didn't see the light.

Not at first.

When I awoke, I saw only darkness. Not blind dark. Not movie theater dim. The visual disruption you get when your head is draped in a black bag.

My brain was slogging through that semiconscious state, still struggling to adapt, as the coarse fibers of the burlap sack came into focus. Marshaling my active neurons, I endeavored to remember where I was, and why.

Before attempting to unmask my eyes, I surveyed my surroundings with my other senses. I was indoors, slouched in a soft chair. An old armchair by the feel. One that stank of cigarette smoke, stale sweat, and vomit. While my nose revolted, my ears locked onto the subtle sounds of others in the room. Two people fidgeting, fumbling, breathing. Both within striking distance. One before me, one behind.

I began testing my wrists and ankles with tiny gestures.

I was but a few twitches in when the man before me refocused my attention. "I apologize for my employee's exuberance. Bobby takes my security very seriously. Sometimes he errs on the side of caution."

The familiar voice brought everything crashing back. The steady stream of top-secret documents leaking out of London. The months of undercover work. The promise of a covert meeting.

My veins surged with excitement even as my head throbbed with regret. I had made it into the same room with Ernesto Sargon, London's legendary thief and underground information broker. If I, Zachary Chase, lived to tell the tale, I would be the first intelligence officer ever to do so.

I reached up to rub the back of my head, but didn't try to remove the bag. Best to leave it on for now if that was their desire. "What did Bobby use? A two-by-four?"

"Nothing so crude," Sargon replied, speaking from behind me now. "Bobby favors a sap, and I assure you there was no real danger. He's got the Goldilocks touch with that little leather sack of lead."

It didn't feel *just right* to me. "If you say so."

The bag lifted off, and I found myself looking at a laptop on an upturned crate. The clock in the corner of the screen displayed 22:27. If it was accurate, I'd been unconscious for a mere twenty minutes. A good sign.

The room provided no clue that could confirm the hour. It was small, windowless, and dim. Nondescript as the average walk-in closet. At least the part I was permitted to see. By standing behind me, Sargon was sending a message. *Don't turn around.*

I tried to catch the criminal's reflection on the computer screen.

"This is how it's going to work," Sargon said, pacing enough to give me reflected glimpses of a dark suit, gray hair, and silver-framed glasses. "First you're going to show me an account with sufficient funds. Then I'm going to show you the documents. Then you're going to make the transfer."

I began nodding acknowledgment, but immediately regretted it. My head was sore from the sap strike. "That works for me. But I need to verify the authenticity of the documents first."

Sargon's reflection put hands on hips. "They're ink on paper. What's to verify?"

"Precisely my point. It's easy to put ink on paper. Anyone

can do it. Prove to me that they were actually authored at the U.S. Embassy, rather than on your laptop, and we're good to go."

"That wasn't our deal."

"Neither was a whack on the head."

"I've apologized for that."

"Yet my head still hurts."

Sargon harrumphed. "My reputation is all the proof you need."

"Same problem. How do I know you're really Sargon? Prove to me that you're the thief who stole the Duchess of Cornwall's jewels, the spy who put a camera inside MI5, the con man who sold Rembrandt's *Storm on the Sea of Galilee* three times, and we have a deal."

Sargon resumed pacing the small room, reminding me of a caged tiger. "You're a cautious one," he said. "I can appreciate that. I tend toward caution myself. Show me the money, and I'll show you proof of provenance. Then you pay and I give you the documents."

"That works for me," I said.

The bag went back over my head amidst a flurry of other movements. I heard a keyboard clatter, a few clicks, and then the sounds of passion. Yes, passion. No doubt about that.

The bag came off.

I didn't know exactly what to expect, but this wasn't it. "Is this a joke? Your proof is a porno?"

"It's no joke. In fact, it's very serious." Bobby stepped into view, paused the video, and pointed at a face.

"Do you recognize this woman?" Sargon asked.

I did. It took a second. I'd never seen her naked. But once my mind made the jump I had no doubt. "Who's the other woman?"

"She works for me."

"An excellent hire," I said, putting admiration in my voice.

"Indeed. Now that you know, next time we can skip the silly stuff. Will be better for your health and mine."

I'd positioned myself as an off-the-books advisor to investors who earned outlandish returns using inside information. Hedge fund managers who needed a steady flow of tips without any links to their crimes. Sargon was playing it cool, but I knew he was practically drooling. I was his conduit to a gold mine.

Bobby closed the video and opened an internet browser. Sargon's sap-happy employee looked like typical London muscle. Probably played rugby and served in uniform before turning to more lucrative, less legal pursuits.

I leaned into the keyboard and called up a Cayman bank account containing exactly two million pounds, then looked expectantly at Bobby.

The brute accepted a manila envelope from his boss. He set it on the table beside the laptop but then anchored it beneath his gloved fist.

I opened a transfer window and typed while Sargon dictated instructions.

The two million moved.

The fist lifted.

The bag went back over my head and I got another unwelcome surprise. A screeching sound followed by ticking.

"When the timer dings, you're free to go. Leaving before then would be ill advised."

Sargon and Bobby left through the rear door.

I immediately removed the bag.

The ticking emanated from an old fashioned kitchen timer. Nothing was connected. It was set for ten minutes. I knew the odds were low that Sargon had laid a trap, but for ten minutes, why risk it? I didn't have a gun or even a camera, and catching Sargon wasn't the mission objective anyway. I'd gone undercover to ferret out information. An identity, to be specific.

I'd spent the past two months establishing the underworld connections necessary to place the order that ultimately led to the meeting where I exchanged two million pounds of Uncle Sam's money for a few pieces of paper. For two months, I'd hung out with people I didn't like in places I didn't want to be. For two months, I'd prayed that my true identity would not somehow be sniffed out. The experience had sucked, but it was worth it. I had succeeded. I'd made America stronger and safer while putting a fat plum in my government service record.

The higher-ups in Langley could wait ten more minutes to congratulate themselves.

When the timer rang, I rose and exited the back door. I found myself in the alley behind an aging strip mall. I walked around front and found everything closed. No surprise given the hour. Fortunately, the biker bar across the street was still lit with neon.

I walked in, mentioned a mugging, showed my lump, and sweet-talked the bushy-mustached bartender into letting me use the landline in his back office.

"Barry, it's Chase. I just met with Sargon. I need you to send a car for me. I'm at the Twisted Sister Tavern in Peckham."

"I saw the money move. Are we happy?"

"We are. The source of the leak is Kaitlyn Connors. The spy is her lesbian lover."

I expected a sharp inhalation of breath, followed by a clever comment and a heartfelt attaboy. I got silence instead. When the CIA's London station chief finally spoke, his tone was terse. "The car is on its way. Talk to no one before you get here."

5

The Red Line

BARRY WAS WAITING FOR ME when I arrived in the underground garage of the sail-covered twelve-story billion-dollar cube that was the new U.S. Embassy. The London CIA station chief even stepped between the two beefy Marines to open my door.

"Welcome back." His hand was out, but not to shake. The palm was up.

I handed him the manila envelope we'd just bought for two million pounds.

Langley's senior local officer didn't lead me upstairs to the CIA floor. He took me to the so-called walk-in room we used when outsiders showed up on the embassy doorstep claiming to have valuable information. Nobody was waiting there, but someone was certainly watching from behind the big mirror, either in person or through the hidden camera. By selecting this room, Barry was sending me a message.

It wasn't good.

An open laptop on the desk displayed a familiar dictation program. It would record my voice and convert it into a transcript. An operations report.

Barry made a point of tossing the unopened manila envelope into a burn bag before sitting down. It would come out later, of course, but again a message had been delivered. "Take me through everything that's happened since yesterday's report. You know the drill."

I did. I'd done this for a decade in espionage hotspots all over the world. And since this particular assignment hadn't required me to bunk down with the enemy, I'd been filing reports on a daily basis.

"This is Agent Zachary Chase, speaking from the U.S. Embassy in London. Having made contact with Ernesto

Sargon, I arranged to purchase draft copies of U.S. negotiating strategies for several post-Brexit US-UK agreements. I went to the meet at an abandoned warehouse in Peckham at 2200. I arrived without bag, weapon, watch, phone, or other electronic device, as instructed. Nothing but memorized banking information. I was met by Sargon's enforcer, whom he later identified as Bobby.

"During the pat-down, Bobby clubbed me on the back of my head. I lost consciousness. I woke up approximately twenty minutes later in a small room." I continued through the story without interruption while Barry watched with barely blinking eyes from across the interrogation table. I concluded, as I did daily, "End of report."

Barry closed the laptop, but didn't respond immediately, or even after an appropriate pause. This convinced me that someone was speaking in his ear. The ambassador or the CIA's deputy director for operations were my best guess, given Barry's seniority and the sensitive nature of our discussion.

"Sargon didn't verbally identify the woman?" Barry finally asked.

So that was it. They didn't want to embarrass the ambassador. The president probably had him in mind for a higher appointment. "There was no need. The images were clear."

"That's a no?"

"It's a no."

Again there was an unnatural pause. "How long between the time you regained consciousness and the time you watched the video?"

"A few minutes."

"Well, that explains it, Agent Chase. Nobody will fault you for failing to see clearly so soon after suffering a traumatic brain injury."

Whoa! Looked like the light at the end of my two-month tunnel was actually an accelerating train. "My vision was fine. My thinking was coherent. I clearly saw Kaitlyn Connors, Ambassador Connors' wife."

Barry did not look happy.

"She has an identifying mark," I added. I was about to describe the mismatched shapes of her areolae when Barry held up a halting hand and another man chimed in.

"We're quite certain that you did not see Mrs. Connors." The voice on the speaker was not that of the ambassador or the deputy director. It was the director himself. "You should amend your report accordingly."

I couldn't believe my ears. Well, actually, sadly, I could. The agency had become increasingly political over the past decade. Either that, or I had simply gained a clearer view of the summit as I rose through the ranks. "If the leak isn't identified, the operation is a failure. That's two months of my life and two million pounds of taxpayers' money down the drain."

"We'll get the money back. And I can assure you that your career will not be derailed. You'll be at the front of the line for the next suitable chief of station slot."

Wow! There it was in blood-red script. The demarcation line. The start of the proverbial slippery slope. Sad as the circumstance was, I was fortunate to have it presented so clearly. Usually they sucked you over to the dark side with shades of gray. This was about to get ugly. For me. "I can't falsify a report."

The director had the predictable retort ready. He'd dangled the carrot, now out came the stick. "I believe loss of judgment is another sign of brain damage. We can't have damaged agents in the field—or behind a desk for that matter."

"Look, Chase," Barry said. "We're asking you to acknowledge the possibility that you didn't see what you think you saw, on account of your head injury."

I felt another brick slip from the foundation of my life. Given my economics degree from Princeton, the financial sector would have welcomed me with open arms and a wide wallet. But instead of cashing in on my new diploma, I'd chosen to risk life and limb for a significantly smaller paycheck but a much greater cause.

I'd been at it for ten years now, happily until today.

The truth was, I prized adventure over money and

prioritized country over self. Patriotism meant more to me than pinning a flag on my lapel. It meant living by a time-honored code of conduct and a consistent set of values. Even when inconvenient. Among people who believed and acted the same. My values hadn't changed since graduation, but management's attitude surely had.

"What you do with my report is up to you. You are free to ignore any part of it that you consider questionable. And I'm certainly not going to repeat what I saw. But I'm also not going to lie about an operation on the record, even if that lie is just a lie of omission."

"Well, then we have a problem," Barry said.

6
Trouble in Paradise

Six months later
San Diego, California

DAVID HUME rested his cheek atop the casket of his oldest friend. *His oldest friend.* The irony inherent in that statement and this situation sent a fresh stream of tears down his cheek and onto the polished mahogany. Eric George Curtis Mark—the man with four first names, the extraordinary cellular biologist who had been his first hire and the second Eos employee to experience halted aging— was dead.

"Are you going to be okay?" Allison D'Angelo asked while placing a tender hand upon his shoulder.

David responded without rising. "I'll be fine."

"It's just that you've been standing here a really long time."

David didn't reply.

"I never thought we'd be here either. None of us did. The death of an Immortal is… unexpected. And Eric's is so tragic."

David didn't bother with his usual *halted-aging* correction. This was not the time, place, or occasion for semantic reprimands. In fact, the time might have arrived to stop altogether. Every day their aging continued to be halted made the shorthand more accurate.

As the only MD among the four Immortal research scientists, David was the group physician. For twenty years, he had been taking tissue samples at their semiannual meetings, then testing and charting the results. Their muscles, fat, connective tissues, bone marrow, nerves, lymph nodes, kidneys, lungs, and liver cells all remained completely normal—for adolescents. They'd actually improved since beginning treatment in their mid-thirties.

Their telomere lengths had rebounded to the point where all the Immortals enjoyed 10,000 active base pairs, versus the 5,000 that would be expected among people in their fifties. Furthermore, none had shown any sign of cancers or other abnormalities. Not once in twenty years. In other words, with 0.0000% degradation, the halt Eos placed on their aging appeared to be permanent. With sterility as the only side effect. If they continued to receive their semiannual injections, it was unlikely that they would ever suffer from cancer, neurodegeneration, or old age.

Of course, as this funeral reminded them, the Immortals could still be killed by external causes.

"Why did he do it?" Allison asked when David kept clinging to the coffin. "I have trouble understanding why anyone would risk their life by skydiving. But someone with an eternity to lose? It's just beyond me. Why, Eric? Why?"

A third voice joined their conversation. "Some of us need to risk dying in order to feel like we're living."

David stood upright at the sound of Ries's voice. Along with Allison, Ries was the other surviving member of the research team—and an avid rock climber. He was also one of those rare everybody's-best-friend guys. Always exhibiting a smile, never voicing a cruel word.

"I think that's crazy talk," Allison said, her eyes teary. "And if you intend to continue with your reckless hobby after seeing this"—she gestured to the closed casket—"then I think you need a brain scan."

Ries didn't reply.

David surely wasn't going to step into the line of fire. He understood the adventurous impulse, but this was not the time for a left-brain parade.

As the three stood in silence beside their fallen friend, David noted that the other clique was similarly huddled across the chapel. Aria, Lisa, Pierce, Felix, and Camilla. The five-to-four majority the MBAs historically held over the PhDs had just increased by one.

There wasn't significant tension or even an active rivalry between the corporate coteries, but like tended to attract like—and repel unlike. That was unfortunate. After twenty years, David's group of four had already been feeling too small. Three was going to feel utterly insufficient, like a triangle where a circle ought to be. Perhaps Eric's passing would serve to unite the remaining eight.

"I know this isn't the best time to bring this up," Allison said. "But I'm going to be scaling back my hours."

David felt a tremor run from his tonsils to his toes, causing him to cough. If anything, he'd expected Eric's death to generate the opposite effect. To compel Allison to accomplish more. But he knew his mindset skewed far from the mean.

Among the Eos employees, only he had not altered his research routine after becoming a billionaire Immortal. He'd just switched projects and started anew with the same passion that had driven him before. This time he wanted to replicate the disease-fighting and prevention effects of Eos with a compound that did not halt aging. He wanted to improve life without extending it, thereby preventing suffering without disrupting the natural balance.

Eric and Ries had quickly figured out that Immortals still lived one day at a time, and that money couldn't buy the unbeatable feeling of flow they got from rewarding work. Both had joined him in the lab, part-time. Allison had also returned within a year, also for just two or three days a week. Now she was going to work part-time of part-time?

David couldn't complain. Quarter-time still beat what the MBAs were doing. As far as he could tell, they had all settled into lives of pure leisure. How much tennis and golf could a person play? How many cruises could he take? How many fancy dinners could he eat? David struggled to understand. He loved vacations as much as the next guy, but largely for the contrast. If you didn't have black to make the most of the white, everything was gray.

"Why scale back? What's come up?"

"Nothing has come up, and that's the problem. We've gotten nowhere in twenty years. I find the constant failure depressing, and there are other things I'd like to do."

Lisa interrupted before David could inquire about *other things*. She put a hand on each of their arms. "At least it was quick and painless. The timing is tragic, but he didn't suffer."

It was true. When your parachute snarled up, there was no time to worry. You spent your last seconds attempting to untangle the spaghetti. Eric had died trying. One second he was tugging parachute cords, the next he wasn't anything.

David did not want to discuss the details of his friend's death, so he changed the subject. "Lisa, could I get you to move up the semiannual meeting to tomorrow? That way we won't have to come back in a week."

The former CEO frowned. "I'd love to accommodate you, David, but I'm afraid we need to keep the current calendar. As you'll recall, we're going to be joined by a special guest."

7

The Hook

FOXY'S FAMOUS CHEESEBURGERS were calling Lars as the Sirens had Ulysses, and fate was not on his side. The bastards in the booths on both sides had ordered and received the house specialty, complete with curly fries that still steamed a salty fragrance. And just to rub it in, one had added a milkshake, the other a root beer float.

Having delivered her cargo, the waitress turned her attention to Lars, order pad in hand. "What will you have?"

Lars closed his eyes and pictured himself in the *Sexy Stranger* role for which he'd just auditioned. "I'll take the garden salad. No croutons. No dressing."

"And to drink?" Her tone made it clear she knew what was coming.

"Just a slice of lemon for my water, please."

She walked away without further acknowledgment. Here in Hollywood, wannabe actors were known to be bad tippers, and Lars had just painted a big black A on his forehead.

No sooner had she walked away, ponytail bobbing, than a man slid onto the cracked red vinyl seat across from Lars. He clearly wasn't a bum begging for cash or a dealer looking to hook, but beyond that Lars couldn't read him. Judging by the custom-tailored suit and precisely knotted tie, the man might be an investment banker. His face, by contrast, was straight off the cover of *Soldier of Fortune*. Chiseled cheekbones and strawberry-blond hair cut short on top and tight on the sides. Then there were his eyes. Pale blue and sparkling with both intensity and intelligence. "Mind if I join you?"

Lars gave a quick glance around the diner to confirm that it was half empty. The request wasn't the result of overcrowding. And Lars was absolutely certain he hadn't met this man before. Even accounting for some Hollywood magic, which could radically alter hair and eyes, the cheekbones were too distinctive to forget.

Lars responded with a throwaway line he often used to push peddlers off balance. "I suppose that depends on whether you're selling or buying?"

The intruder shocked Lars again with his answer. "Buying. Definitely buying."

The downside to his witticism struck Lars for the first time as he processed the unexpected reply.

The man read his mind. "Not that kind of buying, Lars."

"You know my name?"

"I know a lot more than that. It's my job to know." He held out a hand. "Tom Bronco, talent scout."

Lars already had an agent—albeit not a great one. In fact, Monty had yet to score Lars a significant role, and lately he was taking his time returning calls. If Tom Bronco was real —if he was from WME or CAA or UTA—this could be the break Lars had waited a decade for.

But it was much more likely to be a scam.

Usually the pimps targeted girls fresh off the bus, Midwestern prom queens and Southern sorority sisters taking their shot at the big dream. But the Tinseltown vultures had a taste for all types.

Rather than ask for credentials, which were easily faked, Lars decided to test the guy. "What do you know about me?"

Tom's expression remained rock solid. "You graduated from Princeton with honors ten years ago this month after double majoring in theater and economics—the latter being a practical concession to your parents, may they rest in peace. Upon graduation, you immediately moved to Hollywood, which has yet to give you the opportunity you crave or show you the respect you deserve. Apart from scoring a coveted waiter position at a popular Wolfgang Puck restaurant, life's been one long string of disappointments ever since."

Talk about sweet and sour. The sixty-second summary was

spot on. And yet, knowing all that, the talent scout had chosen him. He, Lars de Kock, had been chosen. There was no other obvious explanation for Tom's wealth of background knowledge. *But chosen for what?* It had to be something top shelf if they employed a guy this solid. "Which agency are you with?"

Tom cracked a smile. Not a toothy grin, but enough upward trajectory in a corner of his mouth to count as one on his chiseled monolith. "The most powerful, selective, and prestigious agency."

Lars had walked right into that one. If he guessed incorrectly, he'd be shooting himself in the foot. Rather than risk it, he took a different tack. "What kind of role do you have in mind?"

"It's not a single role, Lars. We have a whole career mapped out for you."

This was really happening! He'd worked long, and he'd worked hard, but he'd never, ever, given up hope. Lars had trouble containing his excitement. Maybe he didn't need to. Tom surely knew what this meant to him. "Sounds good. What's next?"

Tom had that answer ready. "An extensive audition." He reached into his jacket pocket and pulled out an envelope, which he slid across the table.

Lars waited for the confirming nod, then opened it. "A plane ticket. For tomorrow morning. To Newport News/ Williamsburg International Airport in Virginia? Is this a set location?"

"It's a training facility location."

"I don't follow."

"I don't recruit for a studio, Lars. I recruit for the CIA."

The waitress returned, dry salad in hand, before Lars had fully digested the surprising twist. She had forgotten the lemon slice, but he chose not to remind her.

"What does the CIA want with me?"

Tom threw the question right back at him, in a lighter tone. "What does the CIA want with a charismatic Princeton honors grad who knows how to act?"

Now that Lars thought about it, the idea wasn't totally

crazy. His college roommate had joined the CIA straight out of school—although he always claimed to work for the State Department. Thinking back, Lars recalled that while Chase had been ROTC, headed for the army, he'd switched teams after a recruiter not unlike Tom came calling.

"We're not asking for a commitment," Tom continued. "In fact, until you pass a polygraph we won't be in a position to extend an offer. But if you do pass, I can assure you that the offer will be an enviable one. Will you take two days to find out what Uncle Sam has to say?"

8

The Line

LARS SPOTTED THE DRIVER outside baggage claim, exactly where Tom had indicated. He was holding a blank name placard with a gray border, just as Tom had said he would.

Lars identified himself with a nod, as instructed.

The handsome black man held out a big hand, palm up. "Your cell phone, please."

"You want my phone?"

"If you want to go any further, you'll need to hand it over."

Tom had warned Lars not to breathe a word to anyone about his potential employment, or tell anyone where he was going. If he found himself backed into a corner, he was to say he had a promising but confidential audition on the East Coast, a story that had the virtue of being entirely true. But no such situation had arisen. Sadly, Lars was an introvert. It was the attribute he blamed for his lack of career progress but was helpless to correct.

"You get a letter and a tablet in return," the driver added, producing the items from behind the blank placard.

Lars traded devices and watched while the driver sealed his phone into what looked like a thick Mylar bag. As they walked toward the airport garage, Lars read the letter. It was short and printed on plain paper.

Welcome to Virginia. Say nothing to the driver. He is not a Company man. Once you are alone in the back seat of the car, unlock the iPad with your right thumb and proceed as instructed.

Unlock it with my thumb. Clearly, and in retrospect not surprisingly, the CIA operated on a different plane.

The driver raised a partition as the car started moving, making the first instruction easy to comply with. Lars followed the second instruction a few seconds later as their town car merged onto I-64 E toward Camp Peary, which he now knew housed the CIA field operations training facility known as The Farm.

The iPad unlocked to reveal a white screen with *Lars de Kock*, the date, and *Part 1: Psychological Profile* printed bold on center screen. The text vanished the instant Lars finished reading and a set of instructions appeared. *Answer quickly and honestly, with 1 being Nothing Like Me and 5 being Just Like Me*. Again the text vanished the instant Lars finished reading, and he realized with astonished admiration that the iPad must be tracking his eye movements.

Q1: I want to work where contagious diseases run rampant.

Lars pressed 1 while wondering if the device captured his eye roll.

Q2: I work well in isolation.

Lars pressed 5.

Q3: I get nervous around guns.

Lars pressed 1.

Q4: I love my country.

Lars pressed 5.

Q5: I have a lot of friends.

Lars considered pressing 1, then pressed 2.

And so it went for five minutes, with a display in the upper left corner clicking off the quantity of responses, a clock in the upper right displaying elapsed time, and a number in the center showing what Lars quickly calculated to be the average number of responses per minute. Confirming his initial suspicion regarding eye movements, Lars noted that the screen went blank whenever he glanced out the window—something he did on only two occasions, given his battle with the clock.

At the five-minute mark, the active question faded and *Part 2: Personal Profile* appeared. *Speak your answers, clearly and concisely*, popped up next. What followed was an extensive background questionnaire focusing on family and friends.

Q1: List the names and locations of all relatives with whom you are in contact. Q2: Who are your five best friends? Q3: What restaurants do you frequent? Q4: How long have you lived at your current address? Q5: Who is your landlord? Q6: Who would come to your funeral?

The questions continued until the town car pulled to a stop before the Brown Pelican Inn, a two-story colonial building that at first glance appeared to have about twenty rooms. He suddenly found himself doing things like that, observing and analyzing. He was stepping into the role of a CIA agent the way he would any other acting job.

It struck him that they had not stopped at a checkpoint during the drive. While Lars had been focused on the iPad, he would have noticed that disruption. Given the absence of a flag on the hood or a windshield sticker, this suggested that they were not on the grounds of Camp Peary.

Lars was still processing the destination twist as the driver came around to open his door. After closing it behind him, the driver handed Lars his phone, still sealed in the thick Mylar bag. "Go straight to room 20. The door will be unlocked. Don't dawdle. Don't attract attention."

Lars accepted the phone and retained the tablet. "Thank you."

The hotel looked normal enough. The outside door didn't appear to be reinforced. No cameras or guards were evident. The receptionist, a fit-looking female in her late twenties, appeared preoccupied with her computer as he entered. Lars took the stairs rather than the elevator, as that choice didn't require him to wait around in her field of view. *He was thinking.*

Room 20 was a corner unit at the far end of the hall. Lars paused outside to take a deep breath and roll his shoulders. With a *You can do this!* he pushed open the door.

Tom Bronco sat behind a laptop on the window side of a desk, which he had rearranged so that Lars could sit across from him. To Tom's right, an aluminum briefcase lay on the desk.

Lars immediately wondered what was inside. "I didn't know Uncle Sam sprang for town cars, but I certainly appreciate the gesture."

"As you'll see if we get that far, Uncle Sam's usual rules don't apply to us." Tom's tone was friendly but businesslike. "Please, have a seat."

Lars sat. "Thank you. I'm a bit surprised to be here. Rather than The Farm, I mean."

Tom held out a hand. "I'll take two apples, please."

Lars spent a second processing the odd request, then produced the iPad and iPhone.

Tom set the phone aside, then unlocked the tablet with his thumb. He began swiping screens and scanning answers.

Lars tried to read his reaction, but failed. Tom might as well have been a machine.

After half a minute with the iPad, Tom hit the power button. He set the tablet down and opened the briefcase.

Lars wanted to strain his neck to see inside but decided that would be bad form.

"Please lift up your shirt."

Lars hadn't known how to dress for the CIA, so he'd worn his conservative suit, a navy-blue Hugo Boss with a lot of miles on it, and a plain white shirt, no tie, accessorized with polished black leather lace-ups and a matching belt. He had a very limited wardrobe, but it was all quality stuff. "Pardon?"

Tom pulled a black strap from the briefcase. It was attached to a curly cord. "Or unbutton it, your choice."

As he untucked and unbuttoned, Lars knew what would come next. A polygraph.

9
The Sinker

THE POLYGRAPH PROVED to be less stressful and antagonistic than Lars had anticipated. It was more like a methodical mining of his past than a criminal interrogation, with the focus on friends and family. Since he had none of the latter and few of the former, it took only a couple of hours.

After that, they spent ten minutes talking compensation. The salary wouldn't make him rich, but it was considerably better than Lars was expecting, and the benefits were excellent.

"You ready for a steak and a beer?" Tom asked, shutting and locking the briefcase—with the *two apples* inside.

"Sure." Lars wanted to ask how he had done on the test but resolved to play it cool. He had no reason to be concerned, and he didn't want to give the impression that he was. Plus, he figured that Tom wouldn't have bothered discussing the pay package if an obvious problem were present.

Tom rose and motioned toward the door. "There's a good place just across the street."

As they stepped onto the asphalt, Tom used a remote to pop the trunk of a rented Mercedes, further dispelling Lars's impressions of government service. Tom locked the aluminum briefcase inside before they continued across the parking lot.

"You don't live around here?" Lars asked, nodding toward the rental.

"I travel a lot."

Lars noted the evasive answer. Tom had no personal belongings visible in the hotel room, and the bathroom accoutrements had appeared untouched when Lars made use of the facilities.

"Table for Bronco," Tom told the hostess.

The perky coed inside the entrance of Berret's Taphouse Grill checked her log. "You reserved the two-top in the corner of the bar. Right this way."

Berret's had a terra cotta tiled floor and draped white valances decorating the ceiling. Its brick walls were adorned with original paintings by local artists—Lars assumed, spotting price tags—and empty wine glasses accompanied every table setting.

The hostess led them through the main room to one in the back. It featured an old oak bar running the length of the inside wall and offered an atmosphere far more lively and casual than that in the main dining room.

Tom sat with his back to the corner, leaving Lars facing him and nothing else. "This place is known for its seafood, but I tend to order the filet with Brie. It's worth the sin."

Lars pushed his menu aside. When a patron was paying, he would normally go with whatever fish the restaurant served whole, but he was here to seal the deal, not satisfy his stomach. And if this went well, he wouldn't need to remain so watchful of his weight. "Works for me."

A waitress with red hair, a deep dimple, and "Carla" on her name tag appeared. Tom ordered drinks without consulting Lars or the microbrewery menu.

"Two pints of Fearless coming right up," Carla replied.

Once she moved on, Tom released the tension. "The tests you've taken today were all scored live. You did well. Are you still interested in serving your country?"

Lars felt the tight spot between his shoulder blades release as he gave himself a mental high-five. "I find the general idea very interesting, but of course it's the specifics that matter."

Tom's eyes twinkled. "When it comes to working for Uncle Sam, it doesn't get any better than this. My job is better than being president." Tom leaned in and spoke just loud enough for Lars to hear. "I recruit for a division of the Special Operations Group that's formally known as FIFO."

"Like the soccer organization?"

"That's FIFA. Like the accounting term."

Lars had been an economics major, but it had been a decade since his accounting experience ventured beyond balancing his checkbook. Still, the term was readily recalled. "First In, First Out."

"Exactly. The name almost says it all."

"Almost?"

"Our nickname is the 'Dry Cleaners.' It's a direct contrast with our brother group, the *Wet Wipes*. The operative difference being that we solve problems with brains, whereas they solve problems—"

"With blood." Lars got the picture, and he liked it.

His own appearance resembled the traditional depiction of Jesus, with long brown hair, bright brown soulful eyes, and one of those trendy barely beards. He had always appreciated the association with the Savior and would hate to give it up, even if only in his own mind, because of a clashing career choice.

The server reappeared with a frosty mug in each hand. "Two Fearless beers."

"We're going to go with large filets," Tom said with the satisfaction of a man on an unconstrained expense account. "Medium-rare for mine. And a Caesar salad to start."

"Same here," Lars said.

Carla nodded without taking notes, then disappeared.

Tom resumed his pitch while Lars relaxed. "You're an honors graduate from Princeton, so you've got brains. You've spent a decade acting in Hollywood, so you've got the equivalent of undercover skills. Plus you lack any binding ties."

"Binding ties?"

"If you were to go deep undercover tomorrow and be completely cut off from your old life for six months—" Tom trailed off, allowing Lars to complete the sentence.

"Nobody would make a fuss," Lars said as another puzzle piece clicked into place. "Now I understand your questions."

Tom raised his beer in a silent salute and they both took sips.

"Going undercover can be tough and even dangerous, but working with the Dry Cleaners is as rewarding as government service gets. The team is tip-top. The missions are high-impact. And the expense accounts are *very* generous.

"It is an all-in commitment," Tom continued after a second sip. "Like joining the French Foreign Legion or Men in Black. You'll have to cut all ties to your old life. Lars de Kock will virtually vanish. But at the same time, you'll gain a fantastic family, a noble purpose, and all the excitement you can handle."

"What kind of undercover assignments?"

"Overseas, of course. The kind that don't make the news."

"Can you give me an example?" Lars asked, feeling a bit bolder now that he'd crossed the finish line with a winning time.

"I'll give you a few," Tom said, his volume still low but his voice now more congenial than businesslike. "You might be placed on a legitimate team of consultants that's advising a foreign government or corporation, with the goal of obtaining information or recruiting an asset. You might perform the role of a playboy eager to purchase stolen artwork. You might act like a disgruntled CIA agent who can be purchased for a price. We match needs with clever resolutions. Dry cleaning, not wet wiping."

"Got it. Thank you."

The salads arrived, then the steaks. Lars plowed through his meal, working to match Tom's impressive speed. The CIA operative ate like a machine, slicing his steak thin and chewing intensely as if intent on aiding digestion. Lars set his steak knife down for the last time while Tom was draining his beer.

The recruiter picked up a drink napkin and proceeded to roll it into a ball. "Knowing that you've had a long day, I'm going to leave you to eat your dessert in peace. I recommend the chocolate lava cake." He pulled two hundred-dollar bills from a money clip, creased them the long way, and left them tented on the table. "Do me a favor and collect the receipt."

"Sure thing," Lars said, wondering if a man as ripped as Tom ever actually ate cake. Then again, the man had just inhaled a filet covered in Brie. Maybe he ran marathons. He did look like the kind of guy who would suffer for fun.

Tom put the napkin ball on the table. "Tomorrow night at this time, I'm going to pick you up at the hotel. By the way, that was your room, number 20." He pulled a key card from his breast pocket and slid it across the table. "I'll take you either to FIFO HQ or back to the airport. Your choice entirely. In either case, you're not to mention anything we've discussed, or anything you've experienced, now or ever. We'll know if you do, and we'll put you in prison." The business tone was back. "Understood?"

Lars's little bit of boldness faded. "Understood."

"Good. Please remember to collect the receipt. Meanwhile, enjoy the cake. Spies might need to watch their backs, but they don't need to worry about their waistlines."

10
Twists of Fate

LARS LOOKED AROUND Berret's Taphouse as Tom rose from the table. The bar was now packed with a professional-looking crowd. Happy hour. He wondered how many of them were his new peers.

Tom didn't display the swagger one might expect from a master of the clandestine universe now off the clock. He just came across as a tough-as-nails guy in an expensive suit.

As the CIA recruiter pressed through the throng near the door, one of the people he brushed shoulders with caught Lars's eye. It was a guy Lars knew well. A guy Lars had discussed just hours ago during the polygraph test. One of his five best friends. One of the people he'd expect at his funeral.

Zachary Chase had been Lars's roommate at Princeton and a member of the same eating club. After graduation, Chase had stayed on the East Coast, whereas Lars had gone West. Facebook kept them in touch, as did the alumni network, but they'd shared space only twice. Once when Chase crashed on his couch for a week during vacation, the second time more recently at their ten-year reunion. On both occasions, the two had slipped back into their groove with comfort and ease.

Lars stood and waved like an air-traffic controller.

Chase wasn't looking in his direction.

"Chase!"

His fellow Ivy Club diner turned, recognized his old friend, and walked straight over with open arms. "What are you doing at Berret's?"

"Like you don't know."

Chase pulled back from the backslapping hug. "Did I miss an email?"

"That's how you're going to play it?"

Chase scrunched his face but didn't respond directly. "It's great to see you, man. I was just thinking about you. You got time for dinner and a drink? The sea bass here is killer."

"I just ate, but you go ahead."

As Chase took the seat Tom had just vacated, Lars decided this was either a terrific coincidence—or a convenient test. "What brings you to Berret's?"

"I'm in the mood for a drink, and they have a great selection of microbrews." His voice sounded edgy, and his face was fraught with mixed emotions.

"Tough day at work?"

"Last day at work, actually. I just got fired. After ten years."

This was a recruiting tactic Lars didn't see coming. "Seriously? The CIA let you go?"

"State Department," Chase corrected.

"If you're fired, I don't have to pretend not to know any more, right? Besides, Camp Peary isn't State Department, it's CIA."

"Actually, it's DoD."

Chase flagged the red-haired waitress and said, "Two Fierce, please."

Carla nodded but didn't break stride. This was prime tip time.

"Let's forget my woes. What brings you to this little corner of the East Coast?" Chase asked.

Lars decided to go with the vague answer. "I'm auditioning for an interesting role."

Chase sat back and began nodding to himself. He almost started to smile. "Makes sense. Your analytical skills plus your acting talent."

Convincing as Chase was, Lars didn't believe he'd been fired. This was clearly an act to show him how it was done. A live lesson from an expert in his prime. Were they also giving him a chance to ask candid questions? One way to find out. "Why did they let you go?"

Chase rubbed his temples. "There was a go-along-to-get-along situation about six months back. I wouldn't go along.

Firing me would have been awkward, so they pulled me out of the field and parked me at Camp Peary while investigations were conducted. I kept my nose to the grindstone and hoped the political winds would change or the better angels would prevail, but they fired me."

"And you can't fight it?"

"No point. Even a win would be a loss. My career could never progress, and I'm too young for that. I need to know I can grow. And I want to be appreciated. Fortunately, it's not unusual to move on from government service after ten years."

Carla brought the beers. Frosty mugs sloshing foamy heads onto cardboard coasters.

They clinked glasses and sipped while Lars wondered if Chase had just delivered a message. At worst, this opportunity was a great stepping stone. "So what's next? Your résumé must be killer. Pun intended," he added with a wink.

Chase didn't chuckle. "I really don't know. Something very different. You still have the place near Venice Beach?"

Lars had a rent-controlled apartment two blocks from the sand. It was small and old, but the location was prime and the rent was less than half the true market price. He wouldn't give it up until he hit Hollywood's A list. Or at least the B. "I sure do. Why?"

"That's what I wanted to talk to you about. I'm seriously considering renting a Harley and riding the Pacific Coast Highway. The idea has been in the back of my mind for years. Thought I'd crash on your couch for a few days before heading out. Would that be okay?"

"You, on a Harley?" Lars had trouble picturing that scene. Chase was as straitlaced and clean-cut as they came. A star rower who skipped the parties to study and went to church on Sundays.

"As I said, I want to try something very different. Might even let my hair grow longer than an inch if it still can."

Lars had always worn his hair long, Chase always short. "I gotta see that."

"Well, all right then. I'll text you when I have my ticket.

You still have the 7007 number?"

Lars thought about his phone's current whereabouts, and his pending disappearance. For a moment he wasn't sure how to handle this situation. Then he realized that he wouldn't have to. Chase wasn't really coming. This whole run-in was an *acting for espionage* lesson. An excellent lesson. "I sure do."

11
Missing Person

One week later
Venice Beach, California

MY KNOCKING TURNED TO POUNDING as my frustration grew. Lars wasn't answering his phone. Not my calls, not my texts. I wasn't sure what I should do now that he wasn't answering his door either. Should I try to sweet-talk the landlord into letting me in? Should I camp out on the doorstep and wait? Or should I give up and go to a hotel?

I could pick my way into his apartment, of course, but then I'd be a sitting duck if someone spotted me and called the police.

This sucked! I wanted to see my buddy and I needed to save cash. I also preferred not to begin my great getaway in jail.

I decided to start with a note. I'd leave it on the door, then take the Harley on a tour of Venice Beach. If Lars hadn't returned by the time I got back, I'd settle down across the street at his favorite bar and grill to wait. If Lars still wasn't back by the time it got dark, then I'd pick his lock.

But first, I'd stop by the landlord's office and hope to get lucky. I could show the picture from Berret's that was still on my phone and offer a driver's license and credit card as collateral in exchange for a key.

I pulled a pen from my backpack and wrote a note on my used boarding pass. *I'm here with the Harley! Tried texting and calling, but -7007 appears to be an old number. Give me a call or come find me at Foxy's. Chase.*

I wondered if Lars would do a double take, finding me in biker boots and a black leather jacket rather than my habitual polo shirt and sneakers. The image brought a smile to my face.

Free from government service, I'd decided to stretch my boundaries and expand my horizons. Escape myself as much as my old world. Now I understood why Harley-Davidson's marketing focused on *finding freedom.*

While crossing the courtyard, I spotted Lars leaving the apartment office. *Thank goodness!* Spreading my arms in a welcoming gesture that would turn into a hug, I said, "It's about time!"

Lars didn't react.

At least not as expected.

As we closed the gap, I detected panic on my friend's face. Once that distance dropped to a few paces, I saw that it wasn't Lars—just someone with a very similar face, hairstyle, and build. He was even wearing a faded funky-logo T-shirt and old jeans, as was Lars's predilection.

I dropped my arms.

The doppelgänger walked past with an obvious effort not to look me in the eye. *They have all types out here on the fruity fringe.*

I continued to the apartment office, where I found a twenty-something employee stapling papers. "I'm looking for Lars de Kock."

The young manager looked up. "You just missed him."

"That wasn't him. Did look like him though. I'm supposed to be staying with Lars for a few days but haven't been able to contact him. Was hoping you might let me in. I've got pictures and ID."

The manager looked left, then right, a promising start. Apparently satisfied that they were unobserved, he rotated his freshly stapled stack of papers around so I could read the header. "No, that was him. I saw his ID. Mr. de Kock just surrendered his apartment."

"Lars wouldn't do that. It's rent controlled, right?"

The manager smiled. "It was. The next guy will be paying three times the price."

I focused on the signature. It sure looked like Lars', with the framing L and violent Ks. This was one slick impersonation.

I immediately understood the scam. The landlord had figured out how to repossess his rent-controlled units and was using his minimum-wage employees as unwilling accomplices. Shameless bastard. "Do you happen to know where Lars went?"

"I know he didn't go to his room. I've got the keys, and the movers have come and gone."

Of course they had. Lars was in for one hell of a surprise when he returned from whatever acting gig was keeping him away. It couldn't be the CIA. Could it? No way. Their recruiting process took months, and it had only been days.

I sprinted for my Harley.

Given the price of real estate, resident parking in this neighborhood was almost always underground in tight, assigned spaces you needed a key card to access. Like most, Lars's place also had limited visitor parking at the top of the ramp. I had successfully snagged a spot there, given that my vehicle only had two wheels.

The first car exiting as I approached my ride was a BMW i8, the German automaker's $150,000 luxury plug-in hybrid. I would have ignored it had there been movement elsewhere, knowing that neither Lars nor anyone hired for an impersonation gig could afford such a ride. But the driver's nervous sideways glances attracted my attention, and I met his eye.

It was the impostor.

He immediately turned onto the side street and accelerated with a tire screech.

I hopped on the Harley and slammed on my helmet. Ignoring both my bent ears and the dangling chin straps, I hit the keyless ignition, grabbed the handlebars, and screeched out in pursuit.

As the rental company's advertisements had described, the Harley-Davidson *Iron 883* was an appealing amalgam of old and new. The poster bike of the anti-chrome movement, it had a black-powder-coated 883cc engine, with chopped fenders and a short suspension. The low seat was tuck and roll and the handlebars drag-style. Even though I was still getting a feel for the beast, I doubted there was a production car on the planet that could outrun me. Certainly, there'd be no escape in L.A. traffic.

The BMW headed north on Pacific toward Santa Monica. I started off three cars behind but split the lane and soon eliminated the gap. I figured it was best to put the pressure on and eliminate any chance of red-light interference.

I had no way to force the impostor off the road. Not with only two wheels and no weapons at my command. But I could stay on his bumper for the next 170 miles or so. My Harley had a full tank of gas.

I used a red light to adjust my helmet and snug the chinstrap. Adding to the mystery, the impostor made quick use of his cell phone to snap my picture while my helmet was off—as if I were the one committing the crime.

When he shot me a furtive mirror glance at the next light, I gave the engine a rev. The cackle was glorious.

His expression was miserable.

He didn't look again for quite some time.

As Pacific became Neilson Way, he launched into an animated phone conversation. I hoped it was a 911 call. Getting the police involved was one way to resolve this. With the impostor instigating, I could then insist on a police escort back to the apartment complex where the fraud could be documented.

I knew that tactic would be much less likely to work if I made the call. The impostor could say I was a nut job and refuse to go anywhere. No doubt the police in these privileged ZIP codes would favor a resident in his new luxury import over an outsider on a rented bike. Nonetheless, I resolved to place that call if we reached the 100-mile mark.

But that was still a long way off.

Neilson turned into Palisades Beach and then into the Pacific Coast Highway. The impostor returned to eyeballing me in the mirror, although ever less frequently as the city gave way to the meandering cliffside coastline for which

California was famous. He also seemed to be talking on occasion, although whether cursing to himself or into the hands-free phone, I couldn't tell.

As the traffic thinned, the impostor became emboldened and began playing with me. Accelerating and braking for random distances and at odd intervals, testing both the limits of the i8 and my ability to handle the rental bike. Through it all, I stuck behind the BMW's bumper as if attached by a string. Did this guy really think he could outmaneuver a motorcycle? Or was he just burning off nervous energy with a bit of gorilla posturing?

As if in answer to my musings, the i8 turned off PCH and headed up a two-lane road that didn't look like it had been resurfaced since the Eisenhower administration. We added altitude quickly as the snaking asphalt repeatedly lost and regained its view of the shimmering Pacific. Within a minute, we were well off the beaten path.

My CIA instincts flashed a warning.

Suppose my assumption was wrong. What if this was more than the grab of a rent-controlled apartment? That would explain why Lars wasn't answering his phone. What if I was being led to a house in the hills with trigger-happy security guards or hicks with shotguns? Furthermore, just because the impostor had initially been frightened didn't mean he couldn't grow a pair, stop the car, and step out shooting. Up here, the only witnesses would be the birds. The same birds that would then pick my corpse clean to the bone.

I began working defensive scenarios in my mind.

The impostor floored the gas as we took the next tight turn, going from south of 40 mph to north of 80 mph in the span of a second. I kept pace, resolving not to allow him to slip out of sight and into a firing position.

I remained so focused on the i8's rear bumper that I never saw the black SUV accelerating from its hiding spot on the shoulder of the road. It wasn't until I was flying over the guardrail two hundred feet above the canyon floor that the tactic registered and everything clicked. The hands-free calls. The winding routes. The erratic driving. The impostor had summoned assistance to orchestrate an ambush.

12
Close Call

BY THE TIME David reached Lisa's estate, his grip on the BMW's leather-wrapped wheel had almost returned to normal. He wasn't entirely certain that his nervous system ever would. He knew he'd never forget the image of the menacing motorcyclist and his monstrous Harley careening off the road and plunging into the canyon. Why did it have to be a motorcycle? Cars were so much more anonymous.

David checked his watch and did the math. He could have looked at the dashboard clock, but he wanted to see if his hand would shake. One hundred and fifty minutes had passed since he'd U-turned toward San Clemente while Tory Lago waved from his Range Rover. Those two-and-a-half hours had passed in a blur.

David parked his blue BMW between Allison's white Mercedes and Ries's red Ferrari.

Ries opened his door as David's sneakers scrunched onto the crushed stone. "What's with the hair and outfit?"

David had forgotten about his hair extensions. Funny, since they'd bothered him so much at first. He unclipped and tossed them back into his car while answering his brother researcher. "My doppelgänger leads a very different lifestyle. I was just impersonating him and haven't had the opportunity to change. Or shave," he added, rubbing the stylish stubble that these days passed for a beard.

"You look flustered, my friend."

"It's been one hell of a morning."

"Love to hear about it later, but we better get inside. Lisa is anxious to get started. I just came out to get my old phone for the exchange."

David felt his pants pocket, confirming that he had his. The Immortals had begun using anonymous VoIP burner phones to communicate once the replacement process started. As a further security measure, they had agreed to swap them out for fresh ones at every meeting. "What's there to be anxious about? We have plenty of time."

"Funny. You know as well as I do that with Lisa it's an indelible personality trait."

"One can always hope."

As David grabbed his medical bag, Ries said. "Hey, there's no tissue sampling this time, right? We agreed to stop after twenty years of negatives."

"For the tough guy, you're quite the wuss. Yeah, I remember. Just the treatments plus a blood test. But don't expect a lollipop."

David dropped his bag in the den, where he'd later administer their semiannual Eos injections; then he headed straight for the grand room.

"Are you all right, David?" Aria asked as he entered.

He turned toward his financial beneficiary, embarrassed by the attention. She looked the same as always, meaning she probably hadn't been through the replacement process. Allison, by contrast, had a totally new look. She came across as much more glamorous, with a complete makeover, blonde hair extensions, and breast implants.

"I'm fine. Apologies. I had a rough morning. Sorry I'm late."

Felix handed him a pinot noir in one of those crystal wine glasses that could substitute for a fishbowl and put a reassuring palm on his shoulder. Felix also retained his original look—which was prematurely gray. An ironic twist for an Immortal. He'd likely be dyeing it once his replacement came through.

"Thank you, my friend."

As David gave his glass a swirl, Lisa said, "We should get started."

Lisa had the second-most radical change in the room. She had traded her dark hair for a much shorter auburn style and had exchanged her designer wardrobe for one straight from a 1980s Brooks Brothers catalogue. Someone had mentioned that Lisa had replaced a separating Army officer. Despite her commanding personality, David found that an odd choice.

"Given the late start, we'll push new business until after Tory's presentation. Before that, Felix wanted a few words. If you'll all kindly follow me to the theater."

* * *

Felix stood silently beside the big screen while everyone selected a seat. "Since this will be our first group discussion with Tory, I wanted to spend a second on operational security and answer any sensitive questions you might have.

"First the security. Tory knows nothing about us, and we should make every effort to keep it that way, both through concealment and by sowing confusion. For example, you'll notice that I occasionally let a slight Russian accent slip into my speech. You might consider using that tactic as well if you have to talk."

"But he's about to see us!" Camilla interjected. "Should we be disguising ourselves?"

Felix could always count on Camilla to miss the obvious —if it wasn't fashion or society related. When it came to keeping up with the Joneses and manipulating public perception, she was a savant. "By knowing nothing I meant biographical data. He is, of course, intimately familiar with what you look like and sound like from the videos you provided as part of the replacement process. He can't operate without that information."

"Of course. I forgot. Too much wine." Camilla raised her glass.

"Can't he trace this call to our location?" Aria asked.

Aria had a delightfully disarming way about her. Felix

considered it her secret weapon. She was much more savvy and intelligent than you'd think at first glance, because at first glance you were thinking that you'd like to take her clothes off—and she just might let you.

"No. Like your burner phones, this video call operates over a Darknet VoIP service that provides no geolocation."

Felix looked around. "Any other questions?"

"How many people are on his team?" David asked.

"Tory works alone. He subcontracts when necessary—programmers and limo drivers and such—but those people know nothing about how their little piece of action fits into a larger puzzle." Felix's phone vibrated as he spoke.

He checked the screen. "I see that Tory is online, so we'll pause the questions if there are no objections?"

Felix did a quick visual survey of the room, then hit the button that brought the big flat screen to life. Tory's distinctive face, with its chiseled cheekbones and butch-cut strawberry-blond hair, came into focus. He locked his pale blue eyes on the camera and said, "Good afternoon."

13
Tastes and Tactics

LISA COULDN'T HELP being reminded of Vladimir Putin whenever Tory Lago smiled. While the Finn had more hair than the Russian president, and his cheekbones were far more pronounced, the two predators shared the same crocodile stare. Cold, cunning, and clearly willing to make a snack out of her.

While she silently questioned the wisdom of employing such a man, Felix turned toward the freshly illuminated screen. "Good afternoon, Tory. We're all gathered and ready for your update."

Tory's reply came with a two-second delay. A result of the VoIP relay, no doubt. "I'm happy to finally have the opportunity to address you all at once. As you know, I've been at this for six months now. During that time, I've identified replacements for all nine of you and have completed seven."

Despite his militant appearance, Tory had a smooth voice. It came across as intelligent and sincere, again reminding Lisa of the Russian president. Undoubtedly, that charisma was working in the Immortals' favor, given the interactive nature of his assignment.

"So far there has been just one hiccup, and as luck would have it, that hiccup happened earlier this morning. David ran into someone looking for his replacement at the very moment he happened to be there closing out business. Fortunately, David called me right away. I was able to eliminate the security breach before it could become a threat.

"Regardless of that blip, I expect to have the two remaining replacements—those for Aria and Felix—completed within a month."

"Are you confident that you've cured my hiccups?" David asked.

Taking tone into account, Lisa surmised that David considered it closer to a heart attack than a hiccup.

Tory didn't blink. "Well, first of all, that was the one and only time you'll be required to interface with your replacement's life. Now that all his *accounts* have been closed, you're free and clear to operate elsewhere as Lars de Kock.

"Furthermore, as you know, my contract calls for the ongoing monitoring and managing of all replacements. I can't predict the future actions of others, but I can commit to swift resolutions should any such instances occur.

"It's also worth noting that my work in that regard is not just reactive. I put considerable effort into identifying introverted replacement candidates with extremely limited family and friend networks. That said, none of the replacements are actual ghosts, so the potential will always exist. Hence the ongoing contract."

Pierce cleared his throat as David settled back into his chair. "I'd like to learn more about the tactics you're employing to make the transitions work. I'm particularly interested in how you forestall family and law enforcement investigations?"

Tory brushed an imaginary hair off his shoulder before answering. Lisa didn't know him well enough to gauge whether it was a subconscious tell or a conscious suppression tactic. "In each instance, I designed a con that got the replacements to first volunteer extensive background information and then relocate to a place where they had no family or friends. If you think about it, friendships are almost always tied to common geography. If a person isn't family, then when they move, the connections wither and die."

"You can't count on that in the age of social media," Pierce pressed.

"Correct, but people regularly back away from those platforms for other reasons. Facebook accounts are canceled all the time. Turning them off is a growing trend, given rising concerns about privacy, addiction, depression, and other related maladies. In a word, abandoning social media doesn't raise red flags."

While Pierce nodded along, David hopped back in. "Will you give us an example of one of your cons?"

Tory inclined his head. "Most recently, in your case as a matter of fact, I posed as a CIA recruiter. This allowed—"

"I get it," David said. "That's brilliant."

"How do you find our doppelgängers in the first place?" Allison asked. "I'd think that would take an army of spies, but Felix insists that you work alone."

Tory tilted his head the other way, but his facial expression didn't change. "Twenty years ago, it would have taken an army to accomplish. Not today. Everyone we're interested in has a broadband internet connection, and most are actively engaged with social media. These days, people constantly post videos and pictures of themselves. Particularly people in your age group and younger.

"To access and harvest that treasure trove, I contracted with a Russian company. They wrote a program that scours all the major American social media interfaces—and some government ones. It identifies matches for any face I upload. The software is sophisticated enough to ignore alterable characteristics, things like facial hair and blemishes, hairstyle, hair color, and eye color. It can even adjust for weight gains and losses, although I've never needed to use that feature."

"But there's more to it than matching appearances," Allison pressed. "We need loners, and in some cases specific skill sets."

"Indeed you do, and again the software comes through. As I mentioned, most of the matches come from social media sites or government databases. In both instances, profile data accompanies the photos, and with social media it's also paired with posts. Once the software finds a photo it likes, it scans the accompanying documentation for helpful keywords."

"Such as?"

"Words like *relocation, depression, abandoned,* and *orphan.* Please bear in mind, we're dealing with enormous data pools. In any given five-year age band, there are approximately ten million American men and another ten million women. Seventy-two percent of them are Caucasian, like you. That means I get to select from among 7.2 million people who fit your basic demographic profile. That's a lot of job candidates—all of whom have eyes, ears, and noses in roughly the same place you do."

Lisa found herself chuckling along with her peers at Tory's last remark but noted that Felix was busy surveying the room. No doubt he was happy to see the positive reaction to Tory's presentation. Felix had recruited the consultant, and he managed him, so he shared in Tory's successes and failures.

"Has anyone rejected your choice of replacement?" Pierce asked.

"No. But then only three of you asked to be involved in the final selection process."

"Really?" Pierce looked around. "That's surprising."

Lisa was also amazed. "Why wouldn't people want to pick the history they were assuming?"

Tory offered an insightful answer. "While most people enjoy a good hamburger, few want to pet the cow."

14

Reckless Abandon

WITH TORY'S REPORT FINISHED, it was time for more routine business. David's mind wandered as Felix launched into an update of their efforts to sabotage other immortality research programs. Although David shared his peers' interest in preventing others from discovering the secret to halting aging, he already knew what Felix would say.

David had supplied Felix with the intel on what projects they should be sabotaging and which researchers were best positioned to assist in those efforts. All Felix had to do was recruit them. He didn't handle that personally, of course. He hired blind intermediaries. Retired intelligence operatives with experience in the appropriate operating theater, whether in Beijing, Munich, Tel Aviv, or Silicon Valley.

China had been their big adversary in the early years. The Chinese government was all over both glutathione research and telomere shortening. But after Eos's spies orchestrated a few big embarrassments, they abandoned both in favor of more promising programs. These days, the big threat came from Google, with its Calico project. Despite Google's incredible clout, Calico didn't stand a chance. Basic accounting was the reason. Whereas everyone in Silicon Valley was slaving away in hopes of a big payout somewhere down the line, the Immortals could pay even bigger, and they did so without delay.

Nobody asked Felix any questions when he finished his report, so he yielded center stage.

David wasn't surprised by the lack of interest. After twenty years, the medical and mechanical aspects of maintaining halted aging had become routine. Retaining exclusive access to the required pharmaceuticals was now assumed. Kind of like smallpox vaccine.

David was disappointed that interest in the philosophical facets of their special status had also withered on the vine. His fellow Immortals were now fully focused on the daily ups and downs of their personal lives. It was an inevitable development, David knew. Pausing the clock did not change human nature. Still, he wished his peers shared his interest in the big picture.

Lisa and Pierce stood up as Felix sat down. Their body language tripped a switch in David's lizard brain. The forced straightening of Pierce's spine. The firm set of Lisa's lips. Something serious was in the works.

Lisa took a half step forward. "Continuing our discussion of new business, Pierce and I have an announcement. A matter we need to put up for a vote."

The entire audience perked up at that announcement. The only issues requiring votes were those that impacted everyone in a material manner.

"Instead of setting the stage with a long lead-in," Lisa continued, "I'll skip straight to the summit. We've both decided to seek seats in the United States Senate."

David felt his stomach flip as he bit back an impulsive outburst. It was an unthinkable idea. Outrageous, irresponsible, and irrational. What were they thinking?

"I know this is a bit surprising and perhaps contrary to our tenet of leading low-profile lives. But we think we've learned enough over the past twenty years to mitigate the risks, and we believe this is the best way to protect our long-term interests."

"What long-term interests?" Aria asked.

Aria's scornful tone surprised David. Clearly, she had not been privy to this plan. That shed a surprising light on the relationship between the Immortals' alpha females.

Like the professional CEO she was—or like a polished politician, David mused—Lisa remained outwardly calm and upbeat. "Lately, the political Powers That Be seem intent on satisfying special interests. Special industries to be exact. It's gotten to the point where Pierce and I are seriously concerned that we Immortals will eventually fall victim to some manmade global catastrophe. Therefore, we've decided to take preemptive measures."

Ries, usually the happy-go-lucky guy, hopped into the fray with both feet. "We've taken extensive measures to avoid detection, not the least of which is the recent replacement process. For decades we've avoided publicity and public appearances. We've paid handsomely to have professionals scrub our images from the internet. We've even begun masking our continued association, to the extent that we can't congregate or even leave each other voicemails. Now you two want to seek the center of the national spotlight? Forget it! There are other ways to influence policy."

Felix also raised his sword. "I agree with everything Ries said. Find a tactic that keeps us in the shadows."

David's building anger began turning to fear when he noted the nonchalant nature with which Lisa and Pierce were absorbing the backlash. It was as if they knew they had the votes tied up. But they didn't. Not if Aria wasn't on board.

David voiced his vote, even though it was a forgone conclusion. The researchers always stuck together. "I also agree with Ries. It won't take a global catastrophe to end our lives if our status is discovered. The fearful and jealous mobs will manage that."

"If the government doesn't lock us in a lab," Aria added. "And in any case, what makes you think you have a shot at the Senate?"

"Let us worry about that."

David's trepidation grew. He analyzed the vote, even though it was the kind of math first-graders could do on their fingers. Clearly Pierce and Lisa would vote yes. Camilla would back Lisa out of loyalty. But that was only three of the nine Immortals. Well, eight, David corrected himself. Eric was gone. And really only seven since Aria was just a tiebreaker. But Felix, the finance guy, was nothing if not practical, as were all three remaining researchers. That made four against three. Tighter than David would have liked, but sufficient.

Still, his apprehension grew. It was a feeling that had been festering ever since they had voted to obtain new identities by killing innocent people—a tactic none of them would have considered twenty years earlier, during their age of mortal innocence. That incredibly selfish strategy had crossed a line, but at least it was logical. If handled professionally, replacing real people was the safest course for them to take. Running for the Senate, by comparison, was completely crazy.

David decided to put his objection on the record. "I feel compelled to emphasize that secrecy is the cornerstone of our security. It is my strong personal opinion that the Immortals must remain in the shadows. Now and forever."

Lisa turned his way with trademark empathy in her eyes. "I respect your opinion, David. I always have. But twenty years ago, we were living in a very different world. A much more stable world. There was no Facebook or YouTube. No iPhones or wikis. Nobody had heard of Bin Laden or Putin or Kim Jong-un. And there were far fewer nuclear weapons. The world is evolving, and our tactics must evolve with it."

"I call for a vote," Pierce said.

"I second it," Camilla said.

Lisa met David's eye, and he knew he was about to lose. "All those in favor of allowing Pierce and me to seek the U.S. Senate, raise your right hand."

The predicted three hands raised high, then an unexpected fourth. David felt his stomach turn to ice. Allison had switched sides.

"The motion passes," Lisa said, her tone steady rather than smug. "Before we close, there is one more point of new business. This one also requires a vote."

David braced himself. What was next? An Immortals clothing line?

"Allison is also interested in a career change. She wants to become an actress."

15

A Code to Crack

TORY CLOSED HIS LAPTOP and walked to the window of his Signature Suite. He stood still for a second, soaking in the view of the Santa Monica shoreline before raising a fist in victory. "Oorah!"

The incident earlier in the day, when Lars's friend had literally crossed paths with David, could not have happened at a worse time. Coming just hours before his first full client briefing, Tory had worried that it might mark the end of his dream job.

But he'd handled that crisis and he'd managed his clients. His gravy train remained on the rails.

Every private contractor hopes for a humongous score, but Tory had not dared to dream this big. It wasn't the $100,000 he was getting per replacement, or even the $900,000 complete customer satisfaction bonus that might follow. The source of his excitement was the $500,000 annual "maintenance payment" he was set to receive forever after. While technically the half-million was to monitor the replacement identities and manage any complications that might arise, the work involved would likely be next to nothing. It was *hush money,* and he loved it.

Looking around the Huntley Hotel room, he had to concede that the Platinum Business Amex credit card that Felix had furnished was also a pretty sweet perk. Near as he could figure, the account was on autopay. And as Amex liked to advertise, it had no preset credit limit. That made this the first time in his life that he hadn't had to worry about expenses. He didn't even have to file reports. Whatever he needed, and frankly whatever he wanted, he just put on the prestigious titanium card.

That even applied to cash withdrawals. Significant

financial advances. He hired quite a few subcontractors, and he paid a lot of bribes. Most often in cash. Always without pushback. Felix kept an eye on the account to be sure, and he asked the occasional question, but he never demanded spreadsheets or written receipts. Their focus was never on money, just results.

They were an interesting bunch, his employers. Incredibly intelligent, but babes in his woods. Felix was a bit of a prick personally, but reasonable and predictable as a business partner. Pierce seemed to be the only one with a solid backbone, although Tory sensed that Lisa could be tough as nails when pressed. The others appeared malleable, more or less.

Life was good.

In fact, Tory's only frustration was that he had no idea who his employers were, or why they needed replacement identities. They had only provided him with the essential information. Everything he needed to locate American lookalikes, but nothing else.

The most intriguing aspect of the mystery was that none of them had showed up during his doppelgänger searches. Normally, when searching for lookalikes, many if not most of the results would be different pictures of the original person. But during this assignment, Tory's clients hadn't popped up a single time. Not one of them. Not once.

If photographic evidence was all you had to go by, they didn't exist.

He'd scanned every database he could hack or bribe his way into, and he'd searched broadly, catching all Caucasians between the ages of twenty and fifty. Not one hit had been a client. Either they'd all effectively scrubbed their internet presences, a practice requiring high-caliber hackers and sophisticated software packages, or they'd never been there, meaning they likely weren't American.

The other thing that befuddled Tory was the odd assortment of replacement profiles they'd ordered. Of the nine, two had ordered "discharging veterans from swing states with serious political potential," while one had asked for "someone with serious acting credentials from someplace other than Hollywood." Those made sense to Tory. If you were going to become someone else, why not get a leg up on a dream? But the other six had basically just asked for "clean" replacement identities.

He toyed with the idea that some foreign intelligence service, most likely the Russians, was trying to plant moles. But he didn't really believe it. Although Felix appeared to be covering an accent, the Russians would almost certainly be focused on specific geographies. Washington, D.C., for starters.

Unless this espionage ploy was something groundbreaking? An unconventional tactic designed to completely confound the CIA? Putin was as clever as they came, so it certainly wasn't out of the question.

In any case, Tory was dying to learn their true identities, and for more than one reason.

If it wasn't a foreign government op, and he could crack their secret, Tory was certain that he could up his annual hush-money payment to an even million. Actually, given the apparent cash on hand, he was fairly certain he could up it to an even rounder eight figures. But he knew all too well from his days with Finnish Intelligence and Triple Canopy that pigs got slaughtered, so one million dollars it would be.

If he ever cracked the code.

His current best guess was that they were all trying to escape something. But what? He had no idea and little time to speculate. His real job of identifying replacements, running background checks, and setting up scams already had him working eighty hours a week. For now, figuring out the *why* would have to wait. But it would make for one hell of a "retirement" hobby.

Tory turned away from the beautiful beachfront view and returned to the desk. He reopened his laptop and keyed in his eighteen-digit password. He had to get cracking on his next job. It was time to pry Skylar Fawkes from her life—making room for Aria.

16
The Fall Guy

SOMETIMES SCARY DREAMS end with wide-open eyes. They shake us into a consciousness characterized by sweaty palms and a pounding heart. During those first frantic seconds, we struggle to acclimate ourselves while searching for the source of danger. Then, in a revelation that strikes with the speed of a serpent, our minds catch up to our bodies and the world comes into focus. We flop back onto our pillows with empty adrenal glands, exhaling sweet and slow.

I did not flop back down as my eyes flew open. I did not immediately orient myself. I had no pillow.

I wasn't even lying down.

I was crumpled on the side of a cliff, my bent knees pressing against a boulder. Above me, a steep range of rock. Behind me, a short grassy knoll. Below me, some hundred and fifty feet, a canyon floor.

Nothing about my body seemed normal. My hearing was impaired and my vision blurry. I felt like Alice in the rabbit hole.

Everything hurt. My head ached enough to wake the dead. My right knee was on fire. Whoever had hit me hadn't used the Goldilocks touch this time.

I found part of the problem when I attempted to cradle my aching head in my trembling hands. Or more accurately, the solution. And the answer. The explanation for my core condition and incredible circumstance. I was wearing a helmet. A motorcycle helmet.

That finding flipped the switch that brought the story crashing back.

The Lars lookalike. The car chase. The cliffside trap.

As for my survival, I had a one-word explanation. *Hooah!*

I had completed the Army ROTC program at Princeton. That included spending the summer between my junior and senior years at Airborne school in Fort Benning, Georgia. During the first of three weeks, the Black Hats taught me how to fall. During the second, they trained me to fall from fast-moving objects. During the third, I learned how to leap from aircraft and land alive. Of course, each stage stressed surviving the impact without breaking anything required for combat.

The trick was learning to land in a way that transferred momentum through your body and into the ground rather than your organs or bones. This was accomplished by funneling the kinetic energy through a pendulum-like leg swing that planted your heels and stopped your slide.

The reason the Black Hats spent three weeks teaching wasn't to put the right moves in paratroopers' minds; it was to meld them into their muscles. To make them automatic. To train their student soldiers to reflexively tense and twist and adjust just right whenever and wherever they "hit the wind."

I'd passed then, and apparently I'd passed now.

I did not recall making those moves after my motorcycle hit the guardrail. I did not remember properly positioning myself for each of the five prescribed points of contact. But clearly, my conditioning had kicked in. The evidence was obvious and undeniable.

With a deep sense of relief and a satisfying exhale, I began a thorough self-assessment. No cranial contusions. No issues with my neck or shoulders. My hands and arms felt fine. Things got more complicated below the belt. My right knee ached like a mule had kicked it, and my left ankle seemed severely swollen. No doubt the boulder that had ultimately stopped my slide had taken those tolls, but I wasn't about to bicker over the price.

I looked toward the bent guardrail some forty or fifty feet above. I didn't see the Harley. It must have gone over as well. I looked back down the canyon. It was deep and remote. "You are one lucky soldier."

Studying the canyon floor to the extent the foliage

permitted, I thought I caught the glint of sunlight off an orange reflector. Then the lighting itself caught my attention. The source wasn't the afternoon sun. The sun had just cleared the cliffs.

The required calculation wasn't complicated, but given the rattled state of my brain, I eased my cellphone from the breast pocket of my leather jacket. Fortunately, it recognized my face and rewarded me with both time and date. I had lain unconscious for about twenty hours. Through the afternoon, evening, and night. The morning sunlight was likely what had roused me. That and my bladder.

After rolling sideways for a bit of relief, I pressed a button on my phone. "Siri, what's my location?"

"Your location cannot be determined."

Of course not. "What's the nearest road?"

"The nearest road is Deer Creek Road."

I dialed 911 and spoke as soon as the call connected. "I've been in a motorcycle accident. I need an ambulance."

"Are you injured?"

"Yes. I need an ambulance. I'm a mile or two from PCH up Deer Creek Road."

While waiting for help to arrive, I tried calling Lars again. Still no answer.

After a few minutes of spinning my mental wheels on the mysterious implications, my thoughts turned to the bike. With it totaled, the rental company would hit my credit card for ten grand while my insurance company determined the best way to deny reimbursement. That was going to put a serious crimp in my available cash. Cash I might now need for medical bills.

The ambulance and fire truck took forty-eight minutes to reach my location. I could hear the sweet siren coming from a mile away. Then they called and we played warmer/colder until a paramedic spotted me.

Extracting me put another forty-two minutes on the clock. The cliff was steep, and the firefighters didn't rush once they surmised that my injuries weren't life threatening.

X-rays gave me the good news an hour after that. Nothing broken. Just some soft tissue damage. A set of shots, a couple of soft casts, and a pair of ice packs later I found myself in a taxi, headed for the nearest cheap hotel.

I was surprised that the police hadn't confronted me, either at the accident scene or the hospital. Apparently, if no serious injuries or third parties were involved, they couldn't be bothered.

That was fine with me.

I'd been happy to accept assistance from the firemen and ambulance, because there was nothing to lose and everything to gain, not the least of which was a ride back to civilization. But I wasn't about to delegate the law enforcement part of the Lars investigation. That would be an exercise in bureaucratic futility. It would waste time, grate nerves, and go nowhere.

Fortunately, I knew where to start the search.

I hadn't seen the license plate of the skulking SUV, but I had caught a glimpse of the driver. It was my second sighting in as many weeks. The first time I'd seen those chiseled cheekbones had been the last time I'd seen Lars—three thousand miles east of Venice Beach.

17
Bad Day Dawning

LISA AWOKE TO A SENSE OF SATISFACTION and the sound of crows. She had done it! She had gotten the go-ahead to pursue her dream. Sure, it had required some backstage maneuvering and more than a mouthful of guile, but those were the tools it took to make it in Washington. Best to hone them here, on more familiar turf, among friends.

Upon reflection, the meeting itself had been a bit anticlimactic. Immediately prior to the vote, the tension had been taut enough to tune a piano. But afterward, the objections had evaporated faster than margarita ice in the Florida sun. In the aftermath, she had expected David to try talking them around with his trademark logic. How many times had she seen him obliterate opposing views with his unrelenting Socratic wit? But he'd shrugged it off. Apparently Eric's death and Allison's turnabout had taken the fight out of him. Or maybe he was just evolving.

With David's dukes down, Ries had lowered his guard. That left Felix as the lone defender of the old way. Being a paragon of practicality, he swiftly surrendered as well. Aria, of course, went along. She wasn't one to make waves.

No doubt the wine had helped.

Lisa had broken out the best bottles in her cellar. Nothing under a thousand dollars.

She lay still for a minute, staring at the bedroom ceiling, reflecting on where she'd been and contemplating where she had yet to go. The Senate move had been a long time coming. She and Pierce had been discussing it for years. Plotting and preparing, then finally executing.

The external obstacles were the easy ones. Introductions, advice, and endorsements could all be purchased for the right price. Manipulating their fellow Immortals, however, had called for cunning.

The biggest challenge had been getting them to vote for replacing real people rather than assuming false identities. Pierce had steered that situation with subterfuge. He had paid consultants to emphasize and exaggerate the government crackdown on false identities, by tying it to the war on terror.

Once Lisa and Pierce had set themselves up with suitable backgrounds, the challenge was getting permission from their fellow Immortals to run. Uncovering Allison's passion had been the key to that. Paying an agent and casting director to show encouraging interest had sealed the deal. Again, good practice for national-level politics.

Lying there the morning after on her silky sheets, Lisa could admit that the real reason for her Senate run was that she wanted the challenge. She craved the purpose, passion, and power of achieving and holding high office.

The others hadn't felt that pull yet, but they'd be planning their own conquests well before the next twenty-year replacement came around. It was a golden opportunity. Irresistible. The ability to literally step into another person's shoes—and then run with the energy of eternal youth, backed by all the money in the world.

Whoever said you couldn't buy happiness clearly didn't have a billion bucks in the bank. With that kind of cash, one could enjoy an unbelievably lavish lifestyle on the interest alone. She was plenty happy all right, just not content.

Lisa walked to her bedroom balcony window and pulled the curtains aside. She was wearing only a skimpy silk nighty, so it felt a bit exhibitionistic. She liked the feeling, and often dressed that way around the house. She enjoyed the constant reminder that her body remained as sleek and sexy as a runway model's—even if her face wasn't magazine material.

She opened her balcony doors and swung them inward. The motion caused a stir below, scattering crows as if Cruella de Vil were stepping into the morning sun rather than Pennsylvania's next senator.

California was a West Coast state, so it was all about sunsets rather than sunrises. But the Pacific was still beautiful in the morning. Lisa raised her arms to revel in the glory, letting the cool sea breeze caress her body while it blew into her room.

While she sucked in the fragrant air and refreshing atmosphere, the crows returned and their cacophony resumed.

She was twenty feet above the expansive flagstone patio that boasted a sophisticated outdoor kitchen, complete with a fully functional bar and a rotisserie capable of cooking complete beasts. The big black birds were congregating about thirty feet off to her right, directly beneath one of the other balconies.

She couldn't tell why. There were too many of them to identify the attraction. But the shape was foreboding.

A shudder ran down Lisa's spine, leaving a tingling in her toes. Instead of reaching for her robe, she clapped twice to scatter the pests. Paralleling events of the previous night, they protested at first but obeyed after a second round.

As the crows dispersed and the shape took form, Lisa's autonomic nervous system kicked in. Her heart jumped and her lungs jerked and her larynx let loose its first scream in years.

18

A Pattern Emerges

RIES BELIEVED that the secret to eternal youth was running barefoot on the beach. It was an odd conclusion for a biochemistry PhD to make, especially one who could recite the formula for the chemical compound that halted aging. But people were peculiar that way, filled with irony and fenced by incongruity.

It was the connection to eternity that convinced him. Alone on an empty beach at dusk or dawn with the sand squishing between his toes and the water swishing over his ankles, he couldn't help but sense how insignificant he was. If he spent his entire life running up and down that beach, he wouldn't even register as a blip on its timeline. The waves would keep crashing and the water would continue receding for a thousand lifetimes to come. They'd be completely impervious to the fact that he'd ever existed. As they would to the next million men who trod across that sand.

By internalizing the fact that his entire life would almost certainly be entirely inconsequential, Ries never ever had to worry. And when you didn't worry, you didn't age.

At least that was how Ries Robins, Immortal PhD, chose to look at it.

Nonetheless, the scream that capped off his morning run gave Ries cause for concern. Forceful enough to put a dozen crows to flight, it wasn't a simple startle or the overreaction to an insect or mouse. It was a soul-cracking, gut-twisting, glass-shattering shriek of a scream, and it was coming from the back of Lisa's house.

Once the air was free of flapping wings, he saw his friend standing on what he presumed was her bedroom balcony, given the fact that she was barely dressed. Already accelerating toward her in a run, he yelled, "What is it?"

She pointed to the patio two stories beneath her feet.

At first Ries saw a baby-blue bundle splotched with black. Then he made out the human form. A woman in a nightdress, clearly dead. Drawing closer, he recognized the remains of the face. Or rather the hair. Camilla.

He reached the scene a few seconds before David. They both stood staring as the others arrived. "She must have fallen," Ries said, gesturing toward the balcony above her body. "Was she a sleepwalker?"

Nobody answered. Everyone was in shock.

Camilla was lying on her back as though the patio were a bed. A bloody halo indicated that her head had hit hard enough to crack. The imperfect circle surrounding her skull was matted with hair and crisscrossed by crow tracks. Worst of all, the birds had gorged on her eyes. And what lay below. Ries knew that their selection was a simple preference for soft fatty tissue, but as he stood there staring in the dawning light, it sure seemed like a message from God.

David glanced up at the balcony above Camilla, then over at Lisa. "Did you hear anything?"

"Not a peep," Lisa muttered.

"Oh my God!" Allison cried, arriving and immediately turning away.

"Sleepwalking? Suicide? Murder? Drugs?" Ries thought out loud.

"I doubt it's drugs," David replied. "Her bloodwork has always been clean."

"I don't think she was a sleepwalker," Lisa said, answering Ries's question at last. "And she certainly wasn't suicidal." Lisa's voice was returning to normal, although she continued to look away.

"Did anyone pay attention to how much Camilla had to drink?" David asked. Everyone was there now, all seven remaining Immortals.

When none of them answered the question, Felix said, "I'll check her room."

"We can't call the police," Pierce said. "I realize the autopsy likely wouldn't reveal her special status, but we can't be questioned. We aren't prepared to explain our presence, or how we knew her—now that she's no longer Camilla. As far as the government knows, Camilla Rose died earlier this year in Oceanside."

Nobody replied to that. They all stood there staring—everywhere but at each other.

Ries considered the possibility that it might be murder. His thoughts immediately went to the MBA clique, not because he considered any of them capable of homicide, but because they were the A-types. The aggressive personalities. The ruthless achievers. And they had interacted with Camilla much more than the research staff. At least historically. These days, he didn't know if anyone but Lisa had much contact with her. Camilla had always been the odd person out in their crowd.

Pierce would be Ries's first suspect—assuming the choice was among Immortals. The original investor was the oldest member of the team, and the least connected aside from Aria, who would be near the bottom of his list. Next he'd guess either Felix or Lisa. Felix was a man, and men are more likely to commit murder. Lisa had always been cutthroat in the ambitious sense. If poison was involved in Camilla's death, Lisa would move to the top of his list.

Pierce approached David and whispered loud enough for Ries to hear. "Can you do an autopsy?"

David grimaced. "My lab isn't equipped for that, and there's no way I'd take her corpse there in any case."

Pierce reddened and shook his head. "Of course. My lips are moving faster than my brain."

"I could take some blood and run some tests, but I wouldn't be comfortable going beyond that. What are you thinking?"

"Poison."

"Me too," Ries added.

"I'll go grab a couple of syringes," David said.

Felix called down from the balcony. "There's an empty wine glass in her bedroom, and an empty bottle."

David returned with two syringes and bent over the body. Ries watched him draw blood from the femoral vein and urine straight from the bladder. He was quick and discreet.

Given that the corpse's unpleasant appearance had people looking away, Ries doubted anyone saw it happen.

Felix arrived on the patio toting a sheet, a blanket, and two pillowcases. He held the linen out and looked at Pierce. "Give me a hand."

They draped the blanket over Camilla as if making a bed with her on one side—then rolled her up like a burrito. They lifted the roll onto the sheet and folded it from the left and the right. The result was surprisingly neat, respectful even.

Everyone was standing around by that point. The seven surviving Immortals.

Pierce met Felix's eye. "The yacht?"

Felix nodded.

They bent and wrapped the corners of the sheet around their wrists, then stood in unison.

"What are you doing?" Allison asked.

Ries found himself answering the question. "Burial at sea."

19
Cravings and Confessions

ALLISON DIDN'T REMEMBER the walk to the yacht or the ride two miles out. Her mind was as cloudy as the sky, a deep and dreary gray. *Why was this happening to them?* Two Immortal deaths in one month. The first two ever. The analyst in her knew it could not be coincidence. Her inner humanitarian trembled and wept. *Had they angered God?*

It wasn't until Pierce had Camilla's body poised on eternity's precipice that Allison returned to the moment. He was tying off the twisted top of a king pillowcase that she now remembered seeing him fill with rocks.

While the others stood around in silence, Felix reappeared from inside and joined Pierce at the edge of the dive deck. "Nothing. No rope, no cable ties. It's a new yacht, so there's not much lying around. I suppose I could use a kitchen knife to cut strips off a bath towel."

"I'll use my belt," Pierce replied. He pulled the calfskin strap from around his waist and went to work. "Peel back the blanket to expose her ankles."

While Felix complied with the request, Pierce looped the belt around the neck of the pillowcase. He cinched it tight beneath the knot, then wrapped the rest of the long tail around Camilla's ankles and buckled it tight.

"Nice," Felix said, smoothing the wrapping back down.

"Does anyone want to speak?" Pierce asked.

The crowd naturally turned to Lisa. Once their CEO, always their leader. And Camilla's closest friend.

Lisa stood silent for a long second while the waves slapped the side of the yacht and the wind pushed the clouds across the worried sky. Her face contorted a few times, but in the end all she said was, "You were a fine and faithful friend. I'll miss you, dear Camilla. I hope you're in a better place."

When nobody else stepped forward to speak, Pierce guided the makeshift anchor out over the deck's edge, then Felix nudged the body. A *bloop* was followed by a burst of bubbles, and Camilla Rose's body was commended to the sea.

Allison felt a shudder deep within her chest. She looked over at David. He appeared even more shaken. "I'm sorry I blindsided you with my acting and the vote. I know it was a betrayal. I don't feel good about it."

David turned to face her.

She braced for the biting retort about switching sides. Eric, God bless his soul, had always framed things as us vs. them, referring to the PhDs and the MBAs. Ries had taken up the torch in his absence. But David's soulful eyes held sadness wrapped in affection, and his words were anything but biting. "It's different from what we'd expected. Immortality, I mean."

It was the first time she'd heard him refer to their condition using the same shorthand as the rest of them, rather than *halted aging*. Her shoulders relaxed as her defenses dropped. "Yes. So different."

David didn't reply, he just held her eye.

Allison felt a sudden, overwhelming desire to share. To let loose the baggage that bound her heart. "Back at Eos, we were working toward this incredible prize. We had purpose. We had passion. We had hope for fame and fortune and glory. We were going to be the people who cracked the ultimate code. The secret to eternal life. You know?"

"I know," David said, his wise eyes smiling.

"And we did it! Our accomplishment makes landing on the moon look pedestrian. It's like a footnote, whereas we didn't just turn the page, we opened the second volume of human history."

"And nobody knows," David said, completing her thought.

Allison was so relieved to hear her innermost thoughts echoed back. "Nobody knows. And more importantly— something I understand now infinitely better than I did back then—nobody ever should."

"I have no doubt about that."

Allison put her hand on his shoulder. "You always understood me. Don't think I haven't noticed, or that I'm not appreciative."

The yacht rocked abruptly, as if in answer to her words. Allison looked up to see that they were nudging back onto the lift. In a minute, hoists would begin raising the *Sunrise Sailor* out of the sea and up into Lisa's boathouse.

David began to back away, but Allison wasn't finished, so she didn't release her grip. The succession of funerals had uncorked so many emotions. She simply had to let them out. "I got the ultimate prize, and I feel like I earned it. And I got the fortune that's commensurate. On the surface, my life is perfect. Family issues aside, right now there's not a woman in the world who wouldn't trade shoes with me."

David again moved closer. "But those other women don't know."

"Exactly! They don't understand how much you lose by gaining. I was so much happier back in my Eos days than I am now—and it's not because I was younger."

David chuckled and Allison also voiced a nervous laugh. It felt good. She needed that release. "I don't think we're supposed to be happy. I mean the big us, humans. I think we're supposed to struggle. I think that's because there's something more important to our psyche than hedonistic happiness."

"And what's that?" David asked, although she was now certain that he knew darn well.

"Satisfaction. The satisfaction that comes from achievement. From having worked and produced and accomplished. Adults need it the way babies need milk. And like milk, satisfaction has a shelf life. People can feed off past accomplishments for a couple of weeks, but their mood starts to sour after that.

"I have developed the theory that adults wean themselves off the need to achieve as they move beyond middle age. By the time they're seniors, they can sustain a positive attitude off the energy of past accomplishments. But as Immortals, we're stuck with the achievement appetite of youth."

David completed her thought. "And we are inhibited from satisfying it. Secrecy forces us to hide our accomplishments. And since we have no material needs, our struggles aren't the satisfying kind."

She nodded.

"Do you think that acting will give you satisfaction and make you whole again?"

Allison looked down at the deck of the yacht. "To be honest, not really. But I have to try."

David gently lifted her chin. "Why not really?"

"Because I know I'm cheating. Everything we do is cheating. With unlimited time and unlimited money, we're starting on third base." She shook her head. "Funny. You were always the philosophical one. At the first Immortals meeting, when we all announced our plans, you couldn't believe the rest of us weren't planning to keep working."

"But you came around."

"Not as quickly as Eric and Ries."

David gestured toward Lisa and Pierce, who were also engaged in an animated discussion. "But much faster than others. Will you tell me one thing?"

At that moment, in that mood, Allison would have confessed to being a Russian spy—if she had been one.

"Why switch to acting? Why not continue with research? You're so talented. There's lots of satisfaction to be had."

"I'd say I want a change, but that's only a small part of it. Truth is, I feel the same compulsions as Lisa and Pierce. I need a challenge, and I crave glory."

20
Cold Calculation

TEN HOURS AFTER they committed Camilla's body to the deep, Pierce and Lisa approached the Sunset Suite at the Montage Laguna Beach. Her heels echoed purposefully off the marble floor as he checked to ensure that his tie was still knotted tight. He rarely wore one any more and had lost the knack of tying them. Time to get used to it again.

They stopped before the hardwood double doors and turned to meet each other's eyes. This was a big moment. The second that day, as things had turned out. Pierce suddenly felt compelled to comment on that fact. "We've had our ups and downs, but ultimately, you and I have proved to be quite effective together."

"Different, but complementary," she agreed.

"Like an aged filet and a Caesar salad." Pierce knocked three times then added with a wink. "Shouldn't this be the Presidential Suite?"

The door opened as he spoke, revealing the bright blue eyes and thick salt-and-pepper hair of Carl Casteel. "The Montage doesn't have a Presidential Suite. But as you'll see, this one will do. Thank you for arriving precisely on time."

They entered a luxurious room that was poised to capture the oranges and blues of the sun disappearing into the surf. Casteel gave them a moment to soak it in before speaking.

"The color combination reminds me of Monet's 'Twilight, Venice,'" Pierce said. "Albeit with tall palms providing the shadowy contrast rather than the Church of San Giorgio Maggiore."

Lisa gave him the bewildered look of a person who'd just seen a monkey type.

"I own one of the unfinished versions," he said in explanation. "Have it hanging in my bedroom."

"I must say, I'm surprised to see the two of you together," Casteel said. "What with bipartisans being on the endangered species list these days."

"We're closet bipartisans," Pierce said.

Casteel turned from the window, exposing the approval in his eyes. "That's the savvy kind. I look forward to hearing the specifics."

He popped the cork on a bottle of Taittinger Champagne as they took seats around a glass dining table set for six. "The bottle came with the room and a suggestion to enjoy it at sunset."

He poured three flutes, then raised his own. "I thought that was a wonderful idea, especially given the timing of our meeting. But I suggest we toast to rising stars instead."

"To rising stars," Pierce and Lisa repeated.

They all clinked and enjoyed a sip. The Champagne was crisp and dry and instantly reminded Pierce of success. The movie version of James Bond drank vodka, famously shaken, not stirred, but in the books, the British spy drank Taittinger Champagne. Pierce had once been a big Ian Fleming fan.

As an homage during his angel investor days, Pierce had always opened a bottle of Taittinger with management when inking a deal. Both the initial investment and the ultimate exit. Staring at the tiny bubbles, he wondered if this brand of bottle was a coincidence or the result of the good research that made Casteel a legend in his field.

"Now, why don't you tell me precisely what you bipartisans are pursuing, and I'll let you know if it's possible."

Lisa took the lead. She set her flute aside, clasped her hands, and met Casteel's eyes. "We're pursuing sixteen years at 1600 Pennsylvania Avenue."

Pierce noted that Casteel's face revealed nothing of the thoughts within his perfectly coiffed head. Their demand was literally the limit of political possibility, but he didn't even blink. He just moved his head back and forth between his two clients. "Eight plus eight. The math is easy. The rest is incredibly ambitious." His eyes came to rest on Lisa's.

"Ambitious plans are my favorite kind. I'm all ears."

"As you know from our earlier individual meetings, we each have the financial resources to bankroll extensive back-office campaigns. Not just opposition research, but also aggressive offensive tactics."

"Like fabricating sexual assault allegations," Casteel clarified, referencing the specific tactic the two had used to make their senate seats available. He hadn't been involved at that stage, but he knew there were no convenient coincidences in America's Capital. In Washington, brass rings weren't plucked off ribbons, they were ripped from flesh. "I like that you're beginning your quest with a clear understanding of what it takes to play in the major leagues. What I'm not seeing is the bipartisan angle. Cooperation plays well with crowds, but not with donors or special interests. They're motivated by pole positions, not the equator."

Lisa retained her aggressive posture, mirroring Casteel's own. "We're preparing massive propaganda wars. We'll stake out the high ground while financing trench warfare. Since we don't need financing, we can hit our opponents hard on corruption and do so with impunity."

Pierce loved watching Lisa in action. Back in the day, she'd always owned the stage. He was relieved to see that immortality hadn't rusted her mettle. *They were going to make this happen!*

"While that would certainly be easy, it might not necessarily be wise," Casteel cautioned. "You're going to need the support of your respective national committees— and those committees are composed of people who do rely on special interests. If you pee in their pool, don't expect the committee members to want you at the party."

Pierce stepped in for an assist before passing the ball back to Lisa. "Recent history has made it clear that political parties will embrace anybody who can win. Victory is the trump card."

Lisa spread her hands. "We're offering you your dream job, Carl. Unlimited funds—without the need to waste your time or ours passing the hat. That means there's no risk of getting caught lying while pandering this way for one group and that way for another. It means we'll have no need to abandon popular positions to please rich donors." She reached across the table and took Pierce's hand. "We'll speak moderately and respectfully while slipping stilettos into our opponents' sides."

Casteel's face remained impassive, but he leaned back as if momentarily satisfied. "All the while helping each other in subtle ways, with compliments and digs."

"Exactly."

The Washington wise man chewed on that for a minute.

They sipped Champagne.

"If we do it right, the opposition will go hard right and hard left while you each stake claim to your side of the middle ground—perhaps showing off a bit of overlap. But then what? If you both win your primaries, you're stuck facing each other."

Pierce watched with anticipation as Lisa delivered the kicker. "Right before the first convention, we turn to the numbers. By then, there will be plenty of polls pitting us against each other. Whichever of us is losing in those head-to-head battles—joins the bottom of the other's ticket."

Casteel raised his groomed eyebrows. "Creating a unity platform."

Lisa acknowledged his sage insight with a tilt of her head. "And weakening the opposing party, which will be forced to put forward a team the primary voters have already dismissed."

Casteel nodded along. "I like Act One. Tell me about Act Two."

Lisa tented her hands again. "When we're elected, we actually run a bipartisan White House. At that point, the party out of power will know that it's set to win in eight years, so it will be inclined to go along—if the proposals are moderate. And they will be. Lord knows we're overdue for a few of those."

"The special interests will still be funding the fringes," Casteel cautioned.

"We have no delusions about avoiding a state of war. But

we'll have the big microphone, and we'll have the vast majority of the American people on our side. The country is fed up with partisan politics. The middle is a solid sixty percent—which is nine more than we need."

Casteel drained his flute and ran a manicured hand through his George Clooney hair. "This has been contemplated before. More than once. It's fallen apart every time."

Pierce felt his stomach sink, but Lisa kept shining at full power. "Why is that?"

Again Casteel did the back and forth thing with his head. "Politicians look out for number one. Historically, the only times mixed alliances ever survived the flames of political combat were when the two parties were family. I don't suppose you're planning to get married?"

Pierce exhaled in relief as Lisa put her manicured hand on his shoulder. "Suffice it to say we have a deep platonic connection."

21
Stakeout

I LOOKED UP from my book and smiled as Wynter with a *y* replaced my old empty mug with a fresh frosty one. "Thank you."

"What's that mean, *Pushing Brilliance?*"

I turned the paperback around to look at the cover, as if it were going to tell me something I didn't already know. I could flirt if I needed to, and seeing as this was my third evening camped out on a patch of Wynter's prime real estate, I figured flirting was the wise move. "I don't know yet. Part of the fun of a thriller is figuring out what the title means. Often they're intentionally ambiguous."

"Ambiguous?"

"Mysterious." I used my playful voice, mimicking hers.

"You're the mystery. You got the biker jacket and the biker boots, but you're reading books and drinking light beer, night after night, hour after hour. Always leaving alone." Wynter spoke with a bit of a southern twang and had the big blonde hair to match.

I knew I was guilty of bad tradecraft for actually reading a book and allowing myself to be distracted by a waitress, but I wasn't trying to infiltrate the mob. And I would redirect my attention the moment my target arrived. If he arrived.

On the good tradecraft side of things, I was in disguise. I'd grown the start of a handlebar mustache and was wearing a bandanna do-rag. Although typically the straitlaced GQ type, I knew from prior undercover experience that I could pull off the bad-boy look.

I was back at Berret's Taphouse Grill because I couldn't think of a better way to find the mysterious man with chiseled cheekbones. Or Lars.

Since I didn't have the license plate of the Range Rover

that had run me off the road, I had investigated the i8. Turned out it had been reported stolen, then found wiped clean and abandoned. The registration was in the name and rent-controlled address of Lars de Kock.

The lack of automotive leads left me very little data for locating Lars's would-be killer and learning his fate. Nonetheless, I had vowed to do both.

Cheekbones had crossed the big red line. Whoever he was, wherever he was, he was a dead man walking.

I was semi-certain that my nemesis would walk back into Berret's bar sometime soon. My reasoning was based on both logic and experience. If Lars's assailant was willing to write off a $150,000 car, then his disappearance had to be the tip of something much bigger. Lars was no millionaire. Add to that the fact that the CIA con was much too slick and sophisticated to be a one-off, and the odds of a repeat performance were high.

Of course, I had no way to gauge when the next episode would air. I could only hope it would be sometime soon.

Knowing that men are creatures of habit, I installed a bug in the wall lamp beside the corner table where Lars and Cheekbones had dined. I then set myself up in a spot that gave me both a convenient casual view of the entrance, and a reflected view of the suspect table.

I was now three evenings into my costumed stakeout. I wasn't yet discouraged by the lack of action. Stakeouts took time. But I found myself asking how many more days I'd give it.

I ignored Wynter's hint about leaving alone, but gave her a friendly smile. "There's nothing mysterious here. I'm just a man enjoying life between jobs."

She smiled back and moved on.

I mused that I actually was, in fact, just a man enjoying life between jobs. Sitting on a Virginia barstool was a far cry from riding a Harley through Yosemite National Park, but nonetheless I had freedom and purpose and was happy to be catching up on must-read fiction. I'd done so much work-related reading during my days at the CIA that I rarely felt like burying my nose in a book at night. That was a drawback of the job. I wondered if other professions suffered similar side effects. Bartenders, pilots, and gynecologists for example.

I had not set a sunset on my surveillance operation. A date on which I'd fold tent and move on if Cheekbones didn't show. That would clash with the whole freedom aspect of my vacation adventure. I would move on the minute I thought of a better move. That was an additional benefit of my reading selection. Smart espionage thrillers kept me in the right frame of mind and generated new ideas. Was that why they called them novels? I wondered.

I pulled a painkiller from the front pocket of my jeans and washed it down with a swallow of beer. Between those pills and the soft braces on my ankle and knee, I was nearly back to normal. At least neither joint gave me grief while walking to and from my car or sitting on a barstool. It would still be a few days before I'd want to start kicking down doors. Perhaps it was a good thing that Cheekbones hadn't rushed back to Berret's.

They walked in as I turned the last page of the chapter that explained the title of my book. A thirtyish woman with amber eyes, a short blonde hairstyle, and an athletic stride— accompanied by a man whose features created a memorable clash of hard and soft.

The hostess led them straight to the corner table.

22

Iron Woman

THE TOP FEMALE FINISHER in an Ironman race—don't get her started—swims the 2.4 miles, bikes the 112 miles, and then runs the 26.2 miles in about nine hours. Skylar Fawkes had come close to earning that honor a total of seven times. But she didn't remember ever feeling as wrung out as she did that evening, walking into Berret's Taphouse Grill.

Tom's out-of-the-blue recruitment pitch had hit her like the first ray of sunshine falling on Noah's Ark. The truth was, she'd been battling depression, mentally circling the drain.

The purses for peak performers at the pinnacle of the triathlon circuit were usually under $100,000, so very few professional triathletes were able to earn even middle-class wages. Sponsorships were the only way to get rich, but those were limited to the super elite, the known-name winners of multiple championship races.

Skylar hadn't become a triathlete for the money. For her, it was all about passion and personal bests. But still, one had to live. So she had taken a firefighting job that eventually gave her the injury that had cost her the ability to compete. Adding insult to injury, the resultant hypersensitivity to smoke had also disqualified her from her second profession.

It was the injustice and stupidity of that avoidable accident that drove her into and fed her depression. She'd been kicking herself for six straight months, unable to extricate herself from her self-imposed funk but unwilling to ask for help.

Then, in one golden hour, a new opportunity opened before her like the gateway to Heaven. A job that would challenge her mentally and physically while allowing her to serve her country in a starring role. It wasn't a perfect replacement for her chosen profession; it was better. Triathletes had short careers.

She wanted the new job and all it represented so much that she feared it would be yanked away. Easy come, easy go. So she'd sweat the interview and the polygraph even though she had nothing to hide. When Tom finally closed his briefcase with an approving nod, Skylar thought she'd collapse right there on the hotel room floor. Then he proposed dinner so she could ask questions. Her preferred response was, "No, thanks. I just want to hop into a hot bath and put spa music on Pandora." But ironically, that honest answer wasn't an option.

So there they were, ordering drinks at a corner table in her first CIA bar. Skylar didn't drink alcohol, so she passed on Tom's recommended "Fierce" and ordered a club soda with lime. She figured the social slight would be outweighed by the upside of having an agent who didn't drink but knew how to appear as if imbibing.

"This is your time to ask me questions," Tom said as Wynter walked away. "What would you like to know?"

She had her first question tip of tongue. "Where would I be based?"

"This part of Virginia. Langley and the D.C. suburbs up north are for bureaucrats and analysts. Ops works out of *The Woods*."

"The Woods?"

"The Woods surround The Farm."

"Got it."

"That's for training and staging. Our operational work, of course, is overseas."

Wynter dropped off their drinks but chose not to interrupt their conversation.

Tom took a healthy swallow of beer. "As you'll recall, if it isn't all a blur, the Dry Cleaners and Wet Wipes work off the books. We like it that way, removed from the restrictions, inefficiencies, and hypocrisies that always accompany bureaucratic oversight."

Skylar squeezed her lime. "But *you* don't live here?"

"What makes you say that?"

Without releasing her glass, Skylar used her index finger to point at the keys Tom had set on the table. "Your Mercedes is a rental."

"Nice catch. I like that operative eye of yours. It will serve you well.

"My duties involve so much travel that I don't bother with a personal vehicle. I skip the hassle and expense and charge everything to my corporate card. You're going to love FIFO in that regard. Most of the operatives don't own residences either, preferring to pocket more of their paychecks, but not all. Some want a place they can call home, and that's fine too. It's all about personal preference."

Skylar saw the sense in that. She wanted a family someday, and felt the pressure of the biological clock in that regard, but until that time she'd forgo the knickknack mantel in favor of a bigger bank account. Having experienced rainy days, deluge days, she was eager to sock away as much as possible. That might actually be quite a bit, given that they let Tom rent a Mercedes. His Swiss watch was another good indicator.

Wynter returned to their table, holding her order pad. "Have you made your menu selections?"

Skylar ordered the Baked Brie Cheese in Puff Pastry with Grilled Shrimp, Tom the Macadamia Nut–Crusted Mahi-Mahi Fillet. "And another round," he added.

Over their delicious dinners, Tom continued to tout the perks and bennies of FIFO. She was interested but already sold. By the time Wynter cleared their table, Skylar was dreaming of a warm bath, dimmed lights, and soothing music.

Tom finally read her mind. "I know it's been a long day, so I'm going to leave you to enjoy dessert in peace if you'll be so kind as to save the receipt. I recommend the chocolate lava cake." He pulled two hundred-dollar bills from a money clip, creased them the long way, and left them tented on the table. "I'll pick you up at the hotel at this time tomorrow. Then we'll drive to either FIFO HQ or the airport. Your choice entirely. Until then, I have to insist that you have no contact with anyone—even if you're not inclined to take the offer. We're giving you twenty-four hours to reflect. Use it for that purpose, and Skylar—"

"Yes?"

"Congratulations."

23

Role Reversal

I USED THE MIRROR behind the bar to watch Wynter working. She was holding my phone beneath her order pad in a manner that appeared completely casual and relaxed. While photographing car keys was hardly a crime, most people tensed up when acting surreptitiously. Not this one, bless her heart.

With her mission complete, Wynter slipped me my cell phone in a pass-by move that looked like she was leaving a check.

I opened up Photos, hit PLAY on the movie she'd recorded, and watched until I found a frame with the focus I wanted. The license plate number was hand written in pen on the Hertz tag.

Since Cheekbones and his latest victim had just placed their orders, I knew they wouldn't be leaving anytime soon. I left my book and beer to reserve my seat and headed for the parking lot. I expected the Bluetooth transmission to cut out while I walked, but their voices kept coming through my wireless earbuds.

The matching Mercedes took a minute to find. Even though German cars were above most government pay grades, there were plenty of rich college kids in town, and the C 300 appeared to be a popular model with that crowd. I popped a GPS tracker under the rear passenger fender and was back on my barstool before Tom and Skylar received their orders.

The pitch Tom—certainly not his real name—was delivering was undoubtedly the same one Lars had heard. Most of it was fantasy, but all was close enough to the Hollywood portrayal of the CIA that outsiders would eagerly swallow it whole. Especially those hungry to hear their dreams coming true.

I was listening for information that could be identifying. Anything beyond the BS sales pitch. Some hint at Tom's true purpose or the interests of his sponsoring organization. But when the talk wasn't about the fictitious job, it was all about Skylar.

"How'd I do?" Wynter asked, stopping by my stool with empty plates in hand.

I used my watch to lower the volume on my earbuds and tuned Wynter in. "You, my dear, do excellent work."

"I'm guessing this means that I won't be seeing you again after tonight?"

"You're a good guesser. But I'll be back." *After closing, and only to retrieve my bug.*

"Just not tomorrow?"

Technically, it would be tomorrow. "Probably not."

"And tonight? Time to celebrate mission accomplished?" She ran a nail down her forearm.

"I'm afraid my mission is just beginning." I produced a Ben Franklin I'd previously prepared. It was more than I could afford, but less than she deserved.

Wynter winked and straightened up. "Story of my life."

I tuned back into my earpiece in time to hear Tom give Skylar twenty-four hours to think it over. Then he dropped some cash and a balled-up drink napkin and rose to leave. This was the point where I had walked in, two weeks earlier. There was no question of my sitting with Skylar as I had with Lars, but I had to decide which of them to follow.

I decided to play it safe and stick with Skylar. A man with Tom's excellent tradecraft would be on the lookout for a tail, and I could track him electronically in any case. Skylar, meanwhile, was in immediate danger. Lars had disappeared sometime between his leaving Berret's and my arriving in L.A.

Given what I'd just heard, the pickup twenty-four hours from now was likely to mark the beginning of the end. That would be the moment the metallic teeth of Tom's trap snapped around her ankle. But I couldn't be certain. The day he'd given her to think might well be a ploy designed to drop her guard.

Lars had stayed at the hotel across the street, so I assumed Skylar would be sleeping there as well. People followed patterns.

I waited until I saw the tracking dot representing Tom's Mercedes move, then I rose from my barstool. I wanted to get ahead of Skylar. I assumed she'd be skipping dessert despite her host's offer. That she, like me, was only waiting for him to drive off.

I walked past her without a sideward glance, then paused closer to the door. Whipping out my cell phone, I pretended to be consulting it while using the self-portrait feature to keep an eye on Skylar. I'd no sooner focused than she rose, at which point I continued my exit.

Pacing my strides to coincide with her footfalls, I walked straight for the Brown Pelican Inn. Reaching the door a few steps in the lead, I held it open.

"Thank you."

I felt an electric jolt as our eyes met for the first time. "You're welcome."

I followed her up the stairs to the second floor, then down the east hallway. As we approached the second-to-last room, I stopped to make a show of patting my pockets while noting the number, then reversed course while she keyed into the corner room.

Returning to Berret's parking lot, I hopped into my twelve-year-old blue BMW 335i and pulled across the street to park it at the inn. Then I popped the trunk, grabbed my roller bag and backpack, and headed for check-in.

24

Gaining Insight

A PERKY RED-HEADED RECEPTIONIST greeted me with a caffeinated, "Good evening."

I gave her a friendly smile, knowing what the night shift was like. "I'm hoping you have room 21 available for two nights."

"A man who knows what he wants. Clearly you've been with us before Mister—"

"Chase. Zachary Chase. Blackjack's my thing."

She pecked away with a puzzled look, then smiled and said, "I get it. Blackjack, twenty-one. Yes, that room is available. Both nights. But I don't see your name in our system."

Ignoring her last remark, I presented my credit card and hoped it was still working. When the charge for the totaled Harley posted, I'd be over my limit. Given that credit card applications always asked for current income and employment status, getting another was probably out of the question. I was stuck with what I had. "What time's breakfast?"

The receptionist smiled and rewarded me with a card key. "Breakfast is from 6:00 to 10:30 a.m."

In room 21, I immediately put ear to wall. I hoped to hear the TV, but Skylar was playing music instead. Spa music. Not perfect for concealment purposes, but much better than nothing.

Playing a hunch, I went to the bathroom, where I hoped to hear the sound or feel the vibe of running water. No such luck. Thinking about it, I decided that didn't mean anything. The placement of her door indicated that her room layout paralleled mine, rather than mirroring it. That was very good news. It meant that her desk would rest against the opposite wall, and that her laptop screen would also face my direction if she worked on it in bed.

I unzipped my backpack and extracted a small electric drill with a foot-long 4mm bit. After a minute of analyzing angles and accoutrements, I selected a spot on the wall and marked it with the hotel pen. Ready to roll, I turned on *Sports Center* and adjusted the volume to the maximum allowed. Satisfied with the setup, I wrapped a bath towel around the hand holding the drill, pulled the trigger and pushed. I stopped the instant I felt the second sheet of drywall start to give.

I retracted the drill and put my eye to the fresh hole. The light spot was immediately visible—and unobstructed, meaning both that I'd calculated correctly and that Skylar wasn't staring back.

I withdrew a slim fiber-optic camera from my backpack. Not a bit of secret CIA kit, but rather a similar industrial tool: $49 on Amazon. I connected it to my cell phone and used the optics to guide it to the opposite hole. After poking through, I could see the whole bedroom.

Skylar was nowhere to be seen.

Either she was in the bathroom, or she had left the room. The bathroom door was open, but the light did not appear to be on. Since I'd given her very little opportunity to leave undetected, my money was on the bathtub. Dim lighting, soft music, and a stress-relieving soak.

I used the remote to mute the television volume. With my hearing thus restored, I pressed the camera far enough into Skylar's room to allow it to articulate, then began searching for inanimate objects. I didn't spot a laptop or a cell phone on her desk. The bed and nightstand were also unadorned. Perhaps she'd taken her electronics to the tub.

I switched the phone screen over to the feed from the Mercedes. It was only a mile away at the moment, and it wasn't moving. I felt a chill as the obvious conclusion kicked in. The tracker had come off Tom's car. Zooming in, I read the location and relaxed. He'd parked at The Williamsburg Inn.

Google gave the hotel a five-star rating and a $379 nightly

rate. Definitely not on Uncle Sam's approved list for anyone ranking below agency head or three-star general.

I switched back to the camera feed while contemplating that development. Nothing had changed, but the bathroom light flipped on after a few minutes.

I retracted the camera so its eye was flush with the face of the wall. There was a slim chance that she'd notice the dark spot, but given the texturing and the fact that my hole was just two-thirds the diameter of a pencil eraser, I wasn't worried.

Skylar eventually emerged wearing light pink pajamas that hugged her extraordinarily athletic build in a way that required little imagination and left me feeling a bit inadequate. Her feet were bare and her short sun-bleached hair was only towel dried. She was carrying neither cell phone nor laptop.

Did anyone of our generation travel without an internet interface? Not likely. Perhaps she'd pull one or the other out of a drawer. Unless—

Playing a hunch, I looked at my room then surveyed her desk again. Next, I slowly eased the camera back into her room so that I could see the nightstands. Neither held a phone. Both of her landlines had been removed.

Tom had isolated her.

I switched back to the GPS tracker. The Mercedes was still in the parking lot, a mere mile northeast of my current location.

Certain that Skylar was in for the night, I lost the do-rag, shaved the handlebars off my mustache, changed into a business suit, transferred my tools to my roller bag, and headed for The Williamsburg Inn.

25
Just a Number

THE WILLIAMSBURG INN looked like a converted colonial mansion. Its grand three-story central brick building was embraced by shorter wings and topped with a slate roof sporting multiple chimneys. I did a quick window count and estimated that there were about forty-eight rooms in total. That was a good size for my purposes, small enough that locating Tom shouldn't be too challenging, large enough that I might find a vacancy to one side or the other, given that luxury hotels attempted to separate their guests.

Like all five-star hotels, this one had a bellhop, although, given the colonial atmosphere, I guessed they might call him a valet. I appraised the uniformed assistant while approaching from the self-parking lot. Late thirties and fit but not fastidious. The crease in his pants was far from crisp, and his tie was a notch too loose. I put on a friendly smile, read the nametag, and met his eye as he said, "Can I help you, sir?"

"I believe so. I need your help in selecting the right room." I pulled a $100 bill from my pocket to set the hook. Dressed as I was in a suit and tie, I figured I fit the typical tipping-client mold.

"Absolutely, sir," Vincent said, pupils dilating. "It would be my pleasure. What amenities are you hoping to find? The quietest location? The best view?"

"The right number," I corrected.

"I'm not sure I understand, sir."

I pulled out my cellphone and swiped until it displayed a close-up photo of Tom enjoying his Fierce beer. "Do you recognize my buddy, Tom?"

Vincent glanced warily at the photo. "I believe so, yes."

"I need a room next to his. Not across the hall, but right next door." I rubbed the hundred. "Can you recommend a room number?"

Vincent chewed on that.

"Just recommend a room number," I repeated.

Vincent's practiced fingers made the Benjamin vanish. "If you'll follow me, I'll see what's available. What's your name?"

"Chase. Zachary Chase."

We walked to the front desk where Vincent slipped behind the counter. The receptionist gave him a sideways glance but was too occupied with another client to interfere.

Vincent began typing, and typing, and typing. Finally, I got an affirming nod. "Normally I'd recommend either 208 or 212 for someone with your needs, but 208 is occupied. Shall I book you into 212, Mister Chase? It will be $400 after taxes. That includes breakfast."

I pulled out my Visa and said a short prayer. Four hundred dollars would be the most I'd ever paid for a room on my own dime—and I wouldn't even be sleeping there.

"You'll find your room on the second floor. The elevator is to your left." Vincent didn't bother offering to help with my roller bag, given that I had two inches and twenty pounds on him, and had already tipped.

Room 212 was filled with fine furnishings that rested on spindly hardwood legs, supposedly carved by one of Ben Franklin's friends. The fabrics were a cream and ochre combination, as was the wallpaper. I counted four pleated lampshades and an equal number of gold-framed colonial prints. Plenty to block my view.

The sight of silk paper on the walls saddened me. Drilling it would feel sacrilegious. Nonetheless, I unzipped my bag and prepared to do just that. It was a very small hole. Virtually unnoticeable.

The location of the doors told me that Tom's headboard would be back-to-back with my own, separated by the wall, of course. That would be weird, sleeping with the enemy's head literally inches away—were I to stay.

I surveyed the room and selected the point that would

give me the best available angle for seeing a computer screen, whether it was on the desk or in the lap of a man in bed. I repeated the towel and TV trick, then got drilling.

My gizmo showed Tom's room to be lights-off dark, with no one in bed and no light leaking from the bathroom. Were it not for the black roller bag on the sofa, and a white washcloth on the floor by the door, there would be no sign that the room was rented out. I seriously doubted that Tom was soaking in the dark, and thus concluded that he wasn't in the room.

I had seen Tom's car in the valet parking lot, and the chiseled-cheekboned impostor had already dined. Therefore, I concluded that he was either in the bar or at another meeting.

I briefly considered breaking into Tom's room and rummaging through his bag, but given his presence on the property, I decided that would be too reckless. Besides, in a five-star facility like this, entry would not be easy. I'd probably need to swipe a master key card.

I decided to see if he was in the bar.

I returned to the elevator and pressed the down button. It chimed a moment later. The doors opened, and out stepped Tom.

26
Good Question

RIES WADED INTO THE SURF off Point Dume as the midday sun maximized the colors of the Santa Monica Mountains. The exquisite contrast between the reds, golds, and browns of the hardened lava bluffs and the turquoise, azure, and sapphire waters crashing against them always made him smile. This trek into living art kicked off his favorite climb. Ries tried to make it at least once a month—even after his replacement. That was technically a violation of the rules, but one of no consequence, since he was alone.

Most climbers preferred to do the Dume in the morning, so they could climb in the cool of the shade. But Ries was happy to handle the heat in exchange for optimizing the view—and experiencing one of the world's most spectacular cliffs in solitude.

Timing wasn't the only thing that differentiated him from his fellow enthusiasts. Most of them hiked to the top on the landward side and rappelled down before climbing up. No doubt that was easier, safer, and more efficient. But he preferred swimming to the bottom and working without a top rope. In part, this was because top ropes felt to him like cheating. But mainly he just liked meeting life on his own terms, especially when that convergence involved a healthy challenge.

The swim to the boulders at the base of the cliff was no amateur undertaking. You had to stay close enough to the shore to avoid the riptide, but far enough away that the swells wouldn't slap you against the remorseless rock. It was all part of the thrill.

Ries had always felt that he wasn't really living if he didn't occasionally risk dying. It was an ironic juxtaposition that immortality only intensified.

He timed his scramble out of the water and onto the bottom boulders to take assistance from a wave. That was the secret to successful ascents—and most of life for that matter—finding ways to work with nature rather than fight it.

The backpack holding his gear—his helmet, harness, rope, and chalk; his nuts, quickdraws, carabiners, and cams —was waterproof. But the swim had filled his climbing shoes with sand. He removed them one at a time and carefully cleaned each with the assistance of encroaching waves.

Shoes were the secret to rock climbing. Non-climbers had no clue of the magic they held. The way the stiff gummy soles gripped steep rock when he angled his body right still blew his mind. It was just as his instructor had confided the first time they stood at the base of a cliff. Anyone who trusted his shoes and kept his cool could literally walk up walls.

By the time Ries had fitted his footwear and assembled his gear, getting each piece arranged for quick and clean one-handed access, he was dry. He gave his curly sun-bleached hair a quick back-and-forth rubbing, then snugged his helmet, dipped his hands into his bag of chalk, and began the eighty-foot ascent.

The route was rated a 5.10, which meant it was virtually vertical and offered only scant hand and foot holds. Magic shoes and machismo definitely required. Ries knew from experience that it would take him about forty minutes.

Eighty feet doesn't sound like a lot in a world where buildings now soar above two thousand, but sounding and experiencing are two entirely different matters. When there's nothing between you and a quick trip to the ground, most will feel that cool kick of adrenaline before they reach ten feet. Take that up to twenty, and every human heart will start to flutter. By thirty, most are paralyzed with panic. At forty, the fright is enough to make the frail pass out.

Ries paused at that forty-foot halfway point to sip water and enjoy the stunning scenery. Precarious though his position probably looked to laymen, and insane as it undoubtedly appeared to his fellow Immortals, Ries was perfectly safe. About every ten feet, he wedged a nut or a cam into a crack and clipped it to his rope. Even if he slipped or passed out or was struck by lightning, he couldn't fall more than twenty feet before the rope caught. It would stretch out another couple of feet, ending the descent in an experience more like feathering the brakes than slamming them to a full stop. Unpleasant perhaps, but not traumatic. Especially with a helmet.

Much safer than skydiving.

Or stumbling drunk onto a balcony.

Ries didn't actually know how Camilla had ended up with her skull cracked by patio rocks, but now that the initial shock had worn off, he believed drinking was a safe assumption. They'd all over-imbibed after the tense meeting with the shocking announcement and unexpected vote. And Lisa had further facilitated self-medication by having so much fantastic wine on hand.

Camilla's tragic death made Ries all the more determined to feel alive.

The crux of the climb came at a height of sixty-three feet. The crack that he'd been using to anchor his nuts and cams petered out there, leaving seventeen feet of inverted climb with no place to secure a rope. There were two tough alternatives for completing the ascent. Ries could make the rest of the climb without additional anchors for his rope, but that would risk a fall of up to thirty-four feet. Or he could shift to a crack a dozen feet off to his left. The latter was a considerably easier route, with a slope that was dead-on ninety degrees vertical rather than overhanging. But reaching it took serious skill.

The hand and foot holds between the second crack and his present position were little more than blemishes. One- or two-millimeter pimples on the face of the cliff. The first time Ries had attempted the shift, he'd fallen six times, only making it on the lucky seventh. With experience, he now only slipped about once every other climb.

He was halfway there and doing his best starfish

impersonation when he heard the dreaded rattle of gravel overhead. Careful to keep his movement very slow and steady, he rotated his neck in that direction. A coil of rope flew off the clifftop and fell just his side of the last crevice. Due to the overhanging rock, the intruding rope didn't actually touch his. It ran perpendicular to it about two inches out. That overlap was a major breach of both safety and etiquette, as was tossing a coil without first shouting, "Rope!"

"Hey!" Ries shouted. "You're not alone on this rock."

That was another downside to his unusual approach. Some inexperienced climbers, seeing no other lines clipped to the bolt up top, assumed they had the cliff to themselves.

He waited a beat for "Sorry!" but it didn't come.

The climber, however, did.

He backed off over the edge and started to descend. His skin was dark, although whether Asian or African or spray-tanned, Ries couldn't tell. Perhaps the oblivious bastard didn't speak English.

The intruder rappelled down until Ries's rope was at his eye level. Then he stopped, secured his own rope, and looked over. Had he just been surprised by the sight of Ries's line? Perhaps he was deaf.

"You need to shout 'Rope!' before throwing. What you did is very dangerous for your fellow climbers. And you can't have your line crossing mine. You're going to have to reposition."

The man stayed silent while he studied Ries. With his helmet and sunglasses, Ries couldn't tell if there was comprehension on the climber's face, but his mouth didn't appear particularly apologetic.

"Do you understand?" Ries pressed, using his head to gesture ever so slightly toward the rope. "It's very dangerous." Surely his starfish stance said it all.

The man grabbed Ries's rope in his left hand.

"No, no! That's not what I meant! Don't touch my rope!"

While Ries watched in horror, the man pulled a box cutter from his webbing. One of those wicked looking ones with a hooked handle and locking blade. He put it to Ries's rope and severed the multi-strand with a single forceful swipe. There was nothing Ries could do to stop him. Clinging to the rock demanded all his strength and focus.

As the trailing tail of Ries's rope slid back along his path like a retreating snake, making that whispery zippy sound, Ries turned away from the man and locked his eyes on the next crack. His salvation. It was still a good four feet from his grasp. *You've done this before, dozens of times. You don't need the rope.* His hands were sweaty but he hesitated to reach for his chalk. Still, that was the smart move, and this was the time to be—

A tug ripped Ries from the rock face.

The man had pulled Ries's rope.

As he fell into his favorite view and eternal resting place, Ries screamed his last thought. "Why?"

27
The Naked Truth

I STEPPED INTO THE ELEVATOR as Tom turned toward his room. Had the killer recognized me? No way to know. He hadn't reacted, but professionals rarely did.

Fortunately, I had been standing to the side with my face in my phone. That posture was a defensive measure I'd made a habit after a similar event in the Czech Republic had ended with arterial spray all over the elevator of the Prague Castle Suites.

Luck had saved my bacon back then.

Luck and my pet weapon.

The ceramic stiletto blade secured to my forearm with a custom-made 3D-printed clip had been issued to me months earlier for a special op in Switzerland. Pencil thin and just as light, it was invisible to metal detectors, if not to body scans or pat-downs. Once I discovered that I could propel the blade into my hand if I whipped my arm just right—something I often practiced when bored—it became as integral to my wardrobe as my watch.

I stroked my sleeve to verify the stiletto's presence as I rode the elevator down. If Tom had recognized me, he would be running down the stairs at the end of the hall, planning to either flank and eliminate me or make a fast escape.

Exiting into the grand lobby, I used my peripheral vision to check the hallway to my left. Vincent was walking from that direction, but no one else. Inspired by the sighting, I headed the valet's way.

"May I help you, Mister Chase?"

"Did you just see Tom?"

"No, sir."

"Do me a favor, if you'd be so kind. Walk back up the

stairs, then all the way to the other side." I drew a long arc in the air as I spoke. "Then meet me in the lobby and let me know if you see him."

"But of course, sir."

As Vincent reversed course, I moved to a corner of the lobby and pulled up the GPS tracking app on my phone. Tom's Mercedes was still in the lot.

A bit of ruckus in the bar caught my attention, but otherwise the lobby was quiet. Nobody was checking in or out. The receptionist who had given Vincent a sideward glance now gave me a welcoming smile.

I melted into a corner and pulled a twenty from my increasingly slim wallet while keeping an eye on the doors.

Vincent completed his circuit in under two minutes. "No sign of him, Mr. Chase."

"Anybody else about?"

He pointed toward the elevator, which pinged as if prompted. An elderly couple emerged and headed toward the restaurant. "Just them."

I passed Vincent the twenty in a thank-you shake, then took the stairs up to my room.

After quietly opening and closing my door, I hooked my cell phone back up to the fiber optic camera. It gave me another surprise. Tom had pushed the soft furniture aside and was now standing naked in the middle of his room.

It took me a second to recognize the controlled movements of the ancient martial art he was practicing. Memories of Saturday mornings in Hanoi came flooding back as I watched *grasp the sparrow's tail* turn to *ward-off*, and then *roll-back* morph into *gather*. I hit RECORD as Tom exhaled into *press,* while sweat rolled over muscles stretched tight as drumheads.

People out of the know typically scoffed at the lackadaisical looking exercise, but I understood tai chi's power. It exercised the entire body, increasing both flexibility and power while improving balance and training the body to remain relaxed during tense situations.

Watching Tom, I found myself mesmerized by another man's body for the first time in my life. His fat percentage was clearly down in the single digits, but his scar count wasn't. I spotted two bullet holes, three knife wounds, and half a dozen smaller disfigurements that resembled claw marks. Most were on his arms, as if acquired during defensive gestures. Given the scene before me now, it was easy to picture the man practicing martial arts against multiple opponents armed with classic blunt and bladed weapons. I cringed at the thought of facing such a master with my tiny knife.

I kept the recording running as Tom brought hands to heart, then transitioned into calisthenics. He bent forward until his palms were flat on the floor, then slowly shifted his weight and lifted his feet off the ground. He took his legs up through a controlled arc until he was standing vertically on his hands. At this point, Tom's nakedness became particularly distracting, but I still couldn't look away.

It occurred to me that Tom and Skylar would make quite the couple, given their physical fitness fanaticism. If I hadn't heard them speaking and known they had separate rooms, I'd be second-guessing their relationship at this point.

Tom launched off his hands into the most impressive gymnastics display I had seen outside an Olympic competition or mixed martial arts cage match. The man didn't just look healthy, he appeared downright Herculean. I struggled to imagine what it would take to beat him in hand-to-hand combat. What kind of animal I'd have to become to be the one who walked away.

After Tom completed his fortieth inverted pushup, he sprang to his feet and sauntered to the bathroom. I exhaled when I heard the shower engage. Holy smokes! What had Lars stumbled into?

Who was Skylar up against?

Was I crazy for inserting myself?

Tom emerged from the bathroom five minutes later. He threw a towel onto the desk chair, slipped between the sheets and hit the lights. I found myself half-surprised that the man hadn't lit a dozen candles and slaughtered a small animal.

I withdrew the camera carefully so as not to make the

slightest sound, then plugged my side of the hole with a sliver of soap. Satisfied that even without overhearing any phone calls or observing a single laptop screen, the $520 I had dropped at The Williamsburg Inn was money well spent, I headed for my BMW. Hopefully I would soon see a lump in Skylar's bed and hear her snoring.

28
Emergency Stop

SKYLAR ACKNOWLEDGED the wisdom inherent in a twenty-four hour wait. A cooling-off period made sense with decisions as momentous as abandoning one life for another. But she had already lost the only two meaningful things in her old life. Her ability to compete professionally as a triathlete and, as a distant second, her service as a firefighter. Her enthusiasm for the extraordinary new life on offer didn't waiver, even for a second.

She slept well, woke excited, and then burned clock by running thirty miles. Her speed was no longer professionally competitive, but it was still a welcome source of pride.

When at last Tom's Mercedes pulled into the parking lot, she was waiting with a packed bag and a big grin.

"You look like someone who knows what she wants," he said by way of greeting.

"Purpose, service, and elite company? What's not to want?"

"I couldn't agree more."

"So you're in?" he asked, a knowing look in his eyes.

She wasn't about to play hard to get. "I'm in! Take me to HQ."

"Excellent," Tom said, shifting into drive. "This is my favorite part of the job, pulling back the curtain. Prepare to have your mind blown."

"Oh, yeah? In what way?"

"I told you we work outside the bounds of congressional oversight."

"I remember."

"Well, that requires us to base our operation off the grounds of Camp Peary. But of course, by operating beyond the fence line, we expose ourselves to civilian oversight, so to speak. To minimize the unwelcome intrusions, we hide in plain sight."

Skylar understood. "Makes sense. Where do you do that?"

"You tell me," Tom said with a sly wink.

Skylar looked over and saw that he was serious. Given his facial features, he always had a no-nonsense look, but she knew the difference after hours of studying him across tables.

He clarified without prompting. "The office has to be someplace with minimal car and foot traffic, and yet in a location where people can come and go at all hours of the day and night without raising eyebrows. Someplace with natural privacy, where neighbors aren't likely to get curious about what's going on or feel inclined to snoop around. Any guesses as to how we accomplish that?"

Skylar quickly formulated a comfortable guess. "A utility company. Like a power station. Plenty of fences around those, and given the service needs, there would be traffic day and night."

"Nice guess, although most of the cars entering and exiting those are white panel vans." Tom tapped his steering wheel. "We need civilian vehicles to look at home. And we don't want to walk around in hard hats."

"People really pay attention to such things?"

"You'd be amazed. Spend an evening beside a police dispatcher and you'll get a feel for just how many bored and shallow people inhabit our country. It's downright depressing. Next guess?"

Skylar drew a blank. "Nothing's leaping to mind. Where?"

Tom answered by dramatically flipping on the right-turn signal.

Skylar read the road sign. *Good Graces Chapel and Mortuary.* "You're kidding me?"

"No. It's actually a functioning funeral home. Not the kind of place where people are prone to do a lot of mingling, so the business adds cover without increasing exposure."

"I never would have guessed."

"Exactly."

As they drove up the drive, a classic colonial building came into view. Its exterior was illuminated with accent lighting, but there was no glow behind the front windows.

Tom pulled around back and parked near the business entrance. A light over the door was the only sign of life besides half a dozen parked cars.

Skylar couldn't believe this was actually happening. She was about to step into a secret CIA headquarters building—as a new employee. Would a palm reader open a hidden elevator door? Would she be scanned for weapons? Would the old lady behind the reception desk have a gun in her lap? Skylar was about to find out.

"Are you ready for this?"

"Absolutely."

"Good. You can leave your bag in the trunk. We'll only be here an hour or so. Then I'll drop you at your new apartment."

My new apartment. That sounded good. Skylar was expecting something more like a fire station bunk room. She slipped her wallet into her pocket and followed Tom with spring in her step.

He opened the door with a gentlemanly gesture. It appeared to have been unlocked but probably reacted to some transmitter on his person the way luxury cars did these days. There was no reception area, much less a lady behind a desk, but the hallway lights were on.

"Looks pretty normal, doesn't it? Other than the metal detector we just passed."

Skylar whirled around and saw the device she'd been too excited to notice. It was a two-foot-long gray arch placed about eighteen inches inside the door. She turned back to study the hallway, which was generic. "Remarkably normal."

"Hidden in plain sight. It lets car keys and cell phones through, but not guns or knives."

The employee atrium was essentially a wide corridor that gave access to administrative facilities on the left, and public facilities on the right. Tom led her past all that to a set of glass double doors at the end. They pushed through them into a covered walkway with glass walls. It extended about forty feet past flowering gardens until another set of double doors deposited them in an outbuilding. That atrium had double doors on every wall as well, an accommodation for caskets, she realized.

Directly before them was a curtained viewing window. She'd stood before a similar window in a similar building several years back to watch her grandmother's cremation.

Now she understood exactly where they were. "I see what you mean about keeping the neighbors from snooping."

Tom opened the door to the crematory and motioned for her to enter.

"Seriously?"

"No worries. They don't keep cadavers here."

Skylar had never been inside a crematory before. She'd looked through the window, but back then everything either side of the door to the cremation retort had been curtained off.

The room reminded her of a hospital facility. A government hospital. No frills, just the basics. There was a sink to the left of the cremation retort and a pulverizer to the right. Cardboard coffins lined the left wall. Storage cabinets covered the right. Everything you'd need to turn a body into cremains with dignity.

What Skylar didn't see was another door. The entrance to FIFO's secret headquarters.

She turned to Tom, her puzzlement undoubtedly apparent. Her excitement mellowed by the macabre.

Tom's enthusiasm hadn't dimmed. "See if you can find the entrance. Pretend you're a police officer and you got a tip that there's a meth lab hidden on these premises. It's not unknown, using funeral homes for that purpose, given the need drug dealers have to camouflage the heat and fumes from cooking."

Skylar did a 360-degree survey. The cabinets were an obvious choice. Too obvious. Her gaze halted on the cremation controls. Was one a special lever? Perhaps the big red *Emergency Stop*. Perhaps when you pressed it the entire cabinet set swung inward like a large door.

She moved closer to study it.

Tom followed.

She felt the needle prick her thigh, but lost consciousness before her combative muscles could react.

29
Corrupt Practices

DESPITE HIS KNOWLEDGE of her athletic background, Tory was surprised by Skylar's weight as he lifted her unconscious body off the floor and lowered it into a cremation container. Her size-four frame was weighty as a sack of rocks. He automatically adjusted the enclosed pillow but didn't bother unfolding the blanket. Such acts would surely ring hollow, given the circumstances.

He'd skipped the box altogether the first time he did this. That was a mistake. Sliding Ries's replacement into the cremation retort had been unpleasant and awkward. Sleeping bodies weren't rigid.

The fact that a cardboard casket was missing might be noted in the morning, given that the stack at the side of the room no longer reached the ceiling. But that didn't matter. His actions weren't a secret. He'd offered the owner of the family funeral home $100,000 in cash to incinerate *something*. All Mr. Murdoch had to do was leave a few lights on and forget to lock the back door. *Plausible deniability, and a tax-free hundred grand.*

When concocting the scheme, Tory had accurately anticipated an easy sell. He figured that men who made their living by taking advantage of grieving widows would tend to have a me-first mentality.

He'd been right.

The Good Graces Chapel and Mortuary was the fifth funeral home he'd rented. The other owners had all made a show of deliberating before acquiescing with a green light in their eyes, but Murdoch actually made a demand. "No guns."

Tory replied with, "Who said anything about guns?"

Murdoch pushed his thin spectacles up his aquiline nose.

"I am anticipating. Anticipation is how problems are avoided. Wouldn't you agree?"

"I would," Tory said with an appreciative lilt. Cunning was one thing he respected. "No problem."

Murdoch responded by standing in silence for a second, then folding his arms across his chest. "Lest you dismiss this as an unenforceable acquiescence and walk into an unforeseen situation, I should inform you that my brother-in-law works in the law enforcement supply business. If you hand me that envelope, I'm going to use some of that cash to install a metal detector—with an alarm."

Tory suspected that the business owner was bluffing, but hoped he wasn't. A metal detector would add a nice touch of credibility to the ruse. Given the location and the success of his CIA-recruitment scam, he anticipated multiple visits. "No problem, Murdoch. Just be sure to set the sensitivity to ignore phones and keys."

Murdoch nodded and accepted the envelope stuffed with a thousand Benjamins.

Having dismissed the threat as a bluff, Tory wore his weapon to Lars's execution. Fortunately, he spotted the archway in time. He'd mumbled an excuse about forgetting something in the car and run back to deposit his Glock in the glovebox.

The rest of that first op at Murdoch's Mortuary had gone smoothly, so when Tory used the CIA con for a second time, he approached Murdoch again. That time around, the mortician had been nothing but sunshine and rainbows.

Tory opened the retort door but paused before pushing the cremation container into the pyre. Staring into the dark hole with its rings of gas nozzles, he shook his head. This machine would create death when it came to life.

Tory had loved and feared God. Back before the Almighty had taken his wife during childbirth and given the daughter she died for an incurable condition. When his daughter died as well after thirteen difficult years, Tory concluded that if God existed, He had abandoned them. "See what you get when you leave us alone on this rock? We're stuffing each other into incinerators."

With that thought, he shoved Skylar all the way inside. It would take two hours to transform her flesh into four pounds of skeletal remains. He'd have to rake those into the pulverizer to create the cremains that could be dumped into an urn. He hadn't thought to bring a receptacle the first time he used this disposal method, but the mortician kept a supply of biodegradable cardboard cremains containers in one of the cabinets. More than sufficient for a quick trip to the woods.

Tory had taken all the ashes to peaceful natural locations rather than toss them into dumpsters. One had to draw the line somewhere, and his conscience had drawn that one.

His radar pinged as he approached the incinerator control. It wasn't a sight or a sound. More of a sensation. The presence of another person. Could Skylar be stirring? He checked his watch. No, the antipsychotic would have her out cold for at least another hour. Haldol was serious stuff, thank goodness. What a horror that would be, waking up inside an active oven.

As it was, Skylar had effectively died in a good mood, a great mood actually, and without ever knowing what hit her. Everyone should be so lucky. His wife and daughter certainly hadn't been.

Tory cocked his ears, but heard nothing. He decided that what he'd sensed was someone slipping through the outer door. A series of individually undetectable events that somehow registered when combined. Had Murdoch returned? Had curiosity gotten the better of him? No, not curiosity. If Murdoch had returned, it would be to see if he could wring more money from the man who had so easily coughed up two hundred grand.

Tory reflexively flexed his left pec to confirm the presence of his Glock 42 slim subcompact, but it wasn't there. He'd left it in the car on account of the metal detector. Suddenly his situation felt like a setup.

If it was, he might have to make the cremation a twofer. He hoped it didn't come to that. Killing Murdoch would lead to an investigation, and those were something Tory worked very hard to avoid. Just because he could kill, didn't mean he liked it. What he did like was this arrangement. It worked well with his CIA recruitment scam, which was by far his favorite.

There were other funeral homes, of course. But Murdoch's murder would make their owners overly wary. They'd be more likely to report Tory than accept his unconventional offer.

Paying Murdoch extortion money wasn't out of the question. It wasn't Tory's money, and his clients clearly didn't sweat their checkbooks. Pride was the primary consideration. Pride over practicality.

He glanced back toward the mouth of the oven. The *SS Pride* had sailed.

Tory decided to confront the crisis head on. "Come out, Murdoch! This is no time for games."

30
Tough Choice

WATCHING TOM'S MERCEDES whisk Skylar away, I found myself wishing that I'd opted for less surveillance and more sleep. I had spent much of the night going back and forth between the Brown Pelican and The Williamsburg Inn, alternatively spying on Skylar and Tom.

It had been unproductive, but not entirely uneventful. I returned to the Brown Pelican shortly after sunrise to find that Skylar was neither in her room nor in any of the neighborhood restaurants. She returned three hours later, covered in sweat from what must have been a very long run.

My time spying on Tom had started with hope but was soon filled with frustration. His laptop employed a privacy screen. It could only be viewed by a perpendicular observer. I drilled a second hole with the proper perspective, but then Tom's body blocked my view. The two glimpses I stole when he rose to stretch and use the restroom were of Facebook pages, not documents or, better yet, email.

The blue Facebook banner proved to be another tease. Tom was not logged in. He wasn't checking his own feed. He was doing anonymous research. In one case on a woman called Sandy Wallace, in the other on a man named John Maxwell.

That was all I got. The sum total of a dozen hours' worth of surveillance was two Facebook profile sightings.

With the moon and stars again above, I was back behind the wheel of my BMW. I shifted into drive but waited for Tom's Mercedes to disappear from sight before accelerating in pursuit. My plan was to remain half a mile behind since I could follow the red GPS dot just as easily as the car itself—with no risk of being seen.

As I pressed the gas, my knee reminded me that it was

time for another pain pill. I pulled one from my pocket and swallowed it dry. Then I thought about what likely lay ahead, and took another.

I'd altered my appearance from the various versions Tom had glimpsed. The me he'd brushed past while leaving the bar. The me he'd seen sitting on a bar stool. The me he'd encountered exiting the elevator. And the me he'd tried to kill on a motorcycle. Gone now was the entire mustache I'd worn as a biker at the bar and a guest at the hotel. Gone also were my do-rag and side-parted hairstyle. I'd slicked my hair back with pomade and donned lensless horn-rimmed glasses, producing an entirely different look. Somewhere between *Wall Street*'s Gordon Gekko and Agent Smith from *The Matrix*.

About ten minutes after exiting the parking lot, Tom pulled off the main road onto a private drive. I zoomed in on the tracking map to identify the destination. The *Good Graces Chapel and Mortuary*.

I had not seen that twist coming.

An icy finger traced the length of my spine. Was I too late? Had Tom blown Skylar's brains out in the car? Should I have confronted the killer last night? Would I ever forgive myself if she was dead?

I tried consoling myself with logic. A bullet hole in the windshield or blood spatter on the upholstery would attract all kinds of unwanted attention. He was too polished to make an amateur mistake like that.

The answer struck as I pounded the wheel. Pretending that the mortuary was the FIFO HQ was part of Tom's con. He'd told her he would take her there.

So what was his plan? Drug her in the car, then dump her body in the bottom of a freshly dug grave? Toss some dirt on top and hope nobody noticed before she was covered by a coffin? It was a possibility. But that scenario would be a clunky conclusion to the symphony of subterfuge Tom had been conducting. I expected more from him.

Anxious as I'd just become, and eager as I was to intervene before he severed her head with a shovel, I couldn't risk following them up the mortuary drive. I parked on the side of the road and proceeded on foot, knowing the next few minutes would be a tightrope race. I had to move quickly but quietly and carefully, balancing the downside of detection against the consequences of a late arrival.

I stayed in the shadows while sprinting as best I could around the building. The mortuary was the size of a small elementary school, sans playground. I stopped and dropped as soon as Tom's car came into view. It was one of seven.

While counting the cars, I looked down at the Sig Sauer P320 in my hand. "Seventeen rounds."

There in the grass, I saw no movement and heard no activity. I studied the Mercedes to be sure they weren't still inside. It appeared empty, but I made a low dash to confirm the fact with direct visual inspection. The other cars were also empty, but a common detail caught my attention. All seven had rental car barcode stickers on their windshields. Only the Mercedes's hood was warm. Interesting. Had Tom ordered a car company to deliver the other six as window dressing? Or was I about to wish I had more than seventeen rounds?

And now what?

I could call the police and report an abduction. But how long would they take to arrive, and what would happen to Skylar in the interim?

I took a deep breath and ran for the back door.

It proved to be a typical industrial contraption, with a metal skin and a lever handle. Would it be unlocked? For Tom's ruse to work, he would have needed either an unlocked door—presumably picked and left open in advance—or a key. Fifty-fifty. Except he would have wanted the lights inside to be on to augment the appearance of activity. Assuming, of course, that the drivers of the other six autos were back at a rental car office rather than waiting inside with shovels and duct tape.

I put an ear to the door and heard nothing. I pressed the lever, slow and steady. It yielded.

I slipped inside and froze. The hall was arched with a metal detector of the airport variety. A green LED indicated its operational status. That added quite an extravagant touch of authenticity to the HQ ruse. And it meant the mortuary owner was in on Tom's plan.

Metal detectors like the one before me didn't act like Geiger counters. Proximity didn't matter. They only detected disruptions to the field directly between their sensors. While the installation sealed the hallway so as to prevent one from slipping a firearm around the arch, I was able to wedge enough of my Sig into the shelf-like crevice between detector and ceiling to hold it in quasi-concealment until I left. I slid my car key, cell phone, and watch up over the lip as well, both to be certain it wouldn't beep, and to remind me to retrieve my gun.

I slipped past the detector without audible protest and found myself faced with half a dozen choices. There were doors to the left, right, and straight ahead. I strained my ears but heard nothing. That was both good news and bad. The odds that the other six cars were window dressing had just improved. A large group would be hard pressed to remain so silent. But the lack of noise left me without any auditory clue as to which way to go.

I could see lights coming from beyond the glass double doors at the back but knew there might be lights on behind the solid side doors as well. I cracked each, smooth and slow, just enough to check for a lack of lighting. After confirming that each was dark, I pushed through the double doors.

They dumped me into a covered glass walkway that left me totally exposed. I ran to the outbuilding on the opposite side and quickly but quietly slipped inside.

What I found was more doors. Double doors to the left, double doors to the right, a double door straight ahead. The central one had a curtained window beside it, and lights shining on the other side. I'd been in a place like this before. It was the observation room for a crematory.

I crept toward the curtains, ears straining, heart racing.

"Come out, Murdoch! This is no time for games."

Damn! I'd been detected. My eyes flew to the curtain but saw nothing. Of course not. Tom had called me Murdoch, which meant he hadn't seen me. He must have heard me. I'd been quiet, but the door still made a few slight clicks. Perhaps Tom had simply sensed the pressure change during its operation. I wouldn't put that power beyond the capabilities of the fitness freak I'd observed practicing tai chi and extreme calisthenics.

I swiftly considered three responses. I could stay silent and prepare to pounce. I could rush the room. Or I could attempt to bluff my way into striking position.

Could I bluff this man? Not if he recognized me. My disguise was good, but not great. Of course, even if it passed initial muster, the last thing I wanted to do was engage in hand-to-hand combat with a guy whose bedtime routine burned more calories than a mini-marathon. But Skylar's life, if not already extinguished, was at stake. And I had my ceramic knife.

I went with the bluff. "It's not Murdoch. It's Vondreesen. I thought we should talk."

31
Breathless

I WALKED INTO THE CREMATORY like I owned the place—which was precisely the impression I wanted to give.

Tom was alone. Alone and empty-handed and standing across the room beside the control panel of a stainless-steel cremation retort. I had no doubt that Skylar was already inside. But was she unconscious or dead?

If unconscious, there was still hope. The machine was silent. My objective crystalized in that split second. I had to prevent Tom from pressing the ignition switch.

"You need any help getting the retort working?" I asked.

"What are you doing here? Don't tell me you came to help me push a few buttons."

So far, so good. I put on a crafty look and took a step closer. "A man of your means deserves impeccable service. Discreet service."

I could see the calculations churning in Tom's mind as his taut facial features made microexpressions. *Was this a shakedown? Had Murdoch betrayed him? Should he kick me in the nuts? Snap my neck? Or was this all BS?* "Who are you, really?"

It was my turn to calculate, but I had no time. One couldn't waiver while bluffing. I had to either stick with the greedy partner scenario, or go in an entirely different direction. *Which was the more likely to get Skylar out alive?* "Casey McCallum," I said, using the name of a character in the book I was reading. "FBI. I'd show you my badge, but I had to leave it in the bushes outside the door to avoid alarming the metal detector."

"Along with your gun," Tom replied.

I flicked my forearm toward the floor, sending the stiletto to my palm where it snapped open with a swish and locked with a click. "Along with my gun," I repeated.

I was an even six feet tall and weighed 190 pounds, much of it muscle. I was well trained to fight and armed with a familiar weapon. But I didn't give myself even fifty-fifty odds against the smaller, older man with chiseled cheekbones.

Most men wear suits to hide their flaws. This guy wore suits to camouflage his perfections. The strength and discipline Tom had demonstrated as part of his daily routine were Olympic level. Nobody would confuse me with an Olympian.

"I suppose you're going to tell me backup is on the way?" Tom said, his gaze on my eyes, rather than the knife. Would we launch at each other, or pursue alternative actions? The answer to both was *yes*. We were each preparing to pounce while pretending to explore other options.

We both knew it.

But we both played along.

"Would I have exposed myself if backup wasn't coming?"

"You would if you wanted to save the girl."

Save her! That implied she was still alive. Alive in an oven that had yet to ignite.

"What led you here?" Tom pressed.

Time to delay. Not because backup was coming, but to make Tom think that was my tactic. "We've been getting reports of a man posing as a CIA recruiter. Calls that coincide with missing-persons reports. It's amazing how far you can get these days by harnessing the power of big data. The tools are lightyears ahead of what we had even six months ago. Now we can cross-reference airline records with rental car reservations and hotel receipts. Add in IP addresses, voice recognition software, and cell phone calls, and it's almost like having a crystal ball. It's not perfect yet, but hey, here I am." I waved the stiletto.

"You're awfully talkative for an FBI agent. Makes me think either you aren't one, or you're playing a game. In either case, game's over. You have a choice to make."

I tested my hold on the hilt of my blade. It was texturized to add friction, but slim. During combat, I had to grip with gusto to keep it from slipping.

I rehearsed my next moves.

Tom would be expecting me to go for his throat. The quick kill. The arterial spray. That would be the smart move with a normal knife. That or the heart. But my stiletto was not a normal knife. It was four inches long and sharp as a master barber's razor. It would part flesh faster than a guillotine. All I had to do was drag it along a limb. A forearm, a calf, a triceps, a hamstring. Didn't matter. A single swipe could inflict a wound long and deep enough to be instantly crippling. Then blood would gush and consciousness would slip away. "What choice is that?"

"What do you really want to do? Attempt to catch me or try to save the girl?" His left hand shot out fast as a cobra strike, flipping the incinerator ignition switch.

After he struck, Tom stayed still. He didn't run. He didn't pounce. He just stood there blocking access to the *Emergency Stop* button.

In my condition of heightened awareness, I heard the hiss as gas began flowing, then the click-click-click of sparkers bringing flames to life. When the ventilator began humming, I charged. I had no choice. I had never talked to Skylar, and she knew neither my face or my name, but I had studied her biography, and I had shared one of the most important days in her life. And nobody—*almost* nobody—deserved to die this way.

Tom dodged at the last possible instant and put a powerful punch into my solar plexus. He'd set the trap, and I had leapt into it.

I doubled over, struggling to remain on my feet and keep control of the stiletto. Even though I couldn't stand, I could still slash. Still sever fingers and toes. Weren't wounded animals the most dangerous kind?

While I gasped for breath, Tom took my picture with his cell phone. Then he pulled a handkerchief from his pocket, wiped his prints from the ignition switch, and walked out of the room.

32
Custom Catering

FELIX ANSWERED HIS FRONT DOOR rather than let the butler get it. He knew who it was, and experience had taught him that servants sometimes caused coeds to tense up. Even those spending summers working on Jupiter Island, the Southern Florida enclave where the average house cost $4.5 million and residents were more likely to see their neighbors on television than in person.

Her dress was similar in cut and style to the one she'd been wearing when he propositioned her at the Seven Stork Steakhouse, and it immediately had the same effect. The sky-blue pattern even brought out her eyes. "Holly, pleasure to see you again."

"Likewise, Mr. Gentry."

Felix watched her process the revelation that he was dressed for tennis rather than business. "Please, call me Felix. You're this way," he added with a welcoming gesture.

He escorted her through the grand foyer with its dancing waterfall and exotic bird aviary, across the sitting room housing Billy Joel's grand piano and a Chihuly chandelier, then down a wide hallway lined with autographed celebrity photographs. The informal tour ended in a kitchen with an eighteen-foot ceiling and a chef who'd have looked equally at home on the covers of *Maxim Magazine* and *Master Chef.* "Holly, this is Amber. She'll take it from here."

"Thank you, Mr. Gentry. I mean Felix."

He headed upstairs to his bedroom and then out onto the deck. He'd furnished it with an intimate mosaic dining table and a marble sculpture of an angel and nymph about to kiss.

This was the opening sequence of his latest game, his favorite new gig. When he spotted a hostess he wanted—

which was most of them, given the profile for that demographic in the ZIP codes he frequented—Felix would hire her for a four-hour private event. A luncheon at his beachfront estate. Shocked but intrigued, they'd inevitably ask what it paid. His reply was always the same. "Name your price."

Holly's first surprise would come when the chef handed her just two plates. The second would come when she learned that one of them was for her.

Felix's phone rang as he sat down to wait with *The Wall Street Journal.* Perfunctorily checking the display before hitting DECLINE, he saw that the call was forwarded from his Immortals burner phone. *What could Pierce DuBois want?*

Felix, the CFO, and Pierce, the investor, were cut from similar cloth but dyed in different colors. Both were alpha males adept at numbers and politically savvy. But whereas Felix preferred Florida's Gold Coast with its Michelin-starred restaurants and friendly hostesses, Pierce opted for the solitude of Montana's mountains and big sky. This made them both friends and rivals. More rivals than friends now, Felix feared, with Pierce running for Senate and thereby putting all the Immortals in danger.

He brought the phone to his ear. "Hello."

"It's Pierce. Did you hear the news?"

Felix hadn't heard any news, but then he didn't watch much TV any more. He read *The Wall Street Journal* most days and usually leafed through *Forbes* and *The Economist* once or twice a month, but he tried to ignore the talking heads of network news. "Did you get the RNC's endorsement?"

"Ries is dead."

"What! How?"

"A climbing fall, but no accident. His rope was cut."

Felix felt his throat turn dry.

Just then Holly appeared pushing a cart with two lobster salads and an iced bucket of Champagne. He pointed to the phone then held up the palm of his hand. The universal stop sign.

Felix coughed while responding. "That's three in a row."

"I agree. In this light it's clear that Eric's parachute didn't fail by accident."

Holly handed him a glass of water, then backed away. He gave her an appreciative nod and took a sip. "We have to assume the pattern will continue."

"My thoughts exactly."

Someone was executing Immortals. But who? Why? If an outsider had somehow uncovered their special status, why not use that information to join them, rather than beat them? Murder made no sense. But then the alternative was even less likely. Why would one Immortal want to kill the others? There had been no serious conflicts. At least none that he had knowledge of, or had sensed. The disagreement over the Senate runs was their first split vote and only their second controversial one, after the decision to go with replacements.

With murder in mind, Felix ran through a quick mental evaluation of his five surviving peers. Which of them had it in him? Pierce would be his first guess, simply because he was an ambitious alpha male who'd been known to shoot dogs for barking too loud. David was the only other guy, and Felix didn't see that at all. The good doctor was a tree-hugging philosophical vegetarian. Plus Eric and Ries had been his two best friends. Allison was equally absurd. She was ambitious, no doubt, but an artsy scientist much more likely to give a kidney to a homeless woman than pull a homicidal trigger. Among the women, Aria and Lisa were much closer to the murderous type. Both were ruthless and ambitious, but extremely practical. In his opinion, neither would act excessively without a solid logical reason. "I can't think of a motive, can you?"

Pierce didn't ask for clarification. "No. But clearly we have to try. I want to call an emergency meeting."

"In Montana?"

"Sure. We won't be disturbed."

Felix had no intention of visiting a remote ranch anytime soon. Too many horror movies began with that setup.

"How about Seven Star Island instead? Aria has excellent security."

"Fine with me. Anywhere but California. That appears to be the deathbed."

Good point. That common element hadn't occurred to Felix yet. "When?"

"Tomorrow, I hope. Shall we conference Aria into this call?"

Felix looked over at Holly. She looked the part of a professional hostess. Relaxed, discreet, sexy as hell. *Let the games begin.* "I'm sure you can handle it. Text me when you know, I'm about to be stuck in the middle of something."

33
Lost Opportunity

AS TOM LEFT THE ROOM, I lunged for the *Emergency Stop* button, the big red bullseye that might, just might, save Skylar's life.

The gas jets extinguished the instant I slapped the plastic, but the ventilator continued whirring away. As the door at the end slid open with a squeak, smoke struck my olfactory. Thick smoke. Black smoke. But exclusively of the cardboard kind.

Still struggling to regain an upright stance as my solar plexus recovered from Tom's crippling blow, I lumbered toward the smoking hole and looked inside. I saw a long large cardboard box—on fire. It wasn't blazing like a log in full flame. More like it was ringed with birthday cake candles, the pattern corresponding with the placement of the silenced gas jets.

I didn't have time to look for tools or improvise gloves. I just reached in, grabbed the box by the hand-hole in the end, and tugged. Propelled by the momentum I put into it, the cardboard coffin slid out onto the casket bearer in a single swift motion. I used one hand to roll it away from the oven and the other to flip off the flaming lid.

Knowing that every second Skylar stayed inside would do damage, I then grabbed the casket by two fire-free edges and dumped it onto the floor. Her body fell with the limp thud of a fresh corpse.

Not a good sign.

Ignoring my growing sense of dread, I tossed the empty box over the casket bearer to get it out of the way. It landed atop the lid, inadvertently adding fresh fuel to that fire. I scanned the room for an extinguisher. How could there not be one? Surely there was a regulation?

Fearing a fire alarm, I abandoned Skylar long enough to toss the flaming box back into the oven. Fortunately, the incinerator's exhaust fan was still spinning at full force, sucking smoke from the room.

With that emergency averted, I returned to Skylar's side. I rolled her over with a silent prayer.

Her nose was bleeding.

It hadn't been when I lifted the lid.

She must have smacked it when she fell.

I smiled. Not at my accidental handiwork—but because corpses don't bleed. If there was no active pump, the most a body could do was ooze.

Bracing for the moment of truth, I pushed my fingers into the place where her jaw met her windpipe—and felt a pulse. A strong pulse.

She wasn't dead.

She wasn't dying.

She was sedated.

I ran my hands up and down her body, searching for smoldering fabric. I found a few holes and bands of scorched flesh, but nothing that caused me to panic. She was going to be fine. Sore, but fine. I'd be happy to share my pain pills—if I could get us out of there, still free and breathing.

Should the police show up now and catch me carrying Skylar's drugged and damaged body, my explanation would sound insane. Even after Skylar awoke, she could only partly corroborate my story, given that she knew nothing about me.

It would get ugly.

We would suffer delays.

And all the while Tom would slip further away.

The police weren't our only immediate threat. The mortician posed another. Virginia was a stand-your-ground state. If Murdoch was in on this, he could walk in and shoot us without legal consequence. For that matter, Tom could be sitting outside, waiting to shoot us as we walked out the door.

I discounted both threat scenarios.

Tom had exhibited exceptionally rational and detached behavior. A true professional in full control. He hadn't bothered with a combination blow. He'd applied exactly the amount of force required to disable me and enable an easy escape. Nothing more. No gratuitous kick. No gruff threat. No action that made it personal. He had classified his operation as blown, and exfiltrated. *Win some, lose some, on to the next target.* I had worked with a few guys like that. Ice-cold pros.

I grabbed a couple of tissues from a dispenser on the counter and wiped the blood from Skylar's nose. Once it was clean, I returned to the cabinet and found a first aid kit. Automotive size. I stuffed it into the small of my back, then bent over her unconscious body.

With some effort, I hoisted Skylar onto my shoulder and headed for the exit. Pausing in the archway of the metal detector, I reached up to retrieve my gun. My fingers found nothing. *No, please no!*

As my stomach dropped, I laid Skylar gently in the hallway, freeing my fingers for a closer inspection of the crevice. Everything was gone. My gun. My cell. My watch. My car key.

I closed my eyes, and exhaled. *It could be worse. Much worse. For me and for Skylar.*

Latching onto that positive energy, I resumed the fireman's carry and barreled out into the cool Virginia night. There was no sense in moving slow. We were screwed in any case if someone was waiting.

All appeared quiet. Crickets were chirping and the Mercedes was missing. Alas, without my cell phone, I had no way to track it.

I couldn't risk carrying Skylar all the way to my car, given where it was parked. If I was spotted by a patrolling cop or Second Amendment enthusiast, on the side of a rural road, in the dark, with an unconscious woman over my shoulder, I was screwed. Any reasonable person would assume it was an abduction. When Skylar awoke, she would likely confirm as much, given that she'd never met me.

Come to think of it, we couldn't avoid an unthinkable,

unforgettable, unbelievable discussion. One for the record books. One we'd be telling our grandchildren. Whenever and wherever she woke up, the following few minutes were going to be surreal.

I laid her on the grass behind a bush at the top of the drive. Ignoring the growing pain in my ankle and knee, I ran for my BMW.

Years back, I'd attached a hide-a-key behind the rear bumper in a place you had to really hunt to find. I hoped it was still there, with its battery still sparking. For that matter, I hoped my car was still there.

It was.

I hung my suit coat on the side view mirror, put the first aid kit on the roof, and wriggled beneath the back end. Even knowing it was there, the grimy black box took a bit of searching to find. Twenty seconds after sliding back its slippery lid and retrieving my other belongings, I shifted the transmission into drive.

Stopping beside the concealing bush, I put the car in park but left the engine running. I ran around back to open the rear door—then found Skylar sitting up. She was clearly still groggy. As I moved closer to the center of her visual field, she began crab-walking backward. First she mumbled, then she screamed.

34
Reorientation

SKYLAR HAD NEVER BEEN so disoriented in her life. She'd come close once, when her breathing apparatus malfunctioned during the Drew Street apartment fire and she'd had to hold her breath while carrying a kid down six flights of stairs. That was impossible, of course, so she'd sucked in smoke and scorched her lungs before exiting in delirium.

This was worse than that.

She had no idea where she was or why she was there. She was lying on the grass under a night sky rural enough to reveal constellations. Her head ached like she'd just been popped in the nose, and various parts of her body felt like they'd been burned. She looked down at her clothes, half expecting to see firefighting gear, but recognized her interview suit instead.

Then an unfamiliar man appeared. He was wearing a suit and black rimmed glasses. His hair was slicked back in a style that hadn't been popular for decades. Had he punched her in the face? Knocked her to the ground? Was she about to be raped?

She heard screaming, and realized it was coming from her own mouth.

The man spoke as she silenced herself. "It's okay, Skylar. It's okay. You're going to be all right. But you need to calm down, and we need to get out of here."

His voice was imploring. His movements strained, as if he were recovering from a marathon and his joints were hurting.

"Stay away!"

"Okay, okay." He stopped moving and held up empty palms, but he didn't back away.

"Who are you and where are we?"

"My name's Chase, Zachary Chase, and I just saved you from Tom. We're outside the funeral home. Do you remember coming to the funeral home? He fooled you into believing it was a covert CIA location?"

She did remember.

Her hand went to her thigh as the memory returned. She suddenly felt very afraid. "Where is Tom?"

"I don't know. But he might come back, or send someone else. We should leave."

"Send someone else? Why are you here?"

"That's a long story, and I look forward to telling it once we're safe. We are in extreme danger here."

He seemed genuinely wary and concerned, but she wasn't sold. "Where do you intend to take me?"

"Someplace public where we can talk without fear. There's a Denny's a few miles from here off 60. We can be there in five minutes. Or there's an IHOP two minutes further up the road."

Skylar wasn't one to get into cars with strangers, but if Zachary Chase had wanted to harm her, he could have done so already. And what was her alternative? Walk down the road with her thumb out? She had no phone. She'd left everything but her wallet in Tom's trunk. "Conversation and coffee sounds good. Doesn't matter to me where—so long as there are other people around."

Chase closed the back door of his car and opened the passenger door instead. By way of explanation, he said, "I didn't know how long you'd be out."

The horror of her near-death experience sent another shiver up Skylar's spine. "What did he give me? What did Tom inject into my thigh?"

"I have no idea. I didn't see it happen."

He tossed a suit coat from the passenger seat into the back, then handed her a white plastic box labeled First Aid in red letters. "I'm hoping there's burn cream and bandages inside. I haven't had a chance to check."

The box did have antibiotic ointment along with both Band-Aids and gauze. It also held a decent pair of blunt-tipped scissors. The kind used to cut off casts and bandages. Even without points, they would add authority to her punch if slipped around her middle and ring fingers.

Having travelled alone to triathlons all over the world, Skylar knew how to take care of herself. Present circumstances notwithstanding.

She set the scissors on the right side of her seat, uncapped the tiny tube of ointment, and began examining her wounds through the burn holes in her clothes.

Chase U-turned the car and headed toward the highway.

The burns were in bands about twelve inches apart, with the first across her shoulder blades and the last on her calves. The worst were on her buttocks and shoulders.

She pictured the pattern in her mind. It reminded her of grill marks on a steak. Her mind flashed to the last place she'd been, and the last thing she'd seen. As the implication registered, her throat started closing and her flesh began to crawl. "Oh my God! Was I— Did he—" She couldn't complete the questions.

Chase reached out a hand but stopped short of her thigh. Second-guessing himself, he withdrew it. "You're okay now. It was a close call, but you're safe. I'd try not to think about it if I were you."

"What am I supposed to think about? How could I possibly think about anything else, knowing—"

"Where did Tom approach you? The first time? How did you meet?"

Skylar would never forget that encounter. "It was on a run. There's a twenty-six–mile loop I do along Clearwater Beach, from Belleair to Treasure Island and back. He met me at the Treasure Island turnabout and kept pace. After a couple of miles by my side, he motioned for me to take out my earbuds so we could talk. Assuming he was about to hit on me, I complied."

Chase gave her a look.

"He's very athletic. I find that attractive. He pitched me from Madeira Beach to Indian Rocks. We were doing six-minute miles and yet he was talking as comfortably as I am now."

Chase pulled into the restaurant parking lot, but made two laps before parking. On the first lap, she watched him inspect the parked cars. On the second lap, he studied the customers visible through the windows. The precaution put her at ease. As did the fact that he'd given her a choice of restaurant, come to think of it.

He slipped his suit coat over her shoulders as they approached the door. "Probably best if your burn holes aren't on display."

"Good thinking."

They grabbed a corner booth and ordered coffee. On a whim she also asked for a short stack of pancakes. His mention of IHOP had triggered a craving for maple syrup. Not that the brown goo in the plastic bottle would have any relation to the sap of Canada's national tree. *What was the relation between high-fructose corn syrup and maple syrup? Something analogous to second cousins thrice removed? Why was she thinking about such silly stuff at a time like this?* She knew the answer. Her mind was spinning its tires, looking for traction on friendly ground.

With that priming behind her, Skylar met her patient savior's eyes and noted that there were no lenses in the frames of his glasses. He was in disguise. She mapped a path to the door and plotted possible defensive moves. "How did you happen to save me?"

Chase deciphered her gaze and removed his glasses. "Part of a disguise. As is this ridiculous hairstyle." He rolled his eyes.

Skylar immediately felt better, but was anxious to hear his explanation of what came next.

"I'm investigating the disappearance of my college roommate. I don't know all the details because he, like you, must have been sworn to secrecy on pain of imprisonment. But I'm pretty certain he also got a pitch to join an elite group within the CIA."

Her pancakes arrived. She requested more coffee without taking her eyes off Chase. "So what Tom was doing to me —it wasn't his first time?"

"At the very least, it was his second."

"But why? For what purpose. I don't have money or any kind of influence." She got an idea. "Was your college roommate male or female?"

"Lars de Kock was all man."

"De Kock?" she repeated, looking for a bit of levity.

"It's Dutch for *The Cook*, but you can imagine the grief he got. And before you ask, Tom didn't do anything to you beyond the obvious. I wasn't watching, but I know he had no time."

"I almost wish he had," Skylar muttered. "That would be terrible, of course, but I don't remember it, and at least I'd know it was an extraordinary act of perversion. Now, well, I have no idea, and I don't mind saying that it's creeping me out. What do you think he was up to?"

"Honestly, I have no idea. But I'll tell you this, I'm not going to stop investigating until I find out."

35
Bad Connection

STARING AT HIS COMPUTER SCREEN, Tory felt the blood pressure building behind his eyes. He was the worst kind of mad—mad at himself.

He'd blown it big-time by failing to make a connection in time.

His laptop displayed three photographs side by side. The first was the picture he'd taken in the mortuary. The intruder he'd spared. The man still breathing because Tory wasn't a wanton killer—or one to kick a hornet's nest. If the intruder had truly been an FBI agent, his murder would have incited a swarm of investigation likely to leave Tory stung.

Back at the crematory, with his foe doubled over and an easy escape at hand, showing restraint had seemed so sensible, so professional, so wise. But that was before he made the connection.

The face in the second photo on his laptop display matched the face in the first one. It was a twin found by his computer program—and it came coupled with the name Zachary Chase.

Chase was actually ex-CIA rather than current FBI. In some ways that was better, in others worse. Especially in light of the third photo.

The third photo put the whole replacement project in a new light. Or rather, an ominous shadow. It was the picture David had snapped at a stoplight in Santa Monica. A picture of his motorcycle man. A man Tory now knew to be Zachary Chase.

Tory had made the connection just seconds ago while staring at photos one and two. At first, second, and even third glance, the tousled-haired, scruffy-faced, leather-clad motorcycle rider from Los Angeles bore little resemblance to the clean-shaven, suit-sporting, bespectacled man with slicked-back hair that Tory had encountered in suburban Virginia. But when he placed the pixels side by side and focused strictly on the faces, the resemblance was unmistakable. They were the same person.

How was that possible?

What did it mean?

Tory did not know. Not yet.

That was a serious problem.

Tory refused to make another bad move based on incomplete information. Irksome as it was and painful though it might be, he had to let prudence rule. He would place the remaining replacements on hold until he figured out what Zachary Chase knew.

36
The Start of Something

THEY DIDN'T KNOW WHERE TO GO, so they stayed in the booth at Denny's, paying their rent one snack or beverage at a time. The server seemed accustomed to this freeloading behavior—and happy to accommodate. There were plenty of empty booths during the witching hours, seats with no prospect of generating tips.

While Skylar sat in shock, Chase filled her in on everything he knew. He seemed to sense that she needed time to absorb the unbelievable turn of events, and obliged her by doing the talking. He told her about bumping into his roommate at Berret's, and the motorcycle chase in L.A. He described the stakeout at the bar, and spying from an adjoining room. Finally the funeral home, the fight with Tom, and the loss of his cell phone and gun.

Skylar felt whiplashed, mentally speaking. Physically, she literally felt whipped. That was what lines of burns felt like, whip marks. And unfortunately the worst ones were on the parts of her body in contact with the red vinyl booth.

She was at once tremendously grateful to have been rescued from the nightmare of all nightmares, and disappointed that her promised new life had been a scam. She was furious with Tom and frustrated with herself. But at that moment, right there in the booth, the emotion peaking above all others, was rage. The desire to retaliate, to do unto others as they had done unto her.

Skylar found the reaction unsettling. She wasn't a violent or vindictive person. In the back of her mind, she knew the unfamiliar emotion was the culmination of pent-up frustrations. A burning desire to take back control. It bothered her, but she decided not to fight it. Not now. Tomorrow she might wake up with an entirely different perspective. Today, with her skin still smoking and her pulse still pounding, she would indulge her inner demon.

She looked across the table and met Chase's gaze. He was watching her, serene and silent, eyes edged with concern. They were good eyes, kind and patient. A bit more gray than blue at the moment, and sparkling with the light of a bright mind. "I'm going to help you catch him," she said.

He didn't scoff or warn of danger. He didn't frown or sigh. He said, "I thought you might. And, to be honest, I hoped you would."

Skylar found herself taken aback. "Why did you think I might? I never saw myself doing anything like this."

"You were about to join the CIA. That's a pretty good indicator. And you told me you're also a professional triathlete and firefighter."

"Former," she corrected. "On both accounts."

"Neither are for people who shrink from a fight."

She'd never thought of herself that way. As a fighter. Sure, she loved the personal challenge of triathlons. In her opinion they were the ultimate expression of physical fitness. Firefighting was a convenient way to help people while paying the bills. Lots of time off to train, with decent pay and great benefits. The physical demands and potential danger barely registered on her radar. They were a shrug. Perhaps that was Chase's point.

She moved on to the second half of his statement. "You hoped I would?"

"Operations are much easier when you have a partner. It's not purely an additive function, it's a one-plus-one-equals-three situation. Two perspectives, two sets of hands, plus a sounding board. That assumes a competent partner, of course, but I have no doubts." He gave her a wink.

She appreciated the touch of levity. "Even after seeing me duped by Tom?"

"My roommate was very intelligent, *wicked smart* as one of our classmates used to say. But Tom tricked him, too."

Hearing that made her feel a bit better. Slouches didn't get into Princeton. "So what did Lars and I have in common? That's the place to start, right? Backtracking to

Tom's greater objective through a common denominator?"

"You're talking like someone with a business degree."

"Finance from the University of New Mexico."

Chase looked pleased, but not surprised. "Great school. I agree with your starting point, but I'm afraid it won't get us far. Beyond age, IQ, and skin color, you and Lars don't appear to have much in common. Not geography. Not profession. Not interests, organizations, or friends as far as I can gather. Have you been to L.A.?"

"I've done triathlons in California—Oceanside and Sonoma—but not Los Angeles."

Stuck for the moment, they dropped into silence. Chase toyed with the remains of his cinnamon roll.

"Can you still track Tom's car?"

"Not without my cell phone."

"It's not backed up in the cloud?"

"It is, but the serial number I plugged into the GPS tracking app won't be, and I didn't write it down. In any case, it was a rental. Tom will have returned it by now."

Skylar switched gears. "What would happen if we went to the CIA? Told them what was going on."

"They'd send us to the FBI, where we'd waste a few days answering questions, creating a file that would go nowhere. Impersonating a CIA officer is a federal offense, but if it's not linked to a larger investigation, it won't get any resources."

Skylar was about to ask Chase how he knew that when she realized that she knew next to nothing about his background. Not where he lived, not what he did. He'd only talked about his college roommate—from which she surmised that he too had gone to Princeton. "What do you do for a living?"

"I'm between jobs."

Me too, Skylar mused. "What was your last position?"

He popped a piece of cinnamon roll in his mouth. His expression was friendly, but he was clearly buying time to think. "Something similar to the job you were applying for."

He was a CIA agent? "How long ago was that?"

"I was fired an hour before I met Lars at Berret's. That's

why I was there. It's the best bar around. Tom did his research."

She'd wondered about the coincidental roommate run-in when Chase had relayed the story, but hadn't stopped him to ask. Now it made sense.

His answer led to her next question. A sensitive question. Skylar didn't want to offend her knight in pomaded hair, but she had the strong impression that he was more of a man's man than the overly sensitive type. "I'm sorry to hear that. Forgive my bluntness, but does that mean your bridges are burned?"

Chase cracked a grin. "More like the elevator. My issue was with management. Relations with my colleagues are fine. Why do you ask?"

"I'm thinking you might have friends you can ask to investigate?"

"That's not what the CIA does. Our 'I' stands for Intelligence. It's the 'I' in FBI that stands for Investigation. But now that you mention it, if my photos backed up to the cloud during the last twenty-four hours, then I'll get a picture of Tom once I replace and sync my phone." Chase automatically looked at his watch, then rolled his eyes when he saw his empty wrist.

It was still the middle of the night. Skylar didn't need to look at her watch to know that. "And you could have a friend use that picture to identify him?"

"I could indeed. Of course, depending on who he is, she might be prohibited from telling me. She might even send me on a wild goose chase."

37
Two for One

THE BREAKFAST SERVER opened the check folder for the third time to see if the requisite cash or credit card had appeared. Skylar couldn't blame her. This was the start of the morning rush. The restaurant was filling with early-rising patrons forking omelets and pancakes into hungry mouths, fueling up for the day ahead—then leaving tips.

Chase pulled out two twenties while she watched, placed them in the folder, and handed it over. "Thank you very much."

She nodded and was gone.

"Thank you," Skylar said. "I doubt any change will be coming."

"I wouldn't dare wait around to find out."

They walked out into the rising sun. Skylar stopped short just outside the exit.

"What is it?" Chase asked.

"I literally came within a few seconds of never seeing another sunrise."

Chase turned to face east and waited silently by her side. She gave it a few beats, then resumed walking.

They returned to his blue BMW because that was the obvious move. The next step, however, remained a mystery. To her, anyway.

The night had been productive in a calm-down, don't-get-killed sense, but operationally it had yielded no fruit beyond the possibility of having his friend at the CIA match Tom's picture. At least none that Chase had shared.

It had hardened her resolve to see this investigation through. She had told Chase as much.

His reaction to her revelation had been pleasing.

She looked over at him now, expectantly.

He hadn't yet keyed the ignition. "It's not safe for either of us to go home."

"Agreed."

"But we have to go somewhere we can sleep and shower —then plot our next move."

"Where would we be safe?"

Chase shrugged. "Anyplace outside Williamsburg should be fine. We might as well make it someplace conducive to creative thinking. What summons your muse?"

"Running, swimming, biking. A long hot bath or shower. A good cup of coffee. Why are you talking about creative thinking?"

"Tracking down and catching Tom is not going to be easy. The guy's clearly an experienced operative. I have no doubt that he's accustomed to actively thwarting his competition." Chase drummed the wheel while he spoke. "We're in for a battle of wits. I'm with you on the running and showers. Don't have a lot of recent experience with swimming or biking though."

"So where to? A national park? There are plenty of those around here."

Chase stopped tapping. "Actually, Virginia Beach comes to mind."

"Never been."

"I think Guinness considers it the longest pleasure beach in the world. I know they've got a three-mile boardwalk, and they host the annual East Coast Surfing Championship. I had to pretend to participate once as part of a training op."

"You're a surfer?"

"Not a very good one. That was the point of the training. Learning how to fake expertise." Chase brushed the air, pushing the memory aside. "For our purposes, it will be easy to get lost there and pleasant enough. But I have to warn you, the weather will be muggy. Downright oppressive at times."

Skylar felt the tangential realities of her situation begin to sink in. "How long is this going to take? What should I be preparing for? Financially I mean."

She watched his expression as her words emerged. His

eyes grew warm and his cheeks rose. "Being between jobs myself, I share your sensitivity. Let's see what we can find."

They found a Best Western Plus right on the beach. Rather than approach the reception desk, Chase led her through the lobby to the business center. They found two available PCs and the hint of an ocean breeze.

Skylar watched him call up the hotel they were in. He typed in the date and called up the prices. They were surprisingly cheap for someone used to Florida rates. "Online we can get the AAA rate. At the desk you need a card."

She studied the screen over his shoulder. King rooms were $66 with AAA. Rooms with two beds were $75. Both the king and the double came with ocean-view balconies and free high-speed WiFi and included a full breakfast. "It's much cheaper than Florida."

He rose and offered her the chair. "Why don't you pick whatever makes you most comfortable. I'm fine either way."

Skylar didn't need to think about it. She could feed herself with the money saved by sharing a room. Modesty wasn't a question. Triathletes lost that during their first competitive race, skipping changing rooms to shave seconds off their times, and wearing skintight clothing knowing the cameras were constantly rolling.

But she still found herself hesitating to click the mouse.

She realized that his perception mattered to her. What would he think of her if she selected the double? Not about the implied consent, she didn't get the impression that he had expectations, but what he'd conclude about her character. On the other hand, would he feel offended if she selected two king rooms?

This was silly, she told herself. He'd just saved her from being cremated alive. Chase had literally pulled her unconscious body out of the fire. "We're not married, or even dating. In fact, I hardly know you. But at this point, I think it's safe to say that we're a team." She clicked the double.

38
Satisfaction Guarantee

FELIX WELCOMED PIERCE aboard his new Christensen yacht and signaled the captain to set sail.

"I didn't know captains came in the females-under-forty variety," Pierce noted in an admiring tone, after turning his gaze back to Felix.

"They're a rare find—but well worth the search. I've been on a bit of a binge lately, cutting the clutter out of my life."

"Your old captain was clutter?"

"He did his job, but his presence didn't bring me pleasure. That counts as clutter under my new operational paradigm. With Shelly," he gazed toward the bridge, "I smile every time she welcomes me aboard."

The two numbers guys had decided to yacht-pool to Aria's for the Immortals' meeting. Felix had suggested it. He wanted time alone with Pierce, both to brainstorm and to observe. The senatorial wannabe still topped his list of suspects.

They took the outside stairway to the top deck, where an empty 2009 Petrus bottle waited beside a full decanter and two Bordeaux glasses. Felix gestured toward an adjacent seat. "I thought this might smooth the journey."

A waiter appeared while they were settling into the soft white lounge chairs. He poured the wine and vanished without a word. Felix clinked Pierce's glass, then closed his eyes as the first sip passed his lips. It boggled his mind that wine could be so satisfying and complex, whereas grape juice was just another drink. Such were the powers of yeast and time.

He opened his eyes after that satisfying swallow and got straight to business. "What's your latest thinking?"

Pierce needed no clarification. The Immortals faced only

one pressing problem. "I'm thinking we began our earlier analysis with a faulty assumption."

This was exactly the kind of conjecture Felix hoped to hear. "How so?"

"We assumed that any outsider who learned of us would attempt to blackmail his or her way to immortality. That's not necessarily true."

Surprise and intrigue stirred Felix's stomach. "You think we could have wronged someone so much that they'd pick revenge over eternal life? I'd think even the most jaded individual would find immortality irresistible."

Pierce raised his glass to study the wine's color and test its legs. He knew how to tantalize people during pitches. "That was my thinking at first as well, but only because I approached it from a personal perspective. More specifically, from the viewpoint of people like us. Businesspeople. Professionals. If you broaden your outlook, you'll find that there are entire demographic groups who wouldn't make that choice."

"Seriously?"

"I can think of three. There may be more."

Felix didn't know anyone who wouldn't want to live forever. But then, that was Pierce's point. "Prime the pump for me."

Pierce savored a sip of wine while Felix waited. "Our treatment does nothing for the terminally ill."

Felix almost slapped his forehead. He had not thought of that. It was true though. Eos halted aging, but it didn't stop the spread of disease. *Who else? What other demographic?*

He couldn't think of anyone.

Pierce did not leave him hanging this time, but he couldn't resist a bit of intellectual one-upmanship. "Do you remember the Trojan Tithonus from your Eos mythology?"

Everyone had read about the goddess of dawn back when they founded the company bearing her name, but those details had long since faded from Felix's mind. "Refresh my memory."

"Eos asked Zeus to let her lover live forever. But she forgot to also request that Zeus grant Tithonus eternal youth. Like many myths, it did not have a happy ending."

Felix quickly connected the dots. "Point being that immortality is bound to be less appealing to the elderly. I concede that I might not want to go on forever trapped in a wrinkled old sack with a failing mind and leaky colon. That's two I've got to give you."

Pierce raised his glass. "The third group that came to mind is religious fundamentalists. People who believe that death is the doorway to God."

Score three for Pierce. "Huh."

They settled back into their chairs to mull over the implications in shared silence.

Felix was only a few sips into it when his burner cell began vibrating. He pulled it from his pocket, glanced at the display, then showed it to Pierce before answering. "Hello, Tory."

"Good afternoon." Tory's phone voice was unmistakable. No accent per se, more like a sophisticated software program dialed to the Soldier setting. Cool, clean, and devoid of emotion.

"I'm with Pierce. Okay if I put you on speaker?"

"No problem."

"Hold on a sec." Felix gestured toward the yacht's sky lounge where it would be easier to hear. They took their glasses inside and sat at a small table. "Okay, go ahead."

"I've run into an issue with two replacements. David's and Aria's."

"What kind of issue?"

"Interference."

Felix closed his eyes. He'd been dreading a call like this.

"Pierce here, and I'm confused. I thought you'd already replaced David?"

"I did, but the switch was detected. There was a freak coincidence with a man I've since identified as the replacement's college roommate. He showed up in the wrong place at the wrong time and caught David impersonating his friend."

Felix voiced his frustration. "We know that. During the videoconference, you told us you solved that problem."

"I thought I had. I sent him over a cliff on a motorcycle. His survival was a million to one."

"But he beat the odds?"

"He did."

"And then he resurfaced?"

"He did that, too. When I was replacing Aria. In Virginia."

"In Virginia!" Felix felt his bowels turning to water. They'd been discovered. And they were being hunted.

"It's not as bad as it seems," Tory hastened to say.

"We're all ears," Felix said. "Please tell us why."

"Not knowing that the motorcycle man had survived, I used the same con for Aria's replacement. The CIA recruitment ploy I told you about. Apparently, the survivor anticipated that repeat performance and set up a surveillance op at the hotel or restaurant or mortuary. I'm not sure which."

"Mortuary?" Pierce asked.

Felix held up a hand. The others didn't know the details of Tory's disposal tactics, and he figured it was best to keep it that way. "Wait a minute, Tory. You're saying this guy found Aria's replacement through the replacement process itself, not some other leak?"

"I am. I've given it a lot of thought and I'm confident that's the only explanation."

"So he doesn't know about us?"

"There's no way that he could."

Felix desperately hoped that Tory was right.

Pierce chimed back in. "So who is this survivor?"

"Zachary Chase was the college roommate of David's replacement. His Social Security records show employment with the State Department."

"He's a diplomat?"

Tory paused a beat. "After seeing him operate, I think he's a spook. The CIA runs its operatives through the payrolls of other government agencies."

"Let me get this straight," Pierce said. "While a CIA agent is pursuing you, you're doing a CIA recruitment con?"

"Ex-CIA agent. He separated around the time I recruited

David's replacement, which I did near where Chase lives. Given their shared history, and Chase's availability, it's natural that they would hook up. And since the replacement thought he was interviewing for the CIA, and his buddy was CIA, it's natural that they'd talk. It's all an unfortunate coincidence brought about by shared geography."

Felix liked the sound of that, in that it had nothing to do with the Immortals as a group. It was bad luck. With any operation of size, you were bound to get a bit of that. "So where does that leave our operation?"

"We've lost some time, but I think that's it. Obviously, I won't use the CIA con again, and Chase has no other leads, so I'm convinced that he won't get any further."

"But he's seen your face," Pierce said.

"He might as well have seen a ghost. My photo isn't any more available for matching than yours."

Felix looked at Pierce, who gave a satisfied nod. "So what's next?"

"I have to start over with two replacements, and work without my favored con. But I'll have things back on track soon."

Felix felt his digestion returning to normal. He took a healthy swallow of wine while Tory suffered in silence. "Please call Aria and David to let them know. They should hear about this from you directly."

"Will do."

"I also want regular updates."

"Okay. Speaking of updates, is there anything you want to tell me?"

Tory had never used that phrase before, or spoken with a challenging tone. Had he heard about the murders? Felix looked at Pierce, who shook his head. "No."

"Nothing I need to know to do my job?"

"Don't you think I'd tell you if there were?"

"I'm monitoring all of you, as you know. That's part of my job. It's integral to the satisfaction guarantee. Among other measures, I've set up Google alerts for all the new identities." He paused there.

Felix knew what was coming, but held his tongue.

"I know Ries is dead. He's the second member of your group to meet with a fatal accident in a month. What's going on, Felix?"

Felix looked at Pierce. The Eos investor was clearly running calculations parallel to Felix's own—but at a faster pace. Pierce raised three fingers, then rubbed thumb to forefingers.

Felix returned a nod. "We're actually down three. Camilla also passed. Given the increased attention, we're prepared to double your annual maintenance payment. We'll make it an even million dollars for every year you keep all eyes off us. But this raise only applies if you complete your initial assignment in a timely manner and without further interference."

Tory had the tact not to ask for detail about Camilla, but he didn't signal satisfaction either.

Felix pressed forward. "Can you do that? Can you guarantee me that I'll never get another call like this one?"

This time, Tory did not hesitate. "I can."

"Good. Get it done."

39

Capillary Action

SLICED FROM THE STUMP of a giant sequoia, the round table in Aria's library boasted nine matching chairs. Three were empty as the Immortals convened their emergency meeting. Those vacancies were the reason they had assembled.

Attempts at the usual pleasantries had been made as people arrived and mingled, but the beverages imbibed had been nonalcoholic, and the conversations were notably stilted. Weather reports and stock portfolio performances didn't cut it when people feared the Grim Reaper and were searching each other for scythes.

Once the last Immortal arrived, Pierce held up a preemptive finger. "Before we get started, I would like to make one request."

Conversations halted and all eyes turned his way.

"I don't know how to put this delicately, so I won't endeavor to do so. If something should happen to David and Allison, the rest of us will lose our Eos supply. I was hoping that some arrangement could be made."

The room remained silent, but only for a second.

"We worked that out long ago," Lisa said, surprising everyone. "David and I selected two reputable compounding pharmacies, and gave each of them half the recipe, so to speak. Neither knows about the other. Neither knows what they have or why. But they know how to make their ingredient if asked."

"Can we get that contact information?" Pierce asked.

"You'll have it before I leave the island."

"Thank you," Pierce said, taking his seat.

Once everyone was settled, Aria took charge of her meeting. "I propose we stay seated until we have a theory or three, complete with action plans."

Lisa seconded and heads bobbed all around.

Allison surprised everyone by speaking first, "I have a theory."

Five heads turned toward hers.

"Remember all the controversy that arose when scientists first started stem cell research? For years, violent and vehement protests were a part of the nightly news. Although that faded as people became educated, it clearly demonstrated animus out there for any interference in 'God's plan.'" She ended with air quotes.

"You think we're being assassinated by religious fundamentalists?" Lisa asked. "That they somehow uncovered our secret and are now quietly trying to kill us?"

"Probably just one assassin. Someone like that albino monk in *The Da Vinci Code*."

"I'm guessing you recently watched the movie?" Lisa asked.

Allison blushed.

Felix waded in. "While hate groups are certainly worth considering, and I'll be the first to admit I haven't explored that angle," he nodded to Allison, "these aren't terrorist attacks. Nobody is making a public statement. This is private. It is personal." He looked over his left shoulder to redirect the conversation back to Lisa. "I think we need to be looking at people we've wronged."

All eyes turned to the former CEO.

Lisa nodded to herself, then looked around the room. "Felix is talking about Kirsten Besanko."

"What about Kirsten? Why are all of you nodding?" Allison asked, glaring at Lisa. "Are you telling me— Did you — She didn't die from an ischemic stroke?"

Lisa didn't flinch. "I poisoned her energy drink."

Allison gasped and shuddered, her words a tortured whisper. "Kirsten's husband found her floating in the pool."

"We couldn't ask her to leave her family behind."

"We could have brought Chuck with us. Just one more guy. Why are you all shaking your heads again?"

David put an arm around Allison's shoulder. "It wasn't

just Chuck, remember. She was pregnant. She'd unknowingly conceived before taking Eos."

Allison brought hand to mouth as her tears started streaming. "You knew what Lisa did?"

Pierce noted with some surprise that David did not take the politician's escape. "I didn't know. But I suspected."

"And the rest of you?" Allison looked around the table.

"None of them knew," Lisa said.

Allison bowed her head. "They just suspected. I was the only one naïve enough to fall for the coroner's report."

"Where is Chuck now?" Pierce asked, trying to bring this back to a business discussion.

"He's remarried and living in Portland," Lisa said. "He has three kids, two from his wife's previous marriage and one of their own. The marriage looks healthy. I don't think it's him."

"You wouldn't!" Allison said.

"She had a brother," David said.

" 'Had' being the operative word," Lisa replied. "He died of pancreatic cancer."

"We have other enemies," Aria said. "You've been sabotaging other research efforts for over twenty years."

Pierce noted her use of 'you.' He supposed that was fair. She'd just been denied an important vote because she wasn't part of the original Eos team. "Our agents have always been blind. They never know who's paying them to spy and sabotage."

"Maybe one of them figured it out," Aria pressed. "They're criminals, after all. Maybe it's a type of jealous revenge, one team of researchers against another."

"Camilla wasn't a researcher," Pierce said.

"Maybe Camilla's death was an accident, a coincidence."

Pierce understood why Aria would want that to be true. But he also knew that tears tended to warp otherwise logical minds. To save their lives, he needed to dash Aria's hope and refocus the conversation. "Given the fact that these people all sold out their colleagues for money, you can be certain that if one of them did divine who was paying them and why, they'd resort to blackmail, not murder."

"I agree," Felix said. "It's possible, but unlikely. It's far more likely that our killer is someone associated with the replacement process. Regarding Camilla, that can't be a coincidence." He relayed the call from Tory, word for word, while Pierce nodded along.

"So we know there's been a leak on Tory's end," Lisa summarized. "And this friend who popped up twice is a CIA agent?"

"Ex-agent."

"Even worse. That just means he's freed from any constraints on conduct."

"Tory assures me he's been left behind in rural Virginia without any leads to follow," Felix said.

"And in any case, he's not likely to be the killer," Pierce added. "He entered with David's replacement, which was after Eric's demise. I trust that in light of recent events, we're all in agreement that Eric's death wasn't an accident?"

Everyone nodded.

"But where there's one known leak, there's reason to suspect more," Aria persisted. "I want to grill Tory on the subject."

"I can arrange that," Felix replied. "Let's make that number one on our list. Other action plans?"

"I'm in the process of updating security here," Aria said. "I dismissed the workers for our meeting, but they'll be back. I'm turning Seven Star into a fortress. You're all welcome to return indefinitely if it comes to that."

Pierce looked around. He could think of worse prisons.

"Any chance it's Tory himself?" David asked.

"I think it's extremely unlikely," Felix said. "We went to him, he didn't volunteer. And we're his golden ticket. His pension plan."

"And you're certain he's not involving subcontractors?"

"Actually, I'm sure he is, but not in any meaningful way. Just driving jobs and programming gigs. Compartmentalized tasks with no connection to us or our status. For that matter, Tory doesn't know who we are or what our status is so he couldn't share that information even under subpoena or torture."

"I don't actually suspect Tory. I'm just being rigorous." David cleared his throat. "I think it's one of us."

The remark struck with the force of a thunderclap. In a room full of big brainpans, David's tipped the scale. He was the man most responsible for cracking the genetic code that halted aging. An unrivaled expert at exposing hidden patterns.

Everyone's eyes started roaming, looking for the fight-or-flight blush, waiting for David to stand and point a finger.

Pierce didn't observe any reddening.

When it became clear that David would remain seated, Aria asked, "What makes you say that, David?"

"It's the simplest explanation. And statistics back it up. Most murders are committed by friends or family members."

Lungs exhaled as the tension broke. David didn't know anything. He was just applying basic analytical rigor.

Pierce looked up from a contemplative thought to find all eyes on him. "What?"

"You're smiling like a kid just handed chocolate cake," Lisa said.

Pierce realized he was grinning. "I'm relieved."

Four sets of inquisitive eyes turned toward Pierce, as did one bemused smile.

"Relieved?" Lisa asked.

"Nobody reacted, just then. You can't quell the capillary action of an adrenal rush. David just proved that the killer's not one of us."

40
Two Strikes

THE BEST WESTERN had a double room ready for early check-in, so they heard the door lock's inviting click within minutes of making the reservation. Both walked through the room with barely a sideward glance and straight onto the balcony. The weather was muggy, but the view was glorious. All the more so for Skylar, given her brush with death.

Chase turned to meet her gaze.

She felt a funny tingle. "Where do we begin?"

"I'm going to begin in the shower. I'm dying to get this pomade out of my hair. Unless you want to go first?"

She put her hand on the back of the closest lounge chair. "Be my guest. I'll be very happy relaxing here for a while."

Skylar drifted off, waking only when there was a loud commotion on the beach below. She looked over to see Chase standing at the balcony rail. This was the first time she'd seen him in daylight, and with his normal look. She found it somehow comforting. His dark hair was a bit on the long side of corporate norm, and he had a day's worth of stubble despite having just showered. No razor, she realized. The unshaven appearance gave him a carefree look that clashed with the intense intelligence she detected when he turned to look at her with eyes that were now more blue than gray.

"What now?" she asked, feeling a flash of guilt but not knowing why.

"There's a mall about four miles inland with both an Apple and an AT&T store. I'm going to buy a phone and a laptop. If I'm able to pull Tom's picture from the cloud, I'll send it to my friend."

"They've got computers in the business center, but of

course you already know that. What will you be using the computer for? Have you figured out how to backtrack to Tom?"

"I have a theory," Chase said, taking a seat.

As he settled in, Skylar couldn't help but recall the last time she'd done the same thing. Relax on a beachfront balcony with a handsome man. It was in Kona, after the World Championship triathlon. He was the third-place male, she the third-place female. That natural match was only last year, and yet a lifetime ago. A few deep lungfuls of superheated smoke had closed a door that would never open again.

As she looked across the white sand toward the late-morning sun, she felt the first glimmer of hope that happiness might yet find her this side of that door. "Lay it on me."

"I've given more thought to what you and Lars have in common."

"Beyond age, IQ, and skin color," Skylar prodded, recalling exactly where they'd left off. She had a mind for dialogue. Images didn't stick. Neither did reading. But she retained spoken words like a voice recorder. Didn't matter if it was a conversation, a television script, or the lyrics of a song. If she was giving something her attention, she could recall it. Verbatim. She never spoke of her ability, but did use it on occasion to win a bar bet or entertain friends at a cocktail party.

Chase raised an eyebrow. "Right. Except I don't think we need to go beyond them. I've come to realize that those seemingly worthless similarities may actually be significant."

"How so? There must be more than ten million college-educated white people in their early thirties living in the U.S."

"Actually, it's closer to five. There are about twenty million people in any five-year band from birth to sixty. Three-quarters of Americans are white, and thirty percent of us are college educated."

"Well, aren't you an encyclopedia."

"I've sat in on my share of profiling discussions. Shall I

continue?"

"Please."

"If it's graduate school and not just college that counts, we're below two million. On the other hand, if any of those three criteria are irrelevant coincidences, then the number gets significantly larger. But in any case, the pool is at least a couple of million people. Not very helpful on its own."

"But?"

Chase shifted his chair to make it easier to see her face. "When you approach it from the other side, it gets interesting."

"I don't follow."

"Motive. What reason could there be for hiring a professional to make certain members of a population subset disappear without a trace?"

Skylar had been so focused on finding the guy who could tell them why, that she neglected to ask herself the obvious question. She suddenly felt inadequate, sitting there next to Mr. CIA. It was a feeling she'd avoided for many years, but found increasingly common since the fire.

She met Chase's eyes and repeated a line she'd heard John Travolta use in a movie. "Well, possible motives for murder are profit, revenge, jealousy, to conceal a crime, to avoid humiliation and disgrace, or plain old homicidal mania. The first five don't apply to me, and the sixth seems unlikely given the use of a professional killer."

Chase's eyes lit up. Given the lighting and the ocean behind him, they now looked totally blue. "*The General's Daughter*, right? I loved that movie. But I didn't say murder, I said *disappear without a trace*. Makes no difference to the victim, I realize, but I think it's crucial to our investigation."

"How so?"

"If Tom just wanted you dead, he could have stabbed you on Clearwater Beach. One quick thrust and you'd have gone down, while he ran away. Instead, he lured you across the country and then went through an elaborate ruse to leave no clues to your demise."

"I'm with you." *Why hadn't she thought of that? Probably because she was scared, exhausted, and new to the whole P.I. thing.*

"But again, that's something he could have accomplished in Clearwater. Why not lure you onto a boat and feed you to the fishes?"

The clouds parted in her mind, and Skylar suddenly saw the answer as clearly as the sand beyond the boardwalk. "Information. He spent a full day pumping me for biographical information."

"Exactly. I'm sure he did the same thing with Lars. If you think about it, dangling a dream job requiring a background check is the perfect way to get someone to willingly disclose their whole life story."

"I agree. But why would anyone care about my story? I'd understand if I was rich, but stealing my identity isn't going to get anyone very far. And in any case, there are easier ways to get a birthdate and social security number."

Chase raised a finger. "You have to couple it with my initial question."

Skylar repeated it from memory. "What reason could there be for hiring a professional to make certain members of a population subset disappear without a trace?"

Chase nodded.

"So it's identity theft plus disappear without a trace." She processed that for a second, and again felt the joyful jolt of an epiphany. "Someone's not just looking to replace me on paper. She's looking to replace me in person."

"Exactly."

"But why?"

"I suspect we could come up with a dozen reasons if we put our minds to it. Let's save that for later. The operative question is *Who?*"

"Why *Who?*" Skylar asked. "Don't tell me *third base.*"

The Abbott and Costello reference brought a smile to Chase's lips. He had a nice smile, she noted. "Because we can find the *who.*"

"How's that?"

Chase just raised his eyebrows.

"Of course," Skylar said, experiencing yet another lightning strike as she recalled what he'd told her about the man masquerading as Lars. "She has to look like me."

41
Face the Truth

THE RESILIENCE of Skylar's mind astonished me. Less than a day out of the oven and her hard drive was spinning without wobbles or skips. Professional agents often cracked in the wake of their first close call, but she was powering through. Apparently Ironman training transformed nerves from flesh into steel.

After our early-morning breakthrough, I went in search of a razor while Skylar went for a run. A run. I'd offered her the bathtub, certain that she'd want to indulge in a long hot soak as she had after her interview with Tom. I certainly would have felt the urge, both for a bath and a bottle of Bordeaux. But despite the humidity, she'd opted for exercise.

Skylar wasn't even stymied by her lack of workout clothes. She just bought a bathing suit from the drugstore that supplied my shaving tackle and headed out to run barefoot on the sand.

I shaved, then hit the hotel business center. When I returned to the room after a couple of hours on the computer, I expected to find Skylar sawing logs. But there was no sign of her. Instead of searching, I updated the note explaining my whereabouts and left for the mall.

Entering our room upon my return, I heard her singing in the shower. She'd moved the bedside clock radio into the bathroom and was belting it out along with Adele. Unbelievable what endorphins could do.

I knocked twice, cracked the bathroom door, and slid one of my shopping bags into the steamy room as the singing stopped. "I got you some clothes and a few toiletries."

"Thanks. Be right out."

I went to the balcony with the hope that the sun would

soon bring the humidity under control, and booted up my new computer.

Skylar joined me ten minutes later. She looked radiant. Even in basic jeans and a plain cotton shirt. Very healthy. I resolved to get more exercise.

"You're good with sizes. You even nailed the shoes. And the bra."

"I checked your tags. Apologies for the privacy invasion. I weighed the options and pragmatism won."

"No worries." She gestured toward the iPhone on the end table. "Did you get Tom's picture from the cloud."

"I did. I sent it off to Lesley."

"Lesley?"

"Lesley Franna is the friend at the agency I referred to earlier. A crack analyst."

"How long before you hear back?"

"Depends on how busy she is. I gave her the parameters she'll need for an efficient query, so building it won't take long. But she has to get to it first and I won't be a top priority. Then the computer will take a few hours to do its thing. It will give her matches, beginning with the one the program considers the best match, then the second, and so on. Could be a very long list, and she won't be able to share it with me. She'll have to review it, so again that will be a time sink."

Skylar grabbed the empty chair. "What do we do while we're waiting?"

I answered her question with one of my own. "What do you think?"

"I think we look for me."

I pulled a second MacBook Air from the bag at my side. I had been amazed when the charge went through. Perhaps the credit card company knew they had me hooked and was just feeding me more line. "You're exactly right."

She hesitated to take it. "I could use the computer downstairs."

"We can't skimp on equipment or settle for inefficiency if we're going to beat Tom. And Apple has a 30-day return policy," I added.

Her eyes brightened with understanding. "Thank you."

She accepted the laptop and lifted the lid. "Where do we look? I don't suppose you have some special CIA database at your disposal?"

I did, but I wasn't about to mention it, as that particular resource wouldn't help here. "The FBI has the best database, the Facial Analysis, Comparison, and Evaluation Services Unit, or FACE. But it's not at my disposal. Not directly."

"What does that mean, not directly?" Skylar asked, working through the setup screens.

"I can't access it from my computer, and I certainly can't hack the FBI. But my FBI friend Owen has it on his laptop."

"So you want to send him my picture?"

"No. I can't ask him to commit a crime."

Skylar crinkled her blonde brow. "But with Lesley?"

"With Lesley, I had a legitimate, reportable reason. Tom was impersonating a CIA officer. I made her aware of that, as it's well within her purview to run a related search. Reporting the results back to me is where things get a bit sketchy. Kinda depends on what she finds. If Tom actually is a CIA officer who's running something either undercover or off the books, she'll never tell me. On the other hand, if Tom's just some guy off the street, particularly a foreign national, sharing with a former colleague might not get her more than a wrist slapping."

"So how does your FBI friend help you *in*directly?"

"Owen could give me a demonstration of FACE, as a professional courtesy. He doesn't know I'm no longer with the Agency, so by asking him I'll be walking a thin line, implicitly impersonating a CIA employee. It's a gray zone since I'll never actually make the claim, gray enough that he wouldn't be likely to cry foul even if I weren't a friend."

Skylar's laptop emitted a welcoming *bong*. She stopped typing and looked in my direction. "So what's next?"

"I take your picture from a few angles. Then you go to work using those *find my twin* dot-coms while I call Owen and see if he's available to meet after work."

42
Twin Peeks

I CHECKED MY NEW WATCH as I pulled the hotel key from my back pocket. Almost 11:00 p.m. I'd been away visiting my FBI friend for nine hours, and the Do Not Disturb sign was now hanging from the knob. I worked the lock as quietly as possible, but the electronic click was unavoidable.

It didn't matter. Skylar was still up and I even caught the smell of coffee in the air.

She wasn't at the desk where she'd been when I left, but she was still glued to her computer. She was belly-down on the bed with her chest propped up by a couple of pillows and her ankles crossed in the air. Gone were the jeans I'd purchased that morning, but everything else was still on. She probably wanted to air her wounds. Looked like they'd been salved.

She glanced over at me, then hit a few more keys before turning her head. "How was Quantico?" she asked in an upbeat tone.

I snicked the bolt and swiveled the security guard. "Went smoothly. I showed up with a six-pack of Fierce and we worked through it while he demoed FACE." While she watched with wide eyes, I held up the catch of the day, a flash drive. "We found fourteen Skylar Fawkes lookalikes."

"Fourteen! Wow, I only found one." She rotated her laptop in my direction.

My bed was too far from her screen, but I didn't want to sit on hers when she was dressed like that, so I wheeled over the desk chair and sat such that I wouldn't be looking at her long, bare, tan legs. "Sandy Wallace in Miami. The chef. She's on my list too."

"That's an encouraging sign. Show me the others."

I handed her the flash drive.

It was an awkward arrangement, with her on a bed and me on the only chair. "I'm sorry. I should have thought to buy you pajamas."

"Don't worry about it. Not a top priority. Now, if you'd forgotten a toothbrush, that would have been problematic. I hate it when I can't clean my teeth. But seriously, most guys wouldn't have gotten anything at all, much less thought to check my sizes. Of course, you set the bar pretty high last night. On service, I mean. I'm very grateful to you, for everything. And I'm rambling. I do that too, when I have nervous energy. I'll shut up now."

"No worries. But I must say that I'm surprised you didn't burn up all your energy running. You were gone a long time this morning."

"I got a swim in this afternoon too, but no cycling, obviously. I might see if they have a stationary bike in the gym before turning in." Reading my expression, she added. "I know I'm not a professional athlete any more. But the habit is ingrained and I'm addicted to the endorphins. Plus I like to eat and I don't want to get fat. I'm rambling again."

"Actually, I was thinking the salt water would have been painful, given your burn marks."

Skylar grimaced. "Yeah, there was an initial protest, shall we say. But I powered through."

I decided not to dwell on that topic. "Did you get dinner? There's a 24/7 café just down the road. A local place, not a chain. We could take our computers."

Skylar sat up and reached for her jeans. "That sounds fantastic."

The graveyard menu at Rick's Café was heavy on fried food and breakfast items, but Skylar found a grilled, marinated chicken breast and I ordered a mushroom Swiss burger.

We sat side by side in a coveted wraparound corner booth, so both of us could see my computer screen. I inserted the flash drive with the Facial Analysis, Comparison, and Evaluation data, then called up the first of four images deemed to be a match. "Emma Atherton is a day trader from Durango, Colorado."

"I see that FACE ignores hair color and cut," Skylar said. "I'd wondered about that."

Whereas Skylar kept her sun-bleached hair short, presumably for the athletic benefits, Emma's straight brown hair extended a good six inches past her shoulders. "We programmed it to ignore anything easily alterable. Hair color, hairstyle, eyewear, eye color, moles and birthmarks."

"Who's next?"

I hit the forward arrow and Sandy Wallace appeared.

"Same woman I found on Facebook."

I hit the arrow again. "Amy Zabala, a marketing manager from Nashville, Tennessee."

Skylar squirmed. "This is kinda creepy. She could be my long-lost twin."

"She doesn't appear to have your charm."

"It's a driver's license photo. Nobody looks charming in those. But thank you."

I clicked again. "Carmen Rohan, schoolteacher from Michigan's Upper Peninsula."

"She looks like a vampire. A fat vampire."

"The computer ignores skin tone, so long as the race fits. Tanning is easy to manipulate."

"What about weight?"

"I gave it a weight range from one hundred to two hundred. A height range from five feet, four inches to six feet and an age from twenty to forty. Figured it was better to cast too wide a net than too narrow."

"I still don't see the resemblance. Do you?"

I wasn't going to go near that one. "I'd agree that it's the weakest match so far. But remember, Tom isn't trying to match you. He's trying to match someone who looks like you. That someone's probably not a professional triathlete."

The food arrived. I pushed the computer to Skylar's far side so she could click through the ten remaining lookalikes while eating. She did just that, cutting and chewing a single bite of chicken while studying each profile photo. Only one of the images merited two forkfuls.

"So that's it?" she asked after the final arrow click.

I popped the last bite of burger into my mouth and wiped my face with a paper napkin while chewing. "That's what FACE has matching the parameters I used. But FACE is far from complete. While it incorporates most of the federal data from passport, immigration, and licensing applications, less than half the states have supplied data from driver's licenses and such."

"Why is that?"

"It's a privacy-versus-security issue. State legislatures get to decide whether they want to participate or not, and to what degree. Some only provide driver's license photos, others include mugshots as well. The point is, there are a lot more potential matches out there."

"That's discouraging."

"It's not as bad as you think. Tom's ability to search will be limited as well. Social media is the big variable. I'm sure you could write a program like FACE for Facebook, LinkedIn, and YouTube, et cetera. It's just a question of time, talent, and money."

Skylar polished off her chicken and immediately picked up the dessert menu. "So what's next?"

"Pie, I'm guessing."

She licked her lips. "Good guess. But you know what I mean."

The waitress appeared with an expectant look in her eyes. "Can I get you all anything else? The apple pie is my personal favorite."

"Can you warm it?" Skylar said with a smile.

"Sure thing, sweetie. A la mode?"

"Oh yeah."

"Just another slice of lemon for my water," I said when the server turned my way. "Didn't get my swim in today."

She didn't call me sweetie.

Once we were alone again, I turned back to Skylar and answered her earlier question. "Next, we go fishing."

She didn't miss a beat. "With my lookalikes as bait?"

"You got it. Emma, Sandy, and Amy are already dangling. We need to prepare them asap. I also want to create a custom lure."

"What do you mean?"

"I want to set up a new Facebook account. One specifically designed to catch Tom's attention."

43
Astute Observation

ALLISON FOUND DAVID at the bow of the boat, lying on a sky-blue cushion with his hands behind his head. She, David, and Lisa had flown to Seven Star on separate helicopters for the emergency meeting, having arrived in Southern Florida at different times. For the return trip, however, they were all taking Felix's yacht. This gave Allison a welcome opportunity to bounce ideas off the big brain of her fellow research scientist.

She plopped onto the thick cushion beside him, but lay on her side so she could see his face. "I think you're right."

"That's always good to hear," he said with a wink. "About what?"

"About the killer being one of us."

His face darkened. "Actually, I thought Pierce had a good point."

"You and I both know that disciplined minds can exert considerable control over physiological reactions. If the killer knew she couldn't have been uncovered, she'd have remained cool."

"She? You think it's Aria or Lisa?"

"Not Aria. Lisa maybe. She killed Kirsten after all. But I was just avoiding the automatic use of *he*. Actually, I think Pierce is the most likely candidate."

David propped himself up onto one elbow as well, mirroring her pose. "Why's that?"

"For starters, he's an investor. Deep down, they're all carnivores. His relationship to us was always utilitarian. Transactional. I don't know that immortality has changed his perspective on that."

"And now he wants to be a senator."

Allison raised a finger. "He wants to be president."

"Either way, how does killing the other Immortals help?"

His tone was sincere, not judgmental. That, she realized, was why she liked talking to him so much. He never used his enormous intellect to make her feel small. Fortunately, she had already considered his question. "It will help him keep his big secret during the extreme scrutiny that accompanies running for national office. If he's the only Immortal, then the odds of discovery drop to near zero."

David looked up and to the left, an inward stare. She'd piqued his interest. "Excellent point. I hadn't considered that. I'd looked at their ambitions as a danger to us, not vice versa." His expression morphed as he spoke. "But as one of the people whose ambitions are doing the endangering, you've got a different perspective."

Allison absorbed the blow without taking it personally. David had a fair point.

"Let me think about that," he added, giving Allison the opening she needed.

She pulled herself up and sat facing him in a cross-legged position. "I've wanted to be an actress ever since I was a schoolgirl. But my parents took one look at the odds of success and the lifestyles of people trying, then pushed me into science."

David gave her an appreciative smile. "You never told me that before."

She nodded to defuse a bit of nervous tension. "They wanted me to become a doctor. They said a medical degree guaranteed success. Lots of opportunities and universal respect."

"It's a solid, low-risk strategy."

"My senior year of college, I was filling out med school applications when I realized that I didn't want to spend my life around sick people. That led to a big fight with my parents, but we eventually compromised on a career in the life sciences. A PhD rather than a MD. A bit more risk and not quite as much prestige, but still prosperous and infinitely more predictable than acting."

His eyes remained warm and inviting. "I can't believe you never told me that."

It was her turn to wink. "Never told my boss that I'd really rather be doing something else?"

"Good point."

She put her hand on his shoulder. That was twice now, she realized. *Was she subconsciously clinging to him for security during this troubled time?* "You've given us an unprecedented opportunity to reinvent ourselves. Once I started grad school, I never thought I'd get another shot at acting. The window is so short for women. At thirty-one I'm at the upper edge of viability, but immortality gives me infinite shots on goal, so to speak."

"I wish you all the best with it."

She lowered her hand. "Thank you. May I make an observation?"

David canted his head.

"You haven't changed a bit. You drive a nicer car, and now you live on the beach rather than a few blocks back, but that's just Aria's money. Immortality doesn't seem to have impacted your daily routine or your general attitude. You're still the same David Hume."

"I was doing what I loved before we figured out how to halt aging. I still am."

Allison leaned in. "May I make another observation?"

This time he raised his eyebrows in invitation.

"For someone doing what he loves, you don't seem particularly happy."

Ironically, he smiled. "I've always been more Spock than Kirk."

Allison wasn't a Trekkie, but she recognized the character reference and knew Kirk was the charismatic captain and Spock the logic fanatic with pointy ears. "You used to be happier. Or *appear* happier, I should say."

David didn't comment.

"You could start over too, you know. Have you thought about it?"

"Not really."

Allison didn't buy that. "Come on, we're still an hour out of Jupiter. What would you do differently?"

He turned toward the horizon, where blue sky met blue

sea.

Allison waited.

When he turned back, his expression remained pensive. When he met her eye, she knew that he'd done more than take her question seriously. He'd come to a conclusion. Then the spell broke and he began to squirm.

"What is it?"

David pulled a phone from his pocket. It was the burner phone they all used for anonymous internal communication.

"Who is it?" she asked.

"Tory."

44
Unmistakable

I LOOKED LEFT as I lifted my head from the pillow and was pleased to see that Skylar and I had each made it beneath the covers of a bed. I then discovered that I'd also managed to strip to my boxers, though I had no memory of doing so.

After stuffing our stomachs with Rick's late-night fare and establishing our action plan, we had both slumped into recovery mode before the check arrived.

I consulted my watch and experienced a shock. With the balcony blinds snugged tight and a white noise app giving acoustic cover, we'd slept past noon.

Still groggy despite the hour, I slipped into the shower and stood with my head beneath a hot blast long enough for the steam to turn the toilet paper soggy. When I emerged with eyes bright and towel wrapped tight, Skylar was already dressed and working at the desk.

She rose as I appeared. "Good morning."

"Good afternoon."

"That explains it," she said, grabbing the empty mini coffee carafe and heading for the bathroom.

I donned my jeans and shirt while she took care of business. Then I glanced at her computer. Skylar had Facebook open on four tabs. The active one displayed Sandy Wallace, the chef from Miami. I cycled through the others and found three more familiar faces: Amy Zabala, Emma Atherton, and finally *fat vampire* Carmen Rohan.

The toilet flushed. Skylar emerged with the coffee carafe now full of water.

"You found all four promising leads on Facebook," I said.

She dumped the water into the back of the machine and pushed the *Brew* button. "You know, there's a fan in the bathroom. Helps keep the toilet paper dry, among other things."

"Yeah, sorry about that."

"And it's *three* promising leads. I just looked up the vampire out of curiosity."

I decided the wise move was to let Skylar get caffeinated before engaging her further. I opened my own laptop and Googled how to establish a fake Facebook account. Then I went to work. By the time Skylar had sipped her way through half a cup, I had the fundamental structure in place.

"Jenny Johnson," Skylar said, reading over my shoulder. "That's pretty generic."

"Exactly. Harder to home in on electronically, because there's so much noise. Our goal is to get him sniffing around in person."

"Wouldn't that just make him more likely to move on to the next lookalike?"

I turned to look at her. "It would if there were lots of candidates to choose from. But as we saw, there aren't. And meanwhile, we're going to make Jenny irresistible."

"How do we do that?"

I poured myself a cup of coffee while contemplating. "Here's what I'm thinking. Jenny just relocated to Miami from Nebraska to be with her boyfriend. But two weeks after she gets there, he dumps her for an older woman with money. Suddenly she's stuck in Miami, where she has no job and no friends. She's too ashamed to return to Nebraska, which she'd been wanting to escape forever anyway. The only thing going for her is the apartment they shared, which he's agreed to finish out the lease on, since he's now living in a house for free. You with me?"

"I'm with you. In general terms it's not that uncommon a story, other than the rent part."

"So what does she do?" I asked, drawing my partner into the plan.

Skylar downed the last sip of her first cup. "She creates a new Facebook account where she can vent to sympathetic sisters on the web."

"Exactly. Glad to see the coffee working."

"Sorry about earlier. I'm not usually bitchy." She refilled her cup.

"You weren't and I'm sure you're not, but you are entitled. I do apologize for forgetting the fan. I was still half asleep when I stepped into the shower."

She sat on the edge of her bed, which was the one closest to the desk. "Won't Tom suspect a trap?"

"I have no doubt that he's always wary, but he still has to work. I'm hoping the backstory will slip Jenny past his defenses. Plus we'll camouflage the lure by making it difficult for him to locate her. We're not going to include an address, email, or phone number. But we will make it possible for him to identify her apartment building from landmarks in photographs."

"By *her* you mean *me*?"

"Exactly."

"Why not Virginia Beach then? We're here. And here is a lot cheaper and faster than Miami."

I met her question with a question. "Who's the best lookalike on our list?"

She got it right away. "Sandy Wallace in Miami. We need to go there anyway."

"And?"

This time Skylar took two beats to reach the right conclusion. "It makes Tom all the more likely to check her out. Two fish in the same barrel."

"Exactly. When you go shopping today, you'll need to find a wig for Jenny. Meanwhile, why don't you put your bathing suit back on. We'll go take some photos with just sand and water."

"So they could be Miami beach," Skylar said, thinking out loud. "We should put you in a couple of them so I can black you out, as Jenny would be inclined to do with her ex."

"Good thinking. Please pick me up a medium swimsuit while you're shopping. We'll do the beach shoot later." The phone in my pocket vibrated as I spoke. I checked the screen while Skylar watched with raised brows.

"It's an email from Lesley at the CIA."

Skylar moved closer.

I opened the message and read. *Is this him?* A color photo showed a man wearing a foreign military uniform. It was the kind of photo you'd find in a government personnel folder. Posed and proud, looking directly at the camera.

"That's him," Skylar said. "About ten years ago, I'd guess."

"You certainly can't mistake those cheekbones." I tapped REPLY and typed *Yes.*

45
Timing is Everything

ALLISON FELT RELIEVED as she returned home to Laguna Beach from the Immortals' meeting. She knew that wasn't the prevailing sentiment, far from it. Yes, the demise of her colleagues put fear in her heart and grief in her soul, but in her case a greater burden had been lifted. Such was the power of forgiveness.

She'd felt terrible about deceiving her team regarding her aspirations and her secret plan to fulfill it. Knowing that she now had David's blessing clearly meant more than she would have guessed. She hadn't realized how much the guilt was weighing her down until it evaporated under his forgiving gaze.

Now, she just had to make her acting breakthrough.

If only her agent would call.

Suddenly she realized that maybe he had. As per instructions, she'd left her personal cell at home so there wouldn't be a GPS trail linking her to Seven Star Island. She unlocked the garage door and disarmed the alarm, then walked straight to the kitchen and plucked her cell from the charger.

Four messages.

All from her agent.

Rather than listen, she called him right back.

"Mr. Venit's office."

Rubbing her lucky star pendant with her left hand while holding the phone with her right, Allison said, "Jessica, it's Olivia Valesco." In her excitement, she'd almost said Allison DeAngelo. "I—"

"Adam's expecting your call. I'll put you right through."

The hold was brief, but her heart still nearly pounded a hole in her chest. "Olivia. Your career's not yet at the stage where playing hard to get is going to work in your favor." Adam's tone was jovial, but there was some bite in it.

"Apologies. I had to make an unexpected trip and forgot my cell. What's going on?"

"You didn't listen to my messages?"

"When I saw them I called right away."

"You've got an audition for Aaron Sorkin's latest film. He needs a last-minute replacement. His office called and specifically asked for you. Apparently, he saw you in *Nobody's Ghost.*"

What a stroke of luck! Her namesake had been in a dozen plays in New York City. *Nobody's Ghost* had achieved critical acclaim, although Olivia Valesco hadn't been singled out. "What's the role?"

"He wouldn't say. That's not unusual when things aren't going according to plan. The important thing is that the reading is scheduled for 3 p.m. on set in Oceanside."

"Today?"

"That's why you've got so many messages. And why it's so important to promptly return my calls."

Allison looked at her watch. It was 1:15, and Oceanside was at least an hour away at this time of day. "I haven't seen the script."

"They'll give it to you when you get there. The sooner you arrive, the more time you'll have to prepare."

"I'd better run then."

"I'd suggest flying, if you happen to have a helicopter."

Actually, she could easily afford one, but chose not to mention that to Adam. Instead, she headed back to her white Mercedes CLS. "Please text me the address."

"Good luck." Adam hung up.

Oceanside. That might mean a military movie. She wondered if Sorkin was shooting a follow-up to *A Few Good Men.* "Oh my God. I could be in a movie with Tom Cruise!"

She was decently dressed. Designer jeans with Jimmy Choos and an Alexander McQueen top. Knowing that someday she'd have the paparazzi to consider, she'd decided to build discipline and assume she might be photographed whenever she left the house.

She checked the vanity mirror. Her makeup definitely needed a touchup. She'd wait until she parked rather than risk doing a sloppy job at a traffic light.

As she merged onto Laguna Canyon Road, Allison dictated the texted address into her navigation system and waited eagerly while it calculated a 2:21 arrival. By the time she cleared security and found the casting director, she'd be lucky to have ten minutes with the script.

The math wasn't difficult. Every minute she managed to move up her arrival would give her ten percent more time to learn her lines.

She made full use of her 577-horsepower engine, and began beating the clock one car length and yellow light at a time.

It probably wouldn't be the sequel to *A Few Good Men,* she decided. Sorkin was into biographies lately. Mark Zuckerberg and Steve Jobs and Molly somebody. Why hadn't she asked Adam? He'd probably mentioned it in one of his four messages.

The Honda Civic in front of her hit the brakes as she reached for her phone. She avoided its rear end by getting her own foot down in time, but lost her grip and sent her phone sliding between seat and center console. She wanted to scream. This wasn't the first time her phone had fallen into that trap. The last time, she'd lost a nail attempting to retrieve it. With all the fancy options on her hundred-thousand-dollar car, you'd think they could eliminate that pesky gap!

She exhaled long and hard. This was no time to get agitated. At least she had the address plugged in.

Traffic lightened up a few minutes later as she cleared Dana Point. The arrival time now showed 2:18. "A thirty-percent improvement." As Allison spoke the words, she found herself yawning.

Granted, it had been a long day, with the flight back from the East Coast, but wow. Suddenly she could hardly keep her eyes open. What was up with that?

Under normal circumstances, she'd pull over for a catnap. Or at the very least grab a double latte. But of course any delay was out of the question. She was about to audition for Aaron Sorkin! At his personal request! This was her pivotal moment. Her lucky break. Why was she so damn slee—

46
Remote Control

FELIX WAS ON THE SHOOTING RANGE when his watch began to vibrate, alerting him to a call from his special phone. The phone itself was right next to his pile of empty brass, which jumped and jingled as the phone buzzed. For a second, he considered ignoring it, but he knew it would nag him. The caller couldn't leave a message, so he'd wonder.

Before answering, he promised himself that no matter what, he'd go through both boxes of 115-grain Winchester hollow points before leaving. Draw, double-tap, reholster. Draw, double-tap, reholster. Fifty cycles. He was out of practice, and this was no time to be slow on the draw.

On the way back from Seven Star, he had resolved to keep his Beretta PX4 Compact at his side, day and night, until the threat was identified and eliminated. Since July in South Florida wasn't the best weather for a shoulder-holster concealed carry, he had switched to Hawaiian shirts and started wearing the Beretta on his belt.

He pulled off his ear protection and picked up the phone. "Felix."

"It's Aria. Did you hear?"

He clenched the Beretta. "No."

"Allison's dead. She died in a car crash. Apparently she fell asleep at the wheel and—" Aria paused.

Felix waited.

"You know that star pendant she always wore."

"Her good luck charm?"

"It ended up in her neck. That's not what killed her. The police estimate she was going eighty when she hit a lamp post. But it's still kinda creepy."

"Didn't her airbag work?"

"Apparently she still had one of the faulty Takata bags."

"Where did you get your info?"

"From Tory. He just called me. I have him providing me daily updates on my delayed replacement. And that's why I'm calling."

Felix pointed downrange and pulled the trigger, sending a slug of copper-jacketed lead through the six ring on his paper target.

"What was that?"

"The sound of frustration leaving my body."

"Well, then I should be making that sound too. I want to die, but my replacement has been delayed. I'm calling to ask you to put pressure on Tory to get it done. He screwed up. He's the one who has to fix it. Heaven knows we're paying him enough."

"Hold on a minute. What do you mean you want to die?"

"I want the killer to think I'm dead."

Felix hadn't considered that approach.

"As Jacques Eiffel's widow, my death will be reported. I'm planning to fake an accident overseas. I'm thinking Nepal. A Mount Everest climb. But before I fly off to the ever after, I need to know which *dear, dear friend* to put in my will."

"Which is why you need to know your replacement."

"Exactly. So please, put pressure on Tory."

"They say pressure is the first ingredient for making mistakes. Be careful what you wish for."

"I never heard *them* say *that*."

"I kinda just made it up, but that doesn't mean it's not true. Look, Aria, you're in great shape. Better than any of us. You're literally on an island where you can see anybody coming. Did you get those security measures implemented?"

"I did. It's amazing how quickly you can get things done if you throw enough cash at contractors. I've got radar, sonar, guys with guns, and a panic room as posh as any apartment on Fifth Avenue."

"Then quit worrying about the Grim Reaper. I hear worrying ages you."

"Very funny."

"Seriously. You've got to live your life. Just don't pursue

any adrenaline rushes while doing so. No hang gliding or parasailing. Tory will come through before you know it. Meanwhile, stay on your island, stock up on food, kick off everyone you don't trust, and don't let anyone visit."

"That sounds like good advice. Thank you, Felix."

"You're welcome."

Felix had not lied to Aria. He did believe she was safe on her island. He did believe that Tory would come through. But he also thought her idea of disappearing had merit.

His own replacement was set to take place any day now. First Tory would dispose of the original owner. Then there would be a cooling-off period to make sure no alarm bells sounded. No missing-persons filings. No suspicious activity reports. Then he'd swoop into Seattle, tie up any loose ends, and document an exit to someplace far from Washington State. He had been targeting the north shore of Oahu, but Aria had him thinking it might be better to charter a yacht in a fictitious name and head off the grid.

Felix still had no idea who was behind the murder of his friends. But he was growing increasingly confident that the leak was coming from Tory's end. Not Tory himself, and certainly not intentionally, but Aria was right. The presence of one leak did predict others.

Tory would have to go, of course. It would have been much more convenient to have the man who handled the replacement process also manage the monitoring, but that was too risky now. Tory had effectively died the day he reported the Zachary Chase problem. Even if Felix hadn't acknowledged it to himself at the time—a wise tactical move given the operative's elevated ability to sense deception—he had known deep down that offering to double the annual maintenance payment was a diversion.

Speaking of deception, Felix had to figure out how to lure Tory into a trap—once the last three replacements were completed. Preferably a trap he could spring remotely, say from a yacht in the South Pacific. *What to do? What to do?*

47

The Little Things

TORY FOUND HIMSELF SCANNING the road for tailing motorcycles as he exited Interstate 5 onto Fairview and headed north toward the Eastlake area of Seattle. It wasn't rational, he knew, if for no other reason than that the offending motorcycle was rusting away at the bottom of a ravine. But ever since Zachary Chase had foiled the Aria operation, Tory found himself on the lookout for helmeted surveillance.

He told himself there was no way Chase could be here. Seattle was a fresh con, not a repeat performance. Tory himself was a ghost. Born in Finland, he'd come of age completely off the American grid. By the time social media emerged, he knew to keep clear of it. And when he immigrated to the United States, it was for a major private security corporation. Triple Canopy put the C in clandestine. Therefore, to the best of his expert knowledge, not one single picture of him had ever appeared on the internet.

Tory also knew that he had left no fingerprints at the Williamsburg Inn. For decades now he had maintained the habit of mentally cataloging everything he touched and wiping it down before leaving a room. That was why housekeeping always found a dry washcloth just inside his hotel room doors. He'd repeated that procedure at the mortuary before fleeing the scene of the crime, although the handkerchief had gone back into his pocket.

Despite his confidence that Chase had nothing to go on, Tory couldn't slip the annoying, nagging feeling. He knew it was a once-bitten, twice-shy response to having been surprised in that Virginia crematory. But knowing the cause wasn't the same thing as finding the cure.

He surveyed vehicles and scanned faces as he pulled into

the Residence Inn's parking lot. Satisfied that he was surveillance-free, he backed into a visitor spot near a side door.

Despite the name, this Marriott was eight stories of anonymity. Little chance the innkeeper would remember his guests, much less their visitors. That was why he'd selected it. That and the corporate hotel feel.

Tory walked straight through the lobby and into the dining room. He found John Maxwell drinking his morning coffee and looking excited. Exactly as expected. Precisely as instructed.

John rose as Tory approached his table, extending a hand. "Good morning."

Dry palm, Tory noted as they shook. "You ready for the first day of the rest of your life?"

"Yes, sir."

John had been born and raised on the distant outskirts of Louisville, Kentucky. *Horse country* he called it, even though as near as Tory could determine, his mark couldn't tell a colt from a stallion, or a bridle from a halter. John watched whatever sport the Cardinals were playing, and drank whatever beer was cold.

He had worked for UPS ever since graduation, moving as required. For the last five months, home had been Columbus, Ohio. His first shift manager position. The pay was good, very good, but the job was getting boring.

Then one fine day in July, Amazon had come calling. "As you might have heard, we're rapidly expanding."

If there's one important thing you learn at UPS, it's fast and flawless action. John had shown his stripes to the corporate recruiter. Interview offered. Interview completed. Offer extended. *OMG!* Offer accepted.

"If we pay off your apartment lease, can you pack the pickup and be in Seattle Monday morning?"

"Four days, twenty-four hundred miles. No problem."

And here he was: contract signed, fate sealed, body delivered. "Welcome aboard," Tory said, smiling with self-satisfaction.

"I really appreciate the personal service, Mr. Bronco. UPS

would have just had me show up and ask for HR."

"You did the long haul. It's my pleasure to take you the last mile. I see you're packing your car keys and paperwork."

"Yes, sir."

"You won't need them. HR has copies and the realtor will be dropping you off tonight."

"Realtor?"

Tory spread his arms. "Even with the corporate rate, this place is pricy. It's in our best interests to help you get settled. Joan Tiefenthaler will be showing you around after lunch. She's done dozens of relocations for me. Never had a complaint. Sound good?"

"Sure. Thank you."

"Why don't you drop your stuff in your room so you're not stuck lugging it around."

"Okay. Thanks. It will just take a sec. I'm on the first floor."

Tory knew as much. He'd requested the first floor when booking. He just needed to know the room number.

"So will I be with HR all morning?" John asked as they walked.

"Afraid so. As a big company, we've got a lot of forms and a few mandatory videos. But you're a UPS guy, you know the drill."

"That I do."

John left his belongings behind and Tory led him out the side door. Ten minutes earlier the sky had been clear, but now it was raining. "Some people complain about the rain, but I kinda like it. Makes you enjoy the sunny days all the more if you know what I mean. And there's nothing more beautiful than a sunny day in the shadow of Mount Rainier."

"I don't mind one bit, Mr. Bronco. I'm just thrilled to be near an ocean."

Tory's black Camry was a rental, but you'd never know if you didn't notice the bar code on the lower left corner of the windshield. He wasted no time starting the engine and putting it into gear.

John was still struggling with his seatbelt as Tory pulled

back onto Fairview. "Seatbelt's stuck."

"Really? It's never been an issue before. Give it a sec. Maybe you pulled too fast."

Tory kept driving while John tugged. The chime started. Then the voice kicked in. "Please fasten your seatbelt. Please fasten your seatbelt." *Was there anything more annoying?*

"It's really stuck."

"You want me to pull over so you can climb in back?"

"Doesn't matter."

Tory tuned in 102.5, the classic rock station, and learned that Bono still hadn't found what he was looking for. They listened to him lament for a mile while the Camry's chime competed with U2's guitars and drums.

"This is ridiculous," Tory said, turning into a self-service car wash. He pulled into one of the wash bays so they'd be out of the rain and put the transmission in park. "Give it one last try."

When John twisted in his seat to study the feed mechanism, Tory plunged a needle into his thigh.

48
Rat Trap

I GAVE THE MIAMI APARTMENT a 360-degree scan before turning to the realtor with a satisfied smile. "This one feels right."

"It's a rare find," Jeanette confirmed. "You've got location, views, and lots of light. It's a bit smaller than the others, but I think it's a sensible trade."

This was the third apartment we'd visited in South Beach, but the first that had the right view. A view that would allow Tory to pinpoint its location.

Lesley had gotten back to me twenty minutes after my affirmative reply to her email. The man who had introduced himself to Skylar as Tom Bronco was really Tory Lago. A Finnish national with an intelligence background who now lived in the United States. She supplied some basic résumé information, but nothing else, and I hadn't turned up anything additional on my own. Our nemesis was living off the grid.

Skylar and I turned from the high-rise apartment window to address the realtor. "Would you mind giving us a few minutes, Jeanette? I'd like to get a feel for the place."

"Absolutely. Take your time. I'll make some calls in the hall."

Skylar led me to the balcony. I stayed by the sliding glass door while she walked to the rail. The long blonde *Jenny Johnson* wig gave her a completely different look, especially when paired with the oversized black sunglasses, one arm of which Skylar now bit playfully between plump red lips.

I snapped a few photos from various angles, paying as much attention to the background as the fore. Then we did a few together, propping the phone on a light fixture and triggering it with my watch. Finally, Skylar stripped down to her bathing suit and I took a few boyfriend shots from the bedroom balcony. Between the landmarks and the two angles, Tory would have enough to triangulate the address.

Skylar had fun with the shoot, posing playfully and giving the photos an authentic vibe. We'd discussed the scenario earlier. How exciting it would be to move into a South Beach apartment and start a new life with someone you loved.

I couldn't help but notice that Skylar's thigh muscles were enormous. She had swimmers' shoulders as well, of course, but neither were glaring if she didn't flex. Standing there smiling in a bikini that brought out the green ring around her amber eyes, she looked exceptionally healthy.

"Why aren't you married?" The question circumvented my prefrontal cortex, shooting straight from my lizard brain to my tongue.

Skylar reddened as I kicked myself, but she didn't seem put out or offended. "I'll take that as a compliment."

I quickly changed the subject. "I think we're good. I mean, I think we have enough photos."

She pulled her dress back on. White cotton with large daffodils whose stems I now noticed also played off her eyes.

Jeannette hung up her phone as we walked into the hall.

"I don't think we need to look at any more today," I said.

"Are you sure? There's a similar unit a quick two blocks north on Alton."

So much for this being a rare find.

"We need a bit of time to think," Skylar said.

"I understand completely. The process can be overwhelming."

She dropped us at Café Au Lait just after 3 p.m., the start of the slow period between lunch and dinner when chefs did their prep work. The French bistro was almost empty. Just a few late lunchers lingering over croque-madames, steak-frites, and cassoulets. The hostess, an early-twenties knockout who obviously avoided the rich temptations surrounding her, informed me that the kitchen was closed until 6:00.

"We're here to see Sandy Wallace," Skylar said, stepping into view. She'd put on a ponytail wig and applied makeup while studying a Facebook photograph.

The hostess did a double take. "You *are* Sandy Wallace."

"Tell Sandy her twin is here."

"Of course," she said with a pleased appraisal. "If you'd like, you can have a seat." She motioned to the dining room.

We sat on the side of the booth nearest the kitchen. Sandy appeared a minute later, wearing a white chef's coat but no hat. Skylar stood to greet her.

Skylar and I had discussed at length how best to approach the lookalikes on their recruiting missions. Given the high stakes and low number of targets, we agreed that meeting face-to-face was the way to go. We also figured the dramatic *twin* entrance would make the strongest impression and soften the lookalikes for the shocking tale to come.

We were about to put that theory to the test.

"Heather wasn't kidding," Sandy said, approaching our table. "But I know you're not really my twin."

Skylar held out a hand. "My name is Skylar Fawkes. I was recently abducted by a stranger and nearly killed. Mr. Chase saw it happen and helped me escape."

Sandy brought a hand to her chest. "My goodness. Who was he?"

"We're not sure, but we think he was a hired professional," Skylar lied. We'd decided to streamline the story as much as possible, so as not to snag on distracting details. A bit of embellishment further added to the efficiency. "We believe I was targeted because of the way I look. He kept commenting that 'you look just like her.' Since I escaped, we think he might go after someone else."

"Someone who looks like *you*? Who looks like us?" Sandy clarified.

"Exactly."

Sandy's expression morphed into a mixture of skepticism and shock. Nonetheless, she slid into the booth across from me. "How did it happen?

Skylar retook her seat and replied. "I was lured to a quiet location through an elaborate con, drugged, and loaded into a cremation retort. Chase here," Skylar inclined her head in my direction, "literally pulled me out of the fire."

Sandy looked at me, then back at Skylar. Slowly. Twice. "How long ago was that?"

"It seems like a year ago, but it was just a few days."

"Show me the burn marks."

Skylar rose again and turned her back toward Sandy. She pointed to her calves, then, keeping an eye on the other diners, she discreetly lifted the back hem of her dress to expose the angry lines across her thighs.

"*Jesus.*"

Skylar dropped the dress, turned around, and leaned to put her face close to Sandy's. "We're here to warn you, Sandy. And to enlist your help in catching him—and the people who sent him."

49
Bad Taste

A HOT NEW HOSTESS led Felix to the prized table at his favorite restaurant. It was almost as if Raffaele, owner of the landmark Italian eatery, had read his mental wish list.

Felix's standing Friday-night reservations had become awkward after "things didn't work out" with the former hostess. Not awkward enough to make Felix forgo his favorite meal of the week, but uncomfortable enough to ensure that he never arrived without company.

Tonight he was joined by Miami Beach's most successful realtor, the man who had sold Felix his house. Cyrus landed three times as many listings as the number two broker by turning flirtatious lingerie models into real estate agents. "The other realtors curse and complain about me, but they all want to be me," Cyrus had confided during their first dinner.

Felix knew he'd found a friend.

As usual, Cyrus brought a couple of those agents with him. Women eager to allot the day's thousand calories to dishes rating two Michelin stars. Turnover was high at Cyrus Real Estate Services because his agents often developed relationships with the men buying multimillion-dollar Miami vacation houses. Rather than fight it, Cyrus used that turnover statistic as a recruiting tool.

Felix would miss his entrepreneurial friend when the forthcoming identity switch kicked in.

"Felix, meet Nylah and Samone."

The busty redhead and willowy blonde kissed his cheeks and took their seats. Salvatore the sommelier showed up a second later, toting eight big-bowl Bordeaux crystal wine glasses, and a 2007 Sassicaia. Felix ordered the prized Super Tuscan wine by the case, more for the prestige than to save a few hundred a bottle.

As Salvatore presented the cork, he leaned in instead of stepping back. "Excuse me, Mr. Gentry. After this one, we'll be down to two bottles. Shall I order another case? Perhaps the 2010 this time? It's also 97 points." He reached into his apron and produced a second bottle. "I highly recommend it."

Felix turned to the table. "What do you say, girls? Taste test?"

"Sounds good to me," the redhead said. Felix had already forgotten her name.

"I'm allergic to alcohol," the blonde said. "Club soda for me please. With lime."

While Salvatore got busy decanting the bottles and setting two glasses before each imbibing patron, Felix studied the women. If he had to choose, he'd go with the redhead. The blonde was a bit too uptight. But usually he and Cyrus managed to share. They'd get a penthouse suite at the COMO or Mondrian and take the girls up for the view.

"Best to let these breathe for a few minutes," Salvatore said. "Meanwhile, I'll send over some Champagne."

While nodding his appreciation, Felix was distracted by the sight of Raffaele heading his way. The owner had joined Felix for dinner on one of his earlier visits, a time when a last-minute cancellation left Felix dining alone. Raffaele had taken Felix through a chef's tour of the menu, and they had ended the night as fast friends.

That was something Raffaele and Cyrus had in common. They both knew how to take care of customers. They'd give people fitting their target profile something extra special, and turn them into loyal patrons for life. As a result, half the tables at Raffaele's went to regulars. Cyrus's business was similarly stacked with repeat customers.

Felix excused himself and met Raffaele off to the side. After the old friends hugged, Raffaele said, "What's with the Hawaiian shirt? I hope you're not leaving me for the islands?"

"As a matter of fact, that's what I wanted to talk to you about. Not about moving, but about the shirt. He guided

Raffaele back between two potted palms to the place where the dessert cart sat on display when not making the rounds. He twisted halfway to show Raffaele his back, then lifted the printed shirt, exposing the hilt of his Beretta. "There's been a threat on my life."

Raffaele's jaw dropped and his eyes widened.

"Has anyone asked about me? A casual inquiry? Perhaps someone pretending to be a friend? Or looking to do business?"

"No, no. But I'll check with the waiters and ask Giselle. Discreetly of course. You've seen the new girl?" He raised his eyebrows.

"She's lovely."

"And currently unattached, if you can believe that."

Felix wasn't going to go there. Not tonight anyway. "This threat requires me to break my patterns. So for security's sake, I won't be using my table for a few weeks."

Raffaele put his hands on Felix's shoulders. "It will be waiting for you whenever you want to return." He leaned in. "I know a guy who's very good at personal protection. Worked for the Italian version of your Secret Service. Built like a linebacker. One of the leaner players, not the fat ones. He is Italian."

Felix had not considered hiring protection. He asked himself why not, and decided that it was because the other Immortals had all been killed with stealth. Nothing a linebacker's brawn could have prevented, with the possible exception of Ries. "Let me think about that. I appreciate the offer."

Raffaele squeezed his shoulders and released. "Just say the word, my friend."

Felix returned to his seat to find that the Champagne had been poured. Four glasses. Apparently, the blonde had decided she could handle a sip.

"May our evening be as lovely as the ladies we're with," Cyrus said, raising his glass.

They clinked and sipped. Felix hadn't seen the bottle, but he knew it was French, not Italian. Champagne with a capital *c*. The way the bubbles exploded, releasing their acidulous flavors against a rich, smooth background of ripe fruit and exotic wood, was unmistakable. A Blanc de Blanc, he believed, although he couldn't guess the brand.

A waiter reappeared, hands clasped behind his back to indicate that he was above using a pad. "What would delight your palates this evening?"

Felix looked at Cyrus, who nodded. "We're happy to dine at Enzo's discretion."

"The chef's selection. Always an excellent choice. I'll be sure to let Enzo know that you're drinking Sassicaia, and will be right back with an amuse-bouche."

The miniature goat cheese phyllo purses came and went as the foursome discussed their favorite Caribbean beaches. Once the waiter had removed the tiny plates along with their Champagne flutes, Salvatore resurfaced. "Are we ready for the taste test?"

He poured an ounce into each of the six glasses, three from one decanter, three from the other. "Let me know which you prefer, the Sassicaia on the left, or the Sassicaia on the right."

Felix started with the left. He gave it a good swirl and sniffed the bouquet. The rich, fragrant aroma was instantly alluring. The taste was recognizable, complex and fruity. It tickled pleasure centers and triggered sweet emotions as it slid around his tongue and over his palate. Delicious, but not intimately familiar. It must be the 2010.

Salvatore was watching him for a reaction.

"I do like it." Felix then picked up the right glass, which had to be his 2007. Again an utterly alluring bouquet. The taste recognizable, but not completely. That wasn't his bottle either.

"Something wrong, Mr. Gentry?"

Felix grabbed a piece of bread and took a bite to cleanse his palate. Satisfied, he gave the 2007 another swirl, followed by a larger swallow. It was good, but not quite right. "Neither is the 2007."

Salvatore raised his eyebrows. "The one you just drank is the 2007. Your 2007. If you'll indulge me." He poured a half ounce into the silver shell hanging around his neck and gave it a well aerated taste. "You're right. It is a bit off. I wonder if there was some contamination in the bottle. Shall I—"

Salvatore didn't finish his sentence. Felix felt a horse kick his chest. He arched his back and clutched his breast, but neither relieved the pain.

As the sommelier called for help, Felix felt his unresponsive body slide off the chair and onto the floor.

50
Good Call

SKYLAR PLACED HER HAND ON MY ARM as I put the rental car in Park. It was a friendly attention getter.

I looked over at my partner. Today, she was back to short hair, her natural hair, but she'd temporarily darkened it with colored chalk.

We were in Durango, a small town in southwestern Colorado, preparing to give the third of our four planned lookalike briefings. We'd parked on the street in front of a thirty-year-old white one-story starter house with dusty blue shutters. A wooden swing swayed in the breeze on its otherwise empty porch, and a sad silver Chevy with a *Coexist* bumper sticker rested beneath a connected carport. This was the home of Emma Atherton, Skylar's day-trading doppelgänger.

Our first two lookalike recruitment meetings had gone well, thanks to Skylar's appearance and my credentials. Sandy Wallace and Amy Zabala had both been shocked, skeptical, then scared, in that order. The all-important *helpful* remained to be seen, but each had promised to cooperate.

"I've been thinking," Skylar said, closing the car's vanity mirror and turning to face me. "Emma is likely to be more wary than Sandy or Amy was because we're approaching her at home rather than at work."

"I agree."

"She's alone and isolated and in an environment where she frequently fends off solicitors, everyone from telemarketers to landscaping professionals to religious recruiters."

I raised my eyebrows, but didn't comment.

"I think I should start this one alone. By myself, I present an infinitely lower threat profile—even though that's not the case," she added with a smile. "Once I've earned her trust and told our story, I'll call you in. Does that sound like a good plan?"

I've always welcomed insights into the female psyche, and this seemed to be a good one. "It does. I like your thinking. But do me a favor and text me within two minutes of her inviting you in."

Skylar frowned. "That will raise her guard, plus it will take me more than two minutes to get her defenses down."

I persisted. "I just want to know that you're fine. The last time I saw you disappear into a building, things got complicated."

Skylar cocked her head at me. "You really think there's a chance she'll attack me?"

"It's not Emma I'm worried about. Tory might be in there."

Skylar's irises flared; then she looked down at her knees. "I'd never considered that possibility."

"When Tory lost you, he disappointed his client. He's going to be scrambling. Given that we're both urgently hunting the same quarry, overlap is likely."

"Of course. I should have thought of that."

"You still want to go in alone?"

She nodded. "It's still our best chance at success."

Skylar pulled out the burner phone we'd bought for her and called up my number. "I'll pocket text 'OK' if I'm fine. Anything else means I'm not."

"Good plan. Text again after another five minutes if you're still not ready for me."

Skylar popped open the vanity mirror and scrunched her face a few times, working to replace the worry with softer lines. She wanted to appear friendly. Disarming. Satisfied, she closed the flap and opened the door.

While she approached the house, I reclined my seat so that my head wouldn't be obvious when Emma opened up. I stopped at the level where I could still watch with one eye.

Skylar stepped back and to the side after ringing the bell, giving me an unobstructed view. She had good instincts. *Street smarts,* the surveillance experts would say.

Emma's physical reaction resembled Sandy's and Amy's, a full-facial mix of curiosity and surprise. After a few seconds of conversation, the door opened wide and Skylar stepped inside.

To my dismay, they didn't enter the room that was visible from the street. Presumably, Amy had taken her twin back to the kitchen. I kept my eyes locked on the windows, looking for shadows near the edges or the displacement of drapes. Nothing triggered a warning before the *OK* text arrived.

Five minutes after that I got the *Join us* invite.

My knock was met with "Come in."

Emma's house was considerably cheerier inside than out, thanks largely to sunshine-yellow paint and the scent of chicken soup. The owner was pulling mugs from a white laminate cabinet and a tea kettle was beginning to boil as I entered the kitchen. "Skylar was just telling me your remarkable story. Please have a seat. I'm Emma, by the way."

"Chase," I replied, extending a hand. "Thanks for listening."

"Skylar was just about to explain why you don't want to involve the police."

"Actually, Chase will do a better job of that," Skylar said.

I put on my serious face. "Our goal is preventing future assaults—on you, Skylar, and anyone else resembling you. Involving the police won't accomplish that. They're not going to put the A-Team on protecting you, which means there's no way they'll catch this guy. At best, their presence would scare him off. But you couldn't count on that. And even if they did manage to arrest him, you'd still be in danger, because he's just a hired gun. The people who employed him can easily replace him with someone else."

Emma put a box of chamomile tea bags on the table. Her hand shook as she filled the three mugs with boiling water. She did not offer milk or sweetener. "How do you know he's a hired gun? Maybe he's just a homicidal maniac."

I had intended to put a bit of shiver in her spine. Clearly, I'd succeeded. Now it was time to become a beacon of hope. "My background is in the law enforcement field, working at the federal level. I've seen him in action, and I've read his biography. He's a pro. A very high-end pro, which means he's working for people with considerable resources. For you to be safe, we need to identify them."

Emma considered my words while she dipped her tea bag. Far more than was necessary. "What do you want me to do?"

"This guy works using sophisticated cons. If he targets you, he'll likely approach with a friendly offer. When that happens, we want you to play along, then let us know immediately."

"So you can set a trap?"

"Exactly."

"You said he'll *likely approach*. What if he skips the con? What if he just plucks me off the street, plunges a needle into my flesh, and pulls me into a van?"

"Forewarned is forearmed, as they say. And in any case, the police will be no help with that. They don't provide personal protection, and I'm guessing you're not in the position to hire a bodyguard."

Emma nodded grimly.

We sipped tea while the Durango day trader processed how much her life had changed since she answered the door. Eventually, she said, "Show me his picture."

"It's best if you don't know what he looks like. He'll sense it if you recognize him, and then he'll disappear."

"In which case I'll be safe."

"Dead is more likely. At that point you become a witness."

Emma blanched and her mug began to shake.

"Forgive the blunt talk," Skylar said. "It's for your own good. You know everything you need to know to defend yourself. Be extra wary of strangers and special offers, and let us know immediately if you're approached."

"But now I can't help but react, even if I don't know what he looks like."

"To him, you'll appear skeptical and wary," I said. "That's perfectly normal. It's different from facial recognition."

Like the others, Emma maintained her calm and kept a cool head. I attributed their demeanor to a combination of intelligence and the reassuring expression on their twin's face. "Should I buy pepper spray? Or one of those electric-shock things?" she asked.

I shook my head. "Neither would do you any good. Nor would a gun for that matter. This guy is too good for you to beat him in any kind of combat. Now that you've been forewarned, you'll win using your mind."

"So what do I tell him?"

"Just play along," Skylar said. "With me, he made an offer and gave me a day to think. It was a very soft pitch, and in retrospect, very disarming."

"Once people find something that works, they tend to repeat it. That's especially true with high-risk operations," I added.

Emma's expression hardened and I saw resolve reflected in her eyes. "So while I'm 'thinking about' his proposal, I call you."

As she made air quotes, my phone began vibrating. I checked the display. "It's one of your other twins, Sandy Wallace, calling from Miami."

51
No Problem

TORY DID NOT LIKE the way Sandy Wallace reacted to his proposal. Surely most chefs who didn't own equity in their restaurant would jump at the opportunity to double their salary. But her feet remained firmly fixed to the ground.

When he intercepted Sandy in the employee parking lot at Café Au Lait, he hadn't just waved more money. He'd offered to move her out of a hot and crowded kitchen where she made a couple of hundred meals a night onto a yacht where she'd rarely cook for more than a dozen. Not to mention that she'd be off as many nights as she was on, and the scenery would be constantly changing.

He would have understood if she had been in a serious relationship or had just bought a new house, but as far as he could tell, she wasn't attached to Miami in any significant way. Not historically, not financially, not emotionally. She'd grown up in South Carolina and studied in Atlanta.

Sandy had not blown him off. In fact, she'd voiced interest, but there was something behind her eyes. Not just the tinge of suspicion you'd expect, but also a hint of fear. Tory wondered, was it *once bitten, twice shy* he was seeing? Had she been burned by a bogus job offer before? Or was there something more? Was it possible that Zachary Chase had anticipated his move and warned her? That seemed unlikely, but not impossible. Back in Finland, Tory had made a career out of anticipating the Russians' unlikely moves and defending against them.

That's what he would do now.

He didn't want to bail on Sandy. She was the best fit of the remaining candidates, and the quickest solution.

Aria was screaming for a quick solution.

He'd just have to take precautions. Work his own counterintelligence. Set his own traps. This was nothing new for him, and in fact he rather enjoyed it, but it was time consuming.

Tory spent the night thinking about the situation. He researched tactics and reviewed alternatives while drinking Japanese green tea. Then he thought it all through again while practicing tai chi.

The next morning, during his preparations to trap Sandy and satisfy Aria, a new alternative presented itself with a bing. Literally. A fresh Facebook account triggered the facial recognition search he had running in the background. He put his analysis of the Miami Beach Marina's website on hold in order to check her out.

At first glance, the new candidate looked promising. The right face, the right build, and a recent transplant to boot. Unfortunately, she had not submitted any contact information. No phone, no address, no email, not even a full last name. However, Jenny J. was right here in Miami.

He stared at her picture. She had the Aria look. Healthy skin, an athletic physique, and the Snow White nose atop a Scandinavian bone structure. He would definitely keep Jenny J. in mind if Sandy turned sour.

Speaking of which, it was time for that call.

"Sandy, this is Tom. We spoke yesterday in the parking lot."

"Yes, hello." She sounded much less wary today. Her voice seemed deeper and more relaxed.

"Something's come up that's added urgency to my search for a replacement chef. I need to know if you're potentially interested?"

"Absolutely. Sorry if I was less than fully enthusiastic yesterday. You caught me on the heels of some disturbing personal news, so I was a little off-kilter. I'd love to learn more."

Taken at face value, that was good news. Unless the personal matter involved a new relationship. Tory couldn't ask about that now, though. Tomorrow he'd delve deeper. "Excellent! Well, as I mentioned, something's come up. The

Sassones need to sail for Saint Bart's this Friday. So we'd like to have you out to the *Grey Poupon* tomorrow morning to meet them and perhaps cook a couple of omelets."

"Omelets?"

Tory had discovered that the key to effective cons was to provide bits of emotion-driven detail. The little things that helped the mark picture the people inhabiting the fictitious world he was selling. "Mrs. Sassone has it on authority that you can tell all you need to know about a chef from how she works with eggs. I thought I'd give you a heads-up."

"Very kind of you."

"It's in my interest to see you succeed." *And I like the idea of having you cook me breakfast.*

"Should I bring ingredients, or will there be eggs on hand?"

"I was going to say that everything will be provided, but come to think of it, I guess we'll garner additional information from your selections. Thanks for offering."

"But of course.

"The yacht is berthed at the Miami Beach Marina. I'll meet you at the gate to D Dock at eight a.m. sharp."

"Eight a.m. sharp. Okay. Anything else I need to know? What can you tell me about the owners—that I won't find online?"

Tory felt his shoulders relaxing. Aria would soon be thrilled. "The Sassones are fair but demanding. They don't mind paying top dollar for top service, but that's what they expect. As I mentioned yesterday, they are both very health conscious. You'll be cooking lots of fish, all of it fresh, as in straight off the hook. Mr. Sassone and Captain Connor are both good with rod and reel."

"Thank you for the tip."

"As I mentioned earlier, if all goes well with your audition, they'd like you to start on Friday. Is that going to be a problem? You'll only be able to give two days' notice."

"I know someone who can cover for me. Someone who'd love my job. I can make it work."

"Excellent. Thank you, Sandy. I'll see you in the morning."

As Tory hung up the phone, he mused that this was Jenny J's lucky day. Alas, she'd never know how close she'd come to the mortal precipice. Just goes to show you, fate's as fickle as a flipping coin.

52
Fresh Perspective

ALTHOUGH LISA had known Pierce for nearly thirty years, she'd never visited his home. In fact, she'd never been to Montana. Not at ground level.

As she stepped off her G650 onto the private aviation runway at Glacier Park International Airport, the state's nickname suddenly made sense. She'd always considered "Big Sky Country" an attempt to put a shine on desolation. After all, wasn't the sky the same everywhere? But no. Even here at the airport, the mountainous horizon somehow seemed more grand. Perhaps there was something to Pierce's eccentric selection of residence.

The reclusive Immortal had a car waiting for her, as promised. Lisa didn't recognize the model. She asked the driver standing attentively beside the open door. "What is this?"

"It's a Jeep Grand Cherokee, ma'am."

A Jeep. Another first. "It's very nice. Thank you. How long's the drive?"

"Just thirty minutes."

Lisa spent the trip staring at the mountains in a trance of self-reflection. How had her life come to this? How was it that she, CEO of the company that had made the biggest breakthrough in human history, was sneaking off to the sticks in fear for her life? The irony of that actuality was enough to drive a lesser mind crazy. It did have her trembling at times.

Before she knew it, Pierce was opening her door. "Welcome to Whitefish. Thank you for coming."

Lisa had been so absorbed in her thoughts that she'd failed to notice their arrival. She gave Pierce a perfunctory hug while studying the scene behind him. A big, beautiful mountain lodge of a house on the edge of a brilliant blue lake. The air was remarkably fresh and delightfully fragrant with the scent from enormous pines. She immediately felt better. "Glad to be here. I must say, I can already see why you're maximizing your Montana time prior to the full press of a Senate campaign."

"Frankly, I'd rather give up meat and wine. But what we're doing is for the greater good."

She wondered if Pierce actually believed that. No, she was sure he didn't. As much as it pained her to acknowledge it, they weren't that different.

Pierce escorted her through a grand room with a soaring ceiling supported by pine logs toward two overstuffed natural leather chairs arranged before the largest fieldstone fireplace Lisa had ever seen. The rug laid out before it was an elegant sheepskin—rather than some more fearsome creature. The scene reminded her of the romance novels that were her guilty pleasure.

"What are you drinking?" he asked.

Lisa inhaled deeply. She loved the smell of pine smoke almost as much as pine trees. "Green tea, please. I need a clear head."

Pierce turned to the driver, who had followed them inside with her bags. "We'll take a pot of green and a pot of mountain huckleberry, please."

"I must admit, I'm impressed," Lisa said, looking around. "Not just with the house, I knew that would be nice, but with the location. It's so natural. It makes my soul feel like it's come home."

"Glad you approve. I know my place is far from the norm, but with a satellite dish, I'm as connected to the human world as I'd be on Wall Street. Granted, I don't have the same array of dining or entertainment options, but I rotate chefs a month at a time, and as an introvert, I don't miss the other stuff."

The tea arrived. The kettle must have been boiling already.

Pierce poured from his pot first then handed her the cup and saucer. "Have a sip of mine. It's a Montana favorite."

Lisa tasted the dark brown brew. It was as different from her green tea as Montana was from Southern California. Spicy and semisweet with half a dozen distinct flavors. She didn't care for it. Too bold and busy for her palate. But she trusted that the taste could be acquired, and suspected that it packed quite a lift. "I'll keep this cup."

Pierce gave her a gracious nod, then opened the door to business. "What are we going to do?"

The news of Felix's death had really rattled both of them. Felix was part of their contingent, the business-minded Immortals. The other victims had all felt more distant.

Even though the restaurant owner had told the police that Felix was worried for his life, the coroner had labeled his death a heart attack. The other members of his party had consumed the same food and drink, and all three were fine. The autopsy turned up nothing out of the ordinary. But Lisa and Pierce knew it had been murder.

"What can we do?" Lisa asked. "Besides hide."

"Figure it out. We're good at problem solving."

This wouldn't be their first attempt at that. "I keep coming back to the idea that it has to be an insider, but then I get nowhere. I'm here because I know it's not you. We need each other to get to the White House, and I dare say that ambition is the driving force in both our lives. But with Felix gone, that leaves David and Aria. The brilliant, tree-hugging research scientist, and the beautiful island-loving former socialite. Neither strikes me as a killer."

Pierce pushed back with a surprising statement. "They aren't the only insiders remaining."

"What are you talking about?"

"Surely you're not forgetting Kirsten? Obviously she's gone, but she has relatives. That was the whole problem."

Lisa had not forgotten Kirsten. Lisa would never forget Kirsten. "That was over twenty years ago."

"Exactly. Suppose her husband saw one of us, looking like we did back then, and put two and two together? Suppose he then investigated and found that we all looked the same."

"If that were the case, I'd have been the first to die. Don't you think?"

"Not if he doesn't know which of us killed his wife."

Lisa wasn't buying it. "No revenge plot would prioritize Camilla over me."

An attractive Asian woman in a modern chef's uniform approached with a silver platter of sushi. She silently set it on the coffee table with a bow. Lisa concluded that it was Asian cooking month.

"I would agree if it weren't for one thing," Pierce said, refilling their teacups. "None of the victims have suffered. We, the survivors, are the ones suffering. We're suffering from their loss, and we're suffering from fear and anxiety."

The insight struck Lisa like a splash of cold water, chilling her spine and refocusing her attention. She made a mental rundown of the list. Eric had died skydiving. Camilla had cracked her head in her sleep. Ries had slipped after climbing a cliff. Allison had passed out at the wheel. Felix had suffered a heart attack during dinner. In summary, a couple of the killings had included a few short seconds of terror, but that was it. "You're right. Oddly, that makes it more sinister, from my perspective as a survivor."

"I know."

Lisa continued processing out loud. "I had focused on the result, rather than the process. Now that I think about it, we are suffering more than they did. The anticipation is torture."

"Agreed."

"So the question becomes—"

"Who would want to torture us?"

53
Disturbing Pattern

LISA RETURNED from a long contemplative walk in the woods to find Pierce watching from his back porch as she approached. She'd smelled the cigar from a quarter mile away, but hadn't known it was his. "I didn't know you smoked?"

"Only the occasional cigar. But there have been a lot of occasions lately," he added with a wink. "I like to puff back here on the porch while I reflect and deliberate. Lots of cause for that these days."

"Tell me about it."

"I've got a cigar with your name on it if you're interested?" He transferred the Dominican to his left hand, but then hoisted a wine bottle in his right. "I've also opened an Opus One to breathe, in case you're feeling less adventurous."

Lisa's first impulse was to pass on both. She was feeling healthy after burning off calories hiking by the lake. But then she heard her mouth accepting. "You know, in my whole life, I've never once smoked a cigar."

"Well then it's definitely time to try."

He smiled politely, but she knew the same thought had just crossed his mind. This might be her last chance.

She climbed up onto the porch and dropped into a matching teak Adirondack chair. "You really do have a beautiful view."

"Coming from you, that's no small compliment."

"The ocean is also beautiful, but very different. It's wilder. Uncontained. With oceans, you get the full range of emotions, whereas this," she gestured, "must always feel serene."

"It does."

Pierce pulled a fresh cigar from a tube, clipped the end, and applied a torch. "It's a Romeo y Julieta. But don't get any ideas." He winked as he handed it over.

Pierce was a handsome man. He had that rugged outdoorsman look that paired well with flannel shirts and a scruffy beard. Her thoughts flittered back to her books, and his sheepskin rug. *Oh, how far they'd come.*

She mimicked his grasp on the cigar, taking it between two fingers. "This is just tobacco leaf, right? Nothing else?"

"Nothing else. Unlike cigarettes, which have filters and paper and chemical additives, these babies are all natural."

"But they'll still kill you?"

"Oh, yeah."

They chuckled.

"Don't breathe it in," Pierce cautioned, as she moved the cigar toward her mouth.

Lisa stopped. "What?"

"If the smoke goes into your lungs you'll cough like crazy. Just pull some into your mouth, like you're sipping a milkshake you're not sure you'll like."

Who knew? Lisa took a tiny pull.

"Now savor the smoke like you would wine, then exhale it through your mouth. Keep your breathing separate. Do that through your nose."

Lisa complied. The cigar tasted like it smelled, rich and woody and, of course, smoky. She was glad she'd tried it once, but doubted there would be a second time—no matter how long she lived.

"Hold the cigar aside until you're ready for another taste," he advised. "Get a feel for it between your fingers. That's part of the experience. I'll pour the wine."

The cigar had the circumference of her thumb and felt roughly the same, warm and firm but soft when pressure was applied. She could see how some might find it comforting—especially when sitting alone outside. The cigar's band was regal, if not a bit boring, just red and gold with white words, but the box boasted a classic depiction of the young Romeo at Juliet's balcony. Filthy though it might be, this was a classic experience, and she resolved to savor it.

They sat in silence for a while, wine glasses in their left hands, cigars in their right. Lisa knew the isolation of this place would drive her crazy in the long run, but at that moment there was no place she would rather be than with an old friend on that peaceful porch.

"While you were walking, I was thinking about the hypothesis I proposed earlier."

"You and me both. I'm warming to the idea."

"Funny, I'm having second thoughts."

"How so?"

"As I recall, Kirsten's husband had nowhere near her intellectual caliber. His IQ was above average, to be sure, but he didn't strike me as someone with the mental horsepower of a criminal mastermind."

Despite her earlier prediction, Lisa found herself taking a second puff. "Well, now I'm completely confused. Who's the killer then? One of us Immortals, or someone we've offended?"

"If you think about it, the assassinations were brilliant. Each different, each unexpected, each without inflicting suffering or leaving a trace. That exercise led me to consider who could be intellectually capable of such feats."

She swirled her wine while Pierce spoke, then guessed. "David?"

"The CIA."

She coughed, choking on her Cabernet. Was Pierce crazy? Thank goodness it hadn't been the cigar between her lips. She raised her stogie. "Do these contain narcotics?"

Pierce just smiled. "Who controls the CIA?"

She thought about it. "Ultimately the White House, I suppose."

"That's right. The CIA is run by a political appointee, the CIA director, who reports to another political appointee, the Director of National Intelligence, who reports to the president, who, among other things, is the head of a political party."

She took another puff of her cigar without thinking. "So?"

"Do you believe, even for a second, that people like

those, the players at the peak of such professions, aren't acutely attuned to threats against their hold on power? That they're not using the resources at their disposal to stay in place? To fend off potential assaults?" Pierce talked with his hands, threatening to fling ash and slosh wine, but never actually doing either.

"I never really thought about it."

"Well, seeing as politics is your new profession, it's time you started."

"Agreed. But I don't see what that could have to do with the deaths of Allison and Camilla." Lisa noted that despite her cigar being half-gone and her glass nearly empty, her nerves remained on edge.

Pierce followed her gaze toward the tip of her cigar. "You liked it more than you expected."

"Apparently I did. Must be the mountain air."

"Must be. But I'm limiting you to one." He grinned and poured more wine. "Suppose Carl Casteel is on retainer to report emerging threats, like an early warning system. I submit that's not just possible, but likely, given that he's widely regarded as the country's top political strategist."

Lisa started feeling a bit dizzy. She set her cigar on the edge of the big porcelain ashtray, and took a sip of wine. "I'm listening."

"What if Casteel reported us after hearing our individual plans. He clearly took us seriously. Suppose his assessment transferred up the chain of command, or down it, depending on your perspective. In either case, it could have set dangerous dominoes in motion."

Lisa thought it through out loud. "You think the CIA uncovered our real identities, from which they divined our halted-aging status, and then set out to eliminate not just us, but all the Immortals?"

Pierce raised his eyebrows, then rested his cigar in the ashtray next to hers. "It's possible."

"But the killings started before we met Casteel."

"No. They started before we met him together, but after we met with him individually. Because we both crossed the CIA's radar at the same time, it was easier for them to connect us."

"Huh, you're right." A terrifying thought struck as Lisa caught sight of her cigar butt. *Could it have been poisoned? Was this whole talk a smokescreen? Was her throat about to seize up? Her heart about to stop? Had Felix felt this way just before—"*

"You okay?" Pierce asked, his tone sincere, his face concerned. "The nicotine can be overpowering, especially the first time. I should have warned you. I honestly didn't think you'd take more than a puff or two."

She swallowed, then studied his face as she spoke. "I'm fine. You really think the CIA is behind the killings?"

"I think it's worth considering, especially since we don't have another solid explanation. I'm not saying it's specifically the CIA either. That's just a convenient term for black ops. I'm sure POTUS has multiple clandestine resources at his disposal."

Her heartbeat was regular, her breathing normal. She took a deep breath and tried to relax. "Why kill Camilla? She's no political threat."

"Look at the history of political assassinations. When monarchs are killed, their families are typically eliminated as well to avoid comebacks."

"When you explain it that way, I have to admit the idea's not completely crazy. I suppose we should explore it further. But given that we weren't the first to go, I think it's highly unlikely."

Pierce fiddled with his own cigar. "Agreed. That brings me to my second insight."

What now? She found herself reaching for more wine. "I'm listening."

"Regardless of who's behind it, there's a pattern you'll want to bear in mind."

"A pattern?"

Pierce set his glass down, then reached out for hers. A second later, she understood why. "So far, the assassinations have followed a pattern of boy-girl-boy-girl."

Lisa felt the trembling return as her stomach seemed to fill with concrete. "You're right. If it's not a coincidence, then either Aria will die next—or I will."

54
Cooked

TORY SMILED BROADLY as Sandy Wallace walked into sight. She'd opted for the professional look but with a twist. Beneath the short chef's coat she wore black stretch pants. Highlighting her assets was a good sign, as was appearing five minutes early.

She had a black handbag slung over her left shoulder, with something protruding. Tory raised his binoculars and zoomed in. She'd brought her own omelet pan. A true pro.

To access a yacht moored at the Miami Beach Marina, one first had to access its dock. From land, that required a key. A tall, wide gate blocked every dock entrance, each with a frame surrounded by long spikes. If a vandal or voyeur or thief attempted to get around, he risked getting hooked like a fish.

Of course, an intruder could approach from the water. But from Tory's stakeout perch, he had that covered as well. He was confident that once Sandy passed through that gate, she'd effectively be fenced off from the world.

For surveillance purposes, the dock gate made a perfect pinch point. If Zachary Chase had figured out Tory's gig and was somehow working with Sandy, he'd be stuck on the other side. If he approached by water, he'd be a sitting duck. Or a swimming duck. Or a scuba diving duck. Didn't matter to the suppressed automatic Tory held in his hand.

Tory had risen at 5 a.m. to begin his watch two hours before dawn. The captain's chair on the top deck of the 60-foot rental was perfect for surveillance. Literally designed for it—albeit with sandbars and sunfish in mind.

One boating family had left for The Keys an hour earlier. Their voices had carried clearly across the marina's still water. Otherwise, the dock had been quiet.

No surprise there. The fishing charters ran off the less pricy piers. Pleasure craft marinas like this tended to be quiet places, especially during the week. He'd heard that most owners put less than a hundred hours a year on their motors. Such a waste of money when you looked at it that way. Of course, Tory understood that the people who leased slips here tended not to worry about their wallets. He looked forward to adopting a similar attitude sometime soon.

Tory sipped coffee from his thermos while rotating his chair and his attention from land to water and back again. He spotted Sandy as soon as she rounded the corner from the parking lot. Her behavior struck him as entirely normal. No furtive glances, no irregular stride. Just a lone woman walking to a meeting.

He watched her as she waited by the gate while continuing his 360-degree sweeps. For the first six minutes she stood attentively, occasionally glancing at her watch. Once Tom Bronco was officially late, she began thumbing through pages on her smart phone, glancing up every few seconds to look for the man who'd told her 8 a.m. sharp.

At 8:15 she turned to leave.

That was when Tory shouted "Sandy!" and headed in her direction.

She turned.

He bounded down two flights of stairs, across the gangplank, and out onto the dock. Once he'd closed the gap, he said, "So sorry I'm late."

He opened the gate using the tiny knob concealed within a cup and ushered her onto the dock. After it clanged shut behind her, he said, "The bad news is that the Sassones were delayed in New York. The good news is that they've authorized me to make you an offer if I like what I see. And taste."

"So it's just you?"

"Just me. I hope that's all right."

"Only if you're ready for the best omelet of your life."

"I see you brought your own pan."

"The right pan is very important, especially since I'll be

cooking over an unfamiliar stove."

As a bachelor who ate most of his meals out, Tory hadn't considered that aspect of the art. "How so?"

"Making omelets is a very hands-on process, when you do it right. You need to shake the eggs as they cook, forming curd. But it only works when the pan is the right shape and has been properly conditioned."

Always interested in learning new tricks, whatever the field, Tory said, "I usually stir and fold."

"Most people do. It produces an entirely different result. You'll see."

In Tory's experience, one egg rarely varied from the next. Then again, his palate wasn't particularly sophisticated.

The yacht he had rented was called the *Lucky Seven*. To turn it into the *Grey Poupon,* Tory had paid a sign maker to print the new name in nautical blue on two thick vinyl stickers, which he had then applied over the yacht's given name.

There really was a wealthy pair of Miami socialites named Sassone who owned a yacht named the *Grey Poupon,* but of course Tory had no relationship with them. And Sandy would not have been able to learn that latter part during her Google search.

He led the eager chef up the gangplank, through the main saloon, and into the galley. Spreading his arms, he asked, "What do you think?"

Sandy stood in the center and slowly turned around, inspecting each piece of equipment. Cooktop, oven, microwave, refrigerator, freezer, dishwasher, exhaust hood, pots and pans. All of it quality and gently used. "It resembles the kitchen in my apartment much more than the one at Café Au Lait, but then that fits the output requirement. I'm glad to see you use gas burners. I wasn't sure, this being a yacht. And I approve of the French press. Simple is best when it comes to coffee."

"I agree. You'll note that the last chef took his utensils with him, so these are just stand-ins. And the owners asked to have the pantry emptied so everything would be fresh. I did pick up eggs, butter, and Gruyère in case you forgot."

"That's good to hear. Very sensible. But I didn't forget." She extracted a grocery bag from her large purse.

Tory raised a finger. "I've got a few questions and a bit of paperwork, but do you mind if we make the omelet first? I've been up for a while but didn't eat, lest I ruin my appetite." He really was starving. Since he needed the questionnaire completed, he'd have her cook twice, once before and once after the paperwork. But that shouldn't be a problem. She'd likely be flattered. The second time, while watching over her shoulder "to learn her special technique," he'd stick the needle in her thigh.

"Sounds good to me. Cooking calms me, and to be honest, I'm a bit nervous."

She put her personal omelet pan on the front right burner and lit the gas. "This pan's made of five layers, stainless steel sandwiching aluminum sandwiching a copper core. That makes it tough but lightweight, easy to clean, and quick to warm, even on a low flame. And it spreads the heat evenly."

She pulled a small bottle from her shopping bag. "Extra virgin olive oil with black truffles." She poured a healthy portion into the pan. "My secret ingredient."

"So much?"

"You'll see."

"I always use butter."

"Butter's fine, but this is fantastic. I'll show you something in a second."

She cracked three organic free-range eggs into a stainless steel bowl, ground in pink salt and black pepper, then began beating rapidly with a fork. So far, to Tory's eye, she'd done nothing special. But he did like watching her work.

Satisfied with her mixture, Sandy set the eggs aside, ran her forefingers under water and flicked a drop into the pan. It crackled in protest. "Perfect. Now, look at this." She took the omelet pan in her right hand, grabbed the bowl with her left and made room for Tory to watch. "The moment of magic."

Tory stepped closer.

With a jerk fast enough to start a stubborn lawn mower, she brought the pan of crackling hot oil up into his face.

Tory's world erupted in fire as his eyes flared with an excruciating pain more intense than anything he'd ever felt before. His hands flew to his face a second before his left ear exploded, turning everything mercifully black.

55
The Loneliest Place

LISA FELT THE TICKLE of an adrenaline drop hitting her bloodstream as Seven Star Island came into view. The physiological response reinforced what the back of her brain already knew. Coming here was not a safe move.

But she didn't know what other move to make. She'd learned long ago that when every move was risky, the smart step was often bold.

Lisa had known in her gut that Pierce was not the killer. The two of them were fully aligned and completely committed to a codependent plan. They were excited about a future they could only achieve by working together.

Aria was an animal of a different stripe.

Under normal circumstances, or even less extreme abnormal circumstances, Lisa would have scoffed at the suggestion that Aria was capable of killing. Her sorority sister might be cutthroat in the business sense, but not in the literal one. At this point, however, Lisa was willing to consider all options and each candidate. Only four Immortals were left alive.

She jumped in her seat as the pilot's voice came over the intercom, breaking her contemplative trance. "We've got a problem, Ms. Perera." As he spoke, she felt the chartered helicopter pull up and back abruptly as if evading hostile fire.

Red dots of laser light began dancing around the cockpit as the pilot pulled higher. She traced them to the ground. Four men in body armor were braced in firing positions, assault weapons snugged to their shoulders.

The pilot came back on the intercom. "Obviously, I can't land. Do you want me to take you to a neighboring island, or back to the mainland?"

"Just hold on a minute."

Lisa pulled out her burner phone and hit a speed dial. As a security precaution, she had not alerted Aria of her impending arrival. On the off chance that Aria was the killer, Lisa hadn't wanted to give her the opportunity to set a trap, prepare a poison, or arrange a fall. "Aria, it's Lisa. I'm in the helicopter. Just me and the charter pilot. We need to talk about what's going on." She had to speak up to be heard. Even executive helicopters were noisy.

"Oh, thank goodness. The alarm went off when radar detected your approach and I've been locked in the panic room ever since, wondering if today's my day."

"Will you tell your assault squad to stand down so I can land?"

"Of course. I'll see you in a minute."

Lisa hit the comm switch and informed the pilot of the situation and the gratuity that would be forthcoming. Sure enough, the red dots vanished and the welcome party stood down. Sixty seconds later, the pilot put skids on the ground.

Although they'd shouldered their assault rifles, the soldiers remained ready for action, with three standing back while one approached the craft. "It might be best if you remained aboard," she said, straining to keep her voice steady.

The pilot surprised her. "Don't worry about me. I know how to talk to these guys."

After a thorough, unapologetic pat-down, two of the soldiers escorted Lisa to Aria's master suite, one walking in front, the other walking behind. Aria opened the door as they drew near. It was thicker than a brick and seemed to swing open on its own power.

Drawing closer, Lisa noticed that the doorway resembled the entrance to a vault. Clearly Aria's security upgrades extended well beyond the welcome wagon. Lisa took that as a reassuring sign. A killer might camouflage herself behind window dressing, but she'd be unlikely to go whole hog.

The lead guard stepped aside, letting Lisa pass while addressing Aria. "We'll be right outside the door. When you're ready, I'll show Ms. Perera out."

Lisa knew the last remark was for her. The guard wanted her to know that there would be no getaway if any harm befell their charge.

"Thank you, Barry." Aria placed her palm on a wall switch and the door swung shut with a pneumatic hiss.

The Immortals kissed cheeks.

Lisa placed her hands lightly on Aria's shoulders. "I'm impressed. And sorry for the unannounced arrival. I'm taking my own precautions. I'm sure you understand."

The two alpha females did understand each other. Probably better than anyone else understood them. They had shared their formative years, and were now the planet's only Immortal women.

Aria showed her to the sitting room, where herbal tea and fresh fruits were waiting. Another reminder of what they had in common.

"I was just in Whitefish, Montana," Lisa said as an opener.

"Visiting Pierce? I've never been."

"Me either. It was much more alluring than I'd expected. Made me think of what you'd get if the Four Seasons opened a hunting lodge."

Aria poured the tea. "Were you discussing your political plans or our shared predicament?"

"Both, but the accent was on the latter. I've been trying to ignore the threat but have come to realize that I won't be able to focus on my future until I know I have one. Since that won't happen before the killer is unmasked and caught or killed, I figured it was time to get proactive."

Aria handed Lisa a porcelain teacup on a silver saucer. "What did the two of you conclude? Who's behind the mask?"

"Pierce floated the idea that we, he and I, had caused all this by inviting scrutiny." Lisa explained Pierce's train of logic. How their top political consultant might have alerted the political parties to the affluent newcomers, with the ultimate result that the president put the CIA on the case—bringing all their investigative and black bag capabilities to bear.

Aria contemplated the convoluted hypothesis through a few sips of jasmine tea. "A proactive extermination policy would explain why we only get bozos running for national office. The powers that be are suffocating the competent contenders in their cribs. It would also explain the timing and perhaps the tactics. But I agree with your conclusion. If that were the case, you and Pierce would have been the first to go."

Lisa nodded along. "The problem is, we couldn't think of a more likely scenario."

"What about Kirsten's husband?"

"Pierce doesn't think he's smart enough to pull this off."

"I didn't know him. Kirsten was before my time. There were no other Kirstens? No other early Eos casualties?"

"Nobody."

Aria plucked a small stem of purple grapes off an attractive platter. "Do you regret that decision?"

Lisa frowned and shook her head, then spoke with a shrug, "There was no other way. Eliminating Kirsten was the only option for keeping immortality a secret in the long run."

"Remind me why."

"She had a husband and was pregnant. She would have insisted on both becoming immortal of course. Then the child would want a spouse. Soon the Besankos would become like the House of Saud."

"The ruling family of Saudi Arabia?"

"Exactly."

"Reducing the stature of the rest of you given that you couldn't have families of your own. I get it."

Lisa reached out, put her hand on Aria's, and squeezed. "Do you? I've been racked with guilt lately."

"Absolutely. You had no other choice."

Lisa felt a rock roll off her shoulders. "Thank you. That wasn't the only consideration, of course. The family imbalance was bound to lead to conflict, and those have a way of boiling over—especially if you have eternity to simmer.

"Secrecy was our paramount consideration even back

then. We realized early on how disastrous it would be if immortality became widespread. Overpopulation would become so problematic that we'd eventually end up with some kind of culling plan, executions at age 100 or the like. That would turn our Garden of Eden into Hell on earth."

"I know."

Lisa was on a roll. It felt so good to release to someone who truly understood. "Can you imagine growing up, knowing you're going to get a bullet for your hundredth birthday? Granted, we live less as it is, but it's natural. When the time comes, most people are more or less ready. In that scenario, everyone would feel like they're twenty-five when they walk into the execution chamber. What a nightmare."

They sat in silence after that, sipping tea and staring through the bulletproof window at the palm trees waving in the breeze.

When the pot was empty, Lisa turned back to Aria. She had one more dark door to open. "Maybe I should have realized that nothing could end well if it started with killing. Maybe I should have buried Eos instead."

Aria shook her head. "Look at us. We're nearly sixty but we look like we're in our early thirties. We feel like we're in our early thirties. Suppose we died this afternoon. We would still have gotten thirty years' worth of thirties, rather than the ten everyone else gets. And we got the extra years with the benefits of forties and fifties wisdom. Plus, you guys got the money. It was a good deal. A great deal, some might say. Stop second-guessing yourself."

Lisa found herself fighting back tears. What was wrong with her? Was this what mental breakdowns felt like? "I'm not ready to go."

"You might not have a choice. Don't get me wrong," Aria spread her arms and gestured around. "I'm going to fight it with everything I've got. But I'm also preparing myself."

Lisa reached out and put a hand on Aria's shoulder. "I'm glad it wasn't you." She realized her tears were flowing.

"Stay with me," Aria said, her voice soft and reassuring. "It's as safe here as it gets."

"I can't live on an island, or in a fortress for that matter.

It's just not my style."

"I understand it's not your first choice, but it might be the only way to stay alive until we figure this out."

"Not the only way. There are seven billion people out there. How hard can it be to disappear?"

Aria shook her head, but smiled kindly. "You may get lost in a crowd, but you'll be alone."

Lisa took her oldest friend by the hand. "There's no place more lonely than a coffin."

56
Questionable Status

SKYLAR CAUGHT MOVEMENT in her peripheral vision as she extinguished the gas burner. Reasserting her grip on the omelet pan, she turned around.

"I wish I'd caught that on video," Chase said. His tone was light, but his gun arm and gaze were deadly serious. The Sig P320 he usually kept in the small of his back was now pointed directly at Tory's thigh. "It would be a shoo-in to win the Best Revenge Scene category."

Despite what she'd just done, Skylar found that the gun made her nervous. "You can drop the gun. If he wasn't out cold, he'd be squirming and screaming."

Chase kept the gun level. "With anyone else, I'd agree. But this guy's got discipline like I've never seen." With his left hand, Chase proffered a bunch of heavy-duty zip ties. "Start with his ankles. Cross one over the other then double-bind them. Stay out of my line of fire while you work."

Skylar set down her weapon and did as she was told, taking great satisfaction from the zipping sound. "Now his wrists?"

"Yes, same drill. Behind his back."

Tory had been doubled over with his palms pressed to his face when she delivered the knockout blow with the smoking omelet pan. He'd collapsed face down, saving her the trouble of rolling him over.

She pulled one limp muscular arm around in line with his spine, then the other, while Chase kept the gun trained. "Why are you aiming at his leg, rather than his head or heart?"

"I won't hesitate the slightest second to put a bullet through his thigh. It will stop him and leave him alive for questioning."

To Skylar's relief, Chase holstered his Sig once she'd snugged the second wrist tie into place. He then rolled Tory over and they got the first look at the conniving assassin's ruined face. It was splotched with wicked red marks and speckled with big angry blisters. His chiseled cheeks, his strawberry-blond brow, and even his eyes had taken a hit. The left one looked particularly painful. Swollen to the size of an egg, it appeared about to pop.

Skylar gasped, but did not look away. Bad as it was, the damage was far short of cremation.

Chase transferred the cell phones, keys, and wallet from Tory's pockets to his own. Then he disappeared for a few seconds, returning with a blanket. He laid it out flat beside Tory, then rolled their captive like a cigar. Apparently satisfied with his work, Chase hoisted the bundle onto side-by-side bar stools. She recognized the move: he was preparing for a fireman's carry. "You ready to go?" he asked.

Skylar grabbed her bag and pan.

"Check the dock."

She walked to the gangplank, looked around, and ducked her head back into the main saloon. "We're clear."

Chase crouched, worked his right shoulder under Tory's waist, then stood. He followed Skylar off the *Grey Poupon* and down the dock to the 30-foot boat they'd rented.

He dumped Tory below deck, none too gently, still wrapped in the blanket. He unfurled Tory's feet, picked up a chain he had waiting and fastened it tightly around the freshly exposed ankles with a padlock.

Skylar saw that Chase had already attached the other end of the chain to the central leg of the dining table.

"Call me if he moves. I'm going to get us out of here."

Skylar took a seat and readied the omelet pan. She'd found it a most satisfying weapon, despite the stereotype. It was very personal, not like a gun or even a knife. She had felt his skull reverberate through the stainless steel, and found it exhilarating. Not for the violence or dominance, but for the justice. Delivered personally by her to the man who had conned her, lured her, and attempted to burn her alive.

Their plan had worked as expected. Prior to implementation, her primary concern had been passing herself off as Sandy. Not just her appearance but also her voice. At Chase's suggestion, she and Sandy had spent two hours side by side before a mirror, dialing in her diction. Clearly, that had been sufficient.

While they practiced in Sandy's bathroom, Chase rented a yacht that was already slipped at D Dock. Knowing that Tory would be wary and watching, he bought supplies and immediately boarded the *Miami Viceroy*. The three of them continued refining their tactics by phone.

The real break came when Tory mentioned the omelet. With that precious tidbit, the whole takedown plan fell into place. Prior to that, they'd been contemplating pepper spray disguised as cooking spray, and a cry to summon Chase.

The yacht's motor rumbled to life as Skylar pulled a phone from her purse. She called Sandy. "We got him."

"Hallelujah! I can't thank you enough."

"We couldn't have done it without you."

Skylar needed to call Amy and Emma as well, but those calls could wait. Technically, they weren't safe yet—and neither were Sandy and Skylar. None of them would be safe unless and until Tory led them to the people behind this, whatever *this* was. Skylar had no guess as to who *they* were, but when the time came, she'd be happy to *make them omelets* as well.

Skylar didn't consider herself to be a violent person. She carried spiders outside and avoided movies that revolved around guns. But she wasn't horrified by what she'd done. Perhaps waking up with burn marks from the crematory had rewired her brain. Or at least added a new circuit. Whether permanently or temporarily remained to be seen.

Frankly, she was fine with it either way. Shrinking violets had never been her favorite flower. She always cringed when weak women were cast in movies, although she reserved judgment. You never really knew how you'd behave until you wore those same shoes, whether they be sandals, loafers, or heels. Now that she'd been dropped in the jungle, Skylar was pleased to find that she'd grown thorns and was comfortable wearing combat boots.

While that bit of self-realization rolled around her mind, the big burrito before her began writhing. "He's awake!"

The boat slowed immediately, but didn't stop moving. Within a few seconds, Chase was by her side. Gun out and ready.

"We're still cruising."

"Autopilot. I want to get a bit further from shore before we settle down to business." Chase handed his Sig to Skylar, grabbed the edge of the blanket in the middle, and lifted. This caused Tory to roll, which he did until unwrapped.

Ignoring her own discomfort, Skylar pointed the gun at him. She'd never fired a weapon, but had seen enough demonstrations during cop shows to know the basics. Hold firmly, but not too tight. Squeeze the trigger without jerking. Anticipate a powerful recoil, but don't be afraid.

Skylar almost screamed when she saw Tory's face. The blisters were now even larger and beginning to crust. The swelling made him unrecognizable. She was certain that he couldn't see anything from his left eye. His right was questionable. She couldn't believe that he wasn't moaning or sobbing or begging for a doctor. Perhaps his nerve centers had simply been overwhelmed. Or maybe her frying pan had damaged his brain.

"What's my status?" he asked, his tone strained but controlled. His volume was loud as if he was having trouble hearing.

It was a clever question. Simple yet multifaceted. It made her doubt that she'd done cognitive damage.

"Hard to tell at the moment, Tory," Chase said, revealing their knowledge of his true identity. "Depends on how well your mouth works."

57
Cold Conditioning

AARO LAGO HAD TAUGHT HIS SON Tory to ignore pain by teaching him to disregard cold. It was a valuable skill in Oulu, Finland, where the daily high was below freezing for five months out of the year.

Aaro's plan was to drive the sensation of cold, and with it the pain, down below Tory's consciousness to where it no longer registered. Aaro accomplished this by taking his boy out skiing or fishing or chopping wood in the dead of winter, without a hat or coat. Just gloves to keep his fingers limber.

While they were working up a sweat, he'd hit his son with logic problems. Complicated induction or deduction or mathematical puzzles whose solutions required the focused attention of a nimble mind. Tory wasn't allowed in out of the cold until he had the answer. And bless his heart, Aaro stayed right there with him, also baring his body to the great god of the north.

If the sun was shining, they'd skip the riddles in favor of calisthenics, then hike out to the middle of a frozen lake and play chess.

At first, the physics of it boggled Tory's mind. How could his father not be cold? Did his bigger body somehow defy the laws of nature? Why didn't he shiver? Why weren't his lips turning blue? How could he talk in a normal voice when the wind was whipping and the wolves were howling and the dogs were curled tighter than garage door springs? Was it something he'd learned as captain of the national cross-country skiing team? Or had he been born with an abnormal nervous system? If so, had Tory inherited those genes?

"Just ignore it," Father said. He didn't chide or shout. He

just repeated the three-word phrase, then threw another logic puzzle on the pyre of his son's mind, time and again, while Tory's teeth chattered and knees knocked and fingers failed.

As the problems became more complex, the concentration required deepened. Eventually, there wasn't bandwidth for anything else. Solving the riddles required the full range of his mental faculties.

Ultimately, it worked.

By forcing him to push everything else aside, those complex problems trained Tory to ignore the pain.

Once he learned the trick, once his body realized what was possible, Tory found himself capable of exercising it at will. Like juggling or whistling, it became an acquired skill. One that worked against all forms of discomfort and distraction, not just climatic extremes.

Lying on the floor of a boat, tied up tight as a sail in a storm with his face smoldering like an old campfire, Tory found his containment skills strained to their max. It wasn't the physical pain that kept poking its nose under his mental tent. It was the psychological terror. His left eye was blind, probably permanently so. The superheated oil had sent a shock wave of pain directly down his optic nerve and into his brain. He'd never felt such searing white pain. Not from bullets. Not from knives. Not from reindeer antlers or wolverine claws.

His right eye still functioned, but at a greatly reduced level. He could only see through a crack of puffed flesh. That was a torment every boxer knew. Debilitating and frustrating but ultimately transient.

Fortunately, he had the master of all puzzles to occupy his mind, to fill his protective tent. How could he get out of this mess?

"What do you want to know, Mr. Chase?" What Tory could see of the man standing before him was unreliable. But Tory knew this had to be him. Somehow he'd convinced Sandy Wallace what was awaiting her. He must be persuasive, given the conviction it took for her to go through with her frying pan trick.

"I want to know why you're killing people, and who's paying you to do it."

"Anything else?"

"Where we can find your boss?" Sandy added.

That made sense to Tory. Now he needed time to think. To buy time, he turned toward the killer chef. "What did he tell you? How did he convince you to do this to me?"

"No convincing was required. I'm not Sandy, I'm Skylar. You tried to cremate me alive."

Of course! It hadn't occurred to him that the former triathlete might join forces with the ex-CIA agent. Most women would still be curled up in a ball on their therapist's floor. Most men too, for that matter.

"Oh, you get it now," she said.

Tory knew better than to start down that path. He put the conversation back on course. "What are you offering for the answers to your questions?"

"Two-thirds of the American dream," Chase replied.

"I don't understand."

"Life and the pursuit of happiness."

Tory scoffed. "But no liberty."

"That's up to the courts."

If Tory wasn't mistaken, the vision in his right eye was improving. "And if I refuse to answer?"

"Not really an option." Chase walked into the galley, carrying Skylar's bag. It was a different galley, smaller than the one on the *Lucky Seven*. He extracted the omelet pan and placed it on the stove's central burner. Then he turned the dial.

Tory felt an involuntary shudder run down his spine as the gas igniter clicked out sparks. Chase seemed to sense this, as he left it sparking long after the telltale ignition whoosh. "You going to torture me, Zachary?"

By way of answer, Chase emptied the remainder of the olive oil into the pan.

Tory worked himself into a kneeling position, testing his bonds in the process. Both wrists and ankles were tight. A chain tethered him to the fixed table leg. Not good. He needed to get free. Since his arms and legs were uninjured, he could fight his way out of this if given the chance. Even three-quarters blind.

He found himself fantasizing about having his eyelid sliced open to relieve the swelling, the way Mick had done for Rocky before the final round. The sound of water crackling in hot oil brought him out of the trance.

Chase brought the omelet pan over and held it under Tory's chin. The heat coming off it would have been agonizing, given his existing burns, had Tory let the feeling register.

"Tell me why you're killing people, and who's paying you to do it. Or I'm going to press your face into the pan."

"No, you're not."

Tory put conviction in his tone, but Chase showed equal certitude. "You cremated my college roommate alive."

"Yes, I did," Tory admitted, now speaking in a matter-of-fact tone. "So you're going to have to choose. Do you want revenge, or do you want answers?"

"I'll take both. We've got two more liters of oil."

"Doesn't matter."

"And why not?"

"What Skylar did back on the *Grey Poupon* could be construed as self-defense. But now that you've got me, anything additional would be considered torture. By torturing me, you will be eliminating an important option. Specifically, the option of turning me over to the police. That means you really only have two alternatives. You can either kill me when you're done with your questions, or let me go. Given that I don't see you letting me go, I have no reason to answer any of your questions. So you see, logic reduces your available options to exactly one: negotiation."

"You can't negotiate if you can't walk away. Not while I maintain the unlimited ability to inflict pain." Chase spat in the oil, which crackled in protest and sent a furious sprinkle of boiling oil onto Tory's neck and chin.

Tory did not flinch. "That threat may work with most people. But not with me. Look at my face, then try to tell me you need more convincing."

"Plenty of people start off tough. Time changes things.

And there are lots of ways to inflict pain without leaving marks."

"You don't have the time for sleep deprivation and cold therapy. You don't have the pharmaceuticals for chemical inducements. And you don't have the stomach for endless hours of inflicting pain. Even in my condition, I can see your soul straining behind those big gray eyes."

Chase said nothing.

Skylar said nothing.

Tory said nothing.

"What's your offer?" Chase finally asked.

58
Limited Options

AS MUCH AS I WANTED TO, I could not fault Tory's logic. Going to the police would not be an option if I inflicted additional detectable physical harm.

On the other hand, I could kill Tory with a clean conscience—and save the taxpayers a few hundred grand. I had witnessed the crime and heard the confession. Capital punishment was justified. The rest was bureaucracy.

But justice for past actions wasn't my primary goal. Preventing additional attacks took priority. To obtain the information that would empower me to stop Tory's employer from cremating more innocent people, I was prepared to do whatever it took.

Up to a point.

I wasn't certain precisely where that point was. But standing there studying the war-torn face before me, I had to admit that Tory's cracking point was likely well beyond it.

Fortunately, Tory had been wrong about the number of options available. I had more than one. I had two. Negotiation and deception.

"What's your offer?" I asked.

Tory resisted the urge to smile, which must have been tough. "I tell you everything, and then you turn me over to the police—with a clean conscience. Let justice prevail."

I looked at Skylar.

She signaled accord with a slight dip of her head.

"Telling isn't good enough. You'll need to show us. Prove to us that your words are more than an elaborate con. We happen to know that you're good at those."

This time, Tory did smile. "But of course. Consider me the penitent man, ready to cooperate."

Tory's angle was clear. Appear contrite before the court

and police. No doubt play himself off as a pawn. Attempt to cut a deal. Testify against his employers in exchange for lenient sentencing. No doubt they had paid him well enough to provide for a first-rate defense. He'd hire a team of top lawyers, men with courtroom skills and political connections. Enough BS to bamboozle any jury.

Not on my watch.

I set down the omelet pan, then pushed Tory over, off his knees and onto his side. I pulled another zip tie from the packet and hog tied the hitman, binding his ankles to his wrists. "We'll start with your laptop."

"Whatever you like," Tory said, not reacting to the additional restraint.

"Is it on the *Grey Poupon*?"

"No. It's in my hotel room."

"Lie to me and I'll pluck out your other eye."

"It's in my hotel room."

I sailed the *Miami Viceroy* back to the marina, just long enough for Skylar to disembark with Tory's hotel key. He had an executive suite at the Fontainebleau, which was two miles north of the marina on Collins Avenue.

As she set foot on the gangway, I repeated the highlights of our earlier discussion, a move more reflective of my needs than hers. "Be careful, and bring everything. Have the valet hold your car. Tell him you just need to grab your bag."

"I got it."

"I know you do. I'll be listening." I tapped my earbud, then surprised myself by kissing her on the cheek.

What was that about? To camouflage the act, I called down through the hatch to Tory. "At the first sign of foul play, I'll put a fork in your eye."

"She won't have any trouble. I work alone."

I believed it, having watched the Finnish freelancer work in Williamsburg.

Skylar started walking down the dock.

I returned to the helm and immediately pulled away. I didn't want to linger where we could be overheard if Tory started to scream. "Testing, testing."

"I hear you fine," Skylar said, glancing back. "We did it!"

"We don't know that yet. It remains to be seen how much he knows. But in any case, you were amazing."

"It feels fantastic, like I've been freed from a great weight. Now that I've beaten the man who bested me, I'm ready to become my old self again. My old self before the accident." Her tone was absolutely exuberant. "I can hardly believe that I just pulled off a sophisticated covert operation. With your help, of course."

I knew the feeling. "You were fantastic. You're a natural. But please put that elation aside for now and focus on the task at hand. A lot could still go wrong."

"Roger that."

"Seriously, Skylar. Ops are often blown because agents think they're already home."

"Got it," she said. Her voice an octave lower.

I killed the yacht's engine. We were far enough from the marina. "I'm going back below deck to keep an eye on our man. Please talk to me about what's going on."

Skylar did. The valet. The elevator. The five-star executive suite view. The laptop. The toiletries. The search for anything hidden.

She packed all the personal items into Tory's roller bag, and stepped back onto the dock forty minutes after stepping off.

I picked her up and pulled offshore again. Not too far. I needed cell reception to set up a hotspot for Tory's computer.

Before beginning the interrogation, I wanted to search the roller bag. With Skylar watching, I placed the black Travelpro onto the drink table behind the captain's chair and pulled the laptop from its front pocket. Setting the computer aside, I unzipped the main compartment and then went straight for the zippered pockets on the sides. "Bingo!"

"What is it?"

I extracted three items. "My phone, watch, and gun."

"Congratulations."

I set them aside and continued rummaging. I didn't find my car key, and it wasn't until I unzipped the inner pocket of Tory's toiletry bag that I found anything interesting beyond the owner's Glock 19 and lock blade knife. But it was very interesting. Three prefilled syringes. Either an anesthetic or an antipsychotic, I would guess. Probably the latter, given the relatively small size. "Did you check the minibar refrigerator? See any vials?"

"Nothing there but overpriced booze."

"I bet this is his knockout concoction. The one he used on you."

Skylar grimaced.

I set the syringes aside and searched for hidden compartments. I found none.

Satisfied that I'd gleaned all available information from Tory's belongings, I picked up the laptop and led Skylar below deck. I set the computer on the dining table, sliced Tory's hog-tie restraint with his own lock blade knife, and hoisted him onto the bench seat, wrists and ankles still bound. "Scooch to the corner and we'll get started."

Tory complied.

"We'll start with the password for your computer."

"Fly_Eagle-Owls_Fly. With first-letter caps, underlines between words, and a hyphen after Eagle."

There were so many ways this could go wrong.

I walked to the galley and grabbed a teaspoon from a drawer. Turning to Tory, I thumped it on my open palm and said, "I've agreed to go down the path you selected. But if you deviate, my reaction will be extreme. If this password erases your computer, I'm going to pop out your good eye."

"What, no forks?"

I simply stared.

"It's a cheer for the Finnish football team."

Ironically, Tory's handicap also disabled me. I couldn't read his face. Not his expressions, not his eyes. That increased my need to rely on logic and threats. I gave the spoon a final thump. "You've been warned."

I slid around the bench seat until I was sitting close enough to Tory to sense his reactions. Skylar stood where she could see his face.

I typed in the cheer.

The computer unlocked.

I positioned the laptop so Tory could see the screen.

Skylar slid in beside me so she could watch as well. I didn't like being boxed in that way, but with Tory bound and chained I decided not to exclude Skylar. She deserved a seat at the table.

I navigated to Recent Documents. There were ten folders in active use. One called Admin, the other nine designated with first names. Allison, Aria, Camilla, David, Eric, Felix, Lisa, Pierce, and Ries. On a hunch, I used command-space to search for "Lars." The Mac rewarded me with a file nested under David. I clicked it open and was greeted by my college roommate's charismatic face. The file included his picture taken from multiple angles, his biography in great detail, and multiple screens' worth of notes and linked article clippings.

I clicked back out to the parent file named David. The man pictured there was the one I had seen impersonating Lars at his apartment. The man who drove a BMW i8.

"You have nine clients?" I asked.

"A month ago I did. Only six are still alive. Either they're a very unlucky group, or someone has been killing them off."

WITH THE VISION in his right eye now clear, although constricted, Tory studied the opponents seated to his left. Chase had the look of an agent. Clean-cut and athletic. A far cry from the leather-clad scruffy-faced motorcyclist Tory had first glimpsed in California. He wondered if Chase had been undercover. In any case, he was working alone now. Or rather, with a washed-out athlete rather than with fellow officers.

Both his captors were sitting within striking distance. That was bad tradecraft, even with Tory's wrists tied. He hoped the mistakes would continue.

Of course, they'd already made the big one, consenting to his proposal. By agreeing to forgo torture as a means of extracting information, they had shown their true colors, their humanitarian stripes. Now he had the advantage, and they didn't know it.

Chase began opening the other eight named files. Skylar gasped when Aria's face appeared. The woman did look like her. And sure enough, nested inside were folders labeled, Skylar, Sandy, Amy, and Jenny J.

Chase finally turned his attention back to Tory. "Why didn't Aria turn up when we searched for Skylar's lookalikes?"

"None of my clients show up in searches," Tory said, struggling to show his superiority by speaking normally. "Clearly, they've worked hard to avoid and eliminate electronic fingerprints. But I don't know how, and I don't know why."

"All nine?" Chase asked.

"All nine."

"And who are they?" Skylar asked.

"I wish I knew. It would be worth a lot of money to me to figure that out, so I've tried."

"Blackmail?" Chase asked.

"They have money, lots of money, and secrets worth killing for." Tory could see that Chase believed him, but Skylar was still skeptical. The naïveté of one unfamiliar with his world.

"What do they have in common?" she asked.

"You've now seen the same pictures I've seen. Your guess is as good as mine."

"How do you contact them?" Chase asked.

"I work exclusively with Felix. We chat using Darknet services routed over a dedicated phone."

"On one of the phones I found in your pocket?" Chase asked while opening the Felix folder.

"Yes. The generic one. They gave it to me. Each of the nine has a matching device. They're VoIP-based, and specially programmed to go through a Darknet relay in Dallas. Untraceable. Feel free to try."

"Your payment?" Chase pressed.

"My fees are paid from an offshore shell corporation to an offshore shell corporation. For expenses I have a platinum Amex linked to a Delaware shell company, which is funded by the same offshore shell corp that pays me.

"In a nutshell, that's all I know. Now, as anyone can plainly see, I'm in urgent need of serious medical attention. Depriving me of that treatment constitutes torture."

Tory knew they wouldn't give in right away. But he also knew he could wear them down. And once they turned him over to the police, he'd be taken straight to a hospital. There, he'd be a suspect, but nothing more. Security would be inconsequential. Handcuffs with a guard or two at the door. He'd act all weak and feeble, not a hard sell given the appearance of his face. Then *Wham!*

Chase did not look sympathetic to his cause. "We'll talk about your needs once ours are met. Tell me the story from the beginning. I want dates, instructions, and activities. I want the transcripts of your texts plus your personal observations."

Tory told them almost everything. He left out only the special instructions for Allison, Felix, and Lisa. The desire to replace an actress and separating military officers. He wanted something to bargain with, on the off chance that he remained in police custody beyond his hospital visit.

Chase sat in silence after Tory finished round two. His laptop was closed by then, and he was back across the table with Skylar by his side. Eventually, he voiced his conclusion. "So basically, you've become a professional assassin?"

Tory understood this ploy. Chase was painting his captive as less than human. Justifying what he'd done so he could walk away with a clean conscience. Well, Tory wasn't going to give him that psychological crutch. "As an intelligence officer, I was always a professional assassin, of sorts. Now I just work for individuals—rather than a government. The pay is much better. You might consider making the switch yourself."

"I worked for my government to make my country safe."

"So did I. Now I work for individuals to make them safe."

"Safe from what?"

"I don't know. That's not unusual. Soldiers are rarely told what the generals are thinking."

Chase remained unblinking. "Guess."

"My working theory is that they're spies. Some foreign government or organization wants to weave them into the fabric of American society."

"To what end?"

"If I could figure that out, I wouldn't have to guess. As you've just heard, the replacement identities are from random locations. Spies would want specific locations. So it's weak, but I can't think of a better explanation."

"Who do you think is killing them?"

Tory shrugged. "It did occur to me that if the CIA discovered what was going on, they might execute the foreign agents in a way that makes their deaths look like accidents."

"That's what you're giving me? The CIA? That's not going to get you to a hospital."

"What else can I say?"

Chase got up and poured himself a glass of water. He stretched his quads, triceps, and shoulders before sitting back down.

Tory knew the simple actions were designed to make him uncomfortable, to draw focus to his own cramping muscles, constricted blood flow, and overall lack of freedom. He ignored it, as he did his other discomforts, by keeping focused on the future.

"What would happen if you called Felix and asked for a meeting? What if you told him you had to show him something in person?"

"He'd never agree to it. He'd know it was a trap. What could I tempt him with that I couldn't reveal over the phone?"

"You could tell him you've identified the killer," Skylar said, commenting for the first time in a while. "Tell him you need to show him what you've found. That he needs to experience it for himself."

"Experience it?"

"Use those words. It's intriguing. It's BS, and he'll likely suspect as much, but he won't know for sure. And given the level of desperation he's likely feeling, he may bite. Remember, you already know what he looks like, and you know his new name, so what does he have to lose?"

"His new name is worthless. It's just a shell identity. My clients aren't moving into their replacements' houses. Knowing their new Social Security numbers doesn't give me their locations. I couldn't find them if my life depended on it, and they know that. They work very hard to keep it that way."

Chase rose again, this time to stand behind Skylar. "She's right, and it's a good idea. Call Felix. Sell him as if your life depends on it."

Tory couldn't think of an objection. He decided to ask for something instead. Start getting them in the habit of giving, and maybe even free his hands. "Will you brew some coffee while I compose my pitch? A handful of aspirin would also be nice."

Chase walked to the galley where he found a coffee pot and grounds. While it brewed, he rummaged around, obviously looking for something else.

Skylar went to the restroom. She returned before the coffee was done brewing. "No aspirin in the medicine cabinet. It's bare."

Chase poured three mugs, and set one before each of them.

Tory decided not to ask Chase to free a hand. He'd just make a pathetic go at it with his burned lips and hope for the best.

What he got was the plastic straw Chase had extracted from a go-cup.

"What is Felix's number?" Chase asked.

"Speed dial 1."

Chase checked the call log and found a long string of SD 1 entries. It was a smart move, ensuring that Tory had called it often, that it wasn't a warning bell. "How do I display the actual number called?"

"You can't. It's a feature of the Darknet service they use. I told you they're crazy about security."

Chase held the phone close to Tory's mouth so it would sound less like a speaker phone. Another smart move, but one that ultimately made no difference. The other end rang repeatedly without an answer.

Chase ended the call and began tapping the phone against his open palm. "How hard is it to reach Felix?"

"Easy. In seven months, this is only the second time he hasn't answered my call."

"Does he keep tabs on you? Could he know that you've been taken?"

"No. I'd have noticed. He's a numbers guy, not an ops guy. He doesn't think like us."

"Defense, not offense?"

"Exactly."

"What about emergency communication? What's your backup method?"

"They can reach me on my regular phone, but my only link to them is in your hand. Security freaks, remember?"

Chase was clearly getting a headache from running into so many dead ends. He continued tapping the burner phone through an extended silence. "We'll try again in fifteen minutes."

Tory wasn't optimistic. "Okay. But given the developing pattern, I suspect that Felix may never answer a phone again."

60
No Joy

LISA LEFT SEVEN STAR ISLAND with hope and a plan. Forget politics. Forget the United States. Get lost overseas and start a new life. A long life. Someplace with warm weather, blue water, and sandy beaches.

She'd check back in with Aria on occasion. Every six months or so—for as long as Aria was alive. If Aria died, Lisa would forget the other Immortals altogether. She liked Pierce and David just fine, but she wouldn't risk her life to keep in contact with them.

Back home in San Clemente, she gathered everything she couldn't bring herself to leave behind. Given her deep financial resources and complete lack of family, that amounted to little more than a few photos and awards. Happy days with her mom and dad. College and grad-school shots, yearbooks and awards. All professionally assembled in thick scrapbooks with well-worn edges.

She had a similar catalog from her business career. A collection of newspaper articles and magazine features. Her *Top 30 Under 30* Women in Business Award, and a few others. The Eos company photo had been the real prize, although now it made her cry. Both due to the casualty count, and because it was now considered contraband. Like everything else, it would tie her new identity to her birth identity.

The Immortals were supposed to burn all their memorabilia once their replacement process was complete. She hadn't yet phased out her birth identity, so technically it wouldn't be a violation until Lisa Perera had a death certificate, but she knew she'd never destroy her mementoes. She doubted that any of her peers actually did. She put hers in a small suitcase.

Her only other suitcase was topped with toiletries, two swimsuits, and a change of clothes. Underneath, she filled it with $100 bills. A million dollars' worth. With that cash, she could live for years off the grid.

The trip to the airport went by in a blur, and before she knew it, Lisa was looking back toward the private aviation terminal of John Wayne Airport from the stairs to her G650. She wondered when she'd set foot on American soil again.

"Just you today, Ms. Perera?" the familiar flight attendant asked.

"Just me, Brady. I'm taking a break from everything this time, my staff included." Lisa had not told anyone her plans. Safer that way. Aria knew her general intention, but that was it. Pierce would get a letter explaining her decision by snail mail. She felt she owed him that, given their mutual plans. One of them would let David know. He'd understand. The good doctor was a go-with-the-flow kind of guy.

She settled into her usual seat, then got an idea. "Brady, I'd like a glass of Champagne. The 2004 Krug please."

"Coming right up."

She resolved then and there to make the coming months a celebration. Treat this time like an adventure rather than a retreat. If she thought about it, the only thing she was walking away from was familiarity. That wasn't such a big deal, if you had the right frame of mind. If you concentrated on what you were gaining, rather than what you were losing. Immigrants did it all the time.

Captain Carter came over the intercom. She couldn't recall if Carter was his first name or last, but she liked him. His voice and his look. He reminded her of a movie star. "It's fifteen hours to Sydney. It'll be early morning when we arrive, so you'll want to get as much sleep as you can."

Lisa knew that takeoffs out of John Wayne were steep due to noise abatement ordinances, so she drained her Champagne as Carter came back on to announce that they'd reached the head of the queue.

Once they cleared the coastline and began a more traditional climb, she asked Brady for another glass, then hit the intercom. "Captain, I've had a change of plans. I need to head for Bali instead of Sydney."

"Bali, Indonesia?"

"That's the one."

No quips or sighs or complaints about procedure. Captain Carter snapped straight into make-it-happen mode. "We'll need to refuel. Probably Tokyo or Taipei. I'll check our options and get back to you."

"No need. Do whatever makes sense and update the display. I'm going to take your advice regarding sleep." From her chair, she could see a monitor with the flight map, time and distance covered and remaining, speed and altitude.

"Very well. Good night, Ms. Perera."

Lisa had never been to Bali, so nobody would think to look for her there. Of course she hadn't been lots of places. She'd selected the Indonesian island because it was populated with millions of gentle people and on the other side of the planet. Easy to get lost on it or one of the thousands of surrounding islands.

She closed her eyes and pictured her toes dangling off the end of a long dock into water so clear and blue you felt like you were scuba diving even from the surface. She'd find one of those hotels where the suites were individual huts out over the water. She'd swim herself into the best shape of her life and sunbathe until her skin was such a deep bronze that even Aria wouldn't recognize her without a second, studied glance.

Lisa was almost asleep when a stinging sensation made her wince. "Ouch!"

Brady was instantly at her side. "Can I help you, Ms. Perera?"

Her hand shot to her backside, the source of the pain. "Something bit me!"

As Brady turned to inspect her chair, Lisa felt her lungs turn to lead. She couldn't move them. She wanted to scream but could not produce noise. In desperation she jumped up and flung her chest against the back of a neighboring chair, forcing her lungs to expel carbon dioxide, then suck in fresh breath as they recoiled.

It helped.

She began repeating the procedure, pressing herself against the back of the chair, working her own lungs like a bellows.

It wasn't enough.

The exertion used up more oxygen than she was taking in. Her head began spinning, and she soon lost the strength to continue.

She was aware of Brady screaming as she slid to the floor, and the leaden feeling moving beyond her chest. She felt him start mouth-to-mouth. But it wasn't enough. She pictured her toes in that warm turquoise water. Dangling. Dangling.

Only three Immortals left.

61
Talk is Cheap

THEY GRILLED TORY on everything he knew about his clients. They walked through his computer files, bank accounts, and bookmarks. They had him call Felix a dozen times, without success. Finally, Chase opened the call list on Tory's generic phone. "Who is speed dial 3?"

"That's Aria."

"And 5?"

"David."

Coincidentally, they were the ones that looked like Skylar and Chase's roommate. Or perhaps not coincidentally, Tory realized, given how his captors had gotten involved.

"Will Aria and David know if Felix has been killed?"

"I don't know."

"Call and find out. Explain that he's not answering. Then try to set up a meeting. Same con you were planning to use on Felix. Which of the two is more gullible?"

"They're both razor sharp," Tory said with sincerity. "But my relationship with him isn't so hot, thanks to you. Better to call her."

"Watch me for cues," Chase admonished, setting the phone before Tory.

Aria answered on the first ring. "Hello."

"Aria, it's Tory. I've been trying to reach Felix—"

"Felix is dead." Her voice was strained and clipped.

"Oh, no. Oh, dear. I was afraid of that. I think I know who did it."

"Who?" Her voice rang of desperation tinged with hope.

"Not over the phone. Trust me, there's a reason. We should meet."

Aria didn't reply.

"Aria, are you there?"

"I'm not meeting with you or anyone else. Just tell me."

Tory gave Chase a *see what I mean* look.

Chase shook his head.

"Not over the phone."

"Email me then," Aria suggested.

Chase nodded emphatically.

"That might be acceptable. What's your address?"

"Use SevenStar@HughesNet.com."

Chase held out a hand and waggled it side-to-side.

"All right. If I can figure out a safe way to do that, I will. Otherwise, we'll have to get together. Your terms and the location of your choosing."

When she didn't reply, Chase made a hang-up motion.

"Meanwhile, stay safe and let me know if there's anything I can do."

Chase reached over and disconnected the call.

Tory looked at him with his one working eye. "You're planning to run an email trace."

"You try that with them before?"

"I never had an email before," Tory said, feeling inadequate for the first time in years. If only he hadn't been so busy. "Felix was my single point of contact, and he worked exclusively through a Darknet messaging system. The trace might work."

"I'm not familiar with HughesNet," Skylar said.

Tory turned her way. "It's a satellite-based internet provider. They specialize in locations not serviced by cell towers."

"I'm guessing you used them a lot at Triple Canopy," Chase said. "Doing all that Third World security work."

Tory didn't comment while processing the revelation that they knew more than his name.

Chase grabbed the phone again. "Time to call David and see if he'll meet. Same story."

Tory nodded. "Okay. Expect a hostile call."

It was Chase's turn not to comment. He punched the fifth button and set the phone back down. It rang and rang.

"No way to leave a message?"

"Nope. No message capability on these lines. It's a

security precaution."

After twenty rings, Chase disconnected. "Has David always answered in the past?"

"Technically, yes. But I've only called him twice."

"Your best guess?"

The irony of his honest answer put the bitter taste of bile in Tory's mouth. "It looks like your problem is taking care of itself. You needn't have bothered with me."

Chase dwelled on that in silence while sipping coffee.

Tory seized the opportunity to recite his favorite refrain. "I really need that hospital. You know everything I know, and now you have a way to locate Aria. Assuming she stays alive."

Chase set his mug down a bit more firmly than was necessary. "There's one partner you've been hiding all day. It's time to talk about him now."

"Partner? What partner?" Tory was genuinely surprised, and he let it show.

"The funeral home owner."

Tory would have rolled his eyes were it not for the blistering pain. "He's just a guy I bribed."

"Yeah, right. *Hey, would you mind leaving the back door open so I can cremate someone alive?*"

"Strange as it seems on the surface, that's about right. Except that I don't actually mention a body."

"I don't believe you." Chase sounded angry and sincere, but Tory knew that both were easily faked.

"Virginia wasn't the only location where I used that disposal mechanism. It's just the only one I got the replacements to walk into. The other times, they were already drugged. I actually made special arrangements with a total of five funeral homes."

Skylar stomped on that turd. "You got five separate morticians to give you midnight access to their facilities?"

Tory studied his victim turned captor. "Why are you surprised? Funeral home owners spend their days draining the bank accounts of grieving widows. Why wouldn't they leap at the chance for an easy hundred grand? All they have to do is forget to set the alarm, leave the back door open, and switch on a few lights. I'm in and out like a ghost. The only trace that I've come and gone is the cash under their mattresses, so to speak."

Chase shook his head while Tory talked. "I might believe you if I hadn't seen the metal detector. You can't convince me that funeral homes need those. Therefore, I don't believe your BS story. And because of that, I have to question everything you've told me."

"I don't buy it either," Skylar said. "People aren't like that. Ordinary people aren't that evil, or that willing to take risks. Most would call the police."

Tory knew they'd never buy the actual metal detector explanation. Even to him, the brother-in-law story sounded pretty thin. Still, he refused to hit an impasse. He had no choice in the matter. Not if he wanted to live. Fortunately, there remained one way to convince them. "It's easy enough to prove."

"Nice try," Chase said. "But we're not going to let you out of our sight. And we're not going with you to commit a felony."

Tory shrugged, provoking a wince. His hands were suffering big time from the limited circulation. "I can't do it over the phone. If I'm not there with cash in hand, they'll think it's either a setup or a prank—" Tory stopped himself. He could get Murdoch from Williamsburg to vouch for him. Especially if he offered a referral fee. "Actually, there is a way."

Skylar and Chase waited while Tory thought it through. The money might be a problem. He'd literally shown Murdoch and the others the cash. "If I prove this, are we good?"

His captors rose and walked to the other side of the room, where they whispered words Tory couldn't hear.

"By your own deduction, it's an acid test," Tory called. "Confirmation of my entire story. Proof you have everything I know. Everything you need."

They returned to the table. Chase studied Tory's face before giving him the right answer. "We'll need to copy your hard drive first. The police will confiscate your computer."

62
Hidden Jewel

ARIA CAUGHT SIGHT of her shadow as she strode from the ocean onto the sand. She would never tire of having a thirty-year-old, never-been-pregnant figure. What a joy, to not worry about wrinkles or sags. To never fear the mirror. Forget the immortality, the halted aging alone was priceless.

She spread her arms and studied her shadow. With Allison out of the picture, she was undoubtedly the sexiest fifty-six-year-old alive.

The warm air and gentle breeze had her dry by the time she stepped onto her bedroom's tiled floor. Detecting her presence, the sensors in the wall reported in over a concealed speaker. A feature of her new security system. "Good afternoon, Aria. You missed a call."

She checked her iPhone. No missed calls.

She checked her burner phone. Two missed calls. One from Pierce, one from David. As she considered which to call back first, the phone decided for her. It began to buzz. "Hello."

"Aria, it's David. I'm calling to see if you're all right?" There was something in his voice. *Two calls from David. One from Pierce. None from Lisa.*

"I'm fine. What happened? Is it Lisa?"

"She died on her plane."

Aria flopped onto the bed. "Oh, my goodness. Was there a crash? What happened?"

"The authorities aren't saying, but they're calling it a homicide."

"Not an accident?"

"Not this time."

There was something in David's voice. "What aren't you telling me?"

"She was on her way to Bali. Her bags were packed with cash and mementos."

Aria suddenly felt very alone. "She was running away?"

"Apparently."

Aria needed to set up her own Google alerts. At this rate, she could soon be the only Immortal left alive—and not know it. "Wait a minute. How did the police know it was her, and not her replacement senator veteran person?"

"She hadn't yet fully switched over. She was flying as herself. As Tory will explain when your time comes, there's a transition. A tapering into one identity and out of the other."

When my time comes. That suddenly sounded overly optimistic. "I'm supposed to be getting mine this week. I've been trying not to think about it. Not to think about anything related to —our group."

"Me too."

The soft sound of David's soulful voice sent a tear down her cheek. These were good people. Good friends. Why would someone want to kill them?

Aria lay back on her bed. Suddenly she didn't want to let David off the phone. His voice was like a lifeline.

"How are you protecting yourself?"

"I've taken a sabbatical from the lab, moved to a hotel under a pseudonym, and started driving a rental car. I'm treating it as a vacation, but I have to admit that it's not particularly relaxing."

"I know the feeling. I know I'm safe here, unless the killer has planned a missile strike. There's nobody coming and going."

"Good plan."

"Actually, Lisa was just here a couple of days back. She showed up unannounced in a helicopter. My guards lit her up like a Christmas tree with those red dots they have on their rifles."

"What did she want?"

"Advice."

David was tactful enough not to pry. "I'm glad you're okay. Just don't leave your island."

What was she doing? Lying there whimpering like a kicked dog. That wasn't her. Aria Eiffel was a smart, beautiful, resourceful fighter. She didn't demur. She rallied the troops, set the agenda, and called the shots.

She sat up, then stood up as steel filled her spine. "I'm going to phone Tory now. Take care, David."

Aria changed out of her swimsuit and into a fluffy white robe. *Time to call my contract killer.*

Tory didn't answer.

She couldn't leave a message because this was one of their special phones. She threw the cell onto the bed and turned to the bathroom. She wanted to hit the shower. It would help clear her mind and give her something to do. But first she walked to the entrance and placed her palm on the glass pad, activating the lock-down feature that sealed off her suite. She had to make that a habit now, engaging it whenever she'd be in her room for more than a few minutes.

Clicks and swooshes ensued, giving her partial peace of mind.

She dropped the robe on the floor and walked naked to the shower. It was the walk-in kind that could both bring a deluge from above and spray you from three sides. Kind of a standing massage. Aria stepped in and let the warm water pound away.

Part of her wanted to stand there for as long as it took to be safe, but of course that was impossible. What should she do next? The panic room was equipped to support her for a month. She could literally live there quite comfortably, safe as an eaglet high up in a tree.

To some that would have sounded like salvation, but to her the thought was not appealing. That was a retreat, whereas her nature was to advance. Aria Eiffel lived by making the world bend to her demands, not by caving. Add to that the fact that she'd go stir crazy locked in a concrete cage with no one but ghosts to keep her company, and she rejected that option outright.

But what if Tory didn't answer? Not later tonight, not tomorrow. Then again, what if he did? Lisa had tried to disappear, and somehow she'd been killed en route. Murdered in her own plane. How did you kill just one person on a plane—and get away with it? Surely everyone aboard would be suspect? Was there a way to get the details? Of course there was. She could travel to San Clemente and splash some money around. But would it make her feel better, knowing that the killer had once again outwitted everyone? No, it would not.

What would make her feel better?

She turned off the shower and dried herself with a thick white towel from the warming rack. It was a wonderful luxury, caressing your wet body with warm organic cotton. The little things.

Aria knew she wouldn't feel better until she had a definitive plan of action. She'd always been like that. Why would it be different now? But how could she devise a definitive plan when she couldn't leave her house or confide in anyone who wasn't potentially the killer?

From the bathroom, she walked into her huge closet. She went straight to the back, where she parted the hangers on a rack of lingerie. Silk slips and nighties and other lightweight items. She grabbed the bared bar hard with her right hand and gave it a twist. Once. Twice. When she heard the click she backed away, the clothes bar still in her grasp.

The closet moved with her, as if that entire section of the wall were a door. Once she'd swept it aside, she walked around to the exposed vault entrance and pressed her palm against an adjacent reader. The thick stainless steel responded favorably, sweeping open with a satisfying swoosh.

She walked inside.

The eight-by-ten room looked like Aladdin's cave. Thick shelves were packed high with stacks of currency and weighted down with bars of gold. Glass-topped drawers protected important documents and displayed precious jewels.

Aria ignored the treasure trove and went straight for the gray metal box resting atop a pedestal that had once supported a marble bust. Lifting the lid, she removed the lone item lying on sponge padding. Her Ruger LC9.

As her warm, soft fingers took hold of the cold, hard steel, the elusive answer popped into her head. Just like that, she had it. Not foolproof. Not perfect. But a comfortable, convenient, workable plan.

63
Balanced Account

MIAMI WAS PACKED with funeral homes. I shouldn't have been surprised given the demographics of *the retirement state*. But I was. I'd never noticed them before.

Tory had told us how he picked his partner establishments. "Most funeral homes belong to regional or national chains. I ignore those. Among the independents, I disregard the ones claiming 24-hour service, as I don't want anyone around. From the remainder, I focus on those with the worst Yelp ratings, as they're likely the hungriest. Then I go by location."

We picked one for Tory to use in the demonstration that would confirm his entire story, and he made a couple of calls. The first was to offer Murdoch a fee in exchange for a reference. There was some risk in letting Tory talk to an accomplice, but I did the dialing, and Skylar had the omelet pan heated and ready throughout.

The second call, placed two hours later, went to their target operation, the Flowers Funeral Home. It proceeded as Tory had predicted. But then a call was just a call. Skylar and I wouldn't have proof positive until we found the light left on above an unlocked door.

The three of us pulled into Flowers' parking lot just after midnight. Skylar drove while I sat in back with my Sig pressed to Tory's ribs.

"Not a car in the lot. No sign of police on the surrounding blocks. Are you satisfied?" Tory asked, his tone strained.

I didn't have to guess why his voice was starting to give. The Finnish assassin's face was cooked-lobster red, and the boils that covered it were turning crusty yellow. It was painful just to look at him, particularly his left eye. "We'll call the police from inside. Our presence will add credibility."

It was obvious that Tory didn't like my plan.

I knew why.

He was banking on the accusations against him sounding absurd. No doubt he had concocted a tale of assault that made him the victim. Something that sounded more credible than talk of elaborate cons to replace anonymous clients.

But apparently he was also too tired to argue.

I didn't know what technique the assassin was employing, but beyond being remarkable it had to be draining. Tory hadn't screamed or wailed once. He hadn't shed a single tear. Maintaining that discipline had to be depleting his secret reservoir.

Once we parked, I went around to pull our captive out onto the pavement. His ankles were still bound, but I had added a link between the straps so he could hobble. With the hotel room tai chi performance fresh in my mind, I had tripled-up on the zip ties for both ankles and hands.

We stood in silence for a second, the moon shining down, the city asleep. All of us aware of our surreal circumstance.

"This is so déjà vu," Skylar said, looking my way. "I'm glad you're beside me rather than five minutes behind."

The Flowers Funeral Home didn't have a covered glass walkway leading to its outbuilding. The crematory stood separate, like a garage with its own entrance.

I tried the door. It was unlocked.

"Satisfied?" Tory asked, taking his final shot.

I ignored the question and looked inside. The lights were on and the inner door was ajar. "No metal detector."

"As I told you, Murdoch was an exceptionally cautious man."

We hobbled inside.

I glanced at Skylar as the door closed behind us.

She nodded.

I turned back to Tory, looked him in his one functioning eye, and stuck a needle in his thigh. I didn't push the plunger. I waited for him to register what was going on.

The eye told me that he understood. His lips followed. "Go ahead."

I shook my head. "What will you give me to push the plunger?"

Tory's iris widened.

"I know you haven't told me everything. Not even close. I'll give you two minutes to fill in the blanks. Otherwise, you're going in the oven without the needle."

"Which is exactly what you deserve," Skylar added.

Tory leaned his head back as if recoiling in disgust, then he launched his forehead at my nose like a catapulted rock.

I was expecting a big loogie of spittle rather than a physical attack, but in any case my reflexes were primed and prepared. I pushed back hard and I pushed back fast, pressing my left palm against the center of my adversary's chest while my legs sprang into action.

The head-butt missed with an inch to spare.

Tory, hobbled and unbalanced, fell on his hindquarters and bound wrists. I kicked the falling thug under his chin, sending him flat onto his back. Then I rolled him over onto his belly, and tried to force his ankles into the small of his back.

He resisted, knowing the hog-tie was coming.

I rose and kicked him twice where his ribs met his waist, hard enough to splinter bone.

He still resisted.

I pictured Lars as Tory pushed him into the oven, then I kicked again. That did the trick.

With Tory trussed up like a pig, I studied the syringe on the floor. It was still full, but the needle was missing. "It's your lucky day, Tory. I've got another syringe, if you'd like to earn it."

When our captive spoke, his voice was unexpectedly calm and even. Apparently he'd summoned the last of his reserves. "I'm Tory Lago, son of Aaro Lago, and I'm a Viking. I have no interest in fading away. Much better to go out in a blaze of glory."

Even coming from Mr. Tai Chi, I couldn't believe what I was hearing. This wasn't a theoretical discussion. "There is no glory. This is punishment for what you've done, pure and simple."

"No glory?" This time Tory spit the words. "Could you do it?" Tory swiveled his neck in Skylar's direction. "Could you, Miss Fawkes? I think not. I think you lack both the strength and the discipline."

I hoisted the Viking into a cardboard coffin, then slid it onto the casket bearer. While Tory struggled to see me over his shoulder and the rim, I raised the platform level with the mouth of the cremation retort.

Tory remained passive throughout. Dignified some might say.

"Last chance," I offered.

"Get on with it. I'm eager to see the other side."

Skylar looked at me.

I nodded.

She stuck Tory with the second syringe, but he jerked violently and again broke off the needle before any of the antipsychotic was administered.

We didn't bother with the third and final syringe. I slid the assassin into the open oven—but didn't hit the button.

Tory had walked away once when Skylar and I were on the ground. Now, we would be even.

64
Forward Momentum

THE NORTH PALM BEACH executive aviation facility where Aria kept her jet and tiltrotor looked more like a Southern estate than a suburban airport. With a full frontal colonnaded porch and matching balcony above, Pierce half expected to be met by a maid in an apron as he walked into reception.

He was greeted by a concierge resembling a soldier instead. A bulky uniformed man holding two paper shopping bags. "Mr. DuBois, if you'll come with me please. Mr. Hume is already here."

So David would be flying with him.

When Aria called to invite him to her island fortress, she had insisted on arranging travel from the mainland. Pierce had timed his flight from Whitefish accordingly. Apparently, David had been told to arrive at the same time.

The soldierly concierge escorted Pierce to a private lounge, where he found his traveling companion reading an old green book. As Pierce walked in, David closed it, exposing the cover. *An Enquiry Concerning Human Understanding.* The landmark book by his namesake. "Feeling philosophical?" Pierce asked, holding out his hand.

David rose and they shook. "If not now, then when?"

The concierge stepped forward and handed each Immortal a bag. "Please change into these, and place everything you're wearing now into the bag, including watches, shoes, and your tighty-whities." He retreated to stand with his back to the door.

"You're planning on watching us change?" Pierce asked.

"I take Ms. Eiffel's security very seriously."

"I can see that," Pierce said.

He looked at David, who shrugged. "A sensible

precaution."

Their new wardrobes consisted of khaki shorts with pockets sewn shut, white polo shirts, and sandals.

"I'll store your clothes and personal items here."

As David returned his full bag, the concierge held it out and open. "You'll need to leave the book."

David dropped it into the bag. "Probably not the first time it's been banned."

Satisfied, the concierge opened the door, revealing another large man in similar soldierly attire. The first handed the second their bags and then led them back through reception and out onto the tarmac where Aria's AW609 was waiting.

The tiltrotor aircraft looked like a standard small private jet, except that it had two 26-foot triple-bladed propellers instead of twin jet engines. At the moment, those propellers faced the sky like helicopter rotors. "Flight time's just twenty minutes," the concierge said, noting their stares. "Four times faster than a regular bird."

They boarded and took the two rear seats, which were of the standard small private jet sort. Plush cream-colored leather with lots of buttons.

The concierge boarded too. He sat facing them.

"You don't think we're keeping eyes on each other?" David asked.

"How do I know you're not working together?"

Pierce hadn't considered that possibility. All of their discussions had focused on identifying an individual. What if the killer was a team? Could David and Aria be working together? Had they fallen in love? Did they want to start the ruling family? Eos had made them infertile, but what if David had devised a workaround? Was that what he'd been up to the past twenty years?

Pierce looked over at David. "Is this flight the beginning or the end?"

"I was just thinking the same thing. It's got to be one or the other. I assume you received the same call I did? Aria asking to sequester us together until we devise a solution."

"I did. And I have to admit, it seems like a sensible plan."

The propellers revved to full speed and the aircraft lifted straight up. The feel was slightly different from a helicopter. A bit more stable. And with twice the engine, there was twice the noise. They could still speak since they were seated close together, but only with raised voices.

The pilot took them about a thousand feet straight up, then paused and started flying horizontally. Pierce watched through the window while the propeller housings rotated to face straight forward. The transition was a smooth and seamless experience for the user. Once the blades were locked perpendicular to the ground, the aircraft accelerated. He watched the bulkhead readout zip past 300 mph. They began doing double the best speed that his helicopter could muster.

Pierce inclined his head toward David and spoke so that the soldier couldn't overhear. "It's turned out like everything else, don't you think?"

The vague non sequitur didn't tax David's mind. "Immortality?"

"Yeah. It looks like the solution to all your problems, the thing that will bring you everlasting happiness. Until you get it. Then your mind adapts and resets, and you find yourself faced with a new and equally compelling set of wants and wishes."

"I see I'm not the only one feeling philosophical."

"As you said, this has to be either the beginning or the end."

Pierce began playing with the seat buttons, adjusting the footrest and lumbar support. "Even putting our current predicament aside, it's been disappointing. Don't get me wrong, I wouldn't give it up. In fact, I'd do anything to keep it. But after the first few years..." He shrugged.

"I know what you mean."

"It's not different for you?"

"Why would it be?"

"Eos was your creation. Your achievement. I'd think that would bring a whole other set of emotions into play. You didn't get the fame, but you're still the first man to walk on the moon, so to speak. That has to be profoundly gratifying."

"You're comparing me to Armstrong. At the time, I might have agreed with you. But to your earlier point, a better comparison might be Oppenheimer or Nobel."

Pierce hadn't considered that potential perspective. It introduced a whole new calculus. A change in engine hum indicated that he'd have to work the math later.

The aircraft slowed.

Pierce watched out the window as the props rotated upward until they resembled helicopter blades. Then the AW609 began to descend. He couldn't see Seven Star, as it was directly below them and they were still flying at considerable height.

For a few tense seconds, Pierce feared an explosion. The eruption of the great ball of flame that would engulf him and David along with their aircraft, leaving Aria the sole survivor. But the blast never came, and the tiltrotor touched down.

As he disembarked behind David, Pierce felt the strongest sensation that he'd never leave. He paused right there, his feet still on the steps. What would happen if he turned around, if he insisted on returning to the mainland? The answer was obvious. He'd be exactly where he was before, in an untenable position. No, there was only one sensible direction. Forward.

Like Neil Armstrong, he took a figurative leap by putting one foot on the ground.

65
Spicy

IT TOOK SKYLAR AND CHASE a while to figure out how to place a tracer on an email. They tried doing a simple lookup using a paid service, but it just directed them back to the software provider's headquarters in Buffalo, New York. In the end, they subscribed to a commercial service used by companies to track promotional campaigns. It promised to tell them when and where their email was opened.

They composed and sent the email as a one-recipient campaign from Tory2233@hushmail.me. The program then opened up what it called Worldview, a global map where opens and clicks would populate with color-coded pins.

Skylar leaned back in her chair. If the email wasn't opened immediately, she figured it could easily be hours. Maybe even days. But she was hopeful, since Tory had primed Aria with his call.

They were back in a chain hotel room. This one further from the water, thanks to the prices on Miami Beach. Chase's card had been rejected—over his limit he was sure —so it had gone on hers. She added money to her growing list of problems, but without bitterness.

Justice had been served.

Chase had shocked her three times when suggesting his plan for Tory. First with the capture, then with the interrogation, and finally with the payback. Crash! Bam! Boom! They were the three most violent events of her life.

Except for her own near-cremation.

And that, of course, was the point. Fighting fire with fire.

"There are times when ideology should reign supreme, and times when you have to drop to their level to win. Do you want to win?" Chase had asked, sincerely giving her the choice.

She did not regret her decision.

But she was a bit nervous about the new status quo. Chase had assured her that there was a code among intelligence officers, and it would keep Tory in check. Their Finnish foe was now honor bound to respect their balancing act. He would not seek revenge, Chase asserted.

To illustrate his argument with an example, Chase had pointed out that intelligence agencies never targeted the families of their rival officers. They didn't kidnap children. They didn't threaten spouses. For centuries the rule had remained inviolate even between the bitterest of rivals. Skylar had to acknowledge both the existence and the power of the code, and was further comforted by the knowledge that Tory would be stuck in a hospital until this was over. Nonetheless, she retained a nagging feeling.

At that moment, in that lull between storms, as her adrenaline ebbed and her energy rebounded, she found herself battling waves of powerful emotions. They were churning inside her, swaying her this way then that, ever closer to overload.

Chase returned from the bathroom to stand behind her. "No flag on the map yet." It wasn't a question. He could see the screen. "I'm thinking about calling in an order to that Chinese place we saw down the street. Would that work for you?"

Skylar struggled to reorient herself. Food had been the furthest thing from her mind. "You need my credit card?"

"I figure I'll give Tory's Amex a try. Not much risk with takeout. There are a hundred hotels around here." His expression changed as his eyes fixed on hers. Now they were the sweetest shade of blue. And so incredibly kind. "Hey, are you all right?"

She felt a sob welling up from deep within. One of those uncontrollable releases of emotional energy that usually attack at the climax of good dramatic movies. She found herself standing as she struggled to suppress it. Without thinking, she wrapped her arms around Chase's neck and pulled his lips to hers.

He remained a bit rigid at first. No doubt he had his own

conflicting emotions. But her body just powered through, the way it always did when meeting resistance. Her hands ran over his back and through his hair while her mouth worked of its own accord, desperately trying to satisfy an appetite deep within, regardless of cost or consequence.

His gears kicked in before she needed to come up for breath.

Soon his hands leapt into action. Outside her clothes at first, then within. Caressing, petting, pulling, and squeezing. Her shirt flew off, followed by her bra. Pants dropped as they toppled onto the bed, mouths still melded. The fervid kisses continued as their feet began kicking in clumsy attempts to jettison the garments that still clung to their hungry flesh.

Once all their skin was sufficiently exposed, their legs intertwined and a rhythmic motion developed. But he didn't go in. When she reached the point where she couldn't take it any more he pulled away and looked her in the eye. His eyes were bright with desire but tinged with concern. She whispered the answer to his unasked question. "Yes."

He slipped inside and engaged the electricity, a buzzing in her intimate areas that radiated outward in pulses of bright pink light. She closed her eyes and clenched his back, riding her own pent-up emotion as much as his beautiful body. The pulsing grew faster and stronger, slapping her with wave after wave until her world exploded and her body spasmed and she writhed beneath the pleasant tremor of passions released.

He clung tightly until her body went limp and her lungs regained their ability to breathe deeply.

When she finally opened her eyes, Skylar found Chase staring at her, wearing a warm smile. He was propped up on one elbow, his left leg still draped over hers. "You're a dream," he said.

She pulled him close and kissed his lips and it started all over again. A bit less frantic, but ultimately equally satisfying and intense.

The next time she opened her eyes, her tension had vanished. It had vacated her heart and left contentment behind. Almost like giving birth, she imagined. Then her stomach rumbled and they both laughed.

"You said something about Chinese food?"

His reaction surprised her. He tilted his head and grew a broad grin. "You know from now on that's going to be our thing. Someone we're with will suggest Chinese food and we'll be giggling all the way to the bedroom."

Skylar felt another pulse of pink light. He'd just referenced a shared future. Could this be happening? Could it continue? So many questions. Good questions this time. "I love that you think that way." *Oops, she'd said the L word.* She quickly followed up. "I'll take the mapo doufu, please."

"So you like your Chinese spicy?" he said with a wink.

She smiled and stole a quick kiss. "I do."

As Chase rolled off the bed, her computer pinged. Skylar sat up and saw that a single pin had appeared. The email had been opened. On the big map, it wasn't far from their current location. But it also wasn't on land.

66

Strange Arrangement

THE TILTROTOR disgorged David and Pierce into the company of two more guards, both unabashedly brandishing HK MP5s. The one to David's right addressed them. "Please follow me, gentlemen. Ms. Eiffel is expecting you."

"I'd hate to think what would have happened if we hadn't been expected," Pierce said.

"All your worries would have disappeared," David said, forcing a smile.

They marched through the house toward the owner's suite in the back. Marching was the right word, David thought, given how they were sandwiched between men wearing combat boots.

They could see Aria working on her laptop through a doorway that resembled the entrance to a vault. She looked up at the sound of their approach. "Welcome to my safe suite," she said, rising to meet them while closing her computer.

The soldiers peeled off to the side as the guests entered hallowed ground. Once the two Immortals passed her threshold, Aria pressed her palm against a glass plate installed in the wall. The door swung slowly shut, closing them in with a gas-expelling *whoosh*.

To David's eye, the central room of Aria's safe suite mirrored the main room of many modern estates. A full kitchen complete with a long granite island covered the back wall. Luxurious eating and lounging areas occupied the middle, with more intimate seating areas off to the sides. Everything was oriented toward a breathtaking view over her picturesque pool and private beach of sugary sand.

David's focus moved to the middle of the room, where a

table was set for a seven-star feast. Steaming lobsters and chilled oysters and a rainbow of fresh fruits. Wines and juices to the right. Prime rib to the left. Salads and starters and a tiered silver tray full of sweets on the far side.

"The refrigerators and pantry are also fully stocked," Aria said. "We'll be quite comfortable for a week. If it looks like we'll need more time, I'll have a second round brought in."

"More time for what, exactly?" Pierce asked, as Aria settled back into her lounger and they took opposite chairs. "What do you expect the three of us to accomplish?"

David gestured toward the sumptuous table in the center of the room. "She's interrogating us, albeit in seven-star style. It's a simple but effective tactic. You lock people in a room long enough, and they start talking. They can't help it. Ask any police detective."

"It's a brainstorming session," Aria corrected. "The police don't serve lobster and Champagne. And I'm delighted to say that it may all prove to be unnecessary. I just got an email from Tory."

"An email?" Pierce clarified. "That's a first for Tory. Isn't he Mr. Security?"

"He called first to find out if I knew why Felix wasn't answering his phone. Of course I told him. Then he dropped the bomb."

Aria stopped there, savoring the moment while they squirmed forward in their seats. "He told me he knows the killer's identity."

"Who?" Pierce asked, packing a load of excitement into just one word.

"He refused to say over the phone. He wanted to meet."

"That sounds like a trap," Pierce said.

"My thought exactly. So I said he could email me the name if he couldn't talk on the phone."

"And?"

"He said he'd consider it. That was hours ago. But he just did. Sort of. I'm glad I opened it. I've gotten a few junk emails today, so I almost deleted it outright." She lifted the lid of her laptop and read. "It's not a person, it's an organization. The one you'd least suspect."

"Does he reiterate his request for a meeting?"

Aria rotated the computer around on her lap to show them the screen. "No, that's it."

Pierce leaned in. "It's pretty vague. Sounds like he's trying to provoke a reaction. Get you to request a meeting."

David reached for his phone. When his hand found the soft fabric of a sewn-shut pocket, he remembered that they'd surrendered everything back on the mainland. "I got a call from Tory, too. But I didn't answer."

"Why not?" Aria asked.

"I wasn't in the mood to talk about replacements."

Pierce harrumphed. "Apparently that's not what he wanted."

"Who could have guessed?" David turned from Pierce back to Aria, then nodded at the laptop. "How do you plan to reply to Tory?"

"Invite him here," Pierce suggested. "Let him get that warm reception from your security staff. Then we'll interrogate him in person."

David shook his head. "Tory is a first-rate soldier and tactician. He will arrive with overwhelming force—if he's up to something. Personally, I can't imagine why he'd want to be deceitful or antagonistic. We're his gravy train."

"Maybe he's figured out that he can blackmail us into giving him the whole railroad." Pierce held up a finger as an idea struck. "Don't give him the name of the island, just the airport in North Palm Beach. Bring him here the same way you brought us. Preferably blindfolded."

Aria's stomach grumbled. She blushed and rose to her feet. "Gentlemen, please fill a plate. I spent an hour watching them prepare that feast. Clearly, my willpower has reached its limit. We'll get to Tory once we've fueled our brains."

"Sounds good to me," David said, rising. A lobster had caught his eye. He grabbed it along with a candle-warmed pot of drawn butter and made his way to the small round dining table set for three. A crisp white card had his name printed in script, an artifact of Aria's fastidiousness. He set the lobster down and returned to the buffet where he filled a smaller plate with Caesar salad. "Who else is drinking Champagne?"

"You read my mind," Aria said.

"What the heck. I'll switch to Bordeaux later," Pierce said, looking up from the prime rib where he was working a long silver carving knife.

David found it odd that Aria had allowed such a formidable weapon into her sanctuary. Perhaps it was a test. Or perhaps this whole arrangement was more than it seemed.

67
Alternative Approaches

SKYLAR'S BODY was still basking in the afterglow of her amorous outburst as she grabbed her laptop off the desk and returned to the bed beside Chase. Laying it on her bare legs, she noted with some pride that they remained tanned and toned despite her recent lack of exercise. Well, *training,* she corrected.

Chase stood up, causing her stomach to flutter.

Their relationship had crossed the big river, and she wanted to spend some time sunning on the grass. She wanted to find out if it felt as good as it had looked from the other side. If it didn't, she told herself that would be fine. Disappointing but fine. Moving on without taking any time to feel the sand between their toes, however, would be a blow.

She wasn't ready for another kick right now.

Chase pulled on his boxers and snuggled back in beside her, keeping the glow alive. He put an arm around her shoulders and studied the pin that had popped onto her screen, bringing an abrupt end to their first intimate encounter. "That's not a good sign. Looks like a default, the equivalent of an error message. Can you zoom in?"

"Maybe Aria's on a yacht," Skylar said, enjoying his warmth while working the touchpad.

She moved back and forth between zooming in and re-centering until the scale was city size. "It's an island."

One more click revealed the name.

"Seven Star Island," Chase read aloud. "That makes sense. I should have thought to Google it when we got Aria's email address."

Skylar typed in Seven Star and got millions of hits. "It wouldn't have helped."

"Try *Aria Seven Star.*"

Skylar did. They studied the output. "Just garbage. Any more ideas?"

"Tory said he could never find anything on his employers. He explained how he searched and why, and I believed him. But he never had a location, just photos and first names."

"Right. He said they were clearly meticulous about keeping off the grid, and speculated that they'd invested in a serious internet cleanup operation."

Chase raised a finger. "There's one place that cleanup operations can't reach, and that's the NSA archives. The National Security Agency keeps records of cached web pages, kind of like computer backups for the internet. Rumor is they've subcontracted this to Google, but I don't know if that's true. In any case, I can see if Lesley will run an archive search on *Aria Seven Star.* We might get lucky."

Chase retrieved his laptop and began typing.

Skylar waited for him to hit SEND before asking, "Does it matter at this point? Now that we know where to find Aria."

"It might. Although we're definitely going to Seven Star Island, one way or another, I'd like to know what to expect when we get there. Aria might well be a Latin American drug lord, or an East European human trafficker, or an African arms dealer. The only thing we know about her at this point is that she paid a Finnish assassin a lot of money to make people with specific physical descriptions disappear without a trace. The CIA, with all its tricks and toys, would never initiate an infiltration operation with such a paucity of information."

Skylar had never really considered the drug-lord or human-trafficking or arms-dealing options. She'd never really considered the demographics of her assailant at all, beyond *charming con man.* As a professional, Chase had an entirely different perspective. He took the pragmatic block-and-tackle approach of an operative. She needed to start thinking that way too. "How will additional information impact our approach?"

Chase repositioned himself so he was sitting cross-legged

on the bed and they could speak face to face. "It's a question of tactics. Do we make a stealthy assault in the middle of the night, or sail in during the day and knock on the door? Do we take a boat or helicopter—assuming that Tory's Amex is still working? Do we scuba dive, or saunter off the dock? Do we go in heavy or unarmed?"

Skylar was pleased to see Chase stealing glances at her body. "What do you mean by *going in heavy?*"

"Assault rifles, night vision, an assortment of grenades." His intonation altered as he spoke, no doubt in reaction to her facial expression. "Probably not our best option, given the composition of our team. Actually, I feel kind of silly for even considering it. It's just my default scenario, given my background."

"I understand. But you need to know that I've never fired a pistol, much less an assault rifle. And frankly, I'd be nervous about picking up a grenade. I will do it if that's what you're convinced it takes, but I'm hoping we can come up with something more cerebral."

"Like a frying pan?"

Skylar appreciated the injection of levity, but didn't allow it to deviate her train of thought. "I also hope we'll call the police if Aria turns out to be a drug lord or human trafficker or arms dealer."

"You make some excellent points."

Her stomach rumbled again, breaking the tension.

"Let's go out for dinner. Get some air," he suggested. "With luck, Lesley will have responded by the time we're back."

68
Ultimate Relief

DAVID RAISED HIS GLASS as the others took their seats. Given the table's small size, it was easy for them to clink. "To the future."

"To the future," they repeated.

He cracked a claw and forked out the meat, retaining the semicircular shape. One of the things he'd learned as a man of wealth was how to attack shellfish. He dipped the flesh into the warm butter, then popped the whole thing into his mouth, savoring that sumptuous first bite.

Aria went to work with equal aplomb on a slice of honeydew melon. "Before we discuss a reply to Tory's email, have either of you learned exactly what happened to Lisa?" she asked.

"You were the last to see her, right?" Pierce asked. "She paid you a visit?"

"Yes. She showed up unannounced. It provided a timely test for my security contingent. They detected her approach from half an hour out and tracked her all the way here."

David set his fork down softly on the white tablecloth and cleared his throat. He'd hoped to finish his lunch before having this conversation, but it seemed silly to trifle now that Aria had teed it up. "Lisa was killed with a neurotoxin. Batrachotoxin to be precise. An injector hidden in her seat was activated by a trip-switch calibrated to her weight, 120 to 130 pounds. It triggered when the attached altimeter indicated that her G650 had crossed into long-range cruising altitude, 45,000 feet. Ironically, it was her attempt to escape that killed her. Hopefully she died in her sleep."

"You have a contact at the Orange County Sheriff's Department?" Pierce asked, visibly impressed.

David wetted his throat with a swallow of Champagne.

"No. That's just how I designed it. Her seat, her weight, a long-range flight. Safety measures designed to ensure that there wouldn't be an innocent victim."

Pierce's eyes went wide, then turned toward his steak knife. It was the hefty kind, with a riveted hardwood handle and a sharp serrated edge.

"Same thing with Allison?" Aria asked, her voice strained but steady.

"No. I strapped a canister of anesthetic under her seat and triggered it directly. I was in the car right behind hers. I'd phoned her agent with a fake urgent audition to get her going fast on the right road. She fell asleep and the laws of physics did the rest."

"She was innocent!" Pierce shouted. "How could you kill that innocent girl?"

David wiped his lips with a linen napkin. "None of us are innocent, Pierce. Twenty years ago, we killed Kirsten to keep our secret. This year we plotted to kill nine more people to maintain it. In another twenty years, we'd have done it again. Ad infinitum. We're all mass murderers."

Pierce grabbed the knife.

David looked directly into his bulging eyes. "And what are we giving the world in exchange?"

Pierce gritted his teeth, but stayed silent.

Startled by the sanctimony of David's scathing accusations, Aria didn't answer either.

"We're not contributing anything," David continued. "We're living off old money. Collectively, our current lives aren't worth a single one of those we're stealing, much less the tens and hundreds and thousands that we'd eventually have sacrificed. And for what?"

Again David paused.

Again neither answered.

"Have you ever stopped to ask yourself why we deserve to be immortal? Why we should be at the apex of human evolution? Look at us. Look at what we're doing. We're contributing *nothing*." He brought his fist down, rocking the table as at long last he let a little of his rage release.

"It's not a question of deserving," Pierce said, his own

anger barely in check. "We're doing what people always do, and have always done. All people, throughout all of history. We're seizing an opportunity."

"Yes, we are. Is it making you happy, Pierce? Aria?" David swiveled his head like a tank turret as he released the verbal barrage. "Are you in better spirits than you were before I put Eos in your veins? Is that additional glee enough to outweigh the joy you took from the world when you replaced a fellow human being?"

As he studied their stunned faces, David got the impression that he might be breaking through. That his pointed questions and perfect logic stood a chance of hitting home.

"We don't have to keep replacing people. We could go with the less secure solution, if that's what this is all about," Pierce said, practically spitting the words. "I don't remember you taking a mighty moral stance before the big vote— when it would have been productive."

"I do," Aria said, her voice now soft with shock. "Three times David tried to dissuade us, but it was eight to one. So he gave in, and went along."

"Better you had fought us then, in the open, than snipe at us now, in secret," Pierce said. "You're a coward."

David took a deep breath, and willed his blood pressure down. He exhaled slowly, then spoke in a calm voice. "Immortality was a great experiment. But the data is in. We have twenty years' worth. We were the best of society going in. Hard working, highly educated, well intentioned, Mensa members. Honest, forthright, and ambitious. Then we gained the ultimate prize. What happened? We stopped contributing to society and morphed into murderers."

Pierce's face faded from red to pale.

Aria started streaming tears. "You're the killer. You killed Allison and Lisa and Camilla. Felix and Ries and even Eric, your best friend. You killed your best friend, David. First of all."

Pierce hopped in before David could respond, his voice on the verge of hysteria. "The replacements are almost complete. Why now? Why not wait another twenty years?

By then we'd all have lived average lifespans, more or less."

David bowed his head. "I was afraid I'd weaken if I waited. Talking myself into taking your selfish attitude would be the easiest thing in the world. The day we voted in favor of replacements, I knew what I had to do. I'd brought this scourge on the planet, so it was up to me to eradicate it. I didn't want to kill. I don't want to die. But what I want is insignificant compared to the collective need. That's what every hero understands."

Aria gasped. "You think you're a hero?"

"I think I have a lot to make amends for. Like Oppenheimer and Nobel. But even knowing that, I struggled. I procrastinated by devising elaborate plans, so everyone could pass painlessly while happy, rather than crouched in a corner hiding from a gun."

"Why didn't you just set off a bomb at the last meeting?" Pierce asked. "I'm sure you know how to build one of those."

David turned to face the financier. "I considered it. In fact, that was my first impulse—albeit with something more elegant. But as I thought it through, I realized how important it was to spread our deaths around. A mass killing of affluent people like us would lead to an extensive investigation, increasing the odds that our special status would be discovered and our research ultimately replicated. Then some other group would be back where we started, endangering the planet. And we'd have died in vain."

He turned to Aria. "As for Eric, I killed him first so I wouldn't lose my nerve. I knew that if I murdered my best friend, I'd never go back—and the planet would be safe. So I did my homework, then secretly repacked his parachutes.

"Camilla was next. She inhaled a dose of anesthetic, and passed away in her sleep. And so on. You know the details."

Rather than respond with words, Aria conjured up a gun. She probably had it strapped to the bottom of the table. That explained the name cards.

She pointed it at his chest with a practiced grip. "Pierce and I will be keeping your philosophical ramblings in mind —for the next thousand years."

David noted her stance, then studied the black mouth of the unwavering barrel. The safety was off, and a little red flag indicated a chambered round. He wondered when she'd acquired shooting skills.

Aria read his mind. "All that practice with paper targets, but until this moment, I didn't know if I'd have the courage to shoot a person when the time came. Now I know that I needn't have worried. As I point this gun at your heart, the only thing I'm feeling is relief."

LESLEY HAD NOT REPLIED by the time Skylar and I returned to our room after dinner. We'd dined on seafood instead of Chinese, selecting a trendy beachfront restaurant with beautiful views and a vibrant atmosphere instead of grabbing takeout. All successfully charged to Tory's Amex seconds before we skedaddled out the door.

While I was eager to hear if the CIA's cached internet search would shed light on Aria and her island, the slow response was probably a blessing. Our day had been very long and incredibly momentous. It was time to get some sleep.

I wanted to climb beneath the covers beside Skylar, but hesitated to assume. And since our love-making tension-releasing sessions had been in her bed, I couldn't climb into mine and let her decide. Hers was the de facto shared bed.

I decided to punt. "You can use the bathroom first. I'll do a bit of research. Look into yacht charters."

"I was thinking about a bath," Skylar replied.

"Sure. Take your time."

I heard the water start running and then the brushing of teeth, but the door didn't close when the water turned off, and I didn't detect the sound of Skylar settling into the tub. I looked over to see her standing in the bathroom door, wearing only a grin. "I was hoping you'd join me."

I experienced an immediate capillary reaction. Before I knew it, I was kicking my shorts across the bathroom floor.

Refueled by our delicious dinner and once again unhindered by clothes, we kissed with the extreme enthusiasm of kids who'd never locked lips before, hands stroking and heads weaving and bodies bumping about. The first time I came up for breath, I lifted Skylar's naked body onto the bathroom counter. It was scant and slippery but proved just the right height for joining bodies in a second location.

Our third act of love came to a swift conclusion. I wasn't sure if it was practice or just my body signaling that the hour was too late to dillydally.

With her long legs still wrapped around my waist, I carried Skylar into the tub where I slowly dropped to my knees. That went well enough, but I ended up sloshing a wet wave onto the floor as I lowered us into a prone position, drenching our discarded clothes in the process.

While we attempted to get comfortable in the tiny tub, I looked into her eyes. "You're beautiful."

"You're athletic." She winked, and I laughed.

"That's pretty convenient, having the tub topped off and waiting."

"I agree. But I should have put a towel on the counter."

Studying Skylar's smile, I found myself thinking about the future. On impulse, I asked, "What do you want to do next?"

She gave me a *Really, cowboy?* look.

"I mean, after we've beaten these guys. What kind of work will you be looking for?"

She adjusted her position to better meet my eyes. "I wish I knew. By default, it would be something involving physical fitness. But the whole CIA scenario really turned me onto the idea of public service. I haven't figured out how to unite the two yet, but when this is over, I'll head out for a run and keep going until inspiration strikes. How about you?"

"That's what I was supposed to be figuring out right now —on the motorcycle that's rusting away at the bottom of a Ventura County ravine. I know I'm done with government work. For men of my experience, the other obvious employer is a big security firm, but I'm not drawn in that direction either."

Skylar nodded knowingly. "They put Tory on the slippery slope."

"Exactly. So, like you, I'll need to give it a lot of thought. And quickly, given the bills that are about to come due."

I shifted, uncomfortably. My legs were beginning to cramp. "This tub really isn't big enough for two. We need to find a hotel with an oversized spa."

"As long as Tory's Amex is working, there's nothing stopping us."

I wasn't about to pinpoint our overnight location by using the assassin's credit card to reserve a room, but I kept that nugget to myself. Meanwhile, I was glad to have resolved my earlier question about the sleeping arrangement.

We toweled off, hung our sodden clothes to dry, and slid between the sheets. I snuggled up and she shifted toward a spooning arrangement. Fortunately I reacted fast enough to keep my lower arm free, facilitating the inevitable late-night rollover.

It never came. When I awoke, I was right there where I'd been when I closed my eyes.

Skylar's breathing remained regular and deep.

I lay there, thinking about our new romantic arrangement. Could we keep it going? Or would it evolve as vacation romances inevitably did, with geography becoming a wedge? I didn't know.

There was more to it than location, of course.

Skylar was a remarkable woman. Intellectually and physically I found her exceptionally attractive. But I was experienced enough to know that magnetism wasn't powerful enough to forge a lasting relationship. Permanent bonds required similar preferences and perspectives, plus some everyday chemistry. No way to tell what that would be like until we spent some time in everyday situations.

We'd probably never get that.

For financial reasons, both Skylar and I needed to find jobs fast. What were the odds that those jobs would be in close proximity? Not very good.

I decided to ignore that depressing thought for now. My worry plate was already heaped with more than I could eat.

I slid from the sheets as smoothly as possible in an attempt to let Skylar sleep. It worked, so I grabbed my laptop and took it into the bathroom for some multitasking.

Lesley had replied. "Just one hit. Hope it helps," was all

she wrote.

I clicked on the attachment. It was an article from the Living & Lifestyle section of the *Miami Herald,* dated January 2, 2000. "When Five Stars Isn't Enough."

For those readers who didn't score the golden ticket to Seven Star Island this New Year's Eve, allow us to paint you a picture. Hosted by Aria Eiffel, widow of petroleum magnate Jacques Eiffel, the millennial soirée was one to make Julia Roberts swoon and Jay Gatsby blush…

My eyes dropped to the photo montage at the bottom, which included a beachfront buffet stacked high with seafood, dozens of black-tie and ball gown couples dancing beneath fireworks on an outdoor dance floor, and the regal hostess raising her flute of Champagne. That woman was Skylar.

70

The Price

ALTHOUGH HER ARM STAYED STEADY, inside Aria was trembling from a torrent of mixed emotions as she pointed her pistol at David. She was about to bring this nightmare to an end. Permanently and definitively.

Despite her bluster, she dreaded pulling the trigger. David wasn't just a fellow human being; he was her friend.

She studied his face, looking for the madman's sneer or some sign of aggression. She saw neither. Oddly enough, he didn't even look scared. Or remorseful. Or worried. His grand plan had just failed and he was about to die, but his expression hadn't changed since before she'd produced a loaded weapon. "Do you have anything else to say?"

He shrugged and spoke with a voice so level and calm that it sent a shiver down her spine. "I already pulled the trigger."

"What are you talking about? You used gizmos and poisons, but never a gun."

David adjusted his gaze from the gun to her eyes. "I couldn't be certain that any of those would work, much less all of them. With Felix, for example, I bet on a compound fatally interacting with his heart medication. It was a gamble that paid off, but success wasn't guaranteed."

"What are you saying?" Pierce asked, his tone nervous, his steak knife poised to strike. *Let him be the one to draw David's blood,* Aria prayed.

David leaned back in his chair, lacing his fingers behind his head. "In Greek mythology, Eos the rosy-fingered goddess of dawn, opened the gates of heaven so the sun could rise."

Pierce sighed and rolled his eyes.

David ignored him. "Eos was married to Astraeus, the

god of dusk. Together they form the perfect team. She brought out the sun, and he put it away."

Aria felt her stomach fill with ice. "You didn't!"

"Didn't what?" Pierce asked, his voice continuing to crack.

"As you'll likely recall, our Eos works by protecting telomeres, keeping them from shortening. It allows cells to refresh without degrading, thereby halting aging. Astraeus, my more recent invention, does the opposite. It destroys telomeres, preventing cellular reproduction."

Aria dropped her gun arm to her side.

David didn't react to the reduced threat.

"You didn't," she repeated, knowing as surely as day becomes night that he had.

David slowly nodded. "At the last meeting. Everyone got Astraeus instead of Eos."

"Are you telling us we're dying?" Pierce asked. "I'm not sick. I feel fine."

A wry smile creased the right half of David's face. "There's an incubation period as Astraeus spreads, but I'm sure you don't feel fine. You've been experiencing gastrointestinal issues. I certainly have."

"You gave it to yourself as well?" Aria asked, knowing it was true and yet unwilling to believe it. Any of it.

"I had some bad bouillabaisse back in Miami," Pierce protested.

"Intestinal cells have some of the shortest life cycles. As do blood cells. You're beginning to experience the rough equivalent of chemotherapy."

"So we'll survive it," Pierce persisted. "Nobody dies from chemotherapy."

"They would if the treatment never stopped. And Astraeus can't be stopped. The damage is done. I'm afraid it's about to get very painful."

"Painful how?" Pierce asked.

"Picture victims of the Ebola virus."

Aria couldn't believe her ears. She again raised her Ruger. "Why are you doing this? Why are you trying to scare us? What happened to your painless, go happy, humanitarian approach?"

David rocked forward again, almost causing her to pull the trigger. "It's still available."

Aria shuddered to think what that meant.

"If you'll check the refrigerator, you'll find a large vial of morphine hidden in a big jar of apple butter. I also left a bag of brown sugar in the pantry on my last visit. It contains five fat syringes."

"Five?" Aria said, fixating on the incongruous number as her mind strained to find purchase.

"I wasn't certain that Felix would pass or Lisa would flee."

"What are you suggesting?" Pierce said, his left hand now rubbing the back of his neck while his right retained a knuckle-whitening grip on the knife.

David turned back to Aria, exposing the faraway look in his eyes. "It's a beautiful day. You have a perfect pool and comfortable floats. Dismiss your staff and security guards with fat bonuses. Empty the island. Even the yacht captain and helicopter pilot. Send them all home."

Aria felt faint. She dropped the gun and flopped down into her chair.

The Ruger clattered in Pierce's direction, but he didn't pick it up.

"Then what?" she whispered.

"Then we'll finish this fine lunch, change into swimming suits, and drift."

"Send the security home?" Pierce challenged, grasping at the last thread of hope. "You'd like that. How do we know this isn't a trick?"

Aria struggled to retain her dignity while waiting for David's reply.

"Besides feeling it in your gut?" David shrugged. "I'll go first if you like. But as a doctor, I thought you might find it more peaceful if I administered the injections."

71

Engage

SKYLAR AND I DECIDED to take a two-pronged approach to Seven Star Island. Our plan was to start covert and high-tech, then switch to casual and direct.

To prepare for the high-tech portion, we visited an electronics store. After discussing our options with an eager salesman, we charged Tory's employers $1,200 for a DJI Phantom photo drone.

The other main purchase we made over the telephone, rather than in person. This allowed us to swap a diligent in-person ID check for the much less rigorous remote one. I rented the biggest yacht the broker was confident we could handle if docking wasn't involved. A 62-foot Azimut luxury yacht. Just $17,000 for the week, plus a $50,000 security deposit given that we were sailing without the included crew.

I dictated the Amex number, then emailed a scan of Tory's driver's license with my own DL photo superimposed. Hefty stacks of paperwork followed. Rules, regulations, safety procedures, liability disclaimers, and an arbitration agreement. I signed and returned them all—in Tory's name.

With the critical purchases squared away, we moved on to the casual prong of the plan. En route to the marina, we stopped at the Lincoln Road Mall, where Tory's employers graciously outfitted us in shorts, shirts, and sunglasses that cost ten times what either of us would normally have spent.

As we were exiting, I spotted a jewelry store. Acting on a whim, I guided Skylar in and raised the platinum card. "Will you promise not to read anything into it if I suggest that we complete your disguise with a bit of bling?"

Skylar studied my face for a long moment, then broke into a big smile. Forty minutes and a couple of complimentary glasses of Champagne later, we walked out of the shop with an $81,000 receipt, a necklace, a tennis bracelet, and an engagement ring. Skylar held her wrist up to her chest. "What do you think? Will I look at home on a yacht?"

"We might need to extend the rental for a second week. Assuming the card's still working."

"I'm surprised it's worked this long."

"I bet you a diamond ring that the card's on autopay. Might work for years." I flashed my eyebrows.

"I'm pretty sure the ring won't fit you," she replied.

We were enjoying a splash of joviality before facing the danger that lay ahead.

Fully outfitted and looking appropriate, we hired a BMW 7 series through Uber Black to drive us the mile from the mall to the marina. Arriving in anything less just wouldn't do.

The marina wasn't particularly fancy. More like a mid-range restaurant than the gateway to luxury, except that it was up on stilts. But the reception we received was classy and cordial. It began with warm handshakes from the captain, who was about to enjoy a week of paid vacation, and continued with two hours of hands-on instruction on how to handle his baby, the *C'est La Vie*.

Once we both understood the yacht's extensive control system, most of which we'd never touch, Captain Stewart piloted us out of the marina. "On the open water, there's nothing to it. You've got plenty of buffer. Docking is what takes practice. Use this manual"—he grabbed a booklet from beside the captain's wheel—"to radio any marina in the Bahamas or Caribbean. Most will send a pilot out for a modest fee. Believe me, it's worth it." He pointed to a number written in black marker on the manual's front cover. "Call me with any questions. When you're on your way back here, let me know and I'll come out to meet you. Got it?"

"Aye, aye, captain."

He nodded sternly, then headed aft, climbed aboard a trailing dinghy, and left us alone with sixty-two feet of ship and an open ocean.

As he motored away, I felt the weight of what we were attempting come crashing down.

Fortunately, as part of our training, and at Skylar's suggestion, Captain Stewart had plugged Fox Town on Grand Abaco into the navigation system, and set the autopilot. All I had to do to get us there was hit ENGAGE.

Of course, getting there was the easy part.

72

Red Light, Green Light

FOX TOWN was the northwestern-most village on the Bahamian isle closest to Seven Star, which lay about ten miles to its northwest. We sailed straight for it, so as not to alert any radar tracking system Aria might have in place.

While the Azimut's motors churned away under the autopilot's steady hand, Skylar studied the drone. She figured out how to program GPS coordinates into its navigation system, something the store clerk had assured us would not be a problem. Then she practiced precision flying it around the yacht's interior, which consisted of three cabins and two saloons spread over two interior decks.

Meanwhile, I continued to familiarize myself with the helm. It wasn't so very different from the dashboard of a car, once I translated from terrestrial to nautical.

I slowed our speed from twenty knots to two and called back to Skylar as we entered the shallower waters of the island chain. "It's about time. Seven Star is three miles northeast of our current position." Three miles was the outer limit of the drone's transmission range.

We took the drone up to the top deck and Skylar set it down. "Here goes," she said, as it took to the sky. "I've programmed the coordinates. We'll know everything we're going to know in about twenty minutes."

"What happens in twenty?"

"It falls out of the sky. Flight time is twenty-eight minutes max, but it's got wind to contend with, so I figure we can only count on twenty. It will take at least five of those to reach the island."

I was curious and excited to see what we'd find. I'd never been to a private island. Never even laid eyes on one. The owner also intrigued me.

The society page article had described Aria Eiffel as the wealthy and childless widow of a petroleum magnate. She'd been a society belle while her husband was alive but had become reclusive shortly after his death. I figured that if I owned a Bahamian island, I might choose to become a recluse myself—particularly if I had a woman like Skylar by my side. What I couldn't fathom was why Aria had hired Tory.

"What do you think Aria's up to?" Skylar asked, as if reading my mind. We'd been so busy planning and preparing this incursion that we hadn't paused to speculate. "She doesn't need money. She doesn't appear to crave power or prestige. What's left?"

"Health," I suggested.

Skylar mulled that over while the drone gained ground. I knew she'd reached my conclusion when her face contorted. "You mean like organ harvesting for some secret medical procedure?"

"That might explain why lookalikes are required. I'm not an expert on the intricacies of transplantation, but beyond matching blood types I'm sure it's best if the donor is young and of a similar size. By that logic, maybe other appearance-related attributes help make a perfect match."

"If that were the case, Tory would have—" she grimaced, "violated me before shoving me into an oven."

"Maybe before I got there he ran some sort of tissue compatibility test, and you failed."

"He didn't mention anything about tests or tissue compatibility when we interrogated him."

"It was in his best interests to provide the prosecution with as little detail as possible."

"Still seems thin."

"I agree. But we'll learn soon enough, one way or another."

The island came into view after eight minutes, rather than the five the published maximum speed predicted. We knew it was Seven Star by the shape, which was a cross between a kidney bean and a chili pepper, matching what we'd seen on Google.

Skylar had the drone flying at an altitude of 1,000 feet, so it couldn't be heard and wouldn't be noticed with a casual skyward glance. She disengaged the autopilot and began a broad circle.

Half the island was covered with natural vegetation, the other half was landscaped. She narrated, since she was holding the controller with its video screen. "I see two piers, but only one boat and it's a go-fast, not a yacht. The tiltrotor we saw on Google is also gone."

"Sounds like the mistress isn't home."

"Is that good or bad?" Skylar asked.

I waggled my hand. "Could go either way. Depends on the disposition of the people left behind. If there are any."

"You think she'll return anytime soon?"

"I expect so. We know she was there yesterday when she opened our email. With money like that, she probably treats flights to the mainland like you and I do drives to the grocery store. Just part of the daily routine. With a tiltrotor, it would be just as fast."

The drone's remote control beeped after it circled the island twice, then its screen pulsed yellow. "We've reached the return to base limit. In thirty seconds it won't have sufficient power to reach the takeoff point."

"We don't need it back—and neither does Tory."

Skylar elbowed me, but continued to circle.

"I don't see any people. Have you spotted any?" I asked, studying the screen from over Skylar's shoulder.

"Not yet. Should I take it lower?"

"How much battery do we have?"

"Just six minutes. The 28-minute spec is way too optimistic."

"Yes. Start with the secondary structures, which I assume are for guests and servants, including guards."

Skylar took the drone down and inspected the cottages. They were situated in a semicircular formation around the back side of the house, the side away from the beach and the pool. She did a flyby on one side, then the other, peering through windows and one open door. Nothing stirred. No one came into view. "Three minutes."

"Now the main house."

She took the drone halfway around so we could peer into the living room but pulled back and up prematurely when three people appeared on the screen. They were lounging in the part of the pool that was under a sunshade. "The mistress is home."

"Doesn't look like anyone spotted the drone. They'd be looking up if they did. In fact, I think they're sleeping. The guards must be too, if she has any," I added, exposing my wishful thinking.

The remote started pulsing red. "We're down to one minute of battery life. In sixty seconds the drone will automatically land."

"Let's risk a look through the big window at the back."

Skylar made a wide arc, then dropped to a hundred feet and zoomed in on the house. The back window was actually a series of ten heavy-duty sliding glass doors, all parted now to open up the back room. Skylar focused the camera on a scene that looked like a still life oil painting from the time of Henry VIII. A table was piled high with fancy foods on silver service, but there wasn't a soul in sight. Not a waiter. Not a cook.

"Switch back to the people in the pool." The remote turned solid red as I spoke.

"The battery is exhausted," Skylar said. "What do you think?"

"I think it's safe for us to pay a visit."

73

Perfect Sense

TORY'S HEART SANK as he piloted his stolen go-fast boat within sight of Seven Star's two piers. No yachts were docked. No people apparent. That left the tiltrotor he'd seen in Google's satellite shot as his best hope of catching Aria at home, but he couldn't see the helipad from his current position.

Tory had sent half a dozen emails to Aria's address. Emails that would look like junk mail if opened, but ones that would slip through filters since she was the only recipient. He'd sent each from a different email. Fresh accounts from the major public providers.

The tactic worked.

He'd acted the minute he learned her location, knowing that Chase and Skylar would be close behind. This forced him to forgo a hospital stay in favor of a cursory exam and quick clean-up from a concierge doctor. Not a big deal. His left eye remained useless, but what could a doctor do? If surgery was an option he'd have that later. Meanwhile, his right eye was fully functional.

His goal was to make the leap from outside consultant to inside confidant by confronting his employers in person. First he'd show them the battle scars he'd suffered on their behalf; then he'd warn them of the impending threat. Their gratitude and guilt, combined with his obvious value and intimate knowledge, should guarantee him either a sweet contract as their permanent fixer or a payoff suitable for a king's ransom.

The thought of ransom drew his eyes to where his raw wrists rested on the wheel. Breaking out of the oven while hog-tied had been a most unpleasant experience—albeit highly preferable to the alternative.

Chase had played him masterfully. Tory had to give the American credit.

By teaming up with Aria, Tory would also solve the dilemma his charitable captors had created. As things stood, Tory was honor-bound not to pursue the meddlesome couple, despite what they'd done to him. Fair was fair, and he wasn't one to break the code. But if they came to him… well, then the counter reset to zero and the game started anew.

And come to him they would, right there on Seven Star Island.

He managed to dock without attracting attention. Securing the ropes involved a few fast back-and-forth leaps. Nothing too tough, but strenuous enough that he paused afterward to apply a bit more salve to each wrist and ankle. He pulled the burn ointment from his pocket as well, intent on giving his facial wounds a fresh shellacking, but decided to leave them angry. Best to let his employers see the scars in their full glory.

Not really sure what to expect, but full of confidence in his ability to cope come what might, Tory tucked his new handgun into the small of his back and headed up the flagstones toward the house. He spotted no one along the way.

Aria's front door was an intricate ornamental arrangement of glass panes and carved exotic hardwood. Probably cost as much as the average car. He peered through but saw no movement. He looked for a doorbell but didn't find one. Of course. This was a private island.

Walking around to the back, he caught his first manmade sound. A waterfall. Probably a large cascade into an oddly shaped pool, one of those designer types with natural stone accents and romantic grottos. He'd ignored that part of the photo.

Peering around the corner from the inside edge of the flagstone path, he spotted three faces he knew well but had never seen in person. Aria, Pierce, and David. They were seated in floating pool chairs, the kind that looked like contoured chaise longues. Each held a Champagne flute and a large white straw in one hand. All were actively engaged in conversation.

Who drank Champagne from a straw?

Tory took a sidestep into concealing vegetation. The waterfall was drowning out their words, but whatever they were saying, it was obviously fraught with emotion. Faces were scrunching. Tears were streaming. Fingers fidgeted nervously.

He'd picked a bad time.

The discussion stopped while Tory stood contemplating his next move. Some kind of an agreement had been reached, or decision had been made. David placed his Champagne and straw in his cup holder and carefully paddled his chair over next to Aria's.

Now Tory could see that it wasn't a straw. It was a syringe. They looked similar enough from a distance, when you had only one eye.

Aria downed the rest of her Champagne, then dropped the flute in the water. She passed David her syringe and held out her arm.

While he found a vein, she leaned back and closed her eyes.

He completed the injection quickly, then kissed her hand, long and slow. He held onto it while she relaxed. The whole scene resembled some taboo ceremony, and Tory found it fascinating.

He had always known that there was something odd about his clients. The random nature of their replacement requests made no sense. Then there was their lax attitude toward money, which clashed with their extremely disciplined informational security. At last he understood. They'd developed some kind of new narcotic. They were white-collar drug dealers.

Tory felt the thrill of pulling back a big curtain. This new theory explained everything.

They were making money by the boatload, no doubt with elite clientele. Going exclusive was the only way to keep such a special product below the radar. Sure, there would be rumors, but if there were no deaths, law enforcement wouldn't get involved.

The cartels, however, would.

They'd consider any illegal drug to be unacceptable competition. And their preferred method for dealing with competitors was cutting them out. Quite literally. With machetes and chainsaws. Hence his clients' obsession with secrecy and need for identity swaps. It all made perfect sense now.

So what should he do?

He definitely did not want to get tangled up in the narcotics business. Best to hit them hard for a payout, then disappear.

Tory studied Aria. She wasn't moving. He would wait until the others were off in whatever la-la land their product took them to, then he'd put them at his mercy. Nothing painful or even overtly hostile, just precarious enough to make it clear that his offer was one they couldn't refuse.

74

Pointed Argument

SOMEWHAT TO OUR SURPRISE, nobody came running as the *C'est La Vie* approached the big pier on Seven Star Island. How could people so obsessed with their informational security leave their home unguarded?

I knew we'd have that answer within the hour.

I brought the yacht in straight and slow as Captain Stewart had advised, then hit reverse as the bow broke even with the end.

Skylar jumped off and did a masterful job with the ropes, first securing and then tightening them.

"You look like you've done that before," I said, hopping off the yacht to join her.

She linked my arm, playing for the audience if one was watching. "Once or twice, on smaller boats. Triathlons are on the water, so I spent a fair amount of time around boaters. Occasionally I scored an invitation."

The pier was long and large, designed to accommodate yachts twice our size. We walked along it toward the seagrass-speckled shore, wearing hats and sunglasses, armed only with our drone's remote control.

Following the KISS principle, we had decided to present ourselves as boaters retrieving a downed drone. It was a plausible scenario given the propensity of the leisure class to play with expensive toys.

We followed the flagstone path around the side of the house, through the manicured garden, and toward the pool where the drone had shown people lounging.

"What exactly should we say?" Skylar asked.

"We can start with 'Sorry to disturb you. We just need to pick up our drone.' Then we'll try to charm them into talking."

"How should I act?"

The burbling swish of cascading water grew louder as we closed in on the pool. It camouflaged our conversation, but I kept my voice quiet anyway. "Act like a pampered society girl with good genes. Compliment the house and garden. Ask about activities in this area. The best places for snorkeling. Restaurants on nearby islands. Stuff like that. Luxurious as it is, living here has to be lonely. If we come across as friendly members of the club, it shouldn't be hard to get them talking."

"What do we want them talking about?"

"In a word—Aria. The goal is to get her measure and take the lay of the land in preparation for a future confrontation."

We rounded the side of the house and came face-to-face with Tory, who was walking in our direction. He held an aluminum briefcase in each hand and had a big black duffel slung over one shoulder. The Finn looked just as surprised as I was when our eyes met. But his reaction was quicker.

Before I knew it, one of the briefcases was spinning toward my head. I ducked as Tory lunged.

Skylar was not so lucky.

As I dodged left, my ears were struck by the sound of a projectile smacking bone. I stole a sideward glance and saw my partner drop like a ripe coconut. She was undoubtedly unconscious, but whether stunned or dead, I couldn't tell. Nor could I check. Not at that moment. Not if we were to survive the assassin's wrath.

Tory didn't immediately continue his attack. In fact, he backed off.

For a second, we sized each other up like gladiators waiting for the king to commence our battle. Then Tory grinned and reached around to the small of his back.

He came out with nothing but a puzzled expression. Clearly he'd gone for a gun that was missing.

I am not a boxer or a wrestler or a martial artist. I rowed crew in college. But standing two steps from Skylar's limp body while staring at our would-be killer, I found myself feeling entirely different than I had the last time Tory and I had grappled. This time I was fueled by all the world's anger —and half an idea.

Tory had a weakness. A sore spot. A chink in his armor. His left eye was painfully swollen and probably sightless. Surely I could capitalize on that.

But how?

I circled right, moving into the blind spot and forcing him to adapt. Tory was new to the whole blind-in-one-eye thing, especially when it came to combat. That had to be disconcerting, although I wouldn't put it past the fitness freak to have honed some eyes-closed fighting technique back when he learned to ignore pain.

Whatever the reason, Tory soon tired of toying around and attacked. He leapt forward, launching into a torrential punching combination that led with his left and followed with his right. Had I not been prepared, I would have gone down—probably never to rise.

I dodged back and launched a punch packed with fury and powered by rage. Everything I had. All the frustrations, all the anger, all the pain and sorrow and suffering. I put every ounce of unspent emotion into that swing. Thanks to the blessed combination of my superior reach with his inferior sight, my right-armed roundhouse skirted his defenses and collided with his jaw. The connection was solid and square, creating a supremely satisfying crunch that sucked the strength from his killer combination.

But it didn't put him down.

Without missing a beat, Tory redirected his momentum into a leg sweep that would have landed me on my backside had it been adequately aimed. But it wasn't. *"Perkele!"* he swore, cursing the devil that had him fighting half-blind.

I didn't let up.

I didn't pause.

I didn't hesitate.

I spun around as he stood from his sweep and brought the back of my left hand through like a slung stone. It smashed against the same spot that my fist had just visited. There was another crunch, but this one included bones from both bodies.

I bit back my yelp.

Tory dropped, but he didn't collapse.

I pressed on.

So did he. He pulled some kind of a rolling backflip that landed him on his feet and poised to pounce—and pounce he did. Before my mind processed the feat, he was at my throat squeezing, pressing, and clawing like a rabid dog on fresh red meat.

I scrunched my shoulders and flexed my neck, but he was simply too strong. I tried putting my own arms into play, but he was too damn close. I didn't have the angle. I didn't have the leverage.

He added to the onslaught with a roar so savage I knew he was releasing all the pain, sorrow, and suffering he'd bottled up under interrogation. I felt like a lone tree in the path of a nuclear blast. The heat and energy were overwhelming.

My consciousness began to flicker, like pulses of black light cascading through my brain. I was seconds from asphyxiation and would soon be powerless to resist.

This was it. The end. The last gasp. The final fade to black.

Desperate times call for desperate measures, and I had one left. I unleashed my inner animal. The big black beast men keep caged for fear of what they'll become after it's freed.

Reversing course, I rushed into the storm. Rather than attempt to extricate myself, I used my final act to embrace the berserk assassin—and bit his nose. I clamped down with everything I had left. Incisors, canines, premolars, and molars. I put them all into play, crimping and grinding and gnashing with the full force of my jaw and the dynamic desperation of one who knows it's now do or die.

The animalistic assault was too much for even his superhuman self-control to bear. He immediately abandoned his attack and pulled back into a concealing posture.

That was when I went for his eye. I whipped around with all the speed I could summon from my back, shoulders, arms, and legs. I put everything into play and planted my elbow deep into that swollen socket.

Tory's mouth flew open, expelling vomit as he dropped to the ground. He convulsed a few times before lying still as a stone. Unconscious at a minimum. Possibly dead.

Possibly was not good enough.

Nor would incapacitation suffice.

This battle wouldn't end until one of us drew his last breath.

Panting like a derby horse, I wiped my face first with one arm and then with the other. Next I turned my attention to the briefcase that had struck Skylar's head. I unlatched it with my functional hand, hoping to find the equivalent of a matador's sword. A .22, a .38, a .45, a 9mm. It didn't matter to me. It wouldn't matter to Tory.

But the case didn't contain the gun that Tory had failed to find tucked into his belt. It held no knife or bludgeon or papers either. Instead, it was jammed full of jewelry.

The necklaces, bracelets, and rings weren't packed in the padded envelopes a wealthy woman would use while traveling. Instead, the precious ornaments had been hastily piled inside, as if snatched during a robbery. *Snatched during a robbery,* I repeated to myself as a theory formed. If correct, the justice I'd just served had been poetic indeed. Tory had been killed by greed.

I was about to move on in search of a suitable rock or stick when a letter opener came into view. The long curved instrument was crafted from platinum and capped with a sapphire the size of a quarter.

Still stoked by adrenaline and fired by rage, I plucked it from the case, pivoted toward my opponent and plunged it through the bloody pulp until it struck the back of his skull.

75
Good Prediction

NOW THAT I KNEW WE WERE SAFE, that the monster would not rise from his grave, I ran to Skylar's side. She was sprawled out flat on her back, still positioned exactly as she'd dropped. I put my ear to her chest while my fingers fumbled for her carotid pulse.

Her heart was strong and her lungs were working. "Oh, thank goodness."

"Skylar. Skylar, can you hear me?" I hesitated to speak too loudly, lest I be overheard by the occupants of the pool. Although, come to think of it, there'd been no reaction to Tory's primal roar...

She didn't stir.

I probed her temples with a tender touch. It wasn't obvious where the briefcase had hit her and I hadn't seen it happen, but her nose wasn't busted so I assumed it had struck the side of her head. That fit with her condition. Knockout blows were caused by the brain bouncing off the side of the skull in a way that throws the central nervous system into shutdown mode, like a fuse tripping for the brain's protection.

Beyond the immediate loss of consciousness, the primary threat from such a blow was a subdural hematoma. Bleeding inside the skull. I couldn't look for that, but I knew how to test for brain function.

I pinched her earlobe.

She flinched. A good sign.

I pinched again.

She made a faint swatting gesture, as if battling bugs in a dream. A great sign.

I pulled back her eyelids.

Both pupils contracted. Her brain was two for two on the

key indicators. I'd have to monitor for changes going forward, but she didn't appear to be in immediate danger.

So what now?

I decided to go with the original plan, only instead of asking for assistance with a drone, I'd beg for help with my wife.

But first, I would arm myself.

And hide the signs of treachery. Hard to charm your way into someone's confidence if midway through the discussion you stumble upon a fresh corpse doing a Polyphemus imitation.

I hated to leave Skylar, even for the sixty seconds it would take me to run to and from the boat—but I did it anyway.

With the Sig P320 secreted in the small of my back, I used my good hand to grab Tory by a heel and haul him beneath a cluster of ferns. Then I dragged the duffel under another clump. The bag was heavy enough to contain a body. Unable to resist, I pulled the zipper back and peered inside. It was stuffed with cash. Stacks of brand-new banded hundred-dollar bills. Judging by the size of the bag and some quick math, I placed the sum in the neighborhood of three million dollars.

I picked up the second briefcase and found it to be as heavy as any barbell I'd ever lifted. Probably sixty pounds. Between it and the hefty duffel, I understood why Tory had been less than completely attentive while walking to his boat.

Once I maneuvered the briefcase beneath the bush, I flipped the latches and lifted the lid. It was packed with gold. Coins and bars. Had to be a million dollars' worth.

I slid it beneath the black duffel, end to end with the other briefcase.

Returning to Skylar, I used my right hand to tent her knees so that I could slip my left arm under her without further injuring my hand. Then I lifted her up and carried her around back.

The two men we'd seen on the drone screen were still lounging in the pool. I could tell it was them by their bathing suits. Both appeared to be sleeping. The woman had gone. "Hello," I called over the waterfall.

Neither of them moved.

"I need your help," I said even louder.

Again, nothing.

Were they snoozing, or dead? Had Tory turned on his masters? Had he killed them in prelude to robbery? I could see no outward signs of violence. No bullet wounds or bludgeon marks, and the water wasn't bloody.

I'd worry about them later.

Skylar was my primary concern.

I carried her into the house in search of a couch. After spotting a chaise longue, I was startled by a set of double doors that opened automatically as I drew near.

When nobody walked through, I pushed a paperback off the plush upholstery and set Skylar down. As the novel fell to the floor, I noted with some surprise that it was the same one I'd been reading at Berret's. Apparently, Aria and I had the same taste. I wasn't sure what to make of that.

Skylar's eyes opened as the double doors slid closed.

"Hey there. Can you hear me? How are you feeling?"

She blinked a few times, then spoke. "My head hurts. What happened?" Her voice was soft, but steady.

"We ran into Tory. He threw a briefcase at me. I ducked and it hit your head."

"I don't remember."

"Just as well. Can you sit up?"

"Your face is a mess."

"It's nothing. Just a bit of blood and vomit."

"Is that all?" she said with a smile.

It was a proper response to my whimsical tone. She was going to be all right.

"Where am I?"

"I just brought you into Aria's house."

"Where's Tory?"

"He's dead. It appears he'd just looted the island when we bumped into him. He was hauling a five million-dollar stash."

"You're not hurt?"

"I think I fractured a bone or two in my left hand.

Nothing serious."

Skylar took my hand and began to study it. "What about Aria?"

"I'm not sure yet. I haven't had the opportunity to look for her. The other two we saw are still in the pool, either drugged or dead." I studied Skylar's eyes while we spoke.

She suddenly sat fully upright. Rubbing her temples, she asked, "Did you say you found five million dollars?"

"I did."

"Presumably taken from the people who tried to burn me alive?"

"Almost certainly."

"And you killed Tory?" The tone of her questions was more excited than inquisitive.

"I did that, too."

"So why aren't we back on our boat at this very minute, speeding someplace far from here? Like to one of those Bahamian banks that doesn't ask questions?" She gripped my hands hard enough that I had to wince. "Sorry. But surely you don't have a problem skipping the lawsuit and going straight to assessing damages for our pain and suffering?"

No brain damage there. She was firing on all cylinders. "Your health was my primary concern."

Her expression broke. She leaned forward and kissed me quickly on the lips before rising to her feet. "I think I'm fine. Let's go."

Apparently waving five million dollars under someone's nose worked better than an ammonia ampule.

I gave Skylar my arm and guided her outside, but instead of turning toward the yacht, I stopped at the pool. "Let's just check."

She rolled her eyes in response. Yet one more sign of healthy brain function.

While she sat on the edge of a chair, I crouched and leaned to grab the toe of Lars's lookalike. I tugged the doppelgänger to the water's edge, then checked his pulse. "He's dead."

Skylar grimaced but didn't gasp. "Where's Aria? Do you

think she did this in cahoots with Tory?"

"I think Tory works alone. But I can guess where Aria might be." As we rose, I again linked her arm. "Come with me."

Skylar resisted as I turned toward the house. "Let's just leave. Someone has to be coming back, right? That go-fast wasn't Aria's. It's clear now that it was Tory's. That means her staff took her yacht out. Probably shopping. They're not going to leave her stranded for long. They'll likely be back any minute, so we should already be gone."

I favored another hypothesis but decided to keep it to myself for now. "This won't take long. And I think the risk will be worth our while."

"I agree that closure is worth a lot, Chase. I'm just not sure I'd risk five million dollars for it."

"Give me five minutes."

Skylar relented.

I wasn't familiar with the layout of Aria's house, but I knew where to find her bedroom. I led Skylar back into the grand room and then through the automatic double doors I'd activated when carrying her inside.

"Wow!" Skylar said. "Talk about a fairy tale gone awry."

The master suite of Aria's estate was something the designers at Disney would draw, complete with canopy bed and breathtaking view. But at the moment, it looked like a beast had just visited the beauty. Every painting had been pulled from the walls and all the furniture stood askew.

I took that as a good sign.

Noting that nothing had been revealed by the rearrangement, I walked toward the closet doors. They were also automatic. They too slid silently aside as they'd undoubtedly done a thousand times before. As if everything was normal. But it wasn't.

Aria's bikini-clad body lay sprawled face down on the floor. Dead. That much was immediately apparent. The rest of the scene took a second to process.

The walk-in closet was enormous. Bigger than most bedrooms. Clothes had been scattered and shoes tossed aside. One section of the back wall had been hinged inward, revealing a vault. Its thick steel door had also been opened. Aria lay in that doorway.

"You think Tory forced her to open the vault, then hit her on the back of the head?" Skylar asked.

I felt the back of Aria's head before answering. It wasn't warm or damaged. Pointing to the glass rectangle embedded in the exposed wall, I said, "I think she died beside the others in the pool. Some kind of drug overdose.

"I think Tory made the mess searching for the safe he knew had to be hidden somewhere. Once he found it, and the palm reader, he hauled her up here."

"And used her dead hand to unlock it," Skylar said with a shudder.

We walked around the heiress's body and stepped inside the stainless steel room. The first thing to catch my eye was a Glock sitting atop a pedestal. Tory's gun. This confirmed my theory. He had set it aside while packing his bags and forgotten it amidst the excitement. Or figured he'd grab it on the last run. Either way, that single, simple lapse of professionalism had saved our lives and cost him his own. I'd be pondering that blessed piece of luck for years to come.

"Look at all this! The five million you saw was just the beginning." Skylar turned to face me, her eyes wide with excitement and understanding. "This was what you meant when you predicted that the risk would be worth our while."

"Don't ever doubt me again," I said with a wink.

She kissed me.

Epilogue

Six months later
London, England

SKYLAR STOOD before the big black door with no number, hesitant to knock. She raised her hand, knuckles flexed, but paused to reflect—on her past, her present, and her future. A series of simple questions had started the complex cascade that led her to this dark doorway—and the ironic ending on the other side.

The first question had been, "What do we do now?" She'd asked it while standing in Aria's vault, surrounded by treasure-laden shelves and the owner's cooling corpse.

Chase had hesitated to answer, but only for a heartbeat. "We load all this on the boat. Then I close the vault door, wipe our prints, and put Aria back in the pool beside her friends." His head and eye movements told her he was thinking out loud.

She didn't interrupt.

"I'll put Tory on the bow of his boat and send it off into the open ocean. The go-fast may never be found, much less the body."

That was exactly what they had done. Once Seven Star Island was a hundred miles in their wake, she asked the second question, knowing full well that Chase's reply would shape the rest of her days. "What happens next?"

He had that answer ready and waiting. "We keep it simple. We buy this boat, then start exploring the Caribbean, moving place to place and lying low while seeing what shakes out. I'm not convinced that Aria's servants planned on returning. Depends on whether her death was accidental or suicide."

"Suicide! I'd never considered that," Skylar interjected.

"Although, come to think of it, radical behavior could be considered their defining characteristic."

"If accidental, then the story will be all over the news. If suicide, we may never hear anything. Between the birds and the bugs and the sun, the bodies may not be found until someone drains the pool and discovers the bones. That could be many months down the road."

They stuck to that plan. They stashed the loot beneath life preservers and spare rolls of toilet paper, bought the yacht with Tory's Amex card—what an amazing call that had been—and spent six months getting acquainted with both boating life and each other.

Every time they docked, they checked the newspapers and internet. Nothing was ever reported. Not on the deaths. Not on the missing millions in treasure.

They spent many an evening speculating on that silence. While there was no clear or obvious answer, Chase was certain that the root cause lay in the identity swapping that got them involved in the first place. Aria and the others had gone off the grid, and therefore the grid didn't miss them. Or their money.

Skylar had posed the penultimate questions a few nights earlier. Chase was serving rum punch on the upper deck of the *C'est La Vie* as the sun set over Antigua when she asked, "Are we criminals?"

He replied with the soft tone of a person who had spent hours thinking through a sensitive topic and was at peace with his answer. "An aggressive prosecutor could certainly get us indicted. But conviction would be difficult. That requires convincing a jury of our peers that we did something they wouldn't do in our shoes. Our attorney could easily make the case that the real criminals got their comeuppance and we, their victims, were fairly compensated. Justice had already been served."

"You're not concerned then?"

"I'm rightfully concerned. The legal process would be long, costly, and unpleasant. We'd be living on pins and needles for months if not years. And not on this boat we've both come to love. Possibly not even together."

She began crying at that point. Not out of worry or fear but out of relief. By voicing his concerns, Chase had affirmed her status, their status, and it filled her heart with joy.

He didn't stop there. "But unless and until we're found not guilty, we have to be very careful. In that regard, these months at sea—just you and me with the islands, waves, and stars—have brought certainty to my thinking."

"What certainty?" she asked with a prayer in her heart.

"I want us to be careful—together."

She wrapped her arms around him. One thing led to another and before they knew it both were drained and sweaty. "How do we be careful together?" she asked across the pillow. That was her final question. The one that brought them to the big black door with no number.

"Go ahead," Chase said with an affirming nod.

Skylar knocked, then stepped back, holding Chase's hand in full view of the discreet surveillance camera.

The door opened with a click, exposing a short, bare brick hallway. There was a similar door at the other end and a large man standing inside.

He tapped a hefty black sap against his palm as they entered but said nothing.

The door behind them swung shut, then the one before them opened. They walked through it and into a windowless room where a gray-haired man wearing a dark suit and silver-framed glasses sat across a bare table. He motioned to them to sit, then got straight to business. "So, you need new identities."

AUTHOR'S NOTE

Dear Reader,

Are you curious about what's next for Skylar and Chase? To get my thoughts and stay informed of my new releases, email me at ThePriceOfTime@timtigner.com.

If you enjoyed THE PRICE OF TIME, I hope you will be so kind as to leave a review on Amazon. Reviews and referrals are as vital to an author's success as a good GPA is to a student's.

Thank you for your kind comments and precious attention.

ALSO BY TIM TIGNER

Standalone Novels
COERCION, BETRAYAL, FLASH

Kyle Achilles Series
PUSHING BRILLIANCE, THE LIES OF SPIES,
FALLING STARS, TWIST AND TURN

Be among the first to learn of new releases by signing up for Tim's *New Releases Newsletter* at timtigner.com

~ ~ ~

Turn the page for a preview of PUSHING BRILLIANCE, book #1 in the Kyle Achilles series.

Pushing Brilliance

Chapter 1

The Kremlin

HOW DO YOU PITCH an audacious plan to the most powerful man in the world? Grigori Barsukov was about to find out.

Technically, the President of Russia was an old friend—although the last time they'd met, his old friend had punched him in the face. That was thirty years ago, but the memory remained fresh, and Grigori's nose still skewed to the right.

Back then, he and President Vladimir Korovin wore KGB lieutenant stars. Now both were clothed in the finest Italian suits. But his former roommate also sported the confidence of one who wielded unrivaled power, and the temper of a man ruthless enough to obtain it.

The world had spun on a different axis when they'd worked together, an east-west axis, running from Moscow to Washington. Now everything revolved around the West. America was the sole superpower.

Grigori could change that.

He could lever Russia back into a pole position.

But only if his old rival would risk joining him—way out on a limb.

As Grigori's footfalls fell into cadence with the boots of his escorts, he coughed twice, attempting to relax the lump in his throat. It didn't work. When the hardwood turned to red carpet, he willed his palms to stop sweating. They didn't listen. Then the big double doors rose before him and it was too late to do anything but take a deep breath, and hope for the best.

The presidential guards each took a single step to the side, then opened their doors with crisp efficiency and a click of their heels. Across the office, a gilded double-headed eagle peered down from atop the dark wood paneling, but the lone living occupant of the Kremlin's inner sanctum did not look up.

President Vladimir Korovin was studying photographs.

Grigori stopped three steps in as the doors were closed behind him, unsure of the proper next move. He wondered if everyone felt this way the first time. Should he stand at attention until acknowledged? Take a seat by the wall?

He strolled to the nearest window, leaned his left shoulder up against the frame, and looked out at the Moscow River. Thirty seconds ticked by with nothing but the sound of shifting photos behind him. *Was it possible that Korovin still held a grudge?*

Desperate to break the ice without looking like a complete fool, he said, "This is much nicer than the view from our academy dorm room."

Korovin said nothing.

Grigori felt his forehead tickle. Drops of sweat were forming, getting ready to roll. As the first broke free, he heard the stack of photos being squared, and then at long last, the familiar voice. It posed a very unfamiliar question: "Ever see a crocodile catch a rabbit?"

Grigori whirled about to meet the Russian President's gaze. "What?"

Korovin waved the stack of photos. His eyes were the same cornflower blue Grigori remembered, but their youthful verve had yielded to something darker. "I recently returned from Venezuela. Nicolas took me crocodile hunting. Of course, we didn't have all day to spend on sport, so our guides cheated. They put rabbits on the riverbank, on the wide strip of dried mud between the water and the tall grass. Kind of like teeing up golf balls. Spaced them out so the critters couldn't see each other and gave each its own pile of alfalfa while we watched in silence from an electric boat." Korovin was clearly enjoying the telling of his intriguing tale. He gestured with broad sweeps as he spoke, but kept his eyes locked on Grigori.

"Nicolas told me these rabbits were brought in special from the hill country, where they'd survived a thousand generations amidst foxes and coyotes. When you put them on the riverbank, however, they're completely clueless. It's not their turf, so they stay where they're dropped, noses quivering, ears scanning, eating alfalfa and watching the wall of vegetation in front of them while crocodiles swim up silently from behind.

"The crocodiles were being fooled like the rabbits, of course. Eyes front, focused on food. Oblivious." Korovin shook his head as though bewildered. "Evolution somehow turned a cold-blooded reptile into a warm white furball, but kept both of the creature's brains the same. Hard to fathom. Anyway, the capture was quite a sight.

"Thing about a crocodile is, it's a log one moment and a set of snapping jaws the next, with nothing but a furious blur in between. One second the rabbit is chewing alfalfa, the next second the rabbit *is* alfalfa. Not because it's too slow or too stupid ... but because it's out of its element."

Grigori resisted the urge to swallow.

"When it comes to eating," Korovin continued, "crocs are like storybook monsters. They swallow their food whole. Unlike their legless cousins, however, they want it dead first. So once they've trapped dinner in their maw, they drag it underwater to drown it. This means the rabbit is usually alive and uninjured in the croc's mouth for a while—unsure what the hell just happened, but pretty damn certain it's not good."

The president leaned back in his chair, placing his feet on the desk and his hands behind his head. He was having fun.

Grigori felt like the rabbit.

"That's when Nicolas had us shoot the crocs. After they clamped down around the rabbits, but before they dragged 'em under. That became the goal, to get the rabbit back alive."

Grigori nodded appreciatively. "Gives a new meaning to the phrase, *catch and release*."

Korovin continued as if Grigori hadn't spoken. "The

trick was putting a bullet directly into the croc's tiny brain, preferably the medulla oblongata, right there where the spine meets the skull. Otherwise the croc would thrash around or go under before you could get off the kill shot, and the rabbit was toast.

"It was good sport, and an experience worth replicating. But we don't have crocodiles anywhere near Moscow, so I've been trying to come up with an equally engaging distraction for my honored guests. Any ideas?"

Grigori felt like he'd been brought in from the hills. The story hadn't helped the lump in his throat either. He managed to say, "Let me give it some thought."

Korovin just looked at him expectantly.

Comprehension struck after an uncomfortable silence. "What happened to the rabbits?"

Korovin returned his feet to the floor, and leaned forward in his chair. "Good question. I was curious to see that myself. I put my first survivor back on the riverbank beside a fresh pile of alfalfa. It ran for the tall grass as if I'd lit its tail on fire. That rabbit had learned life's most important lesson."

Grigori bit. "What's that?"

"Doesn't matter where you are. Doesn't matter if you're a crocodile or a rabbit. You best look around, because you're never safe.

"Now, what have you brought me, Grigori?"

Grigori breathed deeply, forcing the reptiles from his mind. He pictured his future atop a corporate tower, an oligarch on a golden throne. Then he spoke with all the gravitas of a wedding vow. "I brought you a plan, Mister President."

Chapter 2

Brillyanc

PRESIDENT KOROVIN REPEATED Grigori's assertion aloud. "You brought me a plan." He paused for a long second, as though tasting the words.

Grigori felt like he was looking up from the Colosseum floor after a gladiator fight. Would the emperor's thumb point up, or down?

Korovin was savoring the power. Finally, the president gestured toward the chess table abutting his desk, and Grigori's heart resumed beating.

The magnificent antique before which Grigori took a seat was handcrafted of the same highly polished hardwood as Korovin's desk, probably by a French craftsman now centuries dead. Korovin took the opposing chair and pulled a chess clock from his drawer. Setting it on the table, he pressed the button that activated Grigori's timer. "Give me the three-minute version."

Grigori wasn't a competitive chess player, but like any Russian who had risen through government ranks, he was familiar with the sport.

Chess clocks have two timers controlled by seesawing buttons. When one's up, the other's down, and vice versa. After each move, a player slaps his button, stopping his timer and setting his opponent's in motion. If a timer runs out, a little red plastic flag drops, and that player loses. Game over. There's the door. Thank you for playing.

Grigori planted his elbows on the table, leaned forward, and made his opening move. "While my business is oil and gas, my hobby is investing in startups. The heads of Russia's major research centers all know I'm a so-called *angel investor*, so they send me their best early-stage projects. I get everything from social media software, to solar power projects, to electric cars.

"A few years ago, I met a couple of brilliant biomedical researchers out of Kazan State Medical University. They had applied modern analytical tools to the data collected during tens of thousands of medical experiments performed on political prisoners during Stalin's reign. They were looking for factors that accelerated the human metabolism—and they found them. Long story short, a hundred million rubles later I've got a drug compound whose strategic potential I think you'll appreciate."

Grigori slapped his button, pausing his timer and setting the president's clock in motion. It was a risky move. If Korovin wasn't intrigued, Grigori wouldn't get to finish his pitch. But Grigori was confident that his old roommate was hooked. Now he would have to admit as much if he wanted to hear the rest.

The right side of the president's mouth contracted back a couple millimeters. A crocodile smile. He slapped the clock. "Go on."

"The human metabolism converts food and drink into the fuel and building blocks our bodies require. It's an exceptionally complex process that varies greatly from individual to individual, and within individuals over time. Metabolic differences mean some people naturally burn more fat, build more muscle, enjoy more energy, and think more clearly than others. This is obvious from the locker room to the boardroom to the battlefield. The doctors in Kazan focused on the mental aspects of metabolism, on factors that improved clarity of thought–"

Korovin interrupted, "Are you implying that my metabolism impacts my IQ?"

"Sounds a little funny at first, I know, but think about your own experience. Don't you think better after coffee than after vodka? After salad than fries? After a jog and a hot shower than an afternoon at a desk? All those actions impact the mental horsepower you enjoy at any given moment. What my doctors did was figure out what the body needs to optimize cognitive function."

"Something other than healthy food and sufficient rest?"

Perceptive question, Grigori thought. "Picture your metabolism like a funnel, with raw materials such as food and rest going in the top, cognitive power coming out the bottom, and dozens of complex metabolic processes in between."

"Okay," Korovin said, eager to engage in a battle of wits.

"Rather than following in the footsteps of others by attempting to modify one of the many metabolic processes, the doctors in Kazan took an entirely different approach, a brilliant approach. They figured out how to widen the narrow end of the funnel."

"So, bottom line, the brain gets more fuel?"

"Generally speaking, yes."

"With what result? Will every day be like my best day?"

"No," Grigori said, relishing the moment. "Every day will be better than your best day."

Korovin cocked his head. "How much better?"

Who's the rabbit now? "Twenty IQ points."

"Twenty points?"

"Tests show that's the average gain, and that it applies across the scale, regardless of base IQ. But it's most interesting at the high end."

Another few millimeters of smile. "Why is the high end the most interesting?"

"Take a person with an IQ of 140. Give him Brillyanc—that's the drug's name—and he'll score 160. May not sound like a big deal, but roughly speaking, those 20 points take his IQ from 1 in 200, to 1 in 20,000. Suddenly, instead of being the smartest guy in the room, he's the smartest guy in his discipline."

Korovin leaned forward and locked on Grigori's eyes. "Every ambitious scientist, executive, lawyer ... and politician would give his left nut for that competitive advantage. Hell, his left and right."

Grigori nodded.

"And it really works?"

"It really works."

Korovin reached out and leveled the buttons, stopping both timers and pausing to think, his left hand still resting on the clock. "So your plan is to give Russians an intelligence edge over foreign competition? Kind of analogous to what you and I used to do, all those years ago."

Grigori shook his head. "No, that's not my plan."

The edges of the cornflower eyes contracted ever so slightly. "Why not?"

"Let's just say, widening the funnel does more than raise IQ."

Korovin frowned and leaned back, taking a moment to digest this twist. "Why have you brought this to me, Grigori?"

"As I said, Mister President, I have a plan I think you're going to like."

ABOUT THE AUTHOR

Tim began his career in Soviet Counterintelligence with the US Army Special Forces, the Green Berets. With the fall of the Berlin Wall, Tim switched from espionage to arbitrage and moved to Moscow in the midst of Perestroika. In Russia, he led prominent multinational medical companies, worked with cosmonauts on the MIR Space Station (from Earth, alas), and chaired the Association of International Pharmaceutical Manufacturers.

Moving to Brussels during the formation of the EU, Tim ran Europe, Middle East, and Africa for a Johnson & Johnson company and traveled like a character in a Robert Ludlum novel. He eventually landed in Silicon Valley, where he launched new medical technologies as a startup CEO.

Tim began writing thrillers in 1996 from an apartment overlooking Moscow's Gorky Park. Decades later, he's still writing. His home office now overlooks a vineyard in Northern California, where he lives with his wife Elena and their two daughters.

Tim grew up in the Midwest. He earned a BA in Philosophy and Mathematics from Hanover College, and then an MBA in Finance and a MA in International Studies from the University of Pennsylvania's Wharton School.

Made in the USA
San Bernardino, CA
03 July 2019